At the bottom of the road, I saw the Roman chariot sign above the entrance to the Golden Torch. In another few minutes we would be inside. I couldn't wait.

A rush of hot air, the smell of sweating bodies, cigarette smoke, and various scents, some of them fragrant, hit me as I pushed through the glass doors. Then a tingle of excitement raced up my spine – and it wasn't just from the capsules I'd swallowed. Decibels of raw energy were vibrating the air. We paid our money over. Fifty pence for members – sixty for guests – for twelve hours of fantastic, foot-stomping, Northern Soul.

CRACKIN' UP

*A tale of sex, and drugs
. . . and Northern Soul*

Maxwell Murray

MOONSHINE

First published in 1999
by MOONSHINE

ISBN 0 9536440 0 6

British Library Cataloguing in Publication Data:
A catalogue record for this book is available from
the British Library.

Cover design by Julian Bee

Printed and bound by:
MFP Design & Print, Manchester M32 0JT

Published by:
Moonshine Enterprises Ltd
Chesterfield S42 6NW.
Tel: 01246 220967 Fax: 01246 220982

Acknowledgements

Thanks to Dick Richardson of Country Books
for his guidance and assistance

Thanks to Mick Fitzpatrick for the help and assistance
so freely given. I would recommend anyone wishing to
know more about the Northern Soul scene, past or
present, to visit his website (www.night-owl.co.uk)

Last but not least, thanks to all the Soulies
at "Keeping The Faith"

Keep The Faith
Maxwell Murray 1999

1

I Got What It Takes

Friday the fifth of February 1971 was a day I thought would never come. There was nothing special about the date, but now, at last, I could ride my Lambretta. Twelve months of scrimping and saving to buy it, then another three months of hard work rebuilding the machine, and I was ready to hit the road, so to speak.

I sat outside my parents' bungalow for several minutes, with the scooter's engine ticking over, while I tried to build up courage for that first ride. Just go for it Kenny, I finally told myself. I took a deep breath, twisted open the Lambretta's throttle with my right hand, and released the clutch lever gently with my left. The scooter responded immediately, its engine sending a puff of blue smoke into the air as the exhaust expelled unburned oil.

I swayed a little as I lifted my feet from the ground and settled them onto the floorboards of the scooter. 'Watch what you're doing,' I murmured to myself. Didn't want to fall off in the first few yards. I soon got my balance though; I'd cycled many miles on paper rounds and that helped.

I squeezed the clutch lever once more and turned the left twistgrip into second. The mark on the handlebars lined up fine. I was glad about that. It had been a right fiddle of a job to set up the gear-change cables; the tiny grub screws that gripped them were hard to undo and, until now, I'd not been sure if I had got them right.

The Lambretta picked up speed as I changed up to the next gear. The junction at the end of the road was approaching fast. It had only taken seconds to reach it; walking from home to call at the corner shop, or to the nearby bus stop, would normally take me five or six minutes. I closed the throttle and listened appreciatively as the scooter's engine noise changed from a throaty roar to a loud popping. My friends had told me to knock the circular baffle out of my new exhaust, but I had been a bit reluctant to do it as the chromed megaphone had cost me nearly half my wages. Then I had thought what the hell, and hammered a bar into the narrow end of the metal trumpet, ripping away the baffle's welds. Now, I was glad that I had; the Lammy sounded like a proper scooter.

As I slowed for the junction, I wondered whether to give a hand signal for the right turn, then decided against it; better get used to riding the scooter before I let go of the handlebars. Soon, I was accelerating along the main road, away from the town centre. I had wondered, briefly, whether to go into town, but, having bunked off work early, thought I'd better stay clear, in case my boss, Beresford, saw me.

Strands of hair began to whip at my face as the scooter's speed increased. It needed cutting. Either that or buy a hat. Only sissies wore a crash helmet. Perhaps I could get a bob hat, or a beret, like some other scooterists wore. My fingers began to freeze as the cold air rushed past. I ought to have put gloves on too, but had been too excited to think about them. My ears were cold as well, but the sheer exhilaration of the scooter's speed soon made me forget any discomfort.

The Lambretta was everything that I had dreamed it would be. It was only a TV175, but I could never have afforded an SX, or one of the new GP 200's; it had been hard enough to raise the money for this machine. The scooter was one that a friend of my father used to travel to work on. The man had only wanted fifty quid for it, but I'd been forced to sell my bicycle to boost my savings. I had asked my father to loan me the money, I'd even tried to get my mother to sway the old man, but it had been hopeless.

'If you need owt for college – I'll pay for it,' my father had said, 'but not for one of those damned things. You'll only end up killing yourself. Then I'll have to face your mother!'

Luckily for me, the scooter was still for sale by the time I had saved enough.

'I'll throw in the helmet for free,' my father's friend said, when I tried to knock a bit off the asking price.

'That's no good to me,' I laughed, when he produced a white Kangol helmet, complete with side flaps and peak on the front, from his shed. It was the sort that AA Patrolmen or old duffers wore. 'I wouldn't be seen dead in that!' I told him.

'It's supposed to save you from getting killed,' he grinned. 'You can have it if you want – but I'm not letting the bike go for less. It's cheap enough.'

He was right, and if I'd told him to forget it, it would have taken me months to save for another machine. I shook hands on the deal, then pushed the scooter home.

It had been a non-runner then, but now, with a rebuilt engine, it was fast, very fast. The icy wind made tears stream down my face, but I was too much of a novice to lift my hand and wipe them away. I laughed as the needle on the speedo swung towards the end of the scale; I was doing sixty and yet the engine still had power to spare. Fast enough for now I decided, at least until it was run in. And until I was a better rider. I closed the throttle and allowed the Lambretta to lose speed, dropping my feet to the road as it came to a halt. I touched the ground too soon, and nearly fell off as the surface of the road snatched at the soles of my shoes. That was close I told myself, thankful that I'd not gone into town on my first run; what a prat I'd have looked if I'd done that in front of my mates. I waited for a gap in the traffic, then swung the scooter towards home.

The near spill had dented my confidence a bit, so I kept my speed lower and began to practise gear changes. By the time I reached the edge of town I had regained my composure though, and decided I would have a ride along the High Street, just the once, to see if anyone I knew was there; Beresford would not expect to see me on a scooter anyway.

I pulled up at a crossroads, where the road to Manchester blocked my progress, and waited.

A car drew up behind. I sensed that it was close, too close in fact. I cast a glance into the mirror clipped to my handlebars. It was the first time I had used it, and I would not have dared do that if I'd not been at a standstill. Behind me was an old Ford Anglia, painted black and fitted with tinted windows. It belonged to a greaser bastard called Roger Webster; I had often seen him racing the car through town. I looked along the road. No chance of moving off yet. I glanced at the mirror again.

Webster stuck his head out of the driver's window and glared at me. 'Get that fucking hairdryer out of the way, Roberts,' he yelled.

I debated whether to have a go at him. I wasn't scared of Webster, but knew that his mate, Skunk Martin, was usually in the car. Sometimes they were four up. I couldn't see inside the vehicle, but decided that Webster wouldn't be so cocky if he was on his own. Four against one were not very good odds.

'Knock him off, Rog!' a girl's voice screamed from within the car.

That was why Webster was acting hard; he wanted to show off in front of his slag of a girlfriend, Linda Rider. Everyone called her "Easy Rider" when the biker film came out, but she had earned the nickname from about the age of thirteen. It was rumoured that almost every man and boy in town had

10

been through her. I was pretty sure the story was true; I had been one of them myself, after school one night.

Webster revved the Anglia's engine, then nudged the car forwards until its front bumper was almost touching the Lambretta's numberplate. I checked the main road again. I still couldn't go as a truck was thundering down the hill towards the crossroads.

I heard someone shout and looked back over my shoulder. Yes, Skunk was there too; he poked his head out of the passenger side window. 'Shift the fucking thing, you Mod ponce,' he screamed at me.

I was no Mod, had sometimes fought with them in fact, but now was not the time to argue the point with the greasers. The car crept forwards again. I winced as my numberplate buckled under the pressure. Any more, and the rear body and mudguard would be damaged as well; perhaps even the side panels would get bent. I cursed as I thought of the time I'd spent sanding then painting the bodywork. Brush paint looked crappy, so I'd sprayed the scooter with aerosols of metallic blue. They had cost me another small fortune, as each can only covered a small area, but the finish was brilliant. Now Webster was going to wreck it. One more inch and I'd have the bastard!

The Anglia's exhaust growled as Webster shoved the car at the scooter again. I was just about to pull the Lambretta onto its stand, when I realised that it was rolling forwards into the path of the truck! I lifted my foot onto the floorboards and stamped on the brake pedal. The rear wheel locked but then began to slide across the tarmac as Webster continued pushing. I heard the truck driver sound his horn as my scooter suddenly appeared in front of him.

Webster would give in soon; he wouldn't want to kill me, just frighten me. The Anglia inched forwards. I glanced at the truck. It was almost on me. Suddenly, the lorry driver hit his brakes. A cloud of smoke filled the air as the vehicle's rear wheels began to skip along the road. As if in slow motion, I saw the driver struggling for control as the tyres lost their hold. He was not going to be able to stop in time. I glanced the other way. There was a bus approaching. The lorry driver had a choice, hit me and my scooter or the oncoming bus. I suddenly knew which it would be. My bladder almost emptied as I imagined the heavy wheels crushing me into the road. I wrenched the throttle wide open and the Lambretta leapt forwards, its rear tyre spinning as it fought for grip. Then I was hurtling across the junction, swaying from side to side, my feet scraping on the tarmac.

The truck skidded past behind me, but the bus driver blared his horn as my Lambretta sprinted across in front of him. The sudden noise startled me, making me lose my concentration. The front wheel of my scooter hit the kerb on the opposite corner of the junction, bouncing me off the padded seat, but, thankfully, I managed to regain control again and bumped back onto the road.

I snicked the scooter into second gear and cruised towards the market square, taking deep breaths as I rode, trying to calm my nerves. The roar of an engine made me look in the mirror again. The Anglia was coming up fast. Webster was leaning out of the window, his black hair waving in the slipstream. He was shouting something. I couldn't make it out, but wasn't going to stop to find out what he was saying either. I opened the throttle and went up another gear. Damn! There was a zebra crossing ahead. Several people were already part way across. I couldn't stop else Webster would have me. I swerved around the amazed pedestrians. One man shook his fist at me as my scooter whizzed past him; a woman had to drag a pushchair out of my path.

'Sorry,' I mouthed, as I sped on, praying they'd not taken my number; I hadn't had enough money to get the Lambretta's road tax or insurance yet. When I looked back I saw they were too busy arguing with Webster, who was gesturing for them to move out of his way.

Soon, though, the Ford was behind me again. I swerved

12

the scooter down a side street. A squeal of tyres and Webster was there once more. The gap closed, the Anglia almost touching my scooter. I looked ahead and saw another junction coming up. Mustn't stop I told myself. I slowed the scooter, but only slightly, then leaned it into the corner. As I sped out into the other road, I realised that a car was coming. It braked sharply as I hurtled out in front of it, the driver sounding his horn at me. I heard Webster blast his own horn, wanting the car out of his path. The stationary car gave me a short respite, but then, in my mirror, I saw the Anglia circle around the other vehicle.

Despite the cold, I felt sweat trickle down the side of my ribs. My jaw began to ache and I realised that I was clenching my teeth tightly together. 'Please God, don't let him catch me,' I breathed, as the Anglia roared closer again.

Now I was in the market square. Thankfully it wasn't Market Day, else I'd have been blocked in by stalls and hordes of empty-headed shoppers.

Then I saw a way of escape. At the side of the greengrocers, halfway up the square, was a covered passage-way. It led to a cobbled yard behind the Market Hall. It was wide enough for a car but had stone bollards across the entrance, so that only people on foot could use it. I also knew that the greengrocer stacked boxes of fruit and bags of potatoes and things in the alley, using it as a handy store for his goods. Webster wouldn't be able to follow me there. I rattled across the cobbles, then steered the scooter's forks past the stone posts.

The grocer had just prised the lid off a long wooden box, but was forced to step into it, squashing green bananas underfoot, as my Lambretta screamed past him.

'Bloody idiot,' the man yelled, as I struggled to recover my balance.

I ignored the shopkeeper, and peered back through the mirror, beyond him. The black Anglia screeched to a halt, inches from the bollards, and Webster and Martin leapt out.

13

As I turned the corner at the end of the passageway, I saw them get back into the car. They would know that I'd only one other exit from the yard, and would be trying to get there before I did. I swerved around parked cars and just made it out of the narrow street before the greasers trapped me.

Opposite me, another alleyway gave access to the rear yards of some terraced houses. It was wide enough for the Anglia, but only just. I raced into it, guessing that Webster wouldn't like driving at speed in its narrow confines. A service alley led off to my left, to the front of the terrace. I turned into it. The scooter's exhaust echoed back at me as I sped between the high garden walls, almost scraping the handlebars on the brickwork. I shot out into another street, then turned towards home. It would take Webster several minutes to get to this spot, even if the greaser figured out where I had gone to.

Would the greengrocer call the police? I could imagine him on the telephone right now. 'Yes, officer. Young hooligan on a scooter. Long fair hair. Blue eyes. Wearing one of them denim jackets. And jeans too. Looked a bit like Charlie Roberts' boy.'

My parents often shopped at the greengrocers, and several times I'd been with them. I just hoped that it had all happened so fast that he'd not been able to recognise me. Then again, after seeing Webster and his mate, he may realise that I was being chased, and that it was not my fault.

I decided to go home, hide up for a bit. Then I had a better idea; I'd see if my mate Floyd was in. The two of us could go looking for Webster and Martin; the greasers might not be so brave then.

I had known Floyd since he was about twelve years old. We had both gone to the same school, Westside Secondary Modern. On my first day there, my father had given me a lift in the little Fiat he owned. At break time, several lads had gathered around me.

'Your dad's got a car has he?' one of them, who I found

14

out later was called Eddie Duncan, sneered as he swaggered towards me, then began to push me across the playground.

He was about a year older than me, about three or four inches taller, and in the next class at school. A big flabby youth with light brown hair, a moon face, wide mouth, and thick rubbery lips. His breath smelt too.

'Suppose you think you're better than us do you, you Southern ponce?' he growled, prodding at my ribs with his stubby fingers.

I was puzzled. OK, we had moved North but not that far; I had never thought of myself as being a Southerner. 'What do you mean? I was born in Rugby,' I said angrily. I had the feeling though, that wherever I'd come from, Tyneside, or Liverpool, or even the same town as Duncan, he'd still have been after me.

'Anyway, my father's only just bought the car. He needs it for work.' I told him. My old man was on the Gas Board. He'd just been promoted to a supervisor, and was overseeing much of the work being done to fix customers up with Natural Gas. His new job had meant us moving home. After much searching, my parents had found a small bungalow near to the school where they'd enrolled me. When I explained where I lived, I found out that my home was close to Duncan's.

'So you live in that big place on the corner of Derby Street,' Duncan scowled, then spat on the tarmac. 'Told you he thinks he's somebody,' he said to the others.

I'd never pictured our bungalow as being big and was just about to say so, when the bell to signal the end of break sounded. It gave me a reprieve.

Duncan was waiting, with three of his mates, when I made my way home across the recreation ground. They surrounded me. Duncan glared at me, foxy brown eyes below hooded lids burning into mine. I wasn't very tall, and he must have thought he was going to have fun with me. My father, a former Royal Marine Commando and veteran of the Korean

15

War, had taught me, his only son, how to box. I soon put the skills he'd shown me, as well as a few unorthodox ones I'd learned since, to good use. I gave Duncan a black eye. The others ran off.

Apart from the odd jibe, Duncan had left me alone after that, but it was a long time before I made any friends at school. Any boy who tried to team up with me was warned off by Duncan and his cronies. Because of the house move, I had left behind all my friends from Primary School.

Then, about a year later, Floyd Edmonds joined the class. His black skin made him a target for Duncan's taunts. Me, I was relieved that they had found someone else to have a go at. I ignored their bullying of Floyd. I thought that, being almost six feet tall and still growing, he should be able to fight his own battles.

The other boys would stuff a milk carton into Floyd's satchel then thump it, soaking his books with the stuff, or toss his satchel onto the school roof, or steal his pumps before the sports lesson, so that Floyd would be told off by the PE Master. They bullied Floyd in the schoolyard, rolling him into puddles on the tarmac, or sometimes into the mud of the nearby playing field. On it went, day after day, month after month, and I wondered why Floyd never retaliated. I often saw tears in his eyes.

One day, as I was leaving school, I heard a crowd of boys jeering and laughing, next to the bus shelter on the main road. Curious, I walked that way. Several of Duncan's mates had Floyd on the ground again; they were kicking him. Duncan had hold of a young black girl's hair and was tugging at it, making the girl scream with pain.

'Bet the little piccaninny drops her knickers for you,' Duncan shouted, as he dragged the girl behind him. 'You niggers is all the same. Perhaps she'll drop 'em for me too.'

'Leave her alone!' Floyd yelled.

'Yeah, leave the girl alone,' I said as I came up behind Duncan, making him turn in surprise.

16

'Keep out of this Roberts. We've got to teach these black bastards a lesson.'

'And I'll teach a yellow bastard a lesson in a minute,' I growled, 'unless you let go of her.'

Duncan stood watching me, saying nothing. Then he shrugged. 'No use us fighting,' he said as he released the girl. 'We should stick together against the darkies.' He wiped his hands on his trousers, as if he had soiled them on the girl's hair.

'And him,' I said, nodding towards Floyd.

'Don't cross us,' Duncan scowled, 'else we'll be after you again.'

As I stepped towards them, the other boys let go of Floyd.

Duncan looked as if he was about to have another go at me, but turned away when I met his stare.

'You'll regret this, nigger lover,' Duncan yelled back as the gang sauntered away.

I ignored him and bent down to help Floyd to his feet.

'You didn't have to interfere,' Floyd muttered. 'I can take care of myself.'

'Yeah. Looked like you could,' I grinned.

Floyd brushed the dust from his blazer. The sleeve was almost torn off. 'Shit! I'll be in trouble again,' he cursed under his breath.

'Thank you for helping,' the girl smiled at me.

She was a year or two younger than me I guessed, but was about my height. She had a round face but with high cheekbones and a pointed chin. Her hair, a dark reddish-brown, was pulled back into a tight ponytail. She had full lips, which would have given some girls a petulant look, but somehow they made her look sexy. She had the same snub nose as Floyd. Perhaps she was related?

Floyd confirmed my thoughts. 'This is Cheryl, my sister.'

I put my hand forward to shake hers, then realised that was being a bit formal. I stood there awkwardly for a moment, staring into her amber eyes. Cheryl saved me further

17

embarrassment by hugging me briefly. I could smell a fragrance of lemon on her neck.

As she turned to help her brother gather up his schoolbooks, I wondered why Duncan and everyone, me included, called them blacks. Cheryl's skin, like Floyd's, was the colour of strong coffee. Cheryl had nice legs too I noticed, when her grey pleated skirt rode up her thighs as she crouched to grab at a loose piece of paper. She was a bit young now, but would be a cracker in a few years.

Just then, Cheryl looked over her shoulder at me, as if she'd read my thoughts. I reddened then stepped onto another slip of paper before it blew away.

'Thanks, Kenny,' Floyd said as he took it from me and stuffed it into his satchel.

Floyd was taller than his sister, more rangy, his face was longer, his eyes a darker brown, but he had the same broad smile as her. This was probably the first time I had seen anything other than sadness on his face; but then again, he'd not had much to be happy about at school so far.

'They'll be after you too now,' Floyd said as we walked towards home.

I told him not to worry. 'If we stick together we can see them off.'

Since that day, we'd stood shoulder to shoulder against Duncan's bullying and, apart from the odd catcall, he didn't bother us much. When we left school, Duncan spoke to us, and we to him, as if none of it had ever happened. Floyd had remained my friend, and we'd even started work at the same garage.

Now, still shaken, I made my way to the street where Floyd lived, slowing then looking along each road before I turned in to it, expecting to see the Anglia waiting there. I made it though, without seeing Webster again.

Floyd came out of the house, pulling his jacket on, when he heard the sound of the scooter. 'You finished it,' he beamed, circling around the Lambretta.

I pulled the scooter on to its stand, then switched off the ignition. As the engine shuddered to a standstill, I told Floyd of my run in with Webster.

'Let's get the bastard,' he growled, then told me to wait. He ran down the entryway that led to the backyard of his parents' house. He returned, moments later, with a claw hammer tucked underneath his jacket. 'See if Webster likes this through his screen,' he laughed, as he stepped over the pillion seat behind me.

We set off. It took me several minutes to find my balance again, as Floyd didn't lean with the machine when I cornered. Soon, though, we both got the hang of it, and we cruised the streets searching for Webster's car. It would be easy to spot, as there were no other black Anglia's in the town. There was no sign of it though, even in the road where Webster lived.

We went through the market square. Webster wasn't there either.

'That copper's watching us,' Floyd said, tapping my shoulder then pointing to a policeman standing at the corner of the square, next to Woolworths.

I wondered if someone had reported me earlier. 'We'd better get out of here,' I called back. 'Don't want to get done for carrying a passenger.' Although I had ignored most of the legal requirements for my scooter, I had applied for my provisional licence. Neither of us had passed the bike test though, and I wasn't supposed to have Floyd on the back.

The copper would probably do me for not having any "L" Plates as well; I hadn't wanted to stick any onto the Lambretta's paintwork.

'L – Let's go home,' Floyd stammered. 'I'm frozen.'

I nodded. I was getting cold too. Webster would keep. I'd find him on his own one day, and then . . .

2

A Little Togetherness

'I'll give you a lift home after work,' I hissed as I sauntered past Floyd. The foreman, Frank Johnson, was watching, and I had to be quick, not for my sake, but because I knew that Floyd would get a bollocking if he stopped to speak to me. I bent down to tie my bootlace. 'Then we'll have a go at sorting your scooter,' I whispered as I rose to my feet.

Floyd nodded, then wiped his face with a rag. He had been steam cleaning the underside of a truck, and his clothes were soaked with oil and soapy water.

After I'd started as an apprentice at the garage, I'd offered to see if I could get Floyd a job there. He had tried for work at several places before then, but had been unsuccessful.

I'd asked to see Mr Beresford, the garage owner, and told him that my mate was looking for a job. 'He's good with engines and things – my father's shown him what to do,' I told him.

'I don't know as I need anyone – at the moment,' Beresford said. 'Not unless they've already served their time.'

I'd pleaded with him. 'Give him a chance, sir. He'll not let you down. Ask my father.' Beresford knew my old man as they both bowled at the same club; that was how I'd got my apprenticeship.

The garage owner had pondered for a moment, then said that I should tell my friend to come and see him.

Floyd had been over the moon. 'Man! A job – and a wage. I'll be able to buy you a drink for a change,' he laughed, as he slapped my palm.

The next day, I watched as Floyd reported to the garage. He'd borrowed one of his elder brother's suits, and was wearing a shirt and tie; he'd even tried to slick down his wayward curls of hair. 'Good luck,' I shouted, as he went up the stairs to the office.

Some ten minutes later Floyd came back, escorted to the door by Mr Beresford. I couldn't tell, from the expression on my friend's face, whether he had been successful or not.

Beresford had stopped by the side of the car I was working on. 'You didn't tell me that your friend was black.'

'Didn't think it mattered,' I said quietly.'

'Oh, I've given him a job,' Beresford snapped. 'Don't want people to think I'm prejudiced against them.'

True to his word Beresford set Floyd on, not as a trainee mechanic, but as a general labourer. He was given all sorts of menial jobs: cleaning the toilets, sweeping the workshop floor, washing off trucks, anything the other men didn't fancy doing.

'I don't mind,' Floyd told me, when I said I was sorry that I'd only managed to get him such a crap job. 'It pays. I'll soon have what I need for a scooter.'

And Floyd had saved enough, but only because of a stroke of luck.

My father's friend, the one who had sold me the Lambretta, had seen us with the scooter and asked if we wanted another one. 'It's seized up,' he told us, 'but perhaps you could fix it. She doesn't want much for it.'

I took Floyd to look at the scooter. The "she" turned out to be the man's sister, who had bought the scooter to use for shopping, but had got fed up of having it repaired. 'There's always something going wrong. I've just spent twenty

21

pounds having it painted – now the engine's packed in, she told us.'

It was a Vespa GS160, once fashionable with the Mods, but to us, not as good as a Lammy.

'It'll do until I can get something else,' Floyd whispered, as we inspected the machine. 'Perhaps I can trade it in against a Lambretta.'

We struck a bargain, and it was a real bargain; the woman only asked five pounds for it. 'Just get it out of my sight,' she told us.

I towed Floyd and his scooter home, using a washing line tied from my spare wheel carrier to the Vespa's handlebars.

'Slow down,' Floyd had screamed as we wobbled home. It was the first time he'd steered a scooter and he was terrified. The rope around the handlebars didn't help; it pulled the Vespa over as I leaned my machine into corners.

I'd just grinned back at Floyd. Being under pressure was a good way to learn to ride; I knew that from my encounter with Webster.

We had made it safely. Tonight, I hoped to fix the Vespa's engine.

'Will Clinton be in?' I asked as Floyd slid off the pillion. 'Have a quick look,' I said, when he told me that he didn't know.

Floyd had three brothers. Clinton at twenty seven was the eldest; he was hoping to be a doctor. Then there was Lloyd; he was twenty five. He hadn't got a job at the moment, but didn't seem overly bothered. He spent most of his time at the local snooker hall, much to the irritation of his father. Three years younger than him was Winston, who had just begun work, on the nightshift, at the local bakery. Then came Floyd. After him was Cheryl, the Edmonds only daughter.

'I heard pop say that mom can't have any more,' Floyd had told me when I remarked about the size of the family.

I hadn't meant it that way, but kept my silence.

The Edmonds lived in a large terraced house, together with one of Floyd's uncles and his family. The building always seemed to be hustle and bustle to me. I was more used to the ordered tranquillity of my parent's bungalow. Mr and Mrs Edmonds always made me welcome though. Floyd's mother was an excellent cook, and I loved it when she asked me to stay for tea. She had been a typist before coming over from Jamaica, but had settled for a cook's job at the local school. Fed up with boiling vegetables and potatoes, or frying chips at dinnertime, she loved to serve up traditional Jamaican fare to her family; when she could get the right fruit and things that is. The food was strange to me; there would be sweet potatoes and yams, or saltfish eaten with cornmeal dumplings and tomatoes. It was all very tasty though. My mother was hopeless at cookery, and I'd sampled weirder food from her kitchen.

'Your father married me for my looks – not my cooking,' she would tell me, when I complained about a tough piece of meat, or a burnt offering of a pie.

My father would say little. 'True. Very true,' he would nod, then draw on his pipe, sending fragrant blue smoke towards the ceiling.

And it was true; my mother must have been beautiful when she was younger. My father had a picture of her, taken just after he had met her, in his wallet. Except for a trace of wrinkles at the corner of her eyes, and a deepening of the creases at the side of her mouth, she looked much the same as she did in the photograph. A bit fatter maybe, but that was about the only other difference. I hoped that I took after her; I'd inherited her straight fair hair, and the same piercing blue eyes, and long slender nose, but perhaps my face was more square, my chin narrower. My mother's teeth were small and neat and she still had most of them now, giving her a perfect smile.

I brushed my teeth twice a day and, fights permitting, wanted to keep mine looking like hers.

I was glad that I didn't seem to take after my father. I loved my old man, but he was an ugly brute. His skin was like leather from his time in the Marines, and he had lost most of his hair from a young age. I sometimes wondered if I'd end up the same. My hairline formed what my mother called a widows peak. It hadn't started to recede. Mind you I was only sixteen; there was time yet, I knew.

My old man's nose, though bulbous, had been broken at some time and had a permanent twist to the side. He also had the cauliflower ears of a boxer. His eyebrows, thick and strong, like mine, curled around his eyes and, together with his narrow mouth, gave him a slightly bemused look.

I seemed to have his broad shoulders and slim waist, for which I was thankful, but was smaller than him in height. That would be from my mother's genes. My ears were a bit too big and seemed to protrude too much for my liking; perhaps they were something like my father's, but hopefully not quite so bad. And he had a dimple in the centre of his chin, the same as me. Maybe I took after him more than I hoped I did.

My father had told me that he had fought for the Marines in several boxing tournaments, and that was where he'd gained the many scars to his body. Then, when I was about thirteen, I'd overheard my mother talking to her sister; she had been complaining that my old man's appearance embarrassed her sometimes.

'You've got a good man there,' my aunt had snapped. 'You should be thankful that he's put a roof over your head. When I think what he must have suffered . . .'

She had paused as I entered the room. I'd asked them to explain and, grudgingly, my mother and aunt had told me that my father had been captured, tortured, and beaten by the Chinese, even though he had been suffering the agony of frostbite and had lost a couple of toes. That had explained a lot to me; I'd always wondered what had happened to my father's feet, and why he walked with a limp. He would never tell me. It also answered why my old man, normally very easygoing, detested the Chinese.

'Slit eyed bastards,' he would mutter, when we passed the local take-away.

Floyd's brother, Clinton, seemed to loathe me just as much as my father hated the Chinese. 'What you bringin' this white trash home for,' he had shouted at Floyd, when I first went to the Edmonds home with my friend. 'Come to see how us po' niggers live?' Clinton scowled at me, then went out, slamming the door behind him.

Floyd had told me to ignore his brother. 'He was beaten up last year – in London – by a gang of skinheads. Been like that ever since. Doesn't even talk like that normally.'

It was hatred at first sight between Clinton and me. Whenever we met he would scorn me. His features were harder, more chiselled than Floyd's, and his nose was thin, beak-like, with wide flaring nostrils. A cruel sort of face. His high forehead and long chin reminded me a little of Marvin Gaye, who I'd seen on *Ready, Steady, Go*. I could easily see why Clinton had been given a good kicking; I wished I could do it myself.

Now, although I got on all right with Floyd's other brothers, I tried to avoid the Edmonds home when I knew that Clinton was about.

Cheryl skipped down the front path. 'He's out,' she smiled at me before I could ask.

She was growing up fast I thought, as I looked at the jumper stretched tightly across her chest. Cheryl was only fourteen, going on fifteen, but acted older. I knew that she doted on me, ever since that day when I'd stepped in to help her. And I still felt protective towards her. She was like the sister I'd never had, despite our different backgrounds.

All the same, it was hard to tear my eyes away from the swelling of her breasts. And she wasn't wearing a bra. I could tell by the way that the cold wind caused her nipples to poke at her jumper. I thought back to the time when I'd stepped into the Edmonds kitchen and found Cheryl washing herself at the sink. She had been naked to the waist. Cheryl had grabbed for a towel, but smiled as she held it in front of her body. I could still picture the dark circles capping each brown breast, and wondered what it would be like to cup her beautiful tits in my hands, to suck on . . .

Cheryl had been talking to me I suddenly realised. 'Sorry. What did you say,' I asked, glad that I was still seated on the scooter.

'Will you take me for a ride. Pleeease!'

Despite her father's objections, Cheryl was wearing a mini skirt. I pictured it riding up her thighs as she straddled the seat. I shook my head as my prick began to harden again. Must stop thinking like that. 'No, I can't,' I stammered. 'Not until I've passed my test.'

'But you gave Floyd a lift home.'

'That's different. Floyd has his own licence – so that's all right,' I lied. 'Besides – we want to sort his scooter. I'll give you a ride soon, though. I promise.'

That seemed to placate her, and she went back into the house. I took some spanners from my toolbox then set to work. We had to fix the Vespa at the roadside and, although it was the middle of April, it was bitterly cold.

'Hope it doesn't take too long to f – fix,' Floyd stammered through chattering teeth, some ten minutes later. 'Do you know what's wrong with it?'

'I think so. Sit on it and have a go at starting it.'

Floyd climbed aboard the Vespa, turned on the ignition, the petrol, then the choke, and shoved the kick-start down with the sole of his boot. The engine spun over but didn't fire.

'I don't know what's up,' Floyd said, looking down at the engine, exposed to view now the side panel had been removed.

'Well, if it was seized – then it wouldn't turn over. Try the throttle!'

26

Floyd twisted at the handgrip. 'It won't move.'

'That's right. And if you look closer – you'll see why. Whoever painted the scooter has put too much on the handlebars. It's run into the controls.' I picked up a small screwdriver from my toolbox and prodded down the side of the rubber twistgrip. 'Have another go,' I said after a few minutes work.

This time, the throttle moved. Floyd tried the kick-start again. On his third go the engine spluttered into life. 'Well done, Kenny,' he laughed, then selected first gear.

'We'd better . . .' I said, as with a squeal of tyres Floyd drove the Vespa off its stand and hurtled off down the road. 'Check the brakes,' I finished, shaking my head as he disappeared from view.

Cheryl came out with two steaming mugs of tea. 'You got it going,' she smiled, as she handed one to me, then set down the other on the garden wall. 'Perhaps I can ride on the back of your scooter – now Floyd has his own.'

Cheryl had pulled a long black PVC coat on, but it was unbuttoned and my eyes dropped to her chest again. I gulped on the tea, burning my lips on the hot liquid. Cheryl must know what I'd been staring at. She pushed her hands behind her, under her coat. 'We could go for a run to the seaside,' she said. She smiled and, with her feet planted firmly on the pavement, began to twist her body from side to side.

This movement thrust her breasts between the coat flaps, and I watched, spellbound, as they swayed beneath my nose. I looked down the street. Hurry back Floyd, I prayed. I could never betray my best friend. I knew that Floyd would be delighted if me and Cheryl were an item – if she was a few years older! Floyd would be heartbroken though, if I did what was going through my mind right now. I would also beat any lad to pulp if they touched Cheryl. Yet here I was imagining doing the same. It was all right thinking it though, I finally decided. Yeah, that was a compliment to Cheryl's sexy young body; but I must never do anything about it.

I turned and scanned the road, reaching down and adjusting my crotch while my back was to her.

'Your scooter looks nice now,' Cheryl said.

She had seen it when I'd first bought it; I'd been so proud of it, even then, that I'd pushed it to Floyd's house for him to see. Since that day, as well as repainting it, I'd fastened on front and rear crashbars, the spare wheel carrier, a front carrier, and a couple more mirrors. Putting loads of accessories on their scooters had been the fashion with the Mods, then the craze had died a little, and they'd just fitted a few spots, some mirrors, the odd crash bar, and a screen. I wanted my Lambretta to be different, so had gone for the old look; mine would eventually have loads and loads of chrome. I'd also put a new numberplate on the back, where Webster had damaged the old one.

'I'm saving for some Florida bars next,' I told Cheryl.

When she looked puzzled, I told her they were chrome bars that fitted alongside the scooter's floorboards.

Cheryl climbed onto the Lambretta's seat and gripped the handlebars.

As she twisted the controls, as if riding the machine, I fought to keep my eyes away from her slim legs.

'How do you start it?' Cheryl said, looking down at the kick-start. 'Oh, I don't want you to – just show me for when I have my own scooter,' she smiled.

I pointed to the ignition; glad I had something else to think about. 'You make sure the petrol's on – and the choke if it's cold – then turn the key.'

'How do you turn the petrol on,' Cheryl asked, her dark eyes twinkling as they met mine.

'That silver lever – down there,' I said. I pointed to the fuel tap positioned at the base of the tool locker, beneath the front of the seat.

'Where? Show me,' she said, looking down at her feet.

I had the feeling that Cheryl knew exactly where the tap was; she'd watched me start the scooter before. To show her

28

now would mean reaching between her legs, my head close to her knees . . .

'Floyd's coming back,' I breathed with relief. He was pushing the Vespa though. Perhaps he'd run out of petrol; there hadn't been much in the tank. As Floyd came closer I saw that his jeans were torn at the knees, and he had blood streaming down his face.

Cheryl slid off the Lambretta and ran towards her brother, as she too saw that he had been injured.

'It's only a scratch,' Floyd grimaced as Cheryl examined his face. 'Fell off the bastard thing,' he muttered. He told me that the throttle had stuck open when he'd reached the first corner.

Floyd wasn't badly hurt, just sore. He'd scraped his knees and elbows, and the palms of his hands, on the rough tarmac. The blood on his face was from a cut to his forehead. 'I think I did that on the flyscreen,' he told me, as he pointed to the broken Perspex.

'My father says you can't ride a bike until you've fallen off it,' I grinned, relieved that my friend was all right. 'Mind you, I haven't – yet!'

When Floyd went inside with Cheryl, to clean up his wounds, I examined the Vespa. I found that the throttle cable was too slack. The outer sleeve had come out of its bracket when Floyd had accelerated, and had not gone back in again as he released the twistgrip; it would have kept the engine racing.

If Floyd had thought about it, he could have squeezed the clutch in, then braked. He might not have fallen off then. I also knew that it was easy to think that standing here; it would be different when you were screaming towards danger.

Floyd came to the roadside again, with a large pink plaster stuck across his forehead, contrasting vividly with his dark skin. 'I'm in trouble with pop,' he told me. 'Says I've got to get rid of the scooter. It's not safe.'

'He'll come around,' I said. 'My old man did.' I pointed to the Vespa. 'It's not badly damaged – just needs painting again. I'll take it for a spin – see if it's OK otherwise.'

I stepped onto the Vespa. It took a few kicks to start it again, as the petrol had spilled out of the carburettor. The engine finally spluttered into life and I let out the clutch. The Vespa shot forward, its front wheel rising in the air. 'Fucking hell,' I yelled, as I fought to control the scooter. I eased off the throttle and the front tyre bumped back onto the road again.

'It's different than mine,' I shouted to a worried looking Floyd. The seat was further back, putting the centre of balance more over the rear wheel than with my Lambretta. I shook my head with relief then released the clutch again, more slowly this time. I did a few slow circuits of the nearby streets, until I was sure there was nothing else wrong with the Vespa.

It was beginning to go dark when I returned to the Edmonds home. I found Eddie Duncan waiting there, together with another lad, Nutter Taylor.

Duncan now led a bunch of skinheads called the Hole in the Wall Gang. The naff name was Duncan's idea; the group of schoolkids he'd once led had their headquarters in a damp rubbish-filled archway under a railway viaduct. He'd kept the name for his new gang.

Duncan was talking to Floyd. Cheryl had gone inside. I knew she would have disappeared as soon as she heard Duncan's scooter coming up the road; she'd still not forgotten, or forgiven, his behaviour at school.

We had become allies, if not mates, of Duncan and his gang. Necessity had caused us to get together with them; except for the Hole in the Wall Gang, and a few divs, most of the other teenage lads in town were either greasers or hippies. Even now, counting Floyd, there were only eight of us with scooters.

One night, before we'd joined the Hole in the Wall mob, a

gang of greasers had chased after Floyd and me as we walked through town. To add to our problems, we met up with Duncan and his mates coming the other way.

Duncan had scowled at us, when he recognised who it was running towards him. When we told him that he should watch out, as there were a dozen of bikers close behind us, he had asked us where.

Duncan had reached into his pocket. 'Come with us,' he said. 'We'll soon sort the bastards out.'

We had followed him and his gang back along the street. We met the bikers on the corner.

'Come on then, you grebo wankers,' Duncan had yelled, waving a cutthroat razor in the air. 'I'll carve you up,' he screamed at them.

The bikers had looked at the size of Duncan, then the blade flashing in the orange light of the street lamp, then at the other skinheads, then legged it.

'You can buy us a pint for that,' Duncan grinned.

Later, when we were standing in the pub, sipping an illicit mug of Marston's Pedigree, tapping our feet to the sound of Canned Heat on the jukebox, he had suggested to me that I join the gang. 'Let's work together . . .' Duncan sang, echoing the words blaring out of the machine in the corner.

I hadn't been sure; I didn't find it easy to put memories of school behind me. But then again Duncan had a scooter, and at that time I craved one too.

'All right, I will,' I finally said.

'And you too,' Duncan had nodded to Floyd. 'We need someone to run errands,' he laughed. 'Only joking,' he said, when the two of us glared back at him. He ruffled Floyd's black curls. 'Yeah, only joking,' Duncan repeated as my eyes bored into his.

Since then we had held an uneasy alliance; I couldn't take to Duncan but teaming up made sense. Duncan knew, from experience, of my ability with my fists, and I thought there should be safety in numbers.

31

For it to work though, I had to let Duncan act as leader, although I hated following the flabby youth's orders.

Now, I waited to hear what Duncan had got planned for the night.

'We're gonna blitz the Coffee Cup,' he laughed, referring to the café that the local greasers used. 'A couple of the others will be here soon.'

'I'll get changed,' Floyd said. He was still in his oily work clothes and the ragged jeans. 'At least they're not my best Levi's,' he managed to grin.

By the time he came back, two more of the scooter gang, Rocky, and Cadger, had arrived; they sat revving their machines while they waited, causing Floyd's father to pull back a curtain and scowl out at us.

'I'll ride with you,' Floyd said and climbed aboard my Lambretta. 'Don't want to fall off mine again. 'Specially if there's a load of greasers after us.'

We set off, leaving a cloud of oily blue smoke behind us. We stopped once, to collect some broken bricks from a piece of waste ground, then roared along the High Street. The Coffee Cup was down a side street near the bus station, and we coasted our scooters down the hill towards it, keeping the sound of our engines low.

As we turned the corner I saw several bikers standing outside the café, next to their machines.

'Let's go,' Duncan shouted and opened his throttle.

The bikers looked up, in surprise, then alarm, as they heard, then saw, the five scooters hurtling towards them. More greasers began to stumble from the café, with Coke bottles in their hands, ready to throw at us. Those already outside reached beneath their saddles and pulled out bike chains and metal bars; one even had a hammer in his hand.

They were all too late. As our scooters flashed past we hurled lumps of brick at the greasers, and the café's window.

My scooter jerked as Floyd threw his own contribution. 'Missed!' he cursed as we accelerated away.

32

I looked back over my shoulder; most of the missiles had failed to hit their target. It didn't matter though; it let the greasers know they didn't rule the town.

I saw the bikers kicking their machines in to life, ready to give chase. They had no chance; although most of the motorbikes could leave our scooters standing, we would be long gone before the bikers knew which road we'd taken.

I looked down anxiously as the Lambretta's engine began to splutter. I felt Floyd tense behind me. 'Shit!' I mouthed, imagining our fate if it stopped. The engine misfired once more, then picked up its steady beat again.

'I'll change the plug in the morning,' I shouted back to Floyd. I'd found that my Lambretta had a habit of fouling its spark plug with oil, and I'd yet to find the ideal type. Tomorrow was a Saturday, and we planned a trip into the city.

That was no place to break down either!

3

I Feel An Urge Coming On

I was early at the time clock. I wanted to be first out of the door and had considered asking one of the other fitters to clock me off, but knew that I'd have to wait for Floyd anyway. I saw Ramsbottom, the Service Manager, coming my way, and I looked anxiously at the clock face; it was only five to twelve.

Ramsbottom stopped, then stood with his hands on his hips, looking at the clock, then at the toolbox in my hand. 'Finishing early are we? Have you done that gearbox?'

I told him that I had; I'd rushed to complete it, and knew that I'd probably overfilled it with oil in my haste to get away, but didn't tell Ramsbottom that.

'Got a foreigner to do, have we?' the Service Manager asked, then glanced at my toolbox again.

Thankfully, the other fitters were now queuing behind me; the workshop closed at midday on Saturday and only the showroom and parts department remained open after that.

'I'm going to do some work on my scooter,' I said, my face crimson, as I prayed that the hooter would sound. I imagined Ramsbottom having X-ray eyes, and seeing the things I had stolen stowed away at the bottom of the toolbox.

I'd sneaked into the stores, while the Parts Manager had been in the toilet, and grabbed two mirrors from a shelf. I had known exactly where to look for them; I'd watched him collect one from there when I needed it for a customer's car. It was the first time I had stolen anything in my life.

And it would be the last I promised myself, if I could just escape this time.

Eddie Duncan had fitted more mirrors to his scooter; he had nicked most of them from cars parked at the roadside. I had looked enviously at them. I wanted to fit dozens of mirrors to my Lambretta, but knew that I didn't have the bottle to just walk up and pinch them. And there was no way I could buy more, not at the price they were. Then I had seen the opportunity to get some from the stores; now I would lose my job, perhaps get done for theft as well. What would my mother and father say? I saw Floyd looking worriedly in my direction. He knew what was hidden inside the box; he'd tried to talk me out of doing it.

The hooter sounded.

'Come on, kid. Clock off or shift,' the man behind me growled.

'Off you go, Roberts,' Ramsbottom snapped. 'And I'll see that fifteen minutes is knocked off that,' he added as I punched my timecard.

'That was close,' Floyd said as we made our way across the car park to my Lambretta. 'Thought he'd got you!'

'I'll keep them hidden for a week or two,' I murmured with relief. 'Until I know they've not been missed.'

A car swung to a halt close by us. I glanced towards it. Then my heart sank again. It was Beresford. Shit! What was he doing here on a Saturday? Normally, he didn't come in at the weekend; that was why I had decided that today was the ideal time to raid the stores. I walked on. Perhaps if I didn't look at him, he may think I'd not seen him.

'Roberts. Edmonds. Can I have a word,' Beresford shouted after us.

I walked on a few paces, trying to figure a way out. No ideas came. I turned, looking resignedly at Floyd.

Beresford was standing next to a tall sylphlike girl with vivid red hair. Her sparkling green eyes looked down at me over a slender nose. She smiled, revealing flawless white teeth. There were laughter lines at the side of her wide sensuous mouth; she was obviously a happy sort of person. Very pretty I thought, as I waited for the sky to fall in.

'I'd like you to meet my daughter,' Beresford smiled. 'She's coming to work here – from Monday – in the office.'

So this was Maureen! The other men had told me that the boss had a cracker of a daughter.

'Reckon she's still a virgin,' one of them had said, and explained to me how her father kept a close eye on her.

'Can't shake hands,' I apologised to Maureen, turning my palm over to show the grease embedded there; I'd been in such a hurry to leave that I'd not bothered to wash up first.

Maureen smiled again. There were freckles at the side of her nose, I noticed. 'I'm sure that we'll see more of each other,' she said, tossing her hair back to reveal a high forehead.

She seemed to be about two years older than me. If the other men were right, and she had been at college until now, that would make her eighteen. I saw Beresford looking at the toolbox and I reddened again. How embarrassing it would be to be revealed as a thief in front of the girl; that would be worse than anything.

'Not taking work off me I trust?' Beresford said wryly. 'Come on Maureen. I'll show you your desk.'

I placed the box onto my scooter's back carrier; my hands were shaking when I let go of its handles. 'Shit,' I breathed, 'I thought I was well and truly fucked then.'

'Yeah, and I'd like to fuck her too!' Floyd nodded to where Maureen was striding across the car park.

She was wearing a tan sleeveless suede top over a cream roll-neck jumper. She had matching very tight fitting suede trousers above her high heels. I watched spellbound as her buttocks swayed beneath the soft hide. I wondered what it

36

would be like to hold her bottom tightly while I pumped away inside her. 'She can't be a virgin,' I muttered. 'Not when she's built like that.'

'What a waste,' Floyd grinned, then held out his hand. 'A quid says I screw her before you do.'

'You're on,' I laughed. I saw Maureen turn and smile back at us, almost as if she had heard our bet. But who had she smiled at?

'Christ, Kenny! What will your father say?' Floyd shook his head in amazement as he examined my new haircut. 'Go on then – I'll have the same,' he told the barber, as he took his turn in the swivel chair.

I looked at my reflection in the mirror. Fucking hell – it was short! I grinned as I admired my shaven head. I had asked my father, before we set off for the city, if he would lend me some money for the barbers. 'I'll pay for your haircut,' he told me. 'But get it done proper. You look like a tart with hair that long!' Now, I'd done just what he'd told me to do.

My father was lucky; at least I hadn't decided to be a bloody hippie, with hair down my back, like the T. Rex fans. Some of them had even taken to wearing make up. What would he say about that?

I'd decided to go the whole hog and have a skinhead cut, the same as the other lads in the Hole in the Wall Gang. Eddie Duncan had been on at me for months about having it done. He'd had one even before he left school. It made him look a bit tougher; his hair had a natural curl to it when long, and that made him look a bit puffy. When he told me I'd got to do the same I'd protested, said that close-cropped hair was going out of fashion now and suedehead was the way to be. But Duncan wanted all the gang to be the same.

At least he'd given up trying to get me to have a tattoo. Duncan had wanted us all to have "The Hole in the Wall Gang" and a picture of a dagger on our arms, like him and

Nutter had had done. No way I was going to do that; I hated needles. And the police knew who you were straightaway then. Besides, tattoos lasted a bloody long while. Duncan should know that. As well as "Love" and "Hate" on his knuckles, he'd had "Linda" put on his shoulder. Now Easy Rider had gone over to the greasers. Not surprising really; Webster was just a bit less repugnant than Duncan.

I might get away with a skinhead cut, but my old man would blow his top if I came home with a tattoo, even though he'd got one himself. He had a Marines insignia on his upper arm. The result of getting drunk one night in a foreign port, he had grudgingly admitted to me. As a kid I used to think that the words on his arm, "Per Mare – Per Terram," meant by horse and land. Couldn't picture my old man on horseback though. It was "By Sea – By Land," he told me.

Floyd had, at first, said he would just get a trim; now the barber was shearing away at his head too.

Soon the floor was covered with black curls. I knew that Floyd hated it when his hair grew longer. No matter what he tried to do with it, he always ended up looking like one of the Jackson Five. But this was a bit drastic. 'Never mind my old man – what's yours gonna say when he sees you?' My father was pretty easy going compared to Mr Edmonds.

Floyd shrugged. 'He's already on at me 'cause of the scooter. What more can he do?' He stepped out of the chair and began to brush loose hair from his denim jacket.

'Where to next?' he asked, when we left the barbers.

'I want to get a shirt,' I told him. 'Let's look in that shop up the road.' I had managed to squeeze some more cash from my mother. I'd told her that I needed some shirts, but she had offered to buy them for me the next time she was in town. I could imagine what her choice would be, something that only a div would wear, so I had asked for the money instead.

'Get something smart – and sensible,' she told me, as she

handed me what she thought was enough cash for a couple of shirts. 'You'll need something nice to wear when we go on holiday.'

I groaned, but decided that it was not the moment to tell her that, for the first time, I didn't want to go away with them; I had lots more exciting things to do at home, maybe even have a party while they were away. 'I could do with a new pair of trousers,' I said, hoping that, while my mother's purse was out, I could tease more money out of her. It had worked; now I could afford a couple of Ben Shermans, maybe even a pair of Sta-Prest. I had also managed to save some cash myself, but not enough for the Crombie coat that I wanted so badly, that would have to wait a bit longer. Didn't want to buy one of the cheaper Stone-Dri ones.

I led Floyd into a men's outfitters that, more by luck than design, had many of the garments that us skinheads desired. The shop assistants, more used to dealing with elderly male customers, would be overwhelmed by a sudden rush of lads; they needed to be pretty alert, else some of their stock disappeared under coats or into pockets.

After my fright with the mirrors, I decided that I'd pay for my stuff. I riffled through a pile of shirts in boxes, then held one up for Floyd's inspection.

'Yeah, I like that,' my friend nodded.

'Right. That's you fixed up. Now something for me.'

'You – you don't have to,' Floyd murmured.

I knew he was embarrassed at having no cash. 'I'm being selfish,' I said. 'We won't score tonight – with you looking like a tramp.'

It was hard for Floyd; my mate couldn't even tap his parents for funds, they weren't much better off themselves. I picked up another checked shirt, with a button-down collar, then a pair of black trousers. 'That just leaves enough for a burger – then the club later,' I said. 'There's one thing – my parents can't say these aren't neat.'

We made our way to the Wimpy Bar, after first checking

that the Lambretta was safe. It would be smashed if any greasers found it, so we had hidden it in a narrow alley behind a row of shops. Duncan, Cadger, and Rocky's Lambrettas, as well as Nutter's Vespa, were there too, and we met up with the skinheads in the burger bar.

Cadger saw me and Floyd come in. He made his way across to us. 'Buy us a Coke lads?' he said, living up to his nickname.

Cadger had stayed on at school and was trying to pass his "A" Levels. That meant he was always short of money and forever on the scrounge. He had become expert at being the last at the bar, even when the rest of us deliberately took our time.

I didn't have much cash to spare but I paid for Cadger's drink anyway; it was the easiest way to shut him up.

'And a burger?' Cadger said, hopefully.

'Piss off,' I told him, then picked up my change.

'I like the haircuts,' Duncan grinned as we slid onto the plastic seat opposite him. 'What you been buying?'

We showed him our purchases.

'I nicked these,' Duncan said, swinging his feet onto the table.

I moved my coke out of the way and looked at the leather brogues laced on Duncan's feet. 'You pinched them. How?'

'You should've seen him,' Rocky said. 'Takes one off the rack and asks the girl if he can try a pair on. She fetches him the other one – then as soon as they're on his feet he legs it.'

'I left them my old pair behind,' Duncan said. 'I stole them as well – so I ain't lost nothing.'

'Yeah but the manager grabbed hold of me,' Nutter growled. 'Said he was calling the pigs.'

I could guess the outcome; Nutter's nickname was down to his talent for head-butting anyone he disliked, although most people thought it described the state of his mind.

'That's right,' Nutter smiled. 'Silly bastard soon let go when his nose got broke.'

Rocky, a keen record collector, had bought a couple of 45's. 'Managed to get *Double Barrel* – as well as *You're Ready Now*. Show them what you stole Nutter.'

'Bastard!' Nutter scowled. 'You said you wouldn't tell them. Anyway it's in the bin now.'

'He wanted that Hot Chocolate record – *You Could've Been a Lady*.'

Nutter rose from the table. 'I'm goin' for a piss.'

'So he nicks *She's a Lady*. Big fan of Tom Jones is our Nutter!'

The rest of us jeered him as he scurried towards the toilets.

'Are you ordering again?' the middle-aged woman who ran the burger bar asked, as she put our empty cups onto a tray. 'If you're not – there's people waiting for this table.'

'Hiya, Rita,' Duncan said, patting her bottom. 'How about a quick blow job?'

'It would be quick with you,' the woman hissed, as she slapped Duncan's hand away.

'What's up? Husband back – or are you on the rag?' Duncan shouted after her, as she returned to the counter, causing the other customers to turn and look curiously in her direction. 'Rita lives next door to me,' he explained. 'Her old man's on an oil rig. Soon as he's away – I'm in there.' Duncan rose to his feet and we followed him to the door. 'Shall I come round later, Rita?' he called across the café.

'Yeah. Then you can bring back the knickers you stole off my washing line!'

It was Duncan's turn to look embarrassed. His face reddened as people turned to stare at him. 'Lying bitch,' he muttered, but I noticed he made a rapid exit.

'What time are we meeting tonight?' I asked him, as he kicked his scooter into life.

'Nine o'clock at the Red Lion. Then we'll go on to Annabellas. See if your mate Webster's there.'

It was just over two months since the greaser had tried to knock me from my Lambretta; Webster had not been seen in

41

town since. He was either lying low, or busy elsewhere.

Perhaps tonight I would be lucky.

'How much more of this rock'n roll crap do we have to listen to?' Nutter said. He got to his feet and staggered across the crowded dance floor. He pushed his way through the older Teddy Boy types, who were bopping away with their girls to the corny sound of Bill Haley. Nutter reached the small stage at the narrow end of Annabellas dance floor, then beckoned to the DJ. When the DJ bent down, to listen to Nutter, the skinhead grabbed him by his jacket lapels and pulled his head closer.

From where I sat I couldn't hear what Nutter was saying, but I could guess. Something like, "play any more of this crap and I'll kick your teeth down your throat!" I felt sorry for the DJ's who played at Annabellas. They tried their best, but the clubgoers were a mix of Mods, and Skinheads, or greasers who'd left their leathers at home while they wore the obligatory suit and tie, or Teddy Boys with their DA haircuts, as well as a few farmers' sons, down from the hills, wanting to clomp around to *Sugar Sugar*, or the odd squaddie home on leave and determined to have a good time of it. It was difficult to cater for the varied tastes. Keep one lot happy and you'd upset the others.

This happened now as the DJ spun the skinhead favourite, Desmond Dekker's *You Can Get It If You Really Want It*, and we sprang to our feet and began to stomp. The doormen edged closer, sensing trouble, as the Teddy Boys cursed and moved aside. One of the old rockers, wearing brothel creepers, vivid green socks, and a boot lace tie that had gone out of fashion years before, went up to the DJ. I saw the youth shrug, as if to say, "what can I do?"

This was how most nights went at Annabellas Disco; a few records for each faction while the other mob tanked up on ale. There would be trouble later. There was no sign of Webster or Martin though. Perhaps one of the other bikers

42

would tell me where the bastard was. After a few more reggae numbers, I went across to Pete Andrews. He was a biker but, although he hung around with the other greasers for his own safety, he was really only interested in motorbikes. I had fixed his Triumph for him on several occasions, much to the disgust of Duncan.

Andrews told me that Webster had got a job on the motorways, and was now working away from home. Birmingham or somewhere, he wasn't sure. 'He's coming back in a couple of weeks, though,' he told me. 'Says he knows you are after him – so he's gonna find you first.'

Andrews' girlfriend came back from the loo, so I left him to it and went to look for Floyd. He was chatting to two girls, both of whom looked as if they still went to school despite their stylish clothes and make-up.

'Kenny, this is Anne,' Floyd grinned as he put his arm around the blonde-haired girl nearest to him. 'And Debbie,' he nodded to other one.

Floyd was letting me know that he fancied Anne, and was going to have a crack at her; introducing her first was the code we used when we met up with a likely pair of chicks.

Debbie was small, a good few inches shorter than me, with straight black hair framing her round face. She had a long curved nose and plump cheeks. Dark eyebrows arched over her eyes. What did she remind me of? That was it – a puffin. Mind you Floyd seemed struck on Anne, so I decided I would do my bit; he'd often gone out with a girl he didn't fancy just so that I was fixed up. 'I'll get a round of drinks in,' I said, hoping the girls didn't have expensive tastes.

They didn't. Well not too bad anyway, just rum and cokes.

I shouted into Debbie's ear, as a Chuck Berry number began to blast out. 'Help me fetch them?'

She nodded and followed me. I circled the dance floor. It would give Floyd a chance to chat to Anne.

'Is that you who I've seen on that blue Lambretta?' Debbie asked me, while we waited for our drinks.

When I proudly told her that it was, she smiled up at me. 'Have you come on it tonight?'

I nodded.

'Will you give me a lift home on it later?'

'What about your friend – how's she going to get back?' I asked, thinking I would leave the coast clear for Floyd.

'Oh, her brother's here – he'll see she's all right.'

And spoil Floyd's chances, I decided. 'OK, you're on.'

We went to the corner booth where Floyd and Anne had found a seat. Floyd winked at me. He must think he's scored I realised, then shook my head. Floyd nodded, as if to say, "I'm in here," so I thought I wouldn't disillusion him.

'Shall we dance?' Debbie said, tugging at my arm. The music had changed again; the DJ was spinning a soul record.

It would give Floyd the opportunity to talk the other girl out of going home with her brother. I led Debbie onto the floor.

Several drinks and several more dances later, I decided that Puffin – Debbie – was much prettier than I'd first thought. A slow number came on, so I pulled her into my arms. I looked down into her eyes; they shone back at me, reflecting the warm glow of the disco lights. I sank my mouth down onto hers. She pressed herself against me and her tongue slid between my lips. Yes, she wasn't so bad after all. My prick began to rise in anticipation.

Puffin must have sensed my body's response. 'Shall I get my coat?' she murmured into my ear. 'Then you can give me that ride.'

I nodded and followed her back to our friends. Floyd was nuzzling Anne's neck. 'We're going,' I shouted.

'Be good,' Floyd grinned back.

We made our way to the alley where the Lambretta was parked. As we reached the machine, I pushed Puffin against a wall and began to kiss her again. As her mouth responded, I began to unbutton the front of her dress.

'The ride first,' she gasped, gripping my wrist.

I cursed under my breath; I'd had a few too many drinks to balance properly. I could perhaps have wobbled home all right, but didn't want to fall off with her on board, then have her tell her mates about it after. 'Let's stay here for a while,' I suggested hopefully.

'But I have to be in by twelve!'

I glanced towards the clock above the market hall; that gave me thirty minutes. 'OK,' I said, pulling the scooter off its stand and turning the petrol on. I kick-started it, and told her to slide onto the seat behind me. I saw a flash of her white knickers, as she lifted her leg over the saddle, and I felt a stirring in my loins again. Concentrate on driving I told myself, as I eased the Lambretta forward.

Soon we were speeding along the High Street. Puffin didn't know how to lean for the corners, so I slowed more than usual for them. Even so, she shrieked in my ear as the Lambretta banked over, her thighs squeezing against mine. Although I had fitted a KL backrest to the scooter, and she couldn't fall off that way, she gripped my waist tightly, her hands clasped together just above my straining penis. We did a few laps of the town and, eventually, she relaxed enough to wave and shout to some of her friends who were walking home.

I swung the scooter's forks towards the park and cruised along until I found what I was looking for, a shelter that was not occupied by other courting couples. I pulled the Lambretta to a halt just inside the entrance and tugged it back onto its stand. I stepped off the scooter and turned round, kissing Puffin again as I straddled the seat, facing her. 'Where was I?' I reached for her buttons again.

This time she didn't resist, and soon her dress was undone from top to bottom. I pushed the fabric back then slid my hands behind her, and, despite my intoxication, deftly undid her bra strap. 'Jesus,' I breathed, as her fingers reached for my belt. I moved my hands to cup her breasts, then ran them down her sides to grasp the waistband of her knickers and

45

tights. She raised herself from the seat, helping me. I gasped as her black bush was revealed to me, and I teased my fingers through her curls, feeling the wetness of her.

'Have you got – something.' Puffin whispered hoarsely, as she grasped me in her hand.

Had I? There were some Durex in the, appropriately named, toolbox. Puffin's body gaped invitingly before me, and I was tempted, very tempted, to slide into her as I was.

She seemed to read my mind and covered herself with her hand. 'Not without a rubber.'

Where were the damned things I sighed, as I searched among the spanners? Then I had them. I rolled one frantically into place, barely able to contain my excitement. 'Christ,' I hissed when I felt the warmth of her surround me, as I pulled her body towards me on the seat.

Later, when I had dropped her off at her home, I rode back through town, to see if Floyd had been as successful with Anne. There was no sign of him, but I met Rocky, staggering along, with his arm around Nutter.

Nutter's face was covered in blood, a large stain on his shirt front almost black in the light of the street lamps.

'One of the bouncers threw him downstairs,' Rocky told me. 'Just after you and Floyd left – Nutter had another go at the DJ. The doorman grabbed him and tossed him out. I was on me own – didn't know where Eddie was – so I thought I'd better get him home.'

I winced as I pictured the steps leading from the disco. Annabellas was above Burtons the Tailors, and there were at least thirty concrete steps to hit on the way down.

'Nutter was pissed, so he wouldn't have felt much,' Rocky said, as he helped me put the injured youth onto the Lambretta.

'But God help that bouncer when he sobers up.'

4

I Got The Fever

'Hi, Maureen,' I shouted, causing the red-haired girl to pause at the door of her Ford Escort. This was the first chance I'd had to speak to her in the three weeks since she'd started working for her father. I had seen her in the office, through the glass window above the workshop, and I watched her climb the stairs, to go up there, most mornings.

One day, I had been a dozen steps behind her as she crossed the workshop floor. She had been wearing a beige mini-dress, with a wide floral-patterned belt hanging loosely over her hips. I'd stood with my tongue hanging out, as she ascended the metal stairway and I waited, mesmerised, barely breathing, hoping for a glimpse . . .

Then Ramsbottom had come out of his office. 'Nothing to do Roberts?'

I scuttled back to the car I was working on. As I passed Floyd he had given a crude sign with his arm, then whispered, 'She's mine.'

'You've got no chance, the pair of you,' Frank Johnson, who was checking a car on the ramp next to me, had laughed. 'Little Miss Iron Knickers won't let you near her.'

Today, I hoped to prove him wrong. Floyd wasn't working this Saturday morning. Although he needed the overtime, he said he wanted to finish repairing the Vespa ready for the afternoon. We had repainted it earlier in the week, and now all that it required was a polish up and a new fly-screen.

That meant I had a free run at Maureen. At first, I had begun to doubt if she was coming in; I'd even wondered, for a moment, if Floyd had scored with her, and that's where they both were now. Then, just after ten, I heard her heels clattering on the metal steps. I was too late to catch her, and I couldn't go up to the office, even though I knew Maureen was on her own; Ramsbottom was somewhere in the garage.

I clocked off at noon. Maureen's car was still there. As the other men left, they stared at me; they knew that, usually, I was away as soon as the hooter sounded. I tinkered with my scooter as a cover for my being there.

At one stage, Johnson had come across to me. 'Need a hand?'

I told him it was only a petrol leak, and that I had almost fixed it, and was relieved when he went home too.

It had been some fifteen minutes more before Maureen came out, and I had gone across to her.

'Hi, Kenny isn't it?' Maureen said with a voice of pure honey. She brushed a stray wisp of hair from her eyes, with her slender fingers, then smiled at me, her freckles sparkling in the sunshine against her pale skin. Her eyebrows were thin traces of red, over her wide green eyes I noticed, as she arched one, curiously.

I was in love. She was even more beautiful than I remembered now that I was close to her again. 'How are you enjoying your job?' I said. Prat! I chided myself; I had meant to ask her out, not bore her with stupid questions.

'It's – interesting,' Maureen said. 'I'm just finding out what you all do.'

Take her to the pub and tell her what you would like to do, a voice nagged inside my head. 'We're all pretty busy,' I said, instead.

'You've had your hair cut I see.'

'Yeah, do you like it,' I said. Then my world fell apart.

'I think I preferred it how you had it before. It made you look more – mature.'

My confidence waned altogether. 'Must go,' I said, then headed for my Lambretta.

'See you, Kenny,' Maureen called after me.

After a few steps I turned, hopeful that the situation could still be saved, but she was in her car, starting the engine.

Maureen waved as she drove out the car park. I raised my hand disconsolately in reply. I decided not to say anything to Floyd, it may spark his interest if I did. I resolved to let my hair grow again though; perhaps then she might fancy me.

'Here's another one,' Floyd said as he scrambled over a wrecked Austin 1100's bonnet; he was after a mirror on the door of the car stacked on its roof. He could just reach it, and soon it was added to our collection.

After my fright at the workshop door, when I thought Ramsbottom knew about the stolen mirrors, I had decided to find another source.

Floyd had suggested we try the scrapyard. 'They can't ask much for them there.'

Now we had a dozen mirrors. 'Let's call it a day,' I shouted, as I ducked underneath the rear bumper of an overhanging car. I cursed as my feet sank into the cloying mud, causing a smell of petrol, old engine oil, burnt rubber, and God knows what else, to rise into the air.

Then all of that was forgotten. In front of me was an old cream and maroon car. It was an Armstrong Siddeley. On the bonnet was the maker's badge, a chromed sphinx about four inches long. It would look brilliant on my scooter. The TV175 had a bigger mudguard than the newer scooters, so, before painting my machine, I had cut it down in size. Although I'd managed to roll back the edges to make a smooth lip, I was still unhappy with it. The sphinx would set it off just right though, if I fixed it there. I squeezed a screwdriver under the casting and levered; the sphinx

49

popped up, the small bolts that held it to the bonnet pulling through the panel. I stuffed it into my toolbox and covered it with my spanners.

I circled around the savage looking Alsatian, tethered by a long chain that still allowed it to snap at my heels as I passed, and met Floyd at the yard owner's shed, next to the gateway.

'How much for these?' I said, as we deposited our finds onto the greasy wooden counter; I kept the sphinx hidden though.

'Two bob each,' the yard owner grunted.

'But – that's one pound twenty altogether – in the new money,' Floyd said. 'Bet you ain't paid much more than that for the cars.'

'We'll take them,' I said, placing one of my hard-earned notes and a fifty pence coin onto the counter.

'But . . .' Floyd looked at me in disbelief, then shook his head.

I picked up my change and left the shed. As I tied the toolbox to my Lambretta, I heard someone shouting in the yard.

'What fucker's damaged my car? I'll kill the bastard!'

I started my scooter and Floyd climbed behind me. I glanced back through the gate as we pulled away. A fat black-haired man was making his way, belligerently, towards the shed.

'What's up with him?' Floyd shouted into my ear as the scooter picked up speed.

'He's lost something. I'll show you later,' I grinned. I had thought the car was scrap, and was glad the owner hadn't caught me. The silly bastard shouldn't have parked it there.

We made our way back to town. There was nothing to beat this I thought as the Lambretta howled along; it made all the difference when the sun shone. We had tied our denim jackets to the back carrier, with a bungy cord, and the wind whipped at my granddad shirt.

'Something old, something new . . .' I began to sing the words of the Fantastics song that was currently in the charts.

'Something borrowed, something blue,' Floyd chimed in behind me.

As we sped along a straight piece of road, whooping above the clamour of the engine, a motorbike suddenly appeared alongside us, startling me from my reverie. I had just realised what it was, when the biker swung his foot at the scooter. The Lambretta swerved violently to the left, partly from my surprised reaction, partly from the force of the kick. I fought to regain control as the wall of the front tyre scraped the kerb.

'Shit! That was close,' Floyd yelled.

The greaser came back again. This time though I was ready; I braked sharply and the bike overshot us. I accelerated, as much as the Lambretta would do being two up, and drew alongside the other machine. It was a BSA 250. The rider tried once more to kick us off. I swerved the scooter towards the greaser, my Florida bars squeezing him towards the kerb. He swore and kicked again, until another push of the scooter sent him off the road. The Beezer bounced onto the verge, sending grass and loose stones flying into the air. Its rider howled vengeance after us, as he braked sharply. Suddenly, his front wheel hit a milepost, hidden in the grass, and he catapulted over the handlebars.

'Got the bastard,' I laughed as the biker tumbled into a ditch, his mangled machine close behind.

'He bent your Florida bars though,' Floyd said.

'It'll be worth it – just to tell the gang,' I grinned, and began to sing again.

As we rode on, the Lambretta's engine note changed from its clattering beat to a deeper roar. 'Sounds like the exhaust,' I said, slowing then looking down at my feet.

'Something must have come loose when he hit us,' Floyd said, pointing back over his shoulder with his thumb.

'Damn!' I mouthed, hoping it only needed fixing and not

51

replacing. But then – the sound was still there even though we were losing speed. What was it?

'K – Kenny,' Floyd wailed, tugging at my arm.

I turned to see what was up, and saw hundreds of bikers roaring towards us. 'Fucking Hell,' I yelled, and opened the throttle once more. It was hopeless. In that one quick glimpse I had seen that some of them were Hell's Angels, riding the big American-style chopper bikes that had become common over here since *Easy Rider*. There was no way we could outrun them. I tried to picture the road ahead; we were about two miles from town. If we could just reach there we might lose them.

The bikers must have come to the same conclusion and, almost as one, they began to pick up speed.

I could easily imagine what would happen when they caught us, especially after we had knocked one of their mates off. The local greasers were bad enough, and would give you a good kicking if they got hold of you, but these bastards . . . I tried to concentrate on the road. As I leaned the scooter into the next bend, the Lambretta's tyres fought for grip. I was right on the limit. Don't lose it I cautioned myself, almost feeling the bike chains that would lash into me if I lay helpless on the road.

I risked another quick look back; the bikers were fifty yards away and closing. Ahead was a "30" sign, but nowhere to hide. I didn't slacken for the speed limit. I hurtled past a slower moving car then cursed as I saw, in my mirror, the bikers do the same.

The traffic was beginning to build up now, as Saturday afternoon shoppers sought a parking space. I swerved around a row of cars that were waiting to turn into the High Street; again the bikers followed, only ten yards or so behind.

They were slowed, temporarily, by one of the cars doing a right turn across their path. My relief was short-lived; a clamour of horns and angry shouts and the bikers were there again.

I swerved the Lambretta into the alleyway that I had used to escape from Webster. It was futile now though; the bikes could follow us. As my scooter rumbled across the cobbled car park, the sound of the bikes' exhausts rose to a crescendo as they thundered through the alley behind us. The long front forks of the choppers were a hindrance to the riders, at slow speed, but the power of their engines more than made up for that; they could accelerate rapidly on the straight.

Again, I veered into the narrow service alley. Above the echo of my Lambretta's puny two-stroke engine I could hear the motorbikes, just behind us.

'Some have gone round to cut us off,' Floyd yelled.

I bounced off the pavement in front of the terrace and swerved to the right; there was a maze of alleyways that way. 'When I turn the next corner – jump off and hide,' I shouted to Floyd. 'In a garden or somewhere.'

'No. I'm sticking with you,' he screamed back.

Ahead of us the road was blocked with motorcycles, their riders slapping pieces of bike chain, menacingly, into the palms of their leather gloved hands. I didn't need to turn; the roar of engines told me that the others were behind. We'd had it!

'Down there,' Floyd shouted, and pointed to the driveway of a large detached building. 'It's the doctor's house. There's a path out the other side.'

'Get ready,' I called back as I leaned the Lambretta into the turn. The scooter's tyres lost their grip on the loose gravel of the drive. I shoved my feet down, speedway style, as I fought to regain control. 'Now's your chance,' I shrieked, as we approached the porch at the side of the house. The outer door was open, and I doubted the Hell's Angels would follow Floyd in there; they would be too busy chasing me. 'I'll be faster without you,' I said as I squeezed the front brake lever.

'No – don't stop. They're too close,' Floyd said, shaking my shoulders in his agitation.

There was no time to argue, so I accelerated again. As I steered the Lambretta through a small gateway into the back garden, I heard a loud clatter behind us. I glanced back. One of the bikers had lost it; his chopper was sprawled in the driveway, a cloud of dust rising into the air above the brightly painted machine. It would buy us a few seconds but that was all; the other bikes swerved around the fallen rider.

'The gate's shut,' Floyd said, pointing to a green door, set into a high wall at the end of the garden.

The Lambretta skidded as I steered it among the neat rows of cabbages, heading directly for the door, ignoring the curving red-ash pathway. I tugged the handlebars straight again. What if the gate was locked? Jesus Christ, I prayed, as I imagined the bikers' leather boots thumping into my body; many of them had steel toe caps, and I winced at the thought of them smashing into my teeth.

Locked or not, the bikers would have us when we stopped to open the gate. I looked frantically to right and left, desperately seeking an escape. There was nothing; to one side was a row of beanpoles draped with strands of green foliage. There was another brick wall at that end. The other way, there was a jumble of compost bins and cold frames.

We could abandon the scooter and try for the wall, perhaps use one of the bins as a step up. I thought of what the bikers would do to my Lambretta. Mind you, it was better than being caught by them; I could always salvage the scooter, or what was left of it, later.

I was just about to turn that way when the gate opened! I leaned my body to the right and the scooter responded. I made for the opening.

'What the. . ?' The man who had just been about to enter the gateway gasped in surprise, as my scooter roared past him, nearly running over his toes.

It was our doctor. I hoped he hadn't recognised me else I'd be in trouble with my father later.

The doctor had other things to worry about though, as

dozens of motorbikes burst past him, through the gateway, in pursuit of us.

I scanned the road ahead. No sign of other bikers – yet. Somehow, we had to evade the ones following. But how? My hopes rose as a policeman stepped from a shop doorway. We were saved!

The policeman saw the scooter speeding towards him, obviously well above the limit, and strode into the middle of the street.

I sighed. I'd be done for speeding, having no paperwork, and carrying a passenger, but we would live to fight another day.

Behind us, the roar of the motorbikes eased as the Hell's Angels spotted the bobby. I ventured another backward glance, and saw that there were now fifty or more machines cruising to a halt.

Floyd laughed and made a circle with his finger and thumb. 'Wankers,' he shouted back.

I was just about to tell him that he might be better to keep quiet when the bikers, as one, opened their throttles.

'Bollocks!' Floyd yelled, realising at the same time as me that he might have made a mistake.

I turned back towards the bobby. Would one policeman be able to hold them? I doubted it. So did the bobby; he was folding his pocketbook and racing for the pavement.

I wrenched the right hand twistgrip and the scooter began to pick up speed, but not as quickly as the bikes. As my Lambretta screamed past the policeman, he began to write frantically in his notebook.

Shit, he had my number. I cursed under my breath. No time to worry about that now; the bikers were only yards behind. Ahead, a bus was waiting at some traffic lights. I pulled out to go around it. Should I go through the red light I wondered, as bemused passengers stared down at the scooter from the bus's side windows. The lights began to change, then, with a jolt, and a cloud of unburned diesel, the vehicle began to set off. As I drew past its front bumper I swerved to the left. The bus driver stamped on his footbrake, as my Lambretta swung across his bows. I wasn't sure what hissed the loudest, the bus's airbrake, or Floyd on the seat behind me.

I could hear the bikes racing past the other side of the vehicle; it would take them longer to steer the forks of their machines in pursuit, or so I hoped. Another left and I was on the pavement, scattering pedestrians as I raced back the way I'd come.

I took a right turn into another side street. I was still on the pavement, and swerved around the litterbins, lamp posts, and yet more confused shoppers who stood dumbstruck in my path.

The policeman had been walking towards the lights; he would have seen my dangerous manoeuvre. In my mirror, I saw the first motorbike turn into the street behind us. My risky stunt had only bought us a few seconds. The next right turn took me back towards town. Then I saw a possible escape; someone had left a garage door open at a nearby house. I thundered into it, almost tumbling off the scooter as the front wheel slid on a patch of oil.

I was just about to shout to Floyd, to tell him to close the door, but I saw I had no need. He scrambled from the pillion and pulled one of them shut. Seconds later, the other was bolted in place and we were in darkness. A terrible roaring sound echoed around the asbestos panels of the ramshackle building, and for one terrifying moment I thought the bikers had spotted us and we were trapped. Then, to our relief, the noise died away.

Floyd peered through a crack in the door. 'They've gone,' he whispered, as I pulled the scooter on to its stand and joined him.

The bikers went past several times that afternoon; they even stopped to look up the short driveway, at the garage where we were hidden, before resuming their search.

I prayed that the building's owner stayed away for a while longer yet.

'They're in the White Swan,' Eddie Duncan told us when we met up with him and Nutter outside Payne's café. The other scooterists had seen the bikers riding through town and had left their machines at home, but we had called at Floyd's house so that he could collect his Vespa.

Floyd had been in trouble with his old man, because he was going out again without touching the tea Mrs Edmonds had ready. And his father had still not forgiven him for having his hair cut short. 'That boy is leading you astray,' he said, pointing to me. He shook his head as Floyd defied him and rode off with me.

Cautiously, we had ridden to the café that was the haunt of the Hole in the Wall Gang. As we went in, I told Duncan of our narrow escape. 'You should have seen the look on that guy's face when we came out of his garage,' I chuckled. 'He'd just drawn his car up – never heard us start with his engine running – then out we came. Just managed to squeeze past him.'

I ordered a bottle of Coke for myself, and an Orangeade for Floyd. We both preferred to drink something straight from a bottle. Although the café had been a favourite spot for the local Mods, and still was for the skinheads, Mrs Payne's hygiene left a lot to be desired. She would collect up the empty coffee cups, and dinner plates, and dunk them into a basin of greasy water that she changed regularly – every night! By lunchtime it would be awash with fag ends, congealed lumps of chewing gum, soggy baked beans, and bits of uneaten toast.

Mrs Payne made her own pies and cakes. I used to join the others when they bought something to go with their drinks. One day, I had watched her making them while I waited for her to serve me.

'Gets the dirt from under yer fingernails,' she chuckled,

then swished her hands in the bowl, before wiping them on a piece of rag that had, at some time, been a tea towel. 'What can I get yer?'

I had fought back the bile that rose in my throat, and decided that, from then on, it would be Cokes only; they should be safe enough.

Now, I glanced around, expecting Cadger to appear at any moment.

Duncan saw me looking. 'He's gone shopping with his mother and father. Says he'll see us later at the club.'

'I'm looking forward to that,' Nutter growled as he rubbed his flattened nose. 'That bouncer's been away on holiday – but he's supposed to be back tonight.'

'Yeah, as I said, the greasers are in the pub,' Duncan repeated. 'Someone says they've come over from Buxton. They've left their bikes in the multi-storey. We ought to get them.'

'What? Just the four of us?' I said apprehensively, my nerves still not settled from the earlier encounter.

'We could ride around town – see if there's anyone else about,' Duncan said.

'I think everyone's keeping out of the way,' Nutter shook his head.

'Let's just do it,' Floyd said, angry that the bikers would get away with chasing us.

We set off. Duncan riding behind me on the Lambretta.

He was getting fatter I thought as I was forced forwards on the seat, my knees pressed against the legshield. Nutter was on the back of Floyd's Vespa. We cruised warily along the road towards the car park; there was no sign of the bikers, or of other skinheads. I steered the scooter along a pedestrian walkway, into the open-sided concrete box of the multi-storey, followed a few yards behind by Floyd. Several circuits later, we went up the ramp on to the top floor. Row after row of the greasers' bikes were parked there.

'Fuckin' hell,' Duncan breathed behind me; until that

moment it seemed he'd not realised how many of them there were.

I parked the scooter in the centre of the aisle and walked to the parapet of the car park. Although it was nearly dark, I could see the bikers milling about outside a nearby pub.

'We'll have to be quick – and not make too much noise,' Duncan said as he joined me at the wall.

We were quick – but not silent. As we set about the motorbikes, smashing headlamps and tail lamps, tearing out plug leads, slashing seat covers and tyres, Nutter began to get carried away.

'Greaser bastards,' he yelled as he kicked a bike over. Unfortunately, the other machines began to topple like dominoes, as bike fell against bike. There was a tremendous clatter and a cloud of dust rose into the air.

I could smell petrol as the choppers' tanks spilled their fuel.

'Have you got a light,' Nutter shouted, as he saw it spilling across the concrete floor.

I was just about to answer, to say he hadn't better, when Floyd yelled a warning. He had gone to the wall to see if the bikers had heard the racket. They had! He told us they were racing towards the multi-storey, bike chains and knives at the ready.

'Shit! What do we do,' Duncan said, panic in his eyes.

I felt my legs begin to tremble. We were trapped again.

'Shall we jump?' Duncan said.

I looked down. We were six floors and perhaps eighty or ninety feet up. I shook my head. 'Get on the scooters – and we'll coast down. They're coming up the stairs. They might not see us. We'll be gone before they realise.'

Duncan climbed onto the saddle again, and I pushed the scooter along with my feet towards the first ramp. I couldn't have moved it far, Duncan was just too big, but soon we were freewheeling down the slope. I had to brake or else we would never have got around the corner to the next ramp. I winced as the front brake shoes screeched in protest. Would the greasers hear? Too late to worry about that! We rolled down the next slope, then the next, gathering speed again. I prayed that no cars came in as I was hurtling down the entry ramp. I glanced behind. Floyd was still there, lines of concentration on his forehead, gritting his teeth as the Vespa's tyres squealed on the oil-covered floor. A painted sign on the wall said Floor 3. We might just do it. I could hear the bikers shouting as they headed for their machines. They hadn't spotted us yet. Floor 2 came and went. Now there was just the final ramp to the ground floor to go. I let the scooter gather as much momentum as possible on this last slope; I didn't want it to slow when I finally let the clutch out to bump-start it.

We hurtled across the lower floor then bounced onto the pavement, to bypass the closed barriers. As I finally released the clutch, I heard angry yells behind me. I glanced back; dozens of bikers were scrabbling over the lower wall into the car park and had just spotted our scooters. They began to run after us.

As I let go of the clutch lever the Lambretta's engine coughed then burst into life. I whooped with delight as I accelerated away, then turned round to give a triumphant gesture to Floyd. He wasn't there! The Vespa was several yards behind, the bikers closing on it fast. 'We have to go back,' I shouted, and began to turn my scooter.

'No fuckin' way,' Duncan screamed in my ear, as he saw the hordes of irate bikers racing towards us.

The Vespa was still rolling, but hadn't started. 'Have you switched the ignition on?' I yelled to Floyd.

He seemed to act in slow motion. As the scooter decelerated to walking speed, Floyd turned the key. Just as the Vespa was about to stop altogether the engine caught. It spluttered then misfired. Probably a flooded carb. The engine popped again and, just as the first greaser grabbed hold of the rear carrier, Floyd opened the throttle. The biker clung on as the two-stroke motor fought to gain speed.

Now, other denim and leather clad thugs raced to help, their hob-nailed boots sparking on the tarmac. One of them was Webster.

The greaser recognised me at the same moment. 'We'll get you, Roberts,' he yelled, his acne-covered face split into a snarl.

The Hell's Angel clinging to the Vespa was not going to give up his prize easily, his boots were sliding along the road but he was holding back the scooter. Another few seconds and his mates would be there.

Nutter had seen the danger; a quick slash across the man's knuckles, with his razor, finally persuaded him to let go. The Vespa leapt forward, now it no longer had the added burden.

I spun the Lambretta around again and raced off in Floyd's wake. When we were a good mile or so away, Floyd slowed to a halt. 'Th – That was close,' he stammered. 'They'd have had me if you hadn't told me what was wrong,' he said, reaching across and clasping my arm. 'Thanks bro', ' he grinned.

'Bollocks to the club tonight,' I said. Although I'd promised to meet Puffin at Annabellas, I decided that it would be wiser not to go. I'd miss the chance of another leg over, but suspected that I would miss a lot more if the bikers caught me.

I guessed that the Hell's Angels would look for us there.

5

Pay To The Piper

I went to the yard at the back of the garage, to spend my morning break with Floyd. He'd been given the chore of rubbing down the bodywork of a Vauxhall Victor that had just had a wing and its front valance replaced. 'Hi, Floyd. Get home all right?' I said.

Floyd straightened up, then dropped the cork rubbing-block, together with a piece of wet-and-dry paper that he was using, into a bucket of soapy water. 'I think so. What a night,' he grinned. 'My head's still sore this morning – and so's my dick.'

I laughed. 'Mine too. Hope we didn't pick anything up – besides Shagbag. Everyone said she was a goer – and they were right.'

For the last couple of weeks we had decided it was wise to keep a low profile, as there were still dozens of greasers in town, bent on revenge for the damage to their bikes.

Last night, we had gone to the local youth club instead of Annabellas. It was held in a wooden hut next to the church, in a building used by the scouts on a couple of weeknights. Rocky usually took along several boxes of discs, then acted as unofficial DJ for us. We danced to a few soul records, thumping out from his portable record player, swigged a bottle of Coke apiece, then played a bit of table tennis, to keep the youth leader convinced that we intended to behave ourselves.

When he turned his back, I sneaked into the storeroom below the hut, where the scouts kept their tents and stuff. Floyd followed a few seconds later. Here, we usually practised a few dance steps. We had two of bottles of cider hidden in our kit bags for refreshment.

The music was still loud up above and we knew it would mask any noise we made, so long as we remembered not to clap. We drank some cider then, as *Boogaloo Party* sounded out, tried a few of the moves that some of the older boys said was how they danced, at the Mojo in Sheffield, or at the Twisted Wheel, over in Manchester.

Floyd had just done a brilliant spin when we heard footsteps on the wooden staircase. We froze, almost in mid-movement, Floyd poised with one foot in the air, me with my feet splayed.

I thought it was the youth leader, and that we would be banned. It wasn't him though, it was a blonde-haired girl called Sheila, or, as everyone at the youth club knew her, Shagbag Sheila.

'Can I join you?' she'd asked. A few slugs of cider, a slow dance with each of us, and she had begun to live up to her reputation.

Now, as I thought back to the moment when she had rubbed her hand against my crotch, I shook my head. 'I'd heard about her,' I told Floyd, 'but never believed it. She's a fucking nympho. When was the last time we shared a girl?'

Floyd looked thoughtful for a moment then laughed. 'Eddie's mum.'

I nodded. Floyd was right – unfortunately.

We had called at Duncan's house one night after work, to see if he was home. His mother had invited us in. 'He not here yet. Will not be long.'

Although it was half-past five in the evening, she had still been wearing her blue nylon dressing gown. I had wondered if it was true what Rocky said, that she earned money by having sex with other men.

'Drink?' she said, then poured a couple of good measures of a clear liquid into two smeared glass tumblers. She handed them to us.

I had been a bit reluctant to drink. The whole house stank of something awful; I wasn't sure what. When she filled another glass and toasted us, I decided that the spirits would probably kill anything harmful. It was vodka. I had never tasted it before and it seared at my mouth and throat.

Eddie's mother bent to refill my glass again, even though it was still half full. As she leaned over her gown spilled open, and I suddenly realised that she had little or nothing on beneath it. I peered between her pendulous breasts and could see almost to her navel.

She sat on the settee next to me and crossed her legs. The gown slid from her knees.

I glanced at Floyd, sitting opposite us. When he saw me looking in his direction, he raised his eyebrows in a gesture of astonishment.

'So, you're Kenny,' Eddie's mother said, placing a hand on my knee. 'Eddie has spoken of you.'

I felt the heat of her palm against my leg, and tried to avoid looking down at her red-painted fingertips.

'What time . . ?' I struggled to clear my throat then took another sip of the coarse fluid. 'What time will Eddie be home?' I said, hoarsely.

'Soon. You not like my company?' She ran a fingernail along the inside of my thigh.

Despite myself, I felt my body react to her touch. It was obvious what she intended, but – she was the mother of my friend. 'We'd better go, Mrs Duncan,' I managed to stammer out.

'No, you stay an' haf another drink.' She poured a shot of Vodka into my glass. 'And it not Mrs Duncan,' she told me. 'You call me Paulina. Eddie's father not marry me.'

64

Rocky had told me that Duncan's mother was Polish but not said anything about his old man; that was why.

My head began to swim as the drink took effect.

She clinked the bottle against my glass again and, despite my protests, sloshed more vodka into it. 'He left me with baby,' she slurred. 'I only fifteen when he go.'

'I'm sorry,' I said.

'You nice boy.' She leaned towards my neck; an aroma of stale spirits and cheap scent met my nostrils. 'I like nice boy,' she continued, sliding her fingers between the buttons of my shirt, sending a tingle of anticipation down my spine.

'Can I use your loo?' Floyd said, sidling to his feet. He went into the kitchen when she told him that it was out the back. He was walking awkwardly I noticed; he had a hard on too.

Paulina had her tongue down my throat, and her hands grasping at the buttons of my jeans, seconds after Floyd left the room. I tried to resist, but when she tore her robe aside, and straddled me, I was lost. She guided me between her legs then forced herself down onto me. ' 'Tis all right,' she told me. 'I am on the Pill.'

When Floyd returned she was bouncing naked on me, her breasts jiggling in my palms. 'Sorry,' he coughed, then turned to squeeze past the sofa, towards the front door.

'You join us,' she smiled, as I emptied myself into her.

'I – I don't think so,' Floyd stuttered.

I knew he was embarrassed, but not too much; we had both taken turns to screw Easy Rider, so it wouldn't be the first time.

Floyd didn't take a lot of convincing; his black buttocks were soon pounding between her thighs as she lay back on the settee. The erotic sight soon rejuvenated my interest and, glassy-eyed now, I took my turn again.

When Duncan arrived home some two hours later, we dressed hurriedly. His mother lay naked, in a drunken stupor, on the sofa. It was obvious what had been going on but he just ignored her. 'Are we off to the pub?' he said, dropping his haversack on the living room floor. He grinned wryly, then spat on the carpet. 'I see you've met my mother.' After that, he never spoke of her again.

I pulled the gown over her before we left, disgusted by my behaviour. I felt sorry for Duncan. Fancy having your mates screwing your mother, telling everyone else about it. I regrétted that I'd not held myself back, especially when I saw Paulina in the street several days later. She was only in her early thirties but looked a lot older. Sunlight wasn't kind to her complexion either; thick layers of make-up could not hide the sallowness of her skin, or the dark circles below her eyes.

It was no wonder that Duncan didn't mind it when he was sent to Borstal; there he'd at least get a decent meal and not have to watch a procession of men visiting his mother. That was the last time we called for him at the house.

'We should've used something,' Floyd said, bringing my thoughts back to the present. 'After what I've heard about Shagbag. Now, I shall be worryin' that I've got a dose. It was bad enough after Eddie's mum. Every time I itched, I thought it was the clap.'

I laughed but was worried too; pictures of dripping, sore-covered penises and tales of blindness, insanity, and even death, came back to me from my lessons at school. Was it worth it I wondered?

Then I knew that, despite our fears this morning, both of us would probably give Shagbag one again, if we met up with her tonight.

'Ramsbottom's watching,' Floyd said, causing me to start with alarm.

'See you later,' I said, then went back to the workshop.

Maureen was just coming out of the showroom as I made my way back to the car I was fixing. 'Hello, Kenny,' she smiled, causing my heart to thump in my ribcage.

She was gorgeous; none of the other girls that I knew

could compare to her. She had – class – that was it. Speak to her you clod, a voice said inside my head. 'Are you going on holiday,' I asked, then could have bitten my tongue off. What a stupid thing to say again.

'Yes, my parents want me to go to Bournemouth with them. I should like to stay here – perhaps have a party – but Daddy insists . . .'

'You'll have to come to my party then,' I said. 'I'm having one later – in July or August.' Like hell I was. My father had told me there was no way that he was leaving me on my own at the house. I would have to cross that bridge later. 'I'll let you know when it's to be – a bit nearer to,' I smiled. 'Bring a friend if you like.'

'I might just do that,' she smiled back, her green eyes flashing; then she strode away towards the stairway.

I watched her hips swaying. She walked just like a model on the telly. Or one of the girls on Miss World. I tried to picture her in a swimsuit.

Who would the friend be? I prayed it wasn't a boy. I had never seen her with anyone, or heard that there was someone in her life.

'You young lads are like rabbits,' Frank Johnson said, as he saw the look of rapture on my face. He picked up an exhaust pipe and began to twist it into position under the car he was working on. 'Screw anything that moves. Mind you – I was the same myself at your age. Hadn't had a good night out if I didn't get me leg over.' He rested his arms on the platform of the vehicle ramp. 'Wait until you're married and have got kids screaming around you every night – that'll take the smile off your face. You lot have got it made now – with the Pill and all that.'

'You're right,' I grinned. 'The girl I went with last night is on it. There's nothing like having it bareback. Beats wearing a johnny any day. So long as we didn't catch anything off her.'

'We? You mean both you dirty bastards had her? Girls

nowadays.' Johnson shook his head. 'Wish they'd been like that when I was a lad.'

'She was well up for it. We all call her Shagbag. The only thing she worried about – was that we'd come all over her dress.' I laughed. 'What will my mother say if she sees that,' I mimicked Shagbag's high-pitched voice.

'I should imagine the mother of a girl like that would be used to seeing spunk on a dress,' Johnson winked.

'Well, her parents are going away at the weekend – to Scarborough. They're leaving her behind. So – if we can't find anything better – we'll be in there again.'

'Supposed to be all right Scarborough,' Johnson said, selecting a spanner from his toolbox. 'Never been there before, but me and the missus have always said it's somewhere we wanted to go.'

'Well, Sheila will be on her own all week. Her gran's supposed to be keeping an eye on her – but that's only in the day. With luck we'll be seeing to her at night,' I chuckled, then realised that Johnson was staring at me.

'This girl . . . My lass is called Sheila. She's staying . . .'

I felt a sudden panic in my stomach. Shagbag Sheila – Johnson. Her surname suddenly came to my mind as I saw the look of anger on my workmate's face. With a sinking feeling, I knew I was right; Frank Johnson was her father!

'You fucking bastards,' he spat, then threw the spanner onto the ground. It clattered across the oil-soaked floor. 'You dirty fucking bastards,' he repeated, then stormed across the workshop, kicking a waste bin out of his path.

I was dumbstruck. What an idiot I'd been. I had better warn Floyd; Johnson was on the warpath and my mate wouldn't be aware of it.

'What's going on?' Ramsbottom snapped as I set off in Johnson's wake. 'Get back to your work. Now!'

I ignored him and went outside. Johnson was there, ranting and raving, on the other side of the car that Floyd had been working on, but there was no sign of Floyd. Then I saw him.

Johnson had thrown him to the ground. 'Bastard,' he screamed as he kicked at Floyd. 'I'll teach you to leave my daughter alone.'

Johnson must have caught Floyd unawares, to get the advantage of him. Or maybe Floyd was frightened for his job. Perhaps he thought that if he struck back he would be fired. 'Let him go,' I said, tugging at Johnson's arm. 'I'm as much to blame as he is. Have a go at me then.'

'I fucking will,' Johnson howled, spittle dribbling from his chin as he swung a fist at my head.

I ducked then stepped back.

Johnson spun around again and kicked at Floyd's face. Luckily, Floyd managed to swing his head out of the way.

'Stop it.' I moved forward again, but this time received a punch in the ribs for my trouble. Another fist came at my nose. I fended Johnson's arm aside with the back of my left wrist, then planted a right on the foreman's chin. Johnson went down, pole-axed, just as Ramsbottom arrived on the scene.

'Get your coats – and get out. The pair of you,' the Service Manager stormed. 'I'll not have fighting here. You're both fired.' He bent to check on the unconscious foreman. 'Call an ambulance,' he bellowed to another fitter who had come to see what was happening.

'But we . . .' I started to say.

'Still here,' Ramsbottom scowled. 'If you are not gone in the next five minutes, I shall call the police. He may still want to do so,' he said, nodding towards Johnson, who was now sitting up, holding his head in his hands.

I debated whether to stick one on the Service Manager too. What was the saying, "may as well be hanged for a sheep as a lamb?"

Floyd must have read my mind; he sprang to his feet and led me away by the arm. 'It's not worth it, Kenny.'

I passed him my handkerchief; blood was streaming from his nose where one of Johnson's kicks had struck home.

'What the fuck was that all about?' Floyd said, as he dabbed at his face. 'Came at me like a friggin' madman!'

'Shagbag Sheila's his daughter,' I told him as we collected our things from our lockers.

'Say what?' Floyd stared at me. 'An' you told him about last night. Hell, man,' Floyd dissolved into laughter. 'What a prat you are.'

'Guess we won't be seeing her at the weekend now,' I chuckled.

'Well, it wasn't a bad job – while it lasted,' Floyd said as we walked towards our scooters.

'I'm coming back tomorrow,' I told him. 'I'll ask to see Beresford – explain what happened.'

I hoped that the garage owner didn't tell his daughter everything though.

Maureen would be well impressed by my taste in girl-friends.

'I'm going to have my hair cut off,' Cheryl told me. 'Then I can have it like Diana Ross.'

'The girl means a wig,' Mrs Edmonds explained. 'Talk to her Kenny. She might listen to you.'

I still had my mind on earlier events. What was I going to tell my father? My old man, just like Floyd's, had said, when I had my hair cut short, that I looked like one of those troublemakers he'd seen on the TV. I had explained it was the fashion nowadays; it didn't mean I was actually a skinhead. My father had asked me why I hung around with a gang of lads then if that was the case. I didn't reply; I couldn't. Now, I would have to tell my father I'd lost my job. And what would Beresford say to him, when they next met at the Bowling Club?

Footsteps sounded in the hallway, as another member of Floyd's family came home from work. I prayed it wasn't Clinton. 'Sorry,' I said as I realised Mrs Edmonds was waiting for an answer. 'I was miles away.' What had she

70

said? Hair, that was it! Cheryl was going to go skinhead too. 'I think you look nice with it as it is,' I said, smiling then running my fingers through Cheryl's locks. I meant it as well; the wigs that some of the black singers wore seemed so false. And Cheryl's hair looked just right, as it framed her pretty face.

'I t'ink it look nice as it is,' Clinton's voice mocked me, as he took his place at the table.

'Clinton!' Mr Edmonds glared at his eldest son.

Cheryl smiled at me then turned to her mother. 'OK, I'll think about it,' she said. 'I know when I'm beaten. More pudding, Kenny?'

I nodded. The dessert was delicious, a mix of sweet potatoes and pumpkin.

'Eat all you can,' Clinton said generously, although I, as well as the rest of the family, knew that he was taking the piss; he usually complained that I never left enough tea for him.

As Cheryl slid another portion of the pudding onto my plate, her father turned to Floyd. 'What happened to your face, son?'

'Someone had a go at him on his way home from work,' I said, not wanting him, or Cheryl, to know what was behind it all. There was still a small chance that we could get our jobs back, I thought optimistically.

'That right, boy?' Mr Edmonds turned towards Floyd again.

'Yes,' Floyd said. 'Don't know who it was or why. They just came at me.'

'Some folk don't need a reason,' Clinton scowled at me, 'other than the colour of your skin.'

'It was nothing to do with that,' Floyd told him.

But it had been, I suddenly realised. Johnson had gone straight for Floyd, although I had screwed his daughter too. I decided to keep my silence, no reason to give Clinton that satisfaction.

'You boys finish work early?' Mr Edmonds asked, looking at me, then Floyd.

'We're going out tonight,' Floyd told him, 'so we were quick off the mark. Out of the garage as soon as the hooter went.'

'You can help your mother with the dishes first,' his father said.

'I'll do them,' I volunteered; I didn't mind that chore, not when Mrs Edmonds had cooked such wonderful food.

'I'll help dry them,' Cheryl chipped in, as she saw that Clinton was about to say something in reply. 'Where are you going tonight,' she asked me, as she joined me at the kitchen sink. 'The youth club?'

I shook my head; that was another place to avoid for the time being. 'Just for a ride on our scooters.'

'Can I come too?'

'No, we're meeting the rest of the gang,' I lied; Floyd and me had a lot to talk about. I had also worried for the last two weeks, that a summons would drop through the door of my parents house. Or that the doctor would suddenly turn up, complaining about my behaviour. Neither had appeared, but the last thing I wanted now was to be stopped with Cheryl on the back of my scooter.

I had enough problems without that.

6

Keep On Keeping On

'What was the fight about?' Maureen asked, tapping the end of her pen onto the blotter on her desk.

I stared at her carefully manicured fingernails, then down at my dirt ingrained hands. I was embarrassed. How could I tell her that the fight had started because I couldn't keep my prick in my trousers? I didn't know if Maureen had ever seen or knew of Shagbag; I doubted it, but guessed that if she did, any chance I had of going out with her would be blown.

Then I had the answer! 'Well, you know my mate, Floyd,' I said, looking up and meeting her eyes. 'Well, Johnson found out that Floyd was seeing his daughter. Took offence at it and went after him. I tried to stop him but Ramsbottom arrived. Saw us fighting . . .' I shrugged. That would put Floyd out of the running with Maureen too. I tried not to smile.

Maureen stared at me for a few moments. I felt my cheeks begin to redden; it was almost as if she could see into my mind, tell that I was lying.

'I saw it all from the window.'

Did she know the truth then? Was she playing with me? 'I don't know why Johnson got so angry,' I said. 'Rumour is that Floyd was not the first boy she's gone out with.'

'That's what I heard too.'

73

She did know that I had screwed Shagbag I decided as she smiled accusingly at me. 'Floyd was drunk – and so was Johnson's girl. Floyd told me that he regretted it later.'

'Isn't she fifteen? Still at school? Or so I heard Mr Johnson telling my father. He said it was almost like – rape.'

'Thought she was sixteen,' I mumbled as I examined my shoes, specially polished for my appointment with her father. Damn! I'd not expected Maureen to be here. When my old man had said that he'd asked the garage owner to see me, to get at the truth of the matter, I had thought I might have another chance at keeping my job. Now Maureen thought I was a bloody pervert, a rapist. She would never be interested in me. 'I think she was popular – with the lads in town,' I said. I didn't want Maureen to know that the girl I'd screwed was the town bike. 'She looks much older than she really is – especially when she's made up – and dressed up.'

'But not when she's undressed, I'm sure,' Maureen said, quietly.

She was mocking me! Thankfully, I was spared more discomfort by the sound of the buzzer on her desk.

She stood up and went to the door of her father's office. 'You can go in,' she said, pushing it open.

I straightened my tie, tidied the flaps of my jacket pockets, took a deep breath, then stepped into the lion's den.

'Would you like me to take notes,' Maureen asked her father, as he motioned me to sit in the chair opposite him.

Take notes! My heart sank. Maureen sitting there, writing everything down! It would be the death warrant for our relationship – before it even started!

Beresford rubbed at his moustache. 'No, I think we'll keep this informal. For now,' he finally answered, much to my relief. He waited until his daughter had closed the door again. 'Now, Roberts. I have a report here from Mr Ramsbottom,' he said, tapping a manila file that lay on the desk in front of him. 'He thinks you are a trouble maker, and I must say – with that haircut – you certainly look like one.'

'It's just . . .' I started to say.

'Let me finish!' Beresford snapped. 'I have also spoken to Frank Johnson – trying to find out what sparked it all off. He told me some of the details – but has said that he doesn't wish to take the matter further. That may be his choice but not one that I necessarily agree with. Your father had a word with me too. You have shamed a proud man, Roberts. When someone who fought so valiantly for his country has to grovel for his son to keep his job – then that makes me very angry indeed. However, because of who he is I shall give you one last chance. Let me – or your father – down again and you will be out. That's all.'

He pressed a button on his desk, a signal that the interview was ended.

'But what about Floyd? He never did anything. Didn't lift a finger against Johnson,' I stammered. 'It wouldn't be right if . . .'

'Ask Mr Ramsbottom to step in,' Beresford said as Maureen appeared, behind me, in response to the buzzer. As she turned and left, the garage owner glared at me once more. 'I am a fair man. You will both resume work on Monday.' He paused as the Service Manager knocked then entered the office. 'But if I hear of any friction between you and Johnson – or any other bad reports,' he said, nodding towards Ramsbottom, 'then you are gone. From now on, if Mr Ramsbottom tells you to jump – you ask how high! Got that?'

I nodded. 'Thank you, sir. I won't let you down.'

'You'd better not,' Ramsbottom muttered.

As I left the office, Beresford called me back. 'Let Edmonds know, will you?'

I told him that I would, and closed the door behind me. I'd felt like telling Beresford to stick his job; I had my pride after all. But then I thought of what it must have cost my father to go begging to the garage owner. I felt like cursing but saw that Maureen was watching my face. Looking for my

75

reaction to the warning perhaps – so that she could report back to her father?

'Daddy had a terrible argument with Mr Ramsbottom,' Maureen whispered. She touched my arm, making my pulse race. 'Ramsbottom threatened to leave the firm if he had you back. I don't know what your father said but he's given you another chance. Don't make him regret it, please!'

How could I refuse her I wondered, as her eyes bored into mine?

Maureen must suddenly have realised that she was still holding me and moved her hand away, but not before I had seen the blush – of excitement I hoped – rise to the peach smooth skin of her cheeks.

I could smell her scent, a gentle hint of almonds. How I would love to hold her, kiss her . . .

A chair scraped on the floor of the office I had just left; Ramsbottom was coming out!

I decided it would be wise to be gone before he appeared, and I made for the door to the stairs. 'See you on Monday,' I whispered to Maureen.

'We'll talk more then,' she said. 'I want to hear Floyd's version too.'

I sighed. It certainly sounded as if Maureen knew what I had been doing with Shagbag.

Or maybe she fancied Floyd?

'You should thank your father,' my mother said as she cleared the dinner plates.

'Thanks, pop. I know what you did,' I said, squeezing my father's shoulder as I made my way from the table.

'I couldn't just stand by and watch you throw your apprenticeship away, son. You'll always have a job if you have a trade behind you. But I don't want to have to do that again. Next time, you're on your own.' He tugged a few strands of tobacco from the pouch lying on the table next to his elbow, and began to stuff them into the bowl of his pipe.

'Not in here, Charlie,' my mother frowned, as he reached for the box of Swan Vestas that lay next to his baccy.

My father put the matches down again, but left the pipe jammed between his teeth. 'You should thank that girl as well,' he mumbled, his pipe rocking up and down as he spoke. 'Beresford's girl,' he said when I looked puzzled. 'Told her father that she'd seen everything from the office. Watched Frank Johnson attacking Floyd. And she said you didn't hit him until he hit you. I'm glad about that. Didn't bring you up to be a bully.'

So Maureen defended me I thought, my spirits rising. And Floyd, a voice nagged at my brain.

'I reckon you boys owe your jobs to her as much as to me,' my father continued. 'She told Mr Beresford that, to be fair, Johnson should be sacked as well. Anyway, you had better knuckle down to it now. I promised Beresford that you would – if he gave you the chance.'

I told him that I would, but I was still trying to figure out if Maureen fancied me – or Floyd. I would have to ask her; that was the only way to find out.

My father looked at his pipe, as if surprised that it wasn't lit, then put it on top of the pouch. 'You can start by growing your hair.'

I nodded; I already planned to do that and if it pleased my old man as well . . .

'Perhaps if you saw less of Floyd,' my mother said, as she wiped the chequered oilcloth that covered the table, with a damp dishcloth. She waited for my father to move his smoking stuff out of the way. 'You always seem to get in trouble when he's with you.'

'We're friends,' I shook my head. 'It was just a bit of fun, that's all.'

'That's another thing,' my father said, then waited until my mother had returned to the sink. He lowered his voice. 'If you are – um – going out with girls then we need to – to talk about it.'

77

I noticed my father's face had gone red, even the tips of his ears were glowing with his embarrassment. I smiled. This tough old man, hero of Korea, was shy about discussing the facts of life with me.

'There's things you can use . . .' My father paused as my mother came back to the table.

'I know pop,' I smiled, to put him out of his misery. Then my mother spoiled my good mood.

'Have you told Kenny about our holiday?' When my father shook his head, she turned to me. 'Someone who works with your father is going to lend us his caravan, at Mablethorpe, for a couple of weeks. He says it's in a nice spot, not far from the beach or the shops.'

I groaned. We'd been to the seaside town on one of our Sunday outings. It was all right when you were a kid and wanted to build sandcastles, but two whole weeks with my parents . . . 'I can't afford to go away this year,' I said. 'I've got my scooter . . .'

'You could sell that,' my mother answered. 'It's got you into nothing but trouble. Besides, we'll give you some spending money,' she said, looking at my father for confirmation.

'I don't know if I can get the time off. Especially after what's just happened . . .'

'I've already asked Mr Beresford,' my father said, destroying my feeble excuse. 'He says that if you behave yourself – then you can have a few days off.'

'It will be nice to have a holiday together,' my mother smiled. 'Be a family again.'

My father said nothing, as he rose from his chair, then gathered his pipe, and made for the backdoor.

'I think I'll stay at home. Besides, there's college. I have exams soon. I need to study for them,' I stammered out.

'You can do that at the caravan. I'm not letting you stay here on your own. And that's final!' my father growled as he stood in the doorway.

Two weeks in Mablethorpe! And what about my party? I'd already asked Maureen.

Now, while I was away, Floyd could have a crack at her.

'Shit head!' Shagbag scowled at me, as I waited with Floyd at Annabellas bar. 'You owe me a drink for this,' she said, pointing to her cheek.

Despite the extra layers of face powder she'd applied, and the low lighting of the club, I could see the darkened circle of skin around her left eye.

'My father did it,' she grimaced, when she saw me peering at the injury. 'Why the fuck did you have to tell him?'

'Never realised he was your old man.' I fought hard not to smile, and I daren't look at Floyd. We had split our sides earlier, when we talked of the moment when Johnson had realised that the girl I was on about was his daughter. I would never forget the look of horror on Johnson's face.

Floyd had been overwhelmed when I told him about getting his job back. 'Don't mention it. It was mostly my father's doing,' I said. I kept quiet about Maureen's part in the affair; didn't want Floyd to think she was interested in him. I knew that Floyd would do the same if the situation were reversed; a bet was a bet after all! 'What're you having then?' I asked Shagbag, as the girl behind the bar waited for my order.

'Bet it'll be a double,' Floyd winked at me.

'Shut up,' Shagbag said, nudging him in the ribs. 'Reckon it's worth a brandy and Babycham.' She pulled a packet of cigarettes from her handbag.

'I'll have the same – if you're buying,' Puffin's voice said, from behind me, as she wrapped her arms around my waist.

I called to the bargirl. I had arranged to meet Puffin inside the disco this Friday night; that had left me enough money for a few drinks.

Shagbag picked up the cherry from the glass when it was placed in front of her. She sucked it, seductively, between her lips, then, after gently tugging the glistening red fruit from the cocktail stick with her teeth, swallowed it.

Floyd coughed, trying to attract my attention, but I ignored him; I knew I would end up in hysterics and I didn't want to explain to Puffin what we were laughing at.

'See you later boys,' Shagbag said, tucking her handbag under her arm. A lad standing on the other side of her raised a lit match to the cigarette she placed between her lips. 'Perhaps have a dance?' she said as she blew a smoke ring into the air.

Her lips formed a circle, reminding me of when . . .

'The other girl's say she's a right slag,' Puffin whispered into my ear, as Shagbag swayed away from the bar.

By the amount she was drinking, somebody would be screwing Shagbag before long I thought. As Puffin released my waist I turned and smiled at her. When she smiled back, I wondered if, one day, she would take me in her mouth as Shagbag had done that night.

'Is Anne with you,' Floyd asked her, looking over her shoulder for her friend.

'She's over there, chatting to your mates.' Puffin waved towards the corner booth that Eddie Duncan and several of the other lads had taken over for the night.

We made our way across. Anne was talking to Duncan, but slid along the plastic-covered bench when she saw Floyd. I looked at Floyd; I hoped that Duncan hadn't been telling Anne, who would then confide with Puffin, about our scrape with Johnson. I saw Duncan grinning at me and knew that he had.

'Bastard,' I mouthed to him as I sat down in the booth.

'Hi, Debbie,' Duncan leered. 'Fancy a ride later? Or is Kenny giving you one?'

Puffin looked into my eyes, then, when I nodded, she told Duncan she would be going home with me.

'Like riding two-up, Kenny?' Duncan said, making a rude gesture behind Puffin's back.

Anne saw it I noticed, and she blushed. She shook Puffin's arm. 'Toilets?'

Puffin nodded and picked up her handbag; they disappeared across the dance floor towards the Ladies.

'Just keep your fucking mouth shut will you,' I yelled into Duncan's ear; *Groovin' with Mr. Bloe* was thumping out from the speakers at the side of the stage and it was difficult to make myself heard.

'Keep your hair on,' Duncan said rubbing his hand on my bristly scalp. 'Or what's left of it,' he grinned.

'Suppose you've told Anne everything?'

'Only what I'd heard – and that wasn't much – so I had to make some of it up.'

'Tell her you that made it all up,' I growled. I saw Anne and Puffin come back out of the toilets, then make their way towards the far end of the dance floor, at the front of the building. The scowl on Puffin's face told me that Duncan had said enough. Damn! I liked Puffin and had been looking forward to seeing her home later.

Floyd had also seen the two girls scurrying away and shook his head. 'Well done, Eddie,' he said. 'Thanks a lot – mate!'

I suddenly noticed Nutter sitting in the corner next to Rocky. He was almost hidden behind the other skinhead's shoulder. 'Thought you were banned?' I shouted.

'We sneaked him in through the fire escape,' Duncan laughed. 'Keeping him out of sight for a bit.'

'Fucking hell Kenny, look who's just walked in,' Floyd said, then pointed towards the entranceway.

I turned and saw Webster, Easy Rider, Skunk Martin, and a dozen other greasers, and their girls, handing their coats in at the cloakroom. They had left their leather jackets at home and, so that the club would let them in, changed into jackets and trousers, much like my father's de-mob suit, with bootlace ties at the neck of their white shirts.

The girls were wearing short black leather or suede skirts,

but most had legs like tree trunks and looked about as sexy. Easy Rider's skirt was more like a belt. She had dyed her long hair black and, together with the heavy mascara circling her eyes, her white face made her look like an anorexic panda. To think that I had once screwed that! I shook my head, disgusted with myself.

Webster saw me at almost the same moment and nudged Martin.

The other greasers turned and peered into the gloom, then grinned as they realised there were only five of us skinheads.

I didn't mind those odds too much. Just let the bastards start something . . .

Cadger shuffled into the booth.

That made six against fourteen. Even better I thought. And it was unlikely that the greasers would be tooled up; it was hard to smuggle weapons past the bouncers.

'Whose round is it?' Cadger yelled.

'Yours,' everyone shouted as one.

Cadger shrugged. 'Come on lads – I'll get one next time. I'm hoping to get a part-time job this summer.'

Cadger's "next time" would be a long way off if his past performance was anything to go by. 'Go on then, I'll pay if you fetch them,' I told him.

I watched him make his way towards the bar, past Puffin and Anne who were dancing together near the doorway. Duncan must have told Anne everything; the girls were obviously shunning Floyd and me.

Then my view of the dance floor was blocked by several bodies. I looked up to see Webster and his mates. 'The puftas are in town,' the greaser cackled. 'Watch your handbags girls.'

All five of us rose to our feet as one, but three of the club's bouncers suddenly stepped between us.

'No bother – or you're out,' one of them, built like the proverbial, as well as being an ex-Para, wagged his finger at Webster and his cronies. As the greasers sidled away, laughing, the bouncer faced us again. 'You! I told you that you were banned,' he said pointing to Nutter. 'Out!'

'He's not doing' any harm,' Duncan said. 'Just sitting here quietly with us. Why don't you let him alone!'

The bouncer pondered for a moment. Probably trying to decide whether the aggro of removing Nutter was worth it.

'OK, you stay. But any trouble . . .'

'He won't start any trouble,' Duncan said. As the bouncer turned away, he muttered to me. ' 'Cause we will.'

The music changed again as the first beats of *Brown Sugar* began to echo through the disco.

'Say look at that,' Floyd grinned as several of the greasers took to the dance floor. Webster was among them and he began to imitate Mick Jagger's stage performance; he strutted across the floor, bobbing his long neck backwards and forwards in time with the music.

'Just like a fucking chicken,' I laughed as I joined the other skinheads at the side of the floor. 'Same big mouth as well.'

Webster had heard me I knew, as I saw the look of hatred in his dark eyes, but he continued his strutting. Several of the other dancers had spotted the skinheads and, sensing trouble, decided that now was a good time to visit the bar or the toilets. Soon, apart from the bikers and their girls, the dance floor was empty.

The bouncers had noticed the sudden change of mood and moved towards us again.

Nutter had gone across to the stage and was shaking his fist at the DJ.

As the Stones track finished, it was replaced with a soul record; it was one of my favourites, by the Formations. I saw Puffin and Anne standing nearby and beckoned to Floyd. We went across to the girls and I leaned to shout into Puffin's ear. 'Dance?'

'I don't know,' she scowled at me. When her friend joined Floyd on the floor, she relented.

'Is it true,' she asked, as I side-stepped in front of her.

'Is what true?'

'You and – and Sheila Johnson.'

I decided that she knew everything, that we had both screwed Shagbag. There was no getting out of it. 'We were drunk,' I said.

'How – How could you,' Puffin said, tears springing to her eyes. 'I thought you loved me.'

I was spared from replying by a sudden noise near to the doorway. Nutter had moved from the stage. He was standing next to the bouncer who had thrown him down the steps that other night. 'At the top of the stairs there's a – bastard,' Nutter howled, changing the words of the song to suit his mood.

'If you don't shut up – you're out,' the bouncer snarled. Unfortunately, the same line of the song came round again. 'I told you . . .' the bouncer stepped towards Nutter, as he chanted 'bastard' once more. There was a sudden crack of heads and the doorman staggered backwards, his nose smashed and bleeding where Nutter's forehead had struck it. 'Bastard – bastard,' Nutter yelled and began to punch and kick at the dazed man.

More doormen dashed to help but the other skinheads stepped forward too.

'Get out of the way,' I screamed at Puffin, as she stood bemused by events. The greasers were racing to join the fray. I ducked as Webster swung a fist at my head, then guarded against the next blow with my left. One of the other greasers kicked at me, hitting me on the thigh. The blow almost dead-legged me. I didn't fancy lying on the floor at Webster's mercy, so I quickly threw a fist at the other greaser. Cadger leapt on his back, and, with one arm wrapped around the youth's neck, began to thump at his ear.

As they staggered away, I turned back towards Webster. He hit me on the chin, dazing me for a moment. I recovered, then slung a punch at Webster's nose. Webster turned his head, but not quickly enough to evade the blow; it caught him on the cheek, almost spinning his head round. I followed it with my other hand, striking him on the ear. Webster staggered back, but was saved from my next hit as one of his mates stepped between us.

I cursed as my knuckles struck the other greaser's breast pocket and thumped against something hard; he must have had a cigarette tin or something in there I guessed, as the shock travelled along my arm. The blow had been enough to wind the greaser though, and he doubled up in pain. An uppercut to his chin sent the bastard spiralling to the floor.

Behind me, I could hear Rocky's pleading voice. 'You wouldn't hit a lad with glasses on, would you? Wait, while I take 'em off.'

I spun around to see Rocky flailing at the greaser who had generously allowed him to pocket his spectacles. Without his jam-jar bottom glasses Rocky, who worked out most days, was a terrific fighter and could throw punch after punch. The trouble was he couldn't see who was attacking him, so if he saw something move he hit it.

'It's me,' I shouted as Rocky windmilled towards me.

'OK,' Rocky grinned, then peered, myopically, for the blurred outline of his next victim.

I looked for Webster again, to find that he had moved to the edge of the dance floor. Where was Floyd? I spotted him chasing Martin towards the stairway. Both of them stopped in their tracks as a dozen policemen burst through the swing doors into the disco.

Christ, I thought; neither Floyd nor me wanted any bother with the police right now.

'Stand still everybody,' a sergeant bawled. The DJ had stopped the music the minute the fight started. Experience had taught him that his best policy was to save his records and equipment from damage, so the policeman's words echoed through the building. 'Nobody leaves until we've got names and addresses,' the sergeant continued.

85

I looked at Floyd; we were both under age and had used Clinton and Winston's names when we had applied for club membership. We would be in trouble again with our parents, and Floyd's brothers would not be happy if they were dragged into this. When the police checked our names, it would be obvious that Floyd was not my elder brother.

Floyd must have come to the same conclusion; he winked at me then gave a slight nod of his head, towards the fire exit.

As the police moved among the clubgoers, scribbling in their pocket books, I began to inch towards the doorway. Out of the corner of my eye, I saw Floyd doing the same. I ducked down, behind the backs of the waiting crowd, and ran, bent double, to the exit. I knew it was unlocked because Nutter had come in that way. So did Nutter; he scrambled past me as I fled down the metal stairway that led to the rear of the building. Floyd soon joined us.

We hid in a doorway until we were certain that our escape hadn't been spotted.

'You've torn your suit, Kenny,' Floyd whispered into my ear, pointing to the white lining showing through where the arm joined the shoulder.

'Damn!' I muttered. It was only a cheap suit that I used for the club but I couldn't afford another just at the moment.

Five minutes later, we felt it would be safe to leave the doorway and make our way along the alleyway to where we had left our scooters.

'Easy! Easy!' Nutter yelled when we were fifty yards or so from the club.

'What're you lot up to,' a voice growled from the darkness. A torch was shone in our faces.

I saw silver badges on the man's shoulders; it was another policeman.

'Not running away from the club are we?'

'I don't run from nuffink,' Nutter said. 'Least not the filth.'

'Clever bastard are you?' the policeman said. 'Come over here, where I can see you.' He pushed us towards the single street lamp that lit the alley.

'Let's do him,' Nutter murmured. It was said loud enough for the bobby to hear.

'Be quiet,' I hissed at him.

'Think you are hard, do you kid? What's your name?'

'Nutter.'

'No, I want your proper name – not your mental state,' the policeman laughed.

'Piss off and leave us alone – or you're dead,' was Nutter's response.

'Shut up, Nutter,' Floyd said, and tugged at his arm.

'He's just had a few,' I told the policeman. We'll just be on our way . . .'

'Plod bastard,' Nutter spat in the direction of the policeman's boots.

'So, a tough guy, hey?' the policeman chuckled. 'You wouldn't be so cocky if you knew who I was.'

'You lot just hide behind your job,' Nutter said.

'One more word – and I'll teach you a lesson – off the record.' The policeman removed his helmet. 'Just so you'll remember who gave you a thrashing,' he grinned in the amber light of the lamp, 'I'm PC Dennis. Police Boxing Champion for . . .'

Where he was the champion of, we were not going to find out.

I winced as Nutter's head thudded off the policeman's forehead. The officer's knees sagged and he tumbled to the ground, his helmet rolling across the cobbles.

'Stop it, Nutter,' I yelled as he kicked at the policeman while he lay on the floor.

Floyd bent down in the gloom and felt at the bobby's neck. 'There's no pulse – you've killed him,' he said, panic in his voice. 'We have to fetch help.'

'Fuck that,' Nutter said and booted the fallen helmet along

87

the alleyway. He ran after it and soon disappeared into the darkness.

I heard him give the helmet another kick and then there was silence.

'Are – Are you sure he's dead?' I asked Floyd, then bent down to check for myself. The policeman's flesh was still warm. I could feel the beginnings of stubble on his chin, but Floyd was right, I couldn't find a pulse.

I heard the sound of Nutter's scooter echoing along the alleyway.

We had better get out of here as well I thought. I was just about to rise to my feet again when a car turned into the alleyway, its headlamps illuminating the scene.

'Police,' Floyd screamed as the car accelerated towards us.

The blue light on its roof began to flash.

'Run!' I yelled. We raced off in Nutter's wake. The car would have to stop; they couldn't get to us without moving the policeman's body.

'Stay where you are!' someone shouted behind us, but another few steps took us into darkness.

Minutes later, we were at the spot where we had hidden our scooters. 'We'll coast downhill, towards the traffic lights,' I wheezed, as I pushed my Lambretta off its stand. I ran along the alley, until I thought the scooter had sufficient momentum, then jumped on to its seat. I could hear the whirr of Floyd's Vespa's wheels and the hum of its tyres on the cobbles, so knew my friend was close behind. I could also hear shouting then the sound of a car racing after us. As we turned out of the alleyway onto the road, I dropped the scooter into second gear and let out the clutch. I had switched everything on while we were rolling down the bank. The Lambretta coughed a few times then fired.

A popping noise behind me told me that Floyd had managed to start his Vespa too. We raced through town, expecting dozens of police cars to give chase.

When we reached the end of the street where I lived, we

cruised to a halt in the shadow of a factory wall and switched off our machines.

'Christ, Kenny, What do we do now?' Floyd sobbed. 'We'll be done for murder. A policeman as well. We'll be locked up for life!'

I shook my head; I had no idea what to do. 'We could tell them it was Nutter,' I shrugged, then knew that neither of us could grass on him, despite the consequences. They didn't like narks inside prison, or so I'd heard. 'Let's think it through. Would they have recognised us – or was it too dark?'

'If they didn't – it wouldn't take much to find out,' Floyd said. 'They must have heard the scooters – there's not that many in town.'

I had never smoked, but could have started now. 'Yeah and they only have to ask in the club. Webster and his mates would soon point us out. That bouncer knows who we are as well.'

'An' he'll be looking for revenge,' Floyd said, rubbing his face.

My friend's hands were shaking I noticed, as Floyd fiddled with the keys hanging from the ignition switch. But then again so were my own. 'Do we go home – or run?'

Floyd was just about to answer when we heard a car driving fast along the road; a blue light reflecting from the house windows opposite told us who it was.

I held my breath as the police car, a Ford Escort, hurtled past us. Thankfully, the police didn't stop to shine their lights into the factory yard, or else they'd have seen the scooters. I leaned forward, over the handlebars, to see if it went to my house; then I would know they had the identity of one of the killers. It carried on and turned the corner at the far end of the street. They either had missed my address or were just searching the town for the culprits.

What could we do? Go home and own up to our parents? I could imagine the scene then. The police might be knocking before long anyway. I looked at Floyd. 'We could go to the police station – admit we were there – but say we were trying to help him . . .'

'Yeah, I'm sure they'd believe us. Why did we run?'

'Because we thought we'd be blamed,' I said.

'We're done for,' Floyd wailed.

'Go home,' I told him. 'Deny everything. Yes, we were at the club, but say it wasn't us in the alley. We must get our story right though.'

We went through our respective alibis then made our way home. To my relief, my parents had already gone to bed; I didn't think I could face them at this particular moment. I collapsed onto my bed, fully dressed, waiting for the dreaded knock on the front door. The sound of another car echoed along the street.

I opened my eyes and saw a strobe of blue light bouncing off my bedroom ceiling.

7

I'm Gonna Change

I was the first to rise on the Saturday morning and I met the paperboy at the front gate. I'd been awake all night, waiting to be dragged off to the cells. The police car had driven straight past my parents' bungalow, and there had been no other flashing lights, but I'd still not been able to sleep.

I spread the newspaper on the kitchen table and scanned it from end to end, then back again. There was no mention of the policeman's murder. Perhaps the news hadn't reached the daily papers in time and it would be in Monday's edition. I would have to check tonight's local paper; it was bound to be in there.

My father came into the kitchen. 'You're looking tired, son. What time did you get in last night? We never heard you – so it must have been late.'

'No, it was early. I wasn't feeling well. Must have been just after ten,' I lied, guessing that, as usual, my parents would have gone to bed about nine o'clock. That would make it sound as if I was home two hours or more before the policeman's death. It might give me an alibi.

'You should stay in a few nights. It's not good for you, out until all hours. You need your sleep.'

'You're right, pop,' I told him. 'In fact, I'm going to stay in tonight. I've got a lot of college work to do.'

I saw the look of pride on my father's face; his son had learned his lesson and was going to knuckle down now. Poor bastard! How disappointed he would be when the police came.

I found it hard to face my mother and father knowing that at any minute the terrible truth would be revealed. They would be devastated. I told them I had lots of revising to do, and I went to my room, only coming out for my lunch. Every car that came down the street, every knock at the door, or ring of the telephone bell, sent my heart racing.

It was a shame that Floyd's parents weren't on the phone. We had agreed not to meet, just in case the police were watching us, but I wanted to find out if my friend was still at home, or if he was in a cell. The Edmonds would have come round in that case, to find out what had happened, I convinced myself as the day wore on.

Puffin didn't appear either. I had thought she'd forgiven me for my fling with Shagbag, but perhaps she hadn't after all.

I heard a scooter coming down the street and prayed for it to come to my house. If the rider was in the Hole in the Wall Gang, I could find out what was happening. But it sped past.

As the hours passed, I became more unsettled. The police were busy tracking me down I decided, probably beating my name out of Floyd at this very moment.

I borrowed my father's transistor radio. 'I'd like to listen to some music while I study,' I told him. To keep up appearances I spread my college books over the bedroom floor. When my mother bought me a cup of tea, some time in the afternoon, I was listening to classical music on one of the channels.

'That's nicer than that awful racket you normally listen to,' she smiled, as she placed the tea, and some chocolate biscuits, on my bedside cabinet.

I smiled back but kept silent about the fact that I was waiting for the news bulletin, to see if I was mentioned in it.

The national news came and went. There was nothing about me, or the murder. I tuned to the local radio station and waited impatiently for the hour to come round again. It did, eventually, but still no mention. Maybe the police didn't know who'd done it, had no clues whatsoever, I thought as I munched on one of the biscuits.

Then the doorknocker rattled and I almost choked. I crept to the window, my knees shaking. It was the paperboy again, but with the evening paper this time. He'd knocked because tonight was when he got paid. I collapsed onto the bed to recover.

A short time later, I went into the living room. My mother was peering over her spectacles at that night's paper. I volunteered to make her a drink, then, as she read, every damned line it seemed to me, I sat in the chair opposite her and tried to make out the headlines on the outer pages. She was reading the middle and had folded the paper so that the sports reports were on the outside; no clue there either. I guessed that the murder would be on the front page of the local rag. Normally the biggest crime they covered was the theft of a milk bottle from someone's doorstep, or vegetables pinched from an allotment.

'Are you waiting for this?' my mother said. 'Shan't be long.'

'Is there much in it, tonight?'

'Been some trouble in town, I see. At that place you go to.' She looked accusingly at me, over her half-moon glasses.

'Must have been after we left,' I stammered.

She resumed reading.

She had just finished with the paper, and was about to fold it again when my father came in from the garden. 'Done with that,' he asked, causing me to sigh with frustration.

'Kenneth wanted it,' she told him.

'Just want to look at the latest cricket scores,' my father said, then picked up the paper and spread it out on the table.

'Don't be long, Charlie. I want to set the table for tea.'

My old man grunted then turned another page.

'I thought with you staying in tonight Kenneth, that we would have something special. Some salmon sandwiches perhaps?' my mother said. 'Not often we sit down together as a family nowadays.'

We won't be doing it many more times either I thought, not when I'm inside for life. I watched my father laboriously working his way down the page. Fucking hell, I cursed under my breath; he would take all night at this rate.

My old man ran a fingernail down the list of results. Two minutes later he shook his head in disgust. 'Wonder how the County went on?' he muttered, then began to search for the report of their match.

I wanted to tell him to hurry, but didn't want to arouse his suspicions; it was not often that I read the local paper. Finally, I could stand the suspense no longer. 'I'll help mom with the tea,' I said then joined her in the kitchen.

'Do you need any clothes for your holiday, Kenneth?' she said as I buttered some bread for her.

I won't need much in gaol I was tempted to say, but decided against it. 'Look mum, I love you and dad but I'm a bit old now for going to the seaside with you. All my mates would laugh. Why don't you two go. Enjoy yourselves. It will be better than having me tagging along.'

'We wanted to give you a holiday, Kenneth.'

'Yeah, but you both need a break. Go without me. Get him to take you shopping,' I said, nodding towards the living room.

'I don't think he'll want you staying here on your own. I'll see what he says. Maybe if you're good . . .'

'Maybe if you're good – what?' my father said as he came into the kitchen.

'Kenneth wants to stay here – so that we can have a holiday on our own. A second honeymoon,' my mother smiled.

'A first one would have been nice,' my old man grumbled.

I knew that their honeymoon had been brief, the day after the wedding he had rejoined his unit and gone to Korea. I went into the living room. My mother was on my side now, so perhaps my father might relent. Now all I had to do was stay out of gaol.

'Look at that when you've had your tea,' my mother scolded as I went to pick up the paper. It was folded so that the top of the first page was visible. "Trouble flares up at local nightclub," said the headline plastered across the page. I had to wait until I had eaten the sandwiches and a piece of cake before I could find out more. I couldn't taste any of the food. At one stage I thought I would be sick, my stomach was in such turmoil.

When I left the table, I sneaked the newspaper to my room. Ten minutes later, I was none the wiser. It just said that a fight had occurred at Annabellas, between rival gangs of youths, and that two of the club doorman had been hurt. The police were still investigating. A local magistrate was quoted as saying, "There's too much of this hooliganism in the town. We shall take strong measures against the perpetrators, when they come before us." There was no mention of murder. Perhaps the police were still trying to get people to talk, and thought they would be reluctant to do so if they were putting their friends in the frame for the policeman's death.

I couldn't take much more of this. It was less than twenty-four hours since Nutter had killed the policeman and my nerves were shattered. What would I do if nothing happened tomorrow? And could I go into work on Monday, my first day back after being reinstated, as if nothing had happened? I would have to.

Or go to gaol for life.

8

Seven Days Too Long

'Let's go out on our scooters after work,' I said to Floyd. 'I'm fed up of staying in the house. If they're gonna get us – they'll find us anyway.'

He looked uncertain. 'I don't know. They might just be waiting. Soon as they see our scooters they'll pull us in.'

'I can't stand it anymore,' I told him. 'Especially the not knowing.' At home, my nerves were becoming ever more frayed at each footstep on the garden path; every bump that I heard was the police scaling the garden wall, ready to kick the door in. It had been Monday, at work, before we'd had a chance to compare notes.

What a day that had been. Ramsbottom had stopped me at the door. 'You'll work over here from now on,' he told me, pointing to the service bay outside his office. 'And I shall be watching you. I am going to get rid of you. One way or another I'll find something,' he had snarled at me.

Frank Johnson had passed me on the way to the stores, but turned his head away. How chuffed both men would be when the police caught up with us.

When I had spoken to Floyd later that morning, my friend was no wiser than I was. 'I've not seen Nutter, or Duncan, or anybody. Do you think they've got them at the station, questioning them?'

I told him I didn't know. He had been well agitated. Like me, he'd had hardly any sleep.

'I've not seen Anne either,' Floyd shook his head. 'Perhaps she knows what happened and is avoiding us.'

Floyd had met up with Ramsbottom that morning though and been given the same warning as me.

Johnson had also spoken to him. 'Only two words,' Floyd told me. 'Just called me a black bastard. He's only trying to rile us, get us to do something,' he said, when I told him we should sort the foreman out. 'We've got enough problems without him.'

I had little chance to talk to Maureen either; every time she came into work Ramsbottom always seemed to be there, as if he knew that I was interested in her. Unless the Service Manager hoped he was in with a chance as well. I quickly dismissed that idea. I had a sneaking suspicion that, even though he was married with kids, Ramsbottom's tendencies were of a different sort; his name might be pretty apt.

Saturday morning had finally arrived, and I had the chance to have a proper talk with Floyd. Ramsbottom had gone out for a test drive in a car that Johnson had repaired. It had broken down. I had jeered at the news, laughing as the red-faced foreman had taken his toolbox to the works van, then gone in search of his boss. Now the workshop was quiet, with only one other fitter at work.

'Yes, if we get the scooters out – at least we'll know,' I said. It had been a glorious summer morning, but we had left our machines at home and walked to work, earning curious looks from both sets of parents in the process; they knew that since we had bought the scooters using our feet seemed to have become alien to us.

'Cheryl was talking to some of her mates last night,' Floyd said. 'They saw an ambulance in the alleyway. Police chasing everywhere. But that's all they know. Some of them were in the club and had their names taken. They were threatened with being done for drinking under age if they didn't split on who they were with. Seems they are trying to get the names of everyone who was there.'

'They'll have ours by now,' I shook my head. 'Webster will have told them we were there. If not, Shagbag will.'

'What are we going to do, Kenny? I can't take much more.'

'Me neither. Like I said, we'll go into town. See who's about. If we get done – then at least we'll have the answer!'

'Is – um – is Debbie in?' I said to the man who I presumed to be Puffin's father.

'Why?' he glared at me, then scowled at the Lambretta that was ticking over at the kerbside.

'I just want to talk to her, see if she's coming for a ride.'

'She's grounded. The police came here. Told me she was in that club – or whatever they call it – in town. She's not old enough. They threatened to act next time. Besides, I don't allow her to go on them things,' he said nodding towards the scooter. 'Too dangerous.'

'Can I just have a quick word . . .'

'No! She's in her room – and staying there,' the man snarled, then shut the door.

'Charming,' I muttered then climbed onto the Lambretta.

Puffin's father was wrong though; she was in the High Street with some of her mates when I rode along it. I drew up next to the group of girls. Anne was there too I noticed as they circled around me, giggling as Puffin gave me a kiss on the cheek.

'You're supposed to be at home,' I chuckled, as she wrapped an arm around me, as if to tell the other girls that I was hers.

'I locked the door then climbed out the window,' Puffin laughed. 'Serves him right if he thinks I'm still in there. Are we going for a spin?'

'Just along the street and back then,' I said, shuffling forward so that she could climb onto the pillion. 'Floyd will be here soon,' I shouted to Anne. I backed the Lambretta away from the kerb then, to cheers from the other girls, raced off along the street. At the end, I pulled up again, on a paved area in front of the War Memorial.

'Wondered where you were all week,' I told Puffin. 'I thought you might have called round my at house.'

'I couldn't get out. And I didn't know if I wanted to see you after I found out you'd slept with – her.'

Puffin couldn't even bring herself to speak Shagbag's name I realised. 'I'm sorry,' I told her, 'but we were all drunk. I won't do it again. Promise.'

Puffin smiled, then rested her chin against my shoulder. 'Better not or we're finished. It's lovely to see you now though. Did you get away all right on Friday night?'

What did she know I wondered? 'Get away? I'm not with you?'

'I saw you sneak out. I couldn't follow you as a policewoman was taking my name. Just my luck. Five minutes later they all went rushing out. I'd have got away myself if they'd done me last. They came round and told my father that I'd been there. They wanted to know who else had been there. I didn't give them your name, or Floyd's.' She nibbled at my ear. 'Are you taking me out tonight? I've missed you. I'll do – anything – that she did,' Puffin said shyly, folding down the collar of my Harrington jacket, and nuzzling her face into my neck.

I would have liked nothing more than to take Puffin somewhere and screw her, but I had other things on my mind. 'Did they say anything about a policeman?'

'What do you mean?'

'As we ran down the alley we found a bobby lying on the floor. I think he was dead.'

Puffin gasped with horror. 'My God. What did you do?'

'We were just seeing if he was still breathing – when a police car came into the entry. It looked like we'd done him. I think they'll be after us. It wasn't us,' I added quickly.

'Oh, Kenny. What will you do? Will you take me with you if you go abroad?'

Go abroad? Maybe that was the answer; perhaps Floyd could find out if there was somewhere we could hide in Jamaica. But how would we get passports? I would have to talk that over with him. There must be a way.

A sudden tooting noise made me turn. Floyd was passing on his Vespa, and shouted that he was going to look for Anne at the other end of the High Street.

I kicked the Lambretta into life and a few minutes later pulled in next to my friend. I tugged the scooter onto its stand and waited for Anne to finish kissing Floyd. 'That's enough,' I said, tugging at Floyd's elbow. 'Down, boy. Save it for later,' I grinned. I stepped onto the pavement as Eddie Duncan swung alongside on his scooter.

'Fuckin' hell Kenny. Is it right what I've heard? Nutter did that . . ?'

I placed a finger across my lips, to caution him to say nothing. The other girls had returned when they heard the scooters pull up, hoping to be taken for a spin; I didn't want them blabbering everything all over town. 'We'll talk about it later,' I told Duncan. 'All I can say is that Nutter's dropped us well and truly in it.'

'Kenny,' Floyd interrupted. 'Look. It's . . .'

I turned to see what had alarmed my friend, and met the fiery gaze of – PC Dennis. I swallowed and took a second look. Yes, it was the same policeman. My bladder felt as if it would betray me as he stepped towards me.

'I recognise you,' he said, jamming a finger into my ribs. 'And you,' he scowled at Floyd. 'Now, I want that Nutter's real name!'

So Nutter hadn't killed him. Why hadn't we found a pulse? But then again, I'd never checked for one before, except my own. One night as I drifted to sleep, I had imagined that my heart had stopped and I had frantically felt my wrist. Thankfully, I had found a pulse. No time to worry

100

about that now, we were both in deep shit. 'I don't know who he is. We'd left the club – just going to fetch our scooters when he came out of the darkness. I've seen him before somewhere. Don't know where it was though,' I lied.

'Suppose you don't know him either,' Dennis said, his face pressed against Floyd's.

'We just tried to help you,' Floyd stammered.

I waited for the policeman to radio for help. We'd be dragged off to the cells, have the truth kicked out of us.

Dennis seemed to read my mind. 'I said it would be off the record – and as far as I'm concerned it still is. I haven't reported any of you. But,' he said, as my shoulders sagged with relief, 'by the time I've finished – you'll wish you were tucked up safely in a cell. Your lives are going to be hell from now on,' he said, jabbing his fingertips into my ribs once more.

Dennis was trying to wind me up, hoping I'd take a swing at him in full view of the passing shoppers. I shook my head; after escaping the sentence for murder that had been hanging over me, I wasn't going to do anything that silly.

'We'll start with checking your scooters,' Dennis said, pulling out his notebook. 'Name?'

I debated whether to give a false name but knew that he would soon find out who I was from one of the girls. I gave my name, then my address when Dennis asked for that too.

'Passed your test then?' The policeman nodded his head towards Puffin, who was still on the Lambretta's pillion.

'She's just sitting on it while we're parked,' I said, motioning with my hand, out of the policeman's view, for her to get off.

'That's right,' Puffin smiled sweetly at him as she slid from the saddle. 'I asked him to take me for a ride on it, but he wouldn't.'

'Humph,' said Dennis, obviously disbelieving her story. He walked around my scooter, inspecting the tyres. 'Where's your tax disc?'

I pointed inside the legshield.

'Should be on display,' Dennis said then wrote in his book.

I exhaled slowly. At least I had one now, as well as insurance; a month ago and the policeman would have had me for that as well.

'Right. Let's see your lights work.'

I cursed under my breath. The rear lamp had failed several weeks before and only the dipped headlamp worked. The horn had packed in as well, but I hadn't bothered to fix them yet; I intended to sort all the electrical repairs when I took the horn casting off to be chromed. I couldn't afford that yet, so had left the other problems too.

Now I would never be able to pay for it; once I had settled the fines for all this, there would be little else left. And that assumed I would still have a licence when Dennis had finished with me. 'I haven't got a battery on the scooter,' I told him. 'My lights only work with the engine running.' That was perfectly legal I knew, so Dennis couldn't have me for that.

'Start it up, then!'

Shit! I cursed silently; I'd thought that the policeman wouldn't bother. Then I had an idea. I turned the ignition key to the auxiliary position. This allowed you to leave the scooter with its parking lamps on, if you had a battery fitted, but wouldn't let the engine start. The petrol was still turned on. I twisted the choke lever, then shoved down on the kick-start. The engine turned over, there was a smell of two-stroke, but nothing happened. I tried again and again. Still the Lambretta didn't start; it couldn't.

'What's up with it?' Dennis snarled, peering at the scooter, certain that I was playing some sort of trick.

I pressed down on the kick-start again. 'No use,' I said, gasping for breath.

The crowd was laughing now. My face began to burn with embarrassment as Dennis told me to have another go.

'I can see what the problem is,' Duncan chimed in helpfully. 'You've turned the key the wrong way.'

I glared at the other skinhead. 'Thanks – mate!' Had Duncan done that on purpose or was he just thick? I would have to think about that later.

Dennis turned the key the other way. 'Right. No more games. Just get it going.'

I looked at Floyd in exasperation. My friend's eyes also told me that he wondered why Duncan had acted so stupidly. I kicked down once more. The engine spun over but didn't fire up.

Dennis looked again, to see if I'd fiddled with the key. 'Start it,' he bellowed.

'I think the engine's flooded,' I shrugged. 'It will have to be push-started now.'

Dennis looked at me then at Duncan, as if the other skinhead would tell him this was a lie. 'He's right,' Duncan said, probably hoping to make amends for his earlier error.

'Get on with it then,' Dennis told me.

Some of the lads who were watching cheered as I pulled the scooter off its stand. To add to my humiliation, I saw that Webster and Skunk Martin, and Easy Rider and Martin's girl were there too. Webster had a wide grin on his face. He flicked his long black hair out of his eyes then gave me a V sign.

I waited for a gap in the traffic and pushed the scooter forward. I selected second gear, then ran, and ran. When I judged I had enough speed, I leapt onto the scooter's seat and released the clutch. The Lambretta spluttered, as it threw out the unburned fuel that my previous efforts had put into the cylinder, then it fired up, expelling the rest in a haze of oil-rich blue smoke.

As the Lambretta surged forwards, I changed up into third, looked back over my shoulder to see Dennis waiting patiently for my return, then accelerated down the street. I didn't stop until the Lambretta was tucked inside my father's

103

garage. I pulled the doors shut then sat on the scooter. I couldn't face my parents yet and hoped they were still out shopping. Now what could I do? I was in a fix again. I began to unscrew the horn casting; at least I could sort the wiring out.

Twenty minutes later, I heard a scooter coming up the road. Floyd swung his Vespa onto the drive. I opened the garage door and went out to him.

'Fucking hell Kenny. Where did you go?'

'Dennis didn't say he wanted me to come back,' I grinned, with more bravado than I actually felt. 'Just told me to get it going.'

'Well he was hopping mad. Gave me this,' Floyd said, waving a ticket under my nose. 'Did Eddie for not having a tax disc and for having a worn tyre. Me for no "L" plates and no front number plate. And I've got to take my papers in to the police station.'

'Sorry,' I said. 'Didn't mean to drop you in it – but my lights weren't working.'

'That's OK, Kenny. That bastard was out to do us anyway.'

'What bastard's that?' someone said, behind us.

I turned to see PC Dennis standing there. I almost wet myself. 'Jesus!'

'No, not Him, lad, but you'll need Him when I've done with you.' Dennis handed me a ticket. 'You forgot this. It tells you to produce your papers as well.' He wagged his finger under my nose. 'Think you're a smart arse, do you? Well, you've got an enemy for life now. Keep looking over your shoulder kid, 'cause I'll always be there.' He spun around and strode away.

I sighed. At least he hadn't checked the scooter again. I looked at the ticket. It just listed the documents that I had to take in to the station and said nothing about my riding off. That was something.

But what else had Dennis got planned for us?

9

Be Young, Be Foolish, Be Happy

'I never thought they'd let you stay behind,' Floyd chuckled. 'My old man wouldn't. I know that for sure.'

He placed another record on the player that he'd borrowed from his brother Winston, then sat down again on the carpet with his back against one of the easy chairs.

A pulsing drumbeat and the sound of marching feet began to reverberate through the living room, as Edwin Starr readied himself to sing *25 Miles*.

'Yeah, a week all to ourselves,' I said, as I waved my hand towards the rest of the house. I debated whether to get up off the floor and have another dance, but my aching legs told me to rest a bit longer.

I reached for another bottle of beer. The crate was almost empty. I would have to get Davenports to drop some more off, before my father returned and realised that we had found the bottles hidden in his garden shed.

'Cheryl says she wants to help on Friday.'

I looked at Floyd. 'If she knows – then your parents might find out.'

'Don't worry mate. Cheryl has promised not to say anything. Just says she'll give a hand with the food – if she can come to the party.'

'I wasn't planning to have much to eat. Just invite lots of

girls, get in loads of booze – some records – maybe a few pills,' I grinned.

My mother and father had eventually agreed for me to stay at home while they went to Mablethorpe. Since the run-in with PC Dennis, I'd stayed away from town, and from Annabellas. Floyd had thought it wise to do the same. My parents must have decided that I was knuckling down to college and things, and that I could be trusted to be left on my own. My old man had asked Mr Edmonds to keep an eye on me while they were away, just in case. 'I don't want to hear you've misbehaved when I come back,' he told me.

You won't hear of me causing any trouble if I can help it I'd thought, but kept my silence.

I told Floyd to keep his father off the scent. 'Tell him we're going to have a few runs out – on our scooters – then he'll not bother coming round here.' So far, it had worked; Mr Edmonds had not shown his face at all. We just had to keep him away next weekend now.

A sudden knock at the front door startled me. I looked around the living room, at the empty bottles and dirty plates scattered there. What if it was Floyd's old man? 'Shit,' I hissed, then crept to the window. I peered around the curtain, thankful that my mother liked to put nets up. It was Duncan. I thought about ignoring him; we were having a good time without him poking his nose in. Then I realised that he would hear the music. I shrugged, went to the door, and opened it.

'Thought the party was Friday?' Duncan said as he sprawled onto the sofa.

'Just a rehearsal,' Floyd told him, then passed him a beer.

'Never mind that,' Duncan said as he fished in the pocket of his denim jacket. 'Managed to get some shit off Adam. You know – him that sells gear in the market place.'

I had seen the brightly-painted Bedford van that the hippie dealer was rumoured to use to hide the drugs he sold, parked in the middle of the Market Square. I had never met or seen

Adam though. The police must have known about him too, but, though they often raided the van, they were never able to find anything. Adam must have the gear hidden well. Unless he swallowed it? Perhaps that was why everyone said he didn't seem bothered by the police raids; he was probably on a high.

'What do you mean – you've got some?' I said, then watched as Duncan unwrapped a fold of silver paper. In it was a brown sticky mess, almost a cube, with a strange oily smell; I could see why it was called shit.

'Looks like a fuckin' Oxo cube to me,' Floyd said. 'Sure he ain't had you over?'

'No. This is the real stuff,' Duncan scowled.

'What do you do with it,' I asked, looking suspiciously at the resin.

'Smoke it, you dipstick,' Duncan laughed. 'Adam says you can smoke it as it is – but it works best with a hooker – whatever one of them is.'

'Perhaps we have to . . .' I was about to suggest we invite his mother then decided against it. 'Carry on,' I said.

'Or I think you can mix it with tobacco,' Duncan continued. 'I managed to get some fags – from the machine in the High Street – so we can split them down for the baccy. All we need then is something to put it in.'

'How about this?' I said, fetching one of my father's pipes from a rack on the mantelpiece.

'That'll do.'

'There's a tin of tobacco here too,' I said, then flicked its lid off with a coin. 'Not much in it, though.'

I handed the tin to Duncan, who stripped the paper off the cigarettes and added them to the pipe tobacco.

'How much of this do we use,' Floyd asked, as he sniffed suspiciously at the brown lump.

Duncan was thoughtful for a moment. He looked at the tobacco, then at the cannabis, then at the tobacco again. 'All of it,' he finally pronounced.

107

I shook my head slowly, deciding that, like me, Duncan hadn't got a clue what we should do, but didn't want us to know that.

A few minutes later the tobacco and resin were mixed, and the pipe bowl stuffed with it.

'Let's listen to something different,' Duncan said, then leaned forward and began to rummage through the box of discs that Rocky had lent to me. 'This should do.' He swapped the record on the turntable with the one he had found, then leaned back against the sofa again. 'Ain't much on this fribo stuff,' he said, as Fleetwood Mac's *Albatross* began its drifting tones. 'Just right when you're smoking this though. I'll go first,' Duncan said, touching one of my father's wax spills to the flames of the living room fire. 'I paid for the stuff,' he puffed as he drew on the pipe stem, 'so I get first crack.' Clouds of fragrant blue smoke rose in the air as he drew another slow breath then exhaled it. He passed the pipe to me.

'I – er. I'm not sure,' I said; I had never tried hash and didn't know if I wanted to. Then again, Duncan would probably laugh and tell the rest of the gang if I didn't have a go. Where was the harm?

'Go on. Before it goes out,' Duncan said. 'Nice and slow,' he told me as I sucked on the pipe.

Nothing happened at first, but a few moments later I felt my head begin to swim. I handed the pipe to Floyd, who also seemed reluctant to smoke it. Is it the cannabis or the tobacco that's affecting me I wondered, as Floyd took his turn?

The fifth time round Floyd staggered to his feet. 'I don't feel . . .' he mumbled, then stumbled out of the lounge.

'What's up with him?' Duncan said as he handed the pipe to me again.

I didn't know. I should go and look, check that my mate was all right, but I felt funny. My head was reeling and I felt as if I was about to be sick.

108

Fifteen minutes later Floyd reappeared in the doorway, crawling on his hands and knees, his face tinged with a grey pallor. 'Just spewed my ring up,' he panted, then collapsed in a heap.

I struggled to my knees, to go to him, but as soon as I moved a wave of nausea rose in my throat. I made it to the toilet just in time, then heaved the contents of my stomach into the bowl, struggling to breathe as the vomit surged, endlessly it seemed, out of my throat. I managed to gasp in a lungful of air, then began to choke, as a bit of the spewed-up food went into my lungs. My mind raced as I tried to cough the blockage out; I'd read of people choking to death on their own puke, now I was about to do the same. I'd be past help by the time the others came looking for me. I would have cried if I had been able to, but another gush of vomit prevented that.

Then, for one wonderful moment, I could breathe; the food particle had been dislodged. I waited, my head hanging limply in the toilet bowl, staring absently at the multi-coloured particles floating there. "Talking on the big white telephone," I had heard it called; now I could see why.

It was almost half an hour before I found the energy to return to the living room.

'Good stuff, man,' Duncan laughed as I crawled across the carpet and sagged down alongside Floyd. 'Another beer?'

'Piss off, Eddie,' I scowled.

It wasn't the shit that had got us I realised, or else Duncan would have reacted the same way. He was grinning inanely at us, obviously enjoying himself. But then Duncan smoked cigarettes. Yes, that was it. We didn't, so the tobacco had affected us, especially as we had inhaled deeply hoping to get the benefit of the cannabis. Never again, I vowed.

If I ever tried anything else, it would be something I didn't have to smoke.

10

Ain't Nothing But A House Party

'Are you sure your mum doesn't know,' I asked, as Cheryl began to unpack a box of food; the stuff inside looked as if it was Mrs Edmonds' handiwork.

'She saw me cooking it – but I told her it was for the youth club. She did us some cakes,' Cheryl said, pointing to another cardboard box.

'It was only meant to be a small do,' I told her, wondering how many other people knew about my party. The point of it after all was to get Maureen on her own; I couldn't do that if there were dozens of folk milling around.

I had managed to catch her at work that morning. Ramsbottom had been somewhere about, so I had been forced to keep it brief. 'My party's tonight,' I told her. 'I'd love it if you could come.' Especially at the same time as me, I thought crudely as I ran my eyes down her body.

Maureen pushed a wisp of hair back from her face. 'I'm not sure. I've something else arranged . . .'

'Please come,' I said. 'You don't have to stop all night – unless you want to.'

She smiled at me. 'You did say I could bring a friend?'

'Yeah. Bring who you want,' I grinned, picturing her turning up at my door with one or more of her old schoolmates. I hadn't told Puffin about the party, as I wanted to have a crack at Maureen, and that meant Anne wasn't coming either. I'd told Floyd that the two girls would cramp our style, and that we would have the chance of a bit of fresh without them. One of Maureen's friends would do nicely for Floyd. 'Just bring a bottle,' I told her.

Finally, she had agreed. I had given her directions and said she could turn up whenever she liked, but it would probably be in full swing about ten o'clock.

The rest of the day had gone in a whirl for me. Maureen was coming to my party! I had to pinch myself to make sure that I wasn't dreaming. I imagined her dancing close to me, while Rocky, who had volunteered to spin a few records, played something slow and sexy. Then later, I would lead her to my bed and make love to her, all night long.

'I'll cook the sausage rolls and things – so they're ready,' Cheryl interrupted my train of thoughts. 'Then I can get changed for the party.' She opened the oven door, then bent down to slide the first tray of food inside.

'You look fine as you are,' I told her, as her mini skirt rode up to reveal the rounded cheeks of her bottom. My plans for Maureen had made me horny. Maybe I could . . . I shook my head. Better be good, save it for later I told myself.

'Don't be rude,' Cheryl told me, as she realised what I had been leering at.

She bent down just the same way though, as she placed the next tray in the oven.

Someone rattled the front door knocker. I went to the door and opened it. 'Brought this,' Cadger said, as he thrust a party-size can of beer into my hands.

Had it given to him by someone who didn't like the taste I thought. 'Rocky's in the living room getting set up,' I said, as I pointed the way. I was just about to close the door, when I heard the roar of several scooters approaching.

'Any good talent here yet,' Duncan asked, as he led the rest of the Hole in the Wall Gang into the house. 'Got these

111

from the off-licence,' he grinned, placing two bottles of whisky on the kitchen table.

Several more bottles joined them as the others deposited their haul.

'Thought the girls might like it,' Nutter scowled, as Duncan held up the bottle of advocaat he'd lifted from the same shop.

The stuff in the bottle reminded me of the outcome of my pot smoking, and I turned quickly away. I heard the hiss of escaping gas as the skinheads began to crack open some of the beers.

In the living room, Rocky began to play the Mod favourite, Jamo Thomas's *I Spy – For the FBI*. 'Get everybody in the party mood,' he yelled as I went in.

I'd be in the mood when Maureen got here. There was another knock at the door.

'I'll get it,' Duncan shouted. 'Hi, girls,' I heard him say. 'Have a dance later?'

Puffin came into the room. 'You never told me you were having a party,' she said crossly, as she shrugged off her coat.

Anne was close behind her. Floyd would be pleased when he got back from the off-licence.

Puffin came up to me and hugged me. She kissed me, then looked up accusingly. 'Not trying to avoid us are you?'

'Last minute thing,' I lied. 'We were going to come and see if you were in.'

'Then how come one of my friends knew about it last week?' Anne said.

'Sausage roll?' Cheryl asked, as she waved a steaming tray of the tit-bits under Puffin's nose. 'There's a lot Kenny forgets to tell you,' she said.

I prayed that Floyd would come back, so that he could take some of the flak. Just be my luck for Maureen to arrive now. 'Get you a drink?' I said, as I shrugged myself free of Puffin's hold. 'Rum and Coke?' When Puffin nodded, I went

112

into the kitchen and poured the drink, adding extra rum for good measure. When she'd had a few of these, she would soon forget that I hadn't invited her – I hoped.

I danced with Puffin to Tami Lynn's *I'm Gonna Run Away From You*. It was pretty appropriate I thought, as I tried to figure out how I could score with Maureen with Puffin in the house. I heard more voices in the hallway, then Floyd and several more girls, schoolmates of Puffin's, came in. No sign of Maureen though.

Anne made a beeline for Floyd, to divert him away from her friends, and, as the record finished, Puffin joined them. While she was chatting, I refilled her glass again.

'Want some gear?' Duncan held a handful of tiny yellow pills under my nose. 'They're Dexys,' he said, when I looked doubtfully at them. 'Help you dance all night.'

'Yeah, and make your dick shrink, or so I've heard,' I said, shaking my head. That was the last thing I wanted to happen when I was lying naked next to Maureen.

'Your choice,' Duncan said, then began to pop the pills into his mouth.

I returned to the living room and gave the glass to Puffin.

'Where's your bedroom?' she said, looking towards the hallway. 'Show me where you sleep,' she shouted, as Rocky began to play *Leap Up And Down – Wave Your Knickers In The Air*.

Rocky grinned wryly at me; he hated the record but it went down a storm at the youth club. He saw where I was leading Puffin, then made a crude sign with his fist, blue eyes wide behind his thick glasses.

I looked at the clock on the mantelpiece. Eight thirty. If Maureen was coming at ten – that left an hour and a half. 'Through here,' I said, steering Puffin into my room. Thankfully, it was tidy. Because I was hoping to bring Maureen in later, I had straightened the room, and dusted it. I'd also changed the sheets; got rid of the horrible nylon ones that my mother said were easy to wash, and replaced them with some imitation silk ones from the market. I'd also made sure there were plenty of rubbers to hand in a bedside drawer.

'It's nice in here,' Puffin said as she sat on the edge of the bed. 'I have to share with my younger sister so I haven't got this much room.'

I sat on the bed beside her, and began to kiss her.

'Later,' Puffin said. 'I'd like to have a dance first. Just thought if I knew where you slept . . . I've told my father I'm staying with Anne. I can be here with you all night,' she said, a flush of red at her cheekbones.

Damn, I cursed silently. At any other time, I would have leapt at the chance. But Maureen was coming. That was later though. 'We could do it now as well,' I said, nibbling at Puffin's ear, then sliding a hand along her thigh. 'It will be wonderful to make love in a bed,' I whispered, as I eased my fingertips under the edge of her knickers.

'Oh Kenny. Don't stop,' Puffin said hoarsely, pulling at my shoulders, as I played with her body.

Soon we were naked between the sheets. The silk was cold despite it being nearly the end of July; James Bond never had that problem when he led some girl into his bed. I soon warmed up though, as Puffin pressed herself against me.

'I'm – I'm taking the Pill,' she smiled, as I leaned out of bed towards the cupboard. 'My father will kill me if he finds out – but . . .' She reached for me and guided me into her body

Just my luck! Now she does it! All other thoughts were lost though as I plunged inside her.

'Oh, yes,' Puffin gasped, digging her fingers into my buttocks. 'Yes. Yes,' she breathed, as I plunged into her.

I felt a warm flush spread from her loins, and then began to spend myself as she writhed beneath me. 'Jesus,' I hissed, as I forced myself deep inside her, my cock throbbing with ecstasy. I bent my body back against her grasping hands, thrusting even deeper – and met the eyes of Cheryl; she was standing in the doorway watching us, a look of horror on her face.

'Just looking for more glasses,' Cheryl stammered, then turned and left, slamming the door behind her.

'What's up with her,' Puffin whispered in my ear as she snuggled against me. 'Jealous? Well, she hadn't better be – 'cause you're mine.'

I was feeling sleepy and would have liked nothing more than to close my eyes, then to wake up in an hour or so and do the same thing again. Maureen was due though! 'We'd better get dressed,' I said, sitting up on the bed. 'Supposed to be my party – so I'd better show my face.'

'Hadn't better show that, though,' Puffin smiled, reaching forward and cupping me in her hand.

I felt the first stirrings again and wondered . . . 'Come on,' I said, as I passed her dress to her. 'We have lots of time.' Well, Maureen and me would have I thought – if I could only find a way to get rid of Puffin. I didn't want to finish with her, just get her out of the way for now, in case things didn't work out with Maureen.

I went back into the living room, tucking my shirt into my jeans, to be met by jeers and hand-clapping from the rest of the gang.

'Starting early,' Duncan leered, as Puffin followed me into the room. 'Saved some for me darling?' he said, patting her bottom.

Puffin's face turned crimson and she moved closer to me. 'Let's dance,' she said, as Rocky began to play *Needle in a Haystack*.

I scanned the room as I jigged from side to side in front of Puffin. There was no sign of Maureen yet I sighed with relief, as the Velvelettes sang out, 'Still water sometimes is very deep.' No sign of Cheryl either.

'She's gone home,' Floyd told me when I went into the kitchen for another drink. 'Said she wasn't feeling well.'

'Caught me 'n Puffin at it,' I explained.

'That's enough to make anyone feel sick,' Floyd laughed.

There was a loud crash from the living room, then the sound of breaking glass. I dashed back in. The front of the china cabinet was in pieces on the carpet. Thankfully, the ornaments inside were still intact.

'Tried to do a spin,' Duncan said, as he began to gather up the shards of glass. 'Sorry, Kenny. It were an accident.'

Jesus! What would my parents say when they saw the damage? 'Leave that – I'll get a box or something to put it in,' I told Duncan. I was too late; he was scrawling among the broken glass.

'Shit! I've cut myself,' Duncan crawled to his feet, then staggered to the kitchen, trailing spots of blood across the floor. 'It's only a scratch,' he slurred, as I bound a tea cloth around the wound.

Only a scratch it might be, but Duncan managed to get blood everywhere; it was on the door handles, the wall, the kitchenette, the sink top; there was even some on the windowsill. I would have lots of cleaning up to do before my parents came back.

There was a knock at the door. Someone let the caller in. I looked up, hoping to see Maureen standing there. Instead, I saw it was Shagbag with a couple of her mates.

'Hi, Kenny. Heard there was a party,' she smiled.'

'At least I'll get my end away tonight now,' Duncan murmured as he reeled towards her.

'Cheeky sod. Not with me you won't,' Shagbag chuckled as she shoved him away.

She was wearing a black skirt, slit almost to the waist. I saw a flash of white thigh; she must have stockings and suspenders on. Shagbag had stretched a red woollen V-neck jumper over her upper body. And it was stretched! I gaped at the valley between her breasts.

'Like what you see?' she smiled. 'Maybe later – but this time don't tell my father.'

'What's she doing here?' Puffin scowled at me, as she

elbowed her way past Shagbag to join me in the kitchen. 'Tell her to go. I don't want her here.'

'I can't say that. It's a party. Everyone's invited.'

'Me and Anne weren't,' Puffin snapped. 'I suppose you wanted us out of the way so that you could screw her.'

'If he don't want you – I do,' Duncan said.

'Get off!' Puffin knocked Duncan's grasping paws away. 'Look, you're getting blood on my dress. Listen Kenny – either she leaves – or I do.'

'She's only here to enjoy herself the same as you,' I said, embarrassed that my mates were eavesdropping on our argument. Mind you, it would help if Puffin left; it was nearly ten o'clock.

'Don't class me the same as her,' Puffin shrieked. 'I'm nothing like that slag.'

I looked up, but Shagbag had gone in to the living room and had not heard that last remark.

'Throw her out – or I'm going,' Puffin gave her final ultimatum.

When I did nothing she stamped off. 'Come on Anne, we're leaving,' I heard her yell above the music. Anne must have declined as a few minutes later Puffin stormed out on her own, not glancing in my direction as she went.

'Don't go in there, it's a dead loss,' I heard her tell someone in the doorway.

'Go after her, mate,' Floyd said, as he came to see what the fuss was about.

I was debating whether to do so, when I heard Maureen's voice.

'Is this Kenny's party?' she said, as she stepped, bemused by Puffin's greeting, into the hallway.

I gasped as I saw Maureen framed in the kitchen doorway; the hall light above her head gave her hair a fiery glow. She was wearing an emerald-green ankle-length knitted dress that clung to every contour of her body. There was a black velvet choker around her slim white neck, and a diamond-studded

117

butterfly-shaped brooch pinned above her heart. She was gorgeous. I stepped towards her.

'Hi, glad you could make it,' I said, then leaned forward to kiss her cheek. It was then that I saw King Mod.

'You said to bring a friend,' Maureen smiled, a sparkle in her green eyes. 'You know Gary, don't you?'

Know Gary? Of course I did. Gary fucking Grant – or King Mod as the other boys in town called him now. He was a few years older than me, in his early twenties, and a right poser. He thought he was as wonderful as the film star with a similar name. We'd nicknamed him Gee Gee and then Horse Face at school, because of his prominent front teeth. He'd had the last laugh though; a few years later, after some expensive dental work, he could pull almost any girl he wished. He only had to smile at them and they'd wet their knickers. And here the bastard was – with Maureen!

Grant worked at the same garage as me, but was one of Beresford's salesmen. He never lowered himself to talk to the lads in the workshop, but he'd obviously found the time to chat with Maureen. He was wearing a flash suit in brown mohair. It fitted him well I must admit; most likely it was made-to-measure and would have cost him fifty or sixty quid, maybe more. No cheapo shoes for him either, his were tan Italian leather; I'd seen a similar pair in Dolcis, priced at just under fifteen quid. I'd never paid more than a fiver for any of mine. Gold rings glittered on his fingers and I knew, from seeing him at work, that his hands were neatly manicured. Grant also had a car, a flashy red MGB, in which he cruised the town, showing off to the girls. How on earth could I compete for Maureen's affections against this smooth bastard?

'Brought you this,' Grant said, handing me a bottle of wine. 'Wondered at first if I should bring pop and crisps,' he smiled, white teeth reflecting the kitchen light.

I smiled back, but felt like planting my fist in King Mod's chops. That wouldn't impress Maureen though I decided.

118

'Go through,' I told them, my jaw clenched. 'There's food on the table behind you, if you want it.'

'Thanks Kenny. Perhaps we'll have a dance later,' Maureen smiled.

Grant scowled at me, as if to say, "No fucking way."

When they had gone into the living room, I dashed out of the house. Maybe it wasn't too late to make up with Puffin. The night wouldn't be wasted then. I ran to her house, but there was no sign of her. I wondered whether to knock. Didn't fancy facing her old man again though. What could I say? "Excuse me but my plan's have gone wrong – and could your daughter come back to the party – so I can shag her all night." No, I would have to try to make it up with Puffin some other time.

I retraced my steps, hoping that she had come back to the party. She hadn't. Rocky was playing a slow one, *Just My Imagination* by the Temptations. King Mod was dancing with Maureen, his body pressed against her as they moved sinuously together. He had one hand on her buttock. And his prick pressed against her no doubt I thought, jealously, as she swayed her hips from side to side. It took all my resolve not to drag him off her and beat him into pulp

'Play something faster,' I yelled at Rocky.

Soon, James and Bobby Purify's *Shake a Tail Feather* was rattling the windows. I saw Grant drop his arms from around Maureen's waist and whisper in her ear.

That stopped him I smiled to myself. The other lads began to spin across the room, clapping to the music, almost pushing the couple out of their way as they tried to make themselves more room.

'We're off to a club,' Grant told me. 'Leave the kids to play,' he sneered, as he nodded his head towards the dancers.

'Let me hit the bastard,' murmured Nutter, who had just overheard Grant.

That would have suited me fine; I wouldn't be blamed, but

I didn't want to upset Maureen. I held out my arm to restrain Nutter.

'Bye, Kenny. Shame we didn't get that dance,' Maureen said as she followed Grant into the night.

I went to close the door. What a fiasco this party was turning into. Just when I thought it couldn't get any worse, I saw our neighbour, Mr Jones, leaning over the hedge.

'Keep the noise down else I'll call the police,' he shouted when he saw me.

'Fuck off,' I muttered, then regretted my words. Now my father would hear all about it. Oh, well – too late now. I went back into the living room. I searched for Duncan. 'Got any of them pills left?'

'Not s'posed to have 'em with drink,' Duncan mumbled. He'd obviously ignored his own advice. He leaned against me for balance, then ferreted in his pockets. 'Here y'are,' he said, handing me some oblong white pills. 'Chalkies is all I've got left.'

He staggered to the sofa then tumbled on to the end, earning muttered curses from the couples who were cuddling on it.

What was I supposed to do with the tablets? I went to the hall and washed them down with a glass of cider. My mouth was dry so I finished the cider off, then opened the bottle of wine that King Mod had brought. It tasted sour, almost as if it had turned to vinegar. Some cheap piss that he'd had lying around for ages no doubt.

Rocky began to play another fast soul record, one that I didn't recognise, but I began to dance to it anyway. As it finished, I heard someone hammering on the front door.

Nutter came in. 'Bloke from next door,' he told me. 'Says it's your last chance. If you don't knock it off – he'll have the police here.'

'Tell him to . . .'

'Already have,' Nutter grinned. 'And no, I didn't hit him.'

Sometime later, the hammering came again. Angrily, I

staggered to the door. 'Fuck off 'n leave us alone,' I yelled as I swung it open.

'Hello, Roberts,' PC Dennis said as he strode inside. 'I've had a complaint about the noise.' He pushed through the crowd and went into the living room. 'Party's over,' he yelled, then ordered Rocky to turn the music off.

'Leave it alone,' I told Rocky. I turned to Dennis. 'You can't – you can't come in 'ere ordering us about.'

'Can't I? We'll see.' the policeman growled as he drew his truncheon. He smashed it across the record player, making the music cease with a hideous screech.

'Shit, that's my brother's,' Floyd wailed, as bits of plastic flew across the room.

Rocky retrieved one of the shattered segments of black vinyl and stared unbelievingly at his damaged record. Then he must have realised what had happened, for he began to stuff the rest of his collection back into his case.

'Let's have him,' Duncan slurred behind me.

He was slumped over the sofa arm I saw, and wouldn't be having anybody. Thankfully, there was no sign of Nutter, else things would only go from bad to worse. 'OK, we're packing in,' I told Dennis, to groans from the other partygoers; I had lost the mood now Maureen had left anyway.

'I'll call round and see your father tomorrow,' Dennis smiled.

You can come back then for all I care, I thought; my parents were not due back until Sunday.

Dennis went out and leaned against the garden wall. 'Just in case any of you are thinking of driving home,' he grinned as my guests staggered out.

I poured myself another drink. I might as well.

Those pills had had fuck all effect.

11

Please Give Me One More Chance

There was that knocking sound again. I rubbed my eyes. If it was that bastard Dennis, I'd have him this time.

As the knocking continued, becoming louder by the minute, I tried to get up, but found I was held down by the weight of a girl's body.

I lifted the corner of the bedsheet. It was Shagbag; she was naked next to me, her head on my chest, her arm around my neck. I cursed when I put my hand in something sticky as I tried to get up. I cursed again when I saw that Duncan was sprawled on the other side of the bed. It was my parents' bed as well!

What the fuck had been going on? I couldn't remember much after Dennis had spoiled the party; I certainly didn't remember giving Shagbag one. I had a vague recollection of trying to screw her, but seemed to think I hadn't been able to. Damned pills! It was right what the lads said. And then again, I could have caught a dose off her. I hadn't done last time; no funny sores or ulcers had shown up yet anyway. But who had screwed Shagbag since then?

'I'm coming,' I yelled, as I dragged my jeans over my bare buttocks and stumbled towards the door. As I passed my bedroom, I saw that Floyd was in my bed. He was naked and entwined with one of the silken sheets, his leg draped over

Anne's thigh. It was the first time I had seen Floyd's girl nude; she was quite fit, and, unlike Shagbag, she was a natural blonde I noticed, as I scratched at my crotch.

There was another couple in the bath, a blanket draped over them. I didn't know who they were but could vaguely recall them being at my party. Several more half-naked bodies were slumped on the sofa and chairs in the living room. Nutter was asleep underneath the dining table, hugging a cushion tightly. There was no sign of Rocky; he must have taken his records home.

I swore as my bare foot squelched in some food spilled onto the carpet. The next step, I crushed an empty beer can underfoot. I kicked it away then turned the key that I'd left in the front door. It was fucking cold as I swung the door open.

'What the hell's been going on here?' my father yelled, as he entered the hall, dumping his suitcase on the floor. Behind him, the lads had parked their scooters all over his flower borders, I saw with horror.

'Oh, my God,' my mother gasped, as she saw the mayhem in her house.

I sobered up rapidly; I don't know if it was from the cold morning air, or from fear. I turned to face my father's wrath.

'Get them out,' my old man stormed. 'It's – it's obscene,' he raged, as he saw the first partly-dressed girl.

'I – I'm sorry pop,' I said, 'I invited a few friends round and it – it just seemed to get out of hand.'

'Our bed!' I heard my mother shriek.

'Out! The lot of you,' my father bawled in his best parade-ground voice, 'before I throw you out.'

My friends began to filter sheepishly past me.

'I'll stay,' Floyd said nervously, as he tried to tug a shoe onto his foot. 'Help you clean up.'

'Just go,' I whispered. 'I'll sort it – somehow.' How, I hadn't a clue. But I knew I was in big trouble.

'That's the last time you stay on your own,' my father raged, as he discovered the broken china cabinet door.

'Oh. Just look at this,' my mother sobbed, as she examined the cigarette burns and water stains on her coffee table. 'And my clock's missing,' she howled, pointing to the now-empty mantelpiece.

'You'll stay in – until you've paid for this,' my father said. 'And you can sell that damned scooter. You've never been the same since you bought that. Well, it's going now!'

I was too shocked by events to argue. I spotted a used Durex on the kitchen floor. Grimacing, I bent down and dropped it into one of the empty party-cans. 'Thought you weren't coming back until Sunday?'

'Mr Jones – next door – rang us,' my mother said. 'We left the caravan site number with him – in case there was any trouble. The shame of it,' she wept. 'Now the whole street will know what's been happening.'

This was the end. I had been in some tight scrapes, but this was the worst. It didn't get any better.

'The door was open,' PC Dennis said, as he stepped inside.

'Yes, you can get rid of that scooter,' my father said. 'You never got into this sort of trouble before you had that damned thing.'

I remained silent, hoping that his rage would soon subside. I had a blinding headache, and no matter how much water I drank couldn't get rid of my thirst.

When PC Dennis had gone I set about clearing up the mess, all the while being moaned at by my father. Everything that Dennis had told him had infuriated him even more, until I thought my old man would have heart failure if he kept ranting on about it.

My mother squeezed past, taking a pile of sheets to the dustbin. 'I shall have to buy new Charlie,' she said. 'I don't fancy sleeping in these after . . .'

My father glared at me again. 'I'm putting your board up to six pounds. Starting now!'

'But that's nearly all my wages,' I protested. 'I'll have nothing left to spend on clothes or anything.'

'We'll buy you any clothes you need – then you won't waste your money on things like those silly boots.'

While my parents were away, I had bought myself a pair of cherry red Doc Martens. Because of the party, I'd not had the chance to wear them yet.

'I've got some old boots in the shed you could have had. Plenty good enough for work.'

I thought it best not to tell him that they weren't for the garage, but for kicking some greaser's head in.

'I reckon you should get the best part of a hundred pounds for your scooter,' my father said as he began to load his pipe. 'That should pay for the table – and another clock. And – at a pound a week – you should have paid for the carpet by this time next year.' He put a match to the pipe bowl then drew deeply on the Bakelite stem.

'What if I want to go out?' I said as I gathered up a handful of cans. I saw another cigarette burn on the hearthrug and, while my father was looking quizzically at his pipe, I rubbed at the pile to disguise it; I didn't want to buy one of those as well.

What was I going to do now? I would be an old duffer by the time my father let me out. All my mates would be having fun while I was cooped up here.

'There's a – a – contraceptive under your bed,' my mother shook her head, as she went to the dustbin again. 'It's disgusting.'

'All right, mother. Let the lad be for now,' my father drawled.

I turned in surprise; I had thought I was in for a day long bollocking at least. My father had a strange look in his eyes. Then I remembered the hash; it was still in his baccy tin! No wonder his mood had improved.

Then my optimism was dashed again. I heard my mother inviting someone inside. It was Mr Edmonds.

'I'm sorry about this Charlie,' Floyd's father said, as he looked at the mess still scattered on the floor.

'I asked you to watch out for the place – and make sure they kept out of trouble,' my old man muttered.

'I did Charlie. But my boy told me that they were off to the city and might not be back 'til late. Never expected them to be here, doin' this.'

'This is all your son's fault,' my mother said, arms folded across her chest. 'Kenneth would never have misbehaved like this, unless Floyd led him on. He's a good boy, not brought up to act this way.'

'What – What do you mean, it's our Floyd's fault?' Edmonds stuttered. 'It's your boy who's the troublemaker. I been trying to stop Floyd from seeing your lad. Ever since he got that motorbike – he's been causing mischief.'

'I won't have that said about our Kenneth. He may not be an angel – but he's a good lad at heart. I'm not standing here – in my own house – listening to this,' my mother said.

'An' I don't have to listen to this rubbish either,' Mr Edmonds snapped, then turned on his heels and left.

'Kenneth, I don't want you having anything more to do with that boy of his,' my father said. 'Is that clear?'

I didn't know what to say. Floyd was my mate.

'Do you understand?'

I nodded; it was better to shut my old man up now then sort the consequences later.

'There's no bread – or anything for tea,' my mother shouted from the kitchen, a few minutes later.

'I'll nip to the corner shop,' I volunteered; I would be out of the way for a bit, and a run on the Lambretta would soon clear my mind.

'You can walk,' my father growled as I searched for my keys. 'That scooter stays here until it's sold.'

'But I could be back in five minutes . . .'

'Walk!' my father said, then began to refill his pipe.

I left the house. I can't stand much more of this I thought

126

as I strolled along the street. I kicked at a pebble sending it rattling along the road.

What if I got my own flat? Then I could do what I wanted. I could take a girl home to my bed without the hassle of worrying about my parents coming home. I could even try having it in the bath. I smiled for the first time that day. And play my records anytime I wanted to – loud as anything – without being moaned at.

I kicked the pebble again. But how would I pay for it? Landlords asked for deposits. I didn't have enough for that, and I doubted that I could afford the rent, never mind buy food and stuff. Perhaps I could share with Floyd.

He would be pissed off with his old man by now.

12

Quick Change Artist

'I thought your father had stopped you using that,' Floyd said, as I pulled up on my Lambretta.

He was parked with the other scooterists, next to the War Memorial.

'He has. But what he doesn't know won't hurt him. He's gone bowling – to an away match – and shouldn't be home until late. And my mother's gone to her sister's. My old man took the keys – but it didn't take long to bypass this,' I said, tapping the empty key-slot at the back of the handlebars.

'Hey, Kenny,' Duncan said. 'What about this for an idea. We all go somewhere this weekend. Blackpool maybe? The city mob is supposed to be going there.' He leaned against his scooter's backrest and lit himself another cigarette. 'The others are willing – and Floyd says he'll go if you do.'

'We could go to the Mecca,' Rocky said, as he punched me on the shoulder. 'My brother's been – says it's great.'

'You can count me out,' I told him. 'I can't afford – even if my old man would let me go. And after the party . . .'

'You'll only need a bit of petrol and some spending money,' Duncan said. 'Won't need much. 'Sides – you got paid today'

'I know. But I've got to pay my board – and some towards the damage. My old man makes me hand my pay packet over. And I'm supposed to be working tomorrow. I need the overtime.'

And I did need the extra money; without it I'd have nothing left over to spend on myself.

But then again, it meant another four hours of Ramsbottom breathing down my neck, waiting to catch me out, hoping to break my balls. The Service Manager had hardly taken his eyes off me since I'd started back, and I'd had no chance to talk to Maureen because of him.

Mind you, did I want to talk to her? Let her go out with that slimeball Grant if that's what she wanted; King Mod usually dumped his girlfriends after a few weeks. That would serve her right.

My stomach began to churn over as I pictured her; she was the most beautiful girl I had ever seen. But did I still want her after King Mod had been through her? No – stuff her.

'We can have a go on the Big Dipper,' Nutter said, interrupting my thoughts. 'Or the Dodgems.'

It would be better than being stuck at home, listening to my old man all weekend.

I couldn't go to Floyd's house to get out of the way; Mr Edmonds had barred me. And Cheryl was being a bit off-hand too. Then Winston was after me for the record player. I'd asked Floyd to tell his brother that I would pay for it, but I didn't know how I'd find the money. Floyd said he was working on Winston to let me off, but he hadn't succeeded yet.

'No, I can't do it,' I said, as I adjusted one of the mirrors fitted to the front of the Lambretta. They looked good but were a pain to keep in place. Despite the brackets I'd made in my father's workshop, at the back of our garage, the scooter only had to hit a small bump and they would move out of line.

Normally, I only set a couple of them so that I could see behind, or else some prat in a car would put his headlamps on main-beam and try to dazzle me. When the mirrors moved though, several shafts of light would sear at my eyes as I rode at night.

Cracker, a lad who'd been allowed to join the Hole in the Wall Gang after he'd bought a scooter, bent down to inspect the chrome sphinx on my front mudguard. 'Come with us Kenny. We'll have a great time,' he said, as he tugged gently at the mascot, checking how it was fastened on.

We all knew he was a bit light-fingered. 'I'll know who's had that – if it goes missing,' I told him. 'Anyway, my old man wouldn't let me go – and he would kill me if I went without telling him.'

'I don't think I can afford neither,' Floyd said. 'I've still got to pay my fine.'

PC Dennis had done him for having no "L" Plates, but dropped the charge of not having a front numberplate. Perhaps the copper had thought that one offence would be enough. The magistrates must have thought so too; they fined Floyd five pounds, which he was paying off at a fifty pence a week.

'I'm fed up with sleeping rough,' I said, as I tried to think up other arguments why I shouldn't go. Normally, when we did a seaside run, we just took a sleeping bag apiece and slept in a beach shelter. It was bloody cold in them though, especially just before dawn. Probably would be now, even though it was the middle of August. When the tide came in, throwing sea-spray up the beach, it was often damp as well.

'I know where I can get a tent,' Duncan said.

'Who do you know who's in to camping?' I laughed.

'No, honest. We could take that and kip in it.'

I was still unsure. My old man would go ballistic.

'Kenny, will you have a look at my kickstart? I think it's loose again,' Floyd said, then pointed to his Vespa.

I was puzzled. I was sure it should have stayed secure after I had tightened it the last time. Floyd hadn't fallen off since, and that was what had loosened it before. I crouched down to check the pinch bolt.

'There's your ex,' Duncan grinned, 'she's . . .'

He exhaled noisily as Floyd elbowed him in the ribs.

What was Duncan on about? I raised my head – and saw Puffin walking along the street, arm in arm with another boy.

Well fuck her too, I decided. I had called at her house, only to be met with hostile glances from her old man, or then, the next time, her mother.

The last time, a young girl, who must have been Puffin's younger sister, had told me haughtily that, 'Debbie wants nothing more to do with you'. Then she had shut the door in my face.

Snooty little cow was like her sister in every way. Now, the lad with Puffin would be getting the benefit of her being on the Pill.

'No leg over tonight,' Duncan chuckled, but fell silent when he saw the look on my face.

'You'll have to take a suit and a tie,' Rocky told us, 'else they won't let you in the Mecca.'

That was another reason for not going. My suit had been damaged in the fight at Annabellas. My mother had patched it up, but her sewing was as good as her cooking. Although the cloth was dark brown, she'd only had white cotton to hand and several enormous stitches now held the sleeve to the body. It looked a mess, but it would have to do for now.

I had been hoping to get a suit specially made. Floyd had been trying to save for one too. It would be a long time before either of us managed to get one at this rate.

'Right boys. Let's have a look at your licences,' a familiar voice said behind me.

I didn't need to turn. I knew it was Dennis. I was right. He came out of an entryway and strode to where we were parked, another policeman close behind him.

'We'll start with yours,' he said, jabbing the end of his truncheon into Nutter's ribs. 'Check the others,' he told his companion, 'while I see to nancy boy here.'

Thankfully, no matter what Dennis did, to intimidate him,

131

Nutter kept his cool, else the policeman would have another tale to tell my father.

Perhaps Nutter suspected that Dennis was waiting for the opportunity to crack the truncheon across his head.

Whatever, Dennis left us some fifteen minutes later, with a handful of paper telling us to produce our documents, or that we would be charged with some minor offence.

He'd been a bit upset that he couldn't find anything wrong with my Lambretta. After his last inspection, I had made doubly sure that everything was legal.

Dennis told me that the mirrors looked as if they could be dangerous accessories, but hadn't booked me for it.

'You'll be taking them off anyway, when you sell the thing,' he had grinned.

'Sod it,' I yelled to the other lads. 'I'm coming with you.'

'And me,' said Floyd, who had just been given a ticket because his horn wasn't working.

I would go to Blackpool and stuff the consequences. A quick dash home, to collect my suit and things before my old man came back, then away.

Yes, bollocks to them all.

'Leave your scooters here,' Duncan told us, 'and follow me.'

He led us along a dark silent street, past the gates to the Park, then pointed to a tent that had been erected on someone's front lawn. 'That's the one,' he muttered, 'but keep your voices down. We haven't got to annoy the neighbours.'

To me, it didn't sound as if he'd got permission to borrow it, after all.

Some of the skinheads, Nutter in particular, found it difficult to keep quiet; they'd had a few too many in the pub, while they waited for us to collect our things.

Nutter fell over one of the guy ropes and cursed.

'Shh,' Duncan hissed.

'Who's there?' a man shouted.

I froze, looking for the source of the voice.

One of the upstairs windows of the house reflected the light of a street lamp as it was opened wider.

'I'll call the police if you don't show yourself,' the man called.

Just what I needed. What would my father say when I was done for stealing?

'Must be a cat,' the man said to someone inside the house, then, to my relief, closed the window again.

As the other lads gathered up the tent, Nutter took the opportunity to piss through the letterbox. 'That's better,' he whispered as he emptied his bladder.

Unfortunately, he lost his concentration and let go of the letterbox lid. 'Fucking hell – it's got me!' he howled as it snapped shut.

A light came on upstairs as Nutter began to wail in pain. 'Bastard thing has trapped me prick,' he squealed. The more he struggled, the tighter the lid held him. 'Help me!'

'Stuff that,' Duncan said, as he made for the gate, the rest of us close behind him.

By the time the householder reached his front door, Nutter had freed himself, and was hobbling, bowlegged, after us. 'Nearly castrated myself,' he murmured, wincing as he climbed onto his scooter.

A howl of rage broke the silence of the night; the householder had noticed the tent was missing.

'Thought you said you were borrowing it,' I glared at Duncan.

'I am. I'll drop it off again on Monday,' Duncan shrugged.

We made our way out of town. We hadn't gone far when a car pulled in behind us.

'It's the pigs,' Nutter shouted to Duncan, who had the tent bundled up on his back carrier. 'You ride off. We'll slow him down.'

Before the rest of us could react, the police car switched on its blue light.

I should've known better than to get involved with stealing the tent; it was Friday the thirteenth after all.

The police car accelerated; it raced past us – but kept on going. 'Thank fuck for that,' I breathed. They must have had a more urgent call, maybe to someone who'd had a tent stolen!

It had just gone out of sight when the slipstream blew the tent off Duncan's scooter. The guy ropes snagged on something though and the tent expanded like a giant parachute.

'Holy Mother,' Duncan shrieked, as he was almost thrown over the handlebars; he didn't have to brake, the tent did that for him.

'Good job it didn't happen while he was behind us,' I said, as I helped Duncan stuff it back on to the scooter again.

Duncan shook his head. He said nothing, but his hands were shaking as he lashed the ropes around the tent.

My hands were trembling too as I put my Lambretta into gear again and rode it off its stand.

If the tent had done that five minutes earlier we would all have been going to a cell, and not to Blackpool.

13

Frantic Escape

'This is the life,' I yelled to Floyd, as he pulled alongside me on the Vespa.

We were racing along the motorway; it was just after six, and Saturday morning, so the lanes were almost empty. We had taken our "L" Plates off, ignoring the fact that learner drivers weren't allowed. Why go miles out of our way when the motorway was there? There had been a trace of mist where the motorway crossed over a river valley, but at least it wasn't raining.

Six more of the Hole in the Wall Gang now had scooters, making fourteen of us altogether. They had all decided to come, some carrying another skinhead, others with their girlfriends on the pillion. Those who were riding two-up were struggling to keep pace with the rest.

We were not all going to fit in the tent and some of us would be sleeping rough.

I wondered how the girls would go on; there was only the one tent after all. It would make a very interesting night. Duncan had wanted both Floyd and me to take a couple of the lads on our machines, but we had refused.

I told him that if anyone was going on my scooter it would be the first girl I picked up in Blackpool. Duncan hadn't brought a passenger either; when I ribbed him about it, he told me that it was because he had the weight of the tent to consider.

Probably thought the same as me; much better to have a girl's thighs wrapped around you than some hairy-arsed skinhead's.

A couple of weeks before, I had fitted new twistgrip rubbers and multi-coloured plastic tassels to my handlebars. They looked really neat I thought, as I leaned against my KL backrest. I had slid backwards along the seat and, to the envy of the other lads, was steering the Lambretta using just my body to balance it, leaning slightly to one side or the other to correct its path. I only had to hold the tassels at full stretch to keep the handlebars straight. I had adjusted the twistgrip so that the throttle didn't self-close; turn it to whatever setting I chose, and it would stay there. Just had to make the odd small adjustment when the scooter began to labour up a gradient.

The week before, Floyd had been on another trip to the scrapyard and had found two black, PVC-covered headrests in an old Morris 1000. They were the type that were sold as an add-on accessory, and had a long narrow saddle at the bottom so that they could be dropped in place on the back of a car seat.

Despite Ramsbottom's regular patrols, I had managed to make two frames at work, so that we could fit the headrests above the bars of our scooters' backrests. Now I could relax in comfort, my head against the padded cushion. Floyd had tried to do the same earlier, but his throttle had kept closing and he had soon given up the idea.

Another day at the garage, I had fitted some new tyres to a customer's Mini. Two of the old tyres still had some mileage left in them, maybe just over half-worn. My Lambretta's tyres were almost bald, and I guessed it wouldn't be long before Dennis would be doing me for them. I wondered if the Mini tyres would fit my scooter; the wheels were the same diameter, but the tyre circumference and tread width was a lot bigger. At lunchtime, I waited until Ramsbottom went out, then sneaked my Lambretta's spare wheel into the workshop. The tyre went on the wheel OK but, when I got it home and fitted it to the rear of my scooter, I found it rubbed against the aluminium crankcase. It only happened when I hit a large bump though, then not by much. Filing the crankcase solved that problem.

I decided to leave it on, then put another Mini tyre on the front wheel; that fitted easily, especially as I'd cut back the mudguard. The bigger diameter of the tyres meant that my Lambretta's acceleration was down, but my top speed was higher, as I found now, cruising along the motorway. I also discovered that I could lean the scooter further into corners, even though it was a bit higher off the ground. Before, as soon as I heard the scooter's folded-up stand touch the floor, I knew that I would skid, and would have to fight to get control of the machine again. Now, I could lean right over and, even if the stand was pushed up against the floor, I was confident I wouldn't crash.

I had even decided that I would, at some time in the future, paint my name underneath each floorboard; I could show it off then, when I went around the roundabout in town. That would give me one up on the other lads.

Yes, it had been worth the trouble I grinned, as I heard Floyd's Vespa struggling to keep pace; his scooter only had a 160cc engine, but he had fewer accessories, and so less weight, to hold him back. It was a shame he still couldn't afford to get a Lammy.

I didn't know if the others could fit the same tyres to their newer scooters, the frames of their machines seemed to be smaller.

The speedo was way out now but that didn't matter; there was no way Dennis could check it. All the work I'd done on the Lambretta, to make it special, would be wasted if my old man made me sell it.

A truck ahead of me was labouring up a shallow gradient.

I checked one of my mirrors then leaned to the right. The Lambretta moved towards the centre lane and I began to overtake the other vehicle. As I drew level with the lorry's cab, things went wrong; a sudden blast of air, deflected from its front, threw the scooter to the right. I tugged at the tassels, but the right hand one popped out of the handlebar. Unfortunately for me, the ball on the end of the left tassel stayed in the hole that I'd poked in the twistgrip, and my surprised reaction snatched the handlebars round. The Lambretta leaned to the right but veered to the left, swerving into the path of the truck. Frantically, I tried to slide along the seat and grab for the handlebars.

I managed to grip the controls again, just as the scooter hurtled towards the hard shoulder. The truck driver sounded his horn but, luckily for me, hit his brakes at the same time; the lorry's front bumper cleared the scooter's back carrier by just a few inches.

I was still in trouble. The throttle was wide open, my first frantic wrench at the handlebars had over-corrected the scooter's course, and I swerved back into the path of the still-braking lorry. It missed me again – somehow. Now, I was crossing the other lanes at speed, towards the central reservation. I snapped the throttle shut and managed to regain control just before I bounced on to the grass. I steered back towards the hard shoulder, passing behind the truck this time.

Luckily, the motorway was still fairly empty.

Empty, except for my mates! The rest of the Hole in the Wall Gang were laughing and jeering at me. I glared at them. My heart began to slow again. Red faced, I pulled in behind the convoy of scooters.

'Are you all right?' Floyd shouted, trying hard not to laugh. 'Sorry Kenny, but you didn't half look a wally.'

'Bastard,' I muttered, but then began to grin. Now that I had escaped unscathed, life felt better after all. The sun began to break through the mist, promising a beautiful day.

Stuff my old man, and Dennis, and Maureen. And Puffin – and Cheryl come to that.

This weekend I was going to enjoy myself.

'Hell's Angels,' Floyd shouted, then pointed towards a load of the leather-jacketed bastards running across the tramlines towards us.

They must have been camped overnight in the beach shelters along Blackpool's sea front; dozens, maybe hundreds, of motorbikes were parked there too. The bikers were too slow; we buzzed past them, shouting abuse, before they could reach the road. I didn't fancy bumping in to them later though.

We rode the full length of the promenade, from Squire's Gate, past the Pleasure Beach, and the Golden Mile, and the North Pier, just taking in the scenery. The Tower was outlined against a cloudless sky and even the distant sea looked blue for a change. It was going to be hot. The run was wonderful at that time of the morning, with not much traffic to get in our way. The only people about were a few souls walking their dogs across the deserted beach, or shopkeepers and amusement arcade owners taking down their shutters, in readiness for the hordes to come later.

I loved the first taste of salt on my lips, and the fresh ozone smell blowing off the Irish Sea. That would soon be replaced by the greasy aroma of chips, fried onions, hotdogs, and jam doughnuts, or the sweet scent of candyfloss.

My stomach growled. I opened my throttle and caught up with Duncan. 'Let's find a café. I'm famished. Didn't have time to get anything to eat last night.'

Duncan nodded then turned into a side road. We went down that street then swung right again into the next, running parallel to the seafront, back the way we had come.

After we had gone a few hundred yards, Duncan suddenly veered to the kerb and nodded towards a little café. 'This'll do us,' he said, as he pulled his Lambretta on to its stand.

'After we've filled our faces – just walk out. Bollocks to paying. They won't dare stop us.'

We went inside.

The owner, an Italian, was just taking the chairs off the tables. He soon had bacon, eggs, sausages, fried bread, and tomatoes, spitting on the griddle though.

As he handed us our espresso coffees, the café owner asked how long we were in town. 'I only say this because there is lot of trouble this week. Motorcycles come – from London I think. They have many fights with boys from here. It bad place to be.'

When we told him we planned to stay the weekend, he warned us to be careful.

I didn't like Duncan's idea of scarpering without paying. The Italian seemed so friendly I was reluctant to do it, even though it meant using some of the money I was saving for the Mecca. When Duncan asked if we were ready to go, I told him to fork out his share.

'Yeah, let's pay,' Floyd joined in. 'Don't want trouble when we've only just got here.'

'What's he going to do against all us lot?' Duncan said, waving his arm towards the skinheads at the other tables.

I was sure the café owner had overheard him. 'Just pay him,' I hissed.

Duncan scowled, but, as we stood up to go, dropped some money on the counter. He told the other lads to do the same.

A police car was sitting on the corner of the street, near to where our scooters were parked; if we had skipped without paying, some of us would have been caught. The policemen in the car scowled at us, but didn't bother us.

I decided that, now that the thirteenth was out of the way, my luck had changed for the better.

We collected our scooters, and then Duncan took us back along the seafront once more.This time the bikers were up and raced after us like a swarm of angry bees. We laughed, gave them the V sign, then sped off again.

Duncan pulled up, just after we'd passed the Central Pier. 'We'll park our scooters safe then hit the town,' he said. 'Might bump into the city mob. Keep your eyes skinned for somewhere to hide the things – where the greasers won't find them.'

We rode up and down several streets, searching for a spot that was not too far from the Pleasure Beach, and then I spotted a likely hideaway. I accelerated to catch up with Duncan. 'How about behind there,' I shouted as he braked to a halt. I pointed to a large advertising hoarding, covering the gap where a building had been knocked down. There was a small space between the board and one of the adjacent houses; it should just be wide enough for our scooters.

'Let's take a look,' Duncan said, then did a U-turn in the road.

We discovered that we could squeeze the scooters through by turning the handlebars slightly. Behind the hoarding was a rubble-strewn garden, but it was flat enough, next to the billboard, for our scooters to stand. On each side of the open space were the gable ends of houses, painted with bitumen and propped up by large timbers; at the rear, the dirty windows of a small warehouse stared vacantly across the plot. The scooters would be hidden from the road by the advertising board, and it seemed unlikely that anyone ever looked out of the warehouse.

'Should be all right here,' Duncan nodded. 'We'll find somewhere to pitch our tent when we've had a look around.'

'Just have to make sure we're not seen going in and out of here too often,' I told him.

'Where we going first?' Floyd asked, as we rolled our coats up and lashed them, and our holdalls, on top of our back carriers.

'We'll see what's happening at the fair,' Duncan said. 'If it's dead – we can always go back again in the afternoon.'

The Pleasure Beach was quiet when we strolled across to it. Even though some of the rides were going, there were only a few people about. Most of these seemed to be the staff who worked on the stalls and arcades, and they were busy winding candyfloss onto sticks, or hanging prizes above the shooting galleries.

We meandered through the rides, past the Mouse, then the Log Flume, the entrance to the roller coaster, then back again.

'Waste of time this,' Rocky said. 'Let's head for the beach.'

'We'll go on the rides later,' Duncan said, 'when there's some skirt about. Fancy going to the bandits?'

I shook my head. Rocky had warned me that the last time he'd been to Blackpool, with Duncan, they'd visited the slot machines and got into trouble. Duncan had gone to one of the coin tables, the sort where you try to knock some coins off the edge by rolling another down a ramp. He'd given it a hefty shove with his hip, hoping to spill some coins down for free. No money fell. All that happened was an alarm screamed out, then four or five bouncer types had chased them.

I could think of better ways, than the one-armed bandits, to spend my money too.

As we passed the Haunted House, one of the Pleasure Beach workers shouted to us. He was putting the shutters back into place on his Hoopla stall. 'I shouldn't go down there,' he said, nodding in the direction we'd been heading. 'There's a load of bikers coming this way – looking for trouble. I'd get out of here quick.'

'We ain't scared of greasers,' Nutter scowled.

The man just shrugged. 'Your choice.' He pulled the last board across, shutting himself inside.

'I'll slice the bastards into pieces,' Nutter said, flicking open his razor.

I didn't carry a weapon; my father would have been horrified if I he thought I did, it was against everything that he'd taught me. I could try out the Doc Martens though. I bent down and rolled my Levi's up another turn, so the greasers would be able to see my polished red boots.

We turned the next corner. The pathway was filled with Hell's Angels, at least a hundred of them. Most had steel toe-capped boots and tight-fitting denim jeans that were streaked with oil and grease. Many had sleeveless Levi jackets over their leathers. Some had German helmets, others black peaked hats draped with silver chains.

They all carried a weapon. Suddenly I felt a bit naked. The bikers had knives, pieces of chain, axes, iron bars, and hammers; my DM's seemed puny in comparison. Some of the Hole in the Wall Gang, like Duncan and Nutter, carried razors or knives, but nothing like the bikers had in their hands. And there were only twenty-two of us, four of whom were girls! I felt my stomach churn. I knew I should run. My legs began to shake and I wondered if they would fail me. I wouldn't be the first to go though I decided, biting my lip.

'Let's get them,' Duncan said, then stepped forward.

The lead biker, over six feet tall and built like a brick shithouse, waved an axe, its sharpened steel edge flashing in the sunlight, then suddenly bellowed, 'Kill them!'

That did it; Duncan turned and fled, almost knocking me over in his panic-stricken flight.

I fought to regain my balance, knowing I would be finished if that lot caught me.

Floyd grabbed at my elbow, then began to propel me in the wake of the other skinheads.

Behind us, a terrifying roar almost made me empty my bladder, but, as I heard the rattle of hob-nailed boots on the concrete, I knew I had to leg it; the Angels were not far behind.

Once I was up and running, Floyd let go of me and began to sprint.

The Hole in the Wall Gang scattered to left and right, swerving between the stalls; the few holidaymakers who were about, dodged quickly out of our way.

143

I dared not look behind; the footsteps seemed to be getting closer.

'Come on Kenny,' Floyd yelled, as he turned back to see how far behind I was.

I was struggling; although I was a fast runner, I couldn't keep pace with Floyd's long legs. 'Just get going,' I panted.

'I ain't leavin' you,' Floyd rasped as we dashed across a road, causing cars to swerve and sound their horns.

Should we make for the scooters? No, that would be a fatal mistake. We would be trapped behind the hoarding. In the street someone would see what was left of us, after the bikers had done with us, and call an ambulance – or a hearse. Our machines would be wrecked as well if we went back to them.

'What the . . .' I cursed, as I ran into Floyd's back.

'Jesus,' Floyd sobbed, then bent over, and put his hands on his knees, gasping for breath.

I glanced behind.

The Hell's Angels were now only fifty yards away. They too had stopped running but were advancing towards the two of us, some slapping their bike chains against the palms of their hands, others holding their knives and axes ready to stab or cut.

I looked over Floyd's shoulder. The road ahead was filled with more bikers, coming towards us the other way. We were trapped; sandwiched between a couple of hundred armed and murderous Hell's Angels.

'Nice knowing you, Kenny,' Floyd said, gripping my wrist, then wheeling to face the oncoming bikers.

There had been tears in Floyd's eyes before he turned away. I felt like crying too. I was too young to die. There was so much I wanted to do. This was it I knew, for like Floyd, I doubted we would survive this. I pictured my father's face when they broke the news; perhaps he would forgive me then.

'In here, quickly,' someone yelled.

I saw a movement out of the corner of my eye and turned my head. It was the Italian café owner. I suddenly realised that we had ended up in the street where we'd called for breakfast.

'Come on, you run in here,' the Italian said, beckoning us into the alleyway at the rear of his business. 'You be safe,' he told us, as he bolted the entry door in place. 'The police – they come soon.'

The police! What could they do against that mob? The bikers would have this flimsy door down and hack us to pieces long before the law could step in.

We followed the Italian into his café. It was full of people, but the large plate-glass windows had now been shuttered, blocking out the sunlight.

Despite the shutters, I could hear angry voices in the street outside. There was a sudden roar, almost like a football crowd made when their team scored a goal, the sound of thundering feet, then several cries of pain.

Something crashed against one of the shutters, vibrating the glass it was protecting. There was a scream of terror. I looked around, expecting to see the greasers burst into the café, but, although I could hear them, there was still no sign of them.

'You like a coffee,' the Italian said, handing me a cup and saucer, then another to Floyd.

My hands were all of a tremble I realised, as I put the cup on a nearby table.

'These young thugs. Come here causing trouble. They should do something about it,' one woman said to another, at the front of the shop.

I looked at her, about to say something, but saw that she was peeping through a gap in the covering over the door; the woman had meant the greasers, not us.

'What's going on,' Floyd whispered, as the shouts outside rose in intensity.

'Them motorbike riders. They're attacking each other,' the

145

man standing next to him said. 'They've been spoiling for a fight all week.'

I looked at Floyd looked with relief. The Hell's Angels had other things to think about now. Hopefully, they would have forgotten about the two skinheads they'd been chasing.

'Is there another way out of here,' I asked the café owner, as sirens began to sound above the din in the nearby street, 'without going past that lot.'

'You go that way,' the Italian pointed to the back door, where he'd led us in earlier. 'Turn right and there is another alley. You go along it, then turn left into another and you come out in the next street.'

'Thank you. How much for these?' I said, pointing to the coffees; my cup was still full though, as I'd not felt like drinking.

The café owner shook his head. 'On the house. You good boys. Not like some. You stay that way, OK.'

I wondered if he'd have thought that if we'd legged it without paying the bill this morning.

Yes, my luck was definitely changing.

14

Going To A Happening

'Jesus! This is high up,' I said as the Big Dipper's car reached the top of the climb and circled round, ready for the descent.

'I ain't looking,' Floyd answered, as he gripped the handrail in front of him.

I looked at the curve of the beach, now packed with trippers, some paddling in the sea, others sprawled on deck chairs. Blackpool had certainly filled up since our escapade with the bikers I thought, as the car rattled along the track.

After we had left the café, we had made our way back to the scooters, checking nervously around each corner as we went. Duncan and the other lads were already there.

'You made it then,' Duncan grinned sheepishly. 'Thought they'd had you.'

'You didn't come back for us though,' I said.

'Oh, I wanted to,' he said, lowering his voice, 'but some of the others wouldn't. You know what they're like.'

'Yeah, you can't rely on some folk in a fight,' I said, staring at him.

Duncan averted his eyes, then changed the subject. 'We're off for a burger or something – then back to the Pleasure Beach. Keep an eye out for them greasers though.'

We'd done just that, and had not seen anything more of

the Hell's Angels – yet! We had met up with other skinhead gangs and scooter clubs though, but, because the Hell's Angels were in town, we hadn't fought with them.

I began to wish I'd not stuffed my face with a greasy hot dog and onions, followed by a couple of pints of ale in Yates's Wine Lodge, as the roller coaster car poised on the summit. 'Fuckin' hell,' I breathed as it began to race downhill. I didn't care much for heights, and, to someone who worked in a garage every day, there didn't seem to be much holding the thing on the rails. The car went over the first hump in the track, making me feel weightless. Bile began to rise in my throat as the roller coaster car plunged onwards. At least if I spewed my guts it would land on Duncan I thought, as the car hurtled into a bend.

Then, thankfully, a few more twists and turns later it squealed to a halt.

'Dodgems next,' Duncan said as we scrambled off the ride.

'Count me out,' I told him, as I leaned against the rail at the side of the Octopus.

'Me too. I'm saving some brass for tonight, ' Floyd said.

'See you later then,' Duncan grinned, then led the others across the funfair.

I stripped off my denim jacket, folded it, and tucked it under my arm. 'It's bloody hot,' I told Floyd, as I brushed the sweat from my face. I moved around the rail a bit, away from the smell of brandy snaps and toffee apples coming from a nearby stand. That was better I thought, as I gasped in a few good breaths of air.

'Look at that,' Floyd said, as the Octopus ride began to swirl into action.

'What?' I said, my brain still befuddled from the roller coaster ride.

'There!' Floyd nudged me, then pointed to one of the revolving seats.

I saw the two girls, almost at the same moment as they

waved to us. Both were wearing mini skirts and were struggling to keep them in place.

'The black haired one's fit,' I murmured. She reminded me a little of Puffin, but must be several years older, in her mid-twenties maybe.

'Don't mind the other one, either,' Floyd chuckled.

When the ride finished, we met up with the girls at the exit. One was called Mandy; the one I fancied was Hazel. They told us that they lived in Blackpool, but still enjoyed visiting the Pleasure Beach when they got the chance.

We had a go on the Mouse, me hoping that my stomach wouldn't betray me. Hazel had great legs I noticed, as she snuggled onto the seat next to me. She was not wearing tights and her legs were nicely tanned; she must get more sun here than we do I thought. I could feel the warmth of her thigh pressed against mine. She smelled nice, a scent of roses or something. After the ride, I slipped my arm through hers, as we strolled around the funfair behind Floyd and Mandy.

'Fancy a ride on the Ghost Train,' I suggested, thinking that it would be dark in there, and that I would be able to have a quick grope.

Hazel nodded, and soon we were squeezed into one of the little cars. As it swerved around the first corner, Hazel shrieked as something brushed at her hair. I put my arm around her shoulder and pulled her close. Her lips closed on mine and her tongue slid between my teeth. I moved my free hand to rest on the swelling of her breast. Hazel didn't resist but slid her hand into the waistband of my jeans. I gasped as her fingers touched me. Her tongue probed deeper. Who the fuck was seducing who?

The car thumped against the door to the outside world and I dropped my hand to rest on her lap. Hazel freed her own hand and smiled at me. 'I don't live far from here,' she said huskily. 'Just before the football ground.'

'You mean . . ?'

Hazel ran her tongue seductively between her lips.

'Just lead the way,' I told her.

Mandy and Floyd were waiting nearby. Hazel told her friend that we were leaving.

'We'll come with you,' Mandy said. 'I'm going to show Floyd my flat anyway.'

Floyd winked at me, as we parted at Mandy's place.

Hazel lived in the next street, in a neat little terraced house. I could see the floodlight towers of Bloomfield Road poking above the rooftops, and, from the number of parked cars, and the noise coming from the direction of the stand, I realised there must be a game in progress. I was keen on football, but decided there were better things to do now.

The house, although small, was nicely furnished, and I wondered how Hazel could afford it. She'd told me she worked in a bingo hall, so she couldn't earn much.

Perhaps I could manage my own place on my wages from the garage after all.

'Like a drink,' Hazel asked, as she motioned for me to sit on the sofa. When I nodded, she took a bottle of Bacardi from a glass-fronted cupboard and poured us both one, then topped it up with Coke from another bottle. 'Take your boots off – if you like.'

I did so, thankful that I hadn't any holes in my socks, and that I wasn't wearing a pair that my mother had attempted to darn. I had often wondered if she was colour blind, her idea of a matching yarn seemed to be something that was white, or red, no matter what the colour of my socks.

'Cheers,' Hazel said, as she sat beside me and touched her glass against mine.

I took a deep swallow, feeling the spirits burn down my throat into my stomach.

Hazel turned to face me, her lipstick red where the Bacardi had wet it. She had a luscious mouth I thought, and I leaned forward to kiss her again.

She pushed me away, but only briefly, so that she could

150

put our glasses on the table at the end of the sofa, then reached for me once more.

We kissed again, and as I fumbled at the buttons of her blouse, she began to tug my T-shirt upwards. Our lips parted once more, as she eased it over my head. I lowered my arms to finish my task, peeled back her blouse, then squeezed her breasts in my hands. They felt wonderful. They felt even better when I had freed them from her bra.

Hazel gasped as I bent forwards and circled one of her nipples with my tongue. She began to tug my belt undone.

I decided to help her. I stood up, pulling her with me, then unhooked the belt catch. As her fingers undid my jean buttons, I slid my hands inside her waistband and pushed her skirt downwards. Her white panties came down as well, and I rubbed my fingers against her, in her, feeling the moistness of her. There was something strange about her body though; my fingers had found none of the tight curls that I expected.

Hazel pulled away, then bent to slip her skirt and knickers free of her feet. She tugged at my underpants.

I almost creamed myself as her lips closed around me, then slid along my body. But there was something much nicer I thought, as I looked down and saw her naked buttocks. 'Better stop that,' I hissed, as I felt my climax rising.

Hazel twisted her head and looked up at me questioningly, her lips still clamped on me.

'That's Heaven,' I rasped, 'but I want to . . .'

Hazel understood. She released me, then sprawled back on the hearthrug, propped on her elbows, smiling at me.

She had shaved herself I realised; her pussy was naked – and pink – just waiting to be fucked. I collapsed between her legs, then ran my tongue along her thighs. As I buried my face in her, I could smell the sweet musk of her body. It was ecstasy for me, and Hazel began to writhe beneath my searching tongue. Much more though of that though, and I would be splashing my load over the carpet; better to be

151

deep inside her when I did that I decided, as I scrambled on top of her.

Hazel hadn't mentioned a rubber, and I was too far-gone to suggest one. 'Jesus!' I exhaled as I slid inside her.

Her lips closed on mine again, and I felt her nipples rubbing against my chest. It wouldn't take many strokes I thought as I plunged deeper.

'Oh, that's so good,' Hazel breathed, as I drew back, almost out of her body, then thrust myself forward again. 'Oh, Kenny, give it to me,' she croaked.

I was just about to explode inside her, when I heard footsteps from the room above. I poised in mid-stroke, following the noise across the ceiling with my eyes. I heard someone cough – it was a man – then the tinkle of water as he urinated into a toilet bowl. 'Who's that,' I whispered as Mandy tugged at my waist, urging me on.

'Oh, him. Just my husband,' she sighed. 'It's all right. He's a bouncer at one of the clubs. He's on tonight – probably been in the boozer at dinnertime. He won't come down.'

Hazel was right. I heard the footsteps retrace their path, then the squeak of bedsprings. It was all too much for me though; I felt my passion wilting. I scrambled to my knees.

'Come back,' Hazel rasped, as she sat up and crossed her legs. 'Me and him have an – understanding. I don't ask what he gets up to . . .'

'Have to go,' I muttered as I tugged my jeans into place. I felt a terrible disappointed aching in my loins, but the last thing I wanted was Hazel's husband to catch me shagging her. Besides, I wouldn't like someone screwing my wife – if I was ever daft enough to get married. The bed creaked again as her old man turned over, spurring me on. I stuffed my feet into my DM's, wishing I had gone for the ten hole boots and not the twelve.

'Bastard!' Hazel spat as I left the room.

Two minutes later, I was sitting on the kerb opposite

Mandy's flat, tucking my Fred Perry shirt back into my jeans. Thankfully, the football crowd had gone home while I was with Hazel, else I might have got a kicking off the local skins. They were a hard bunch of bastards, or so I had heard. Mind you, they needed to be, with a load of Glaswegians visiting the town on their annual holiday, or Scousers and Mancunians making the short trip up the coast, or the Brummies, or lads from Stoke, coming for a week or a fortnight away, all spoiling for a fight when they'd had a bit of sun and a lot of ale.

It was another hour, and there was a red glow in the sky, when Floyd came out. Mandy, her naked body covered only by a flimsy gown, blew a kiss at him as he crossed the street to where I sat on the kerb.

She had been married too, Floyd told me, but she said her husband was away in the army. The ring on her finger had not stopped her taking Floyd to her bedroom though.

'I drew the short straw,' I told him as we went to fetch our scooters. 'I was just on the vinegar stroke too,' I grumbled. And it was supposed to be my lucky day. But then again, maybe fortune had smiled on me; I hadn't been caught on the job by the bouncer. I doubted if I would have been so keen on getting to the Mecca after he'd finished with me.

'They're all in the pub up the road,' Rocky told us when we returned to our scooters, to find him there alone.

I was relieved to see that no one had discovered the hideaway, so we could leave our machines there for a while longer. We had bought fish and chips on the way back, and I offered them to Rocky.

'Silly bastards ain't looked for anywhere to camp yet,' Rocky said, helping himself to one of my chips, then pointing with it to the tent, still bundled on Duncan's back-carrier. He swallowed the chip, then stripped off his jeans and unrolled his suit trousers, cursing when he saw the creases in them. 'Yeah, imagine them trying to put the tent up at three o'clock in the morning – when they're pissed out of their minds.'

'That's a point. Where are we sleeping tonight?' I looked at Floyd.

Rocky answered for him. 'Stick with me,' he said, as he stuffed his jeans into his holdall. 'I've found a caravan site – on the edge of town. Some of them don't seem to have anyone staying in them – and the doors are easy to open.'

'Better than kipping on the ground,' Floyd grinned.

I began to change into my suit.

'Borrowed that off your old man?' Rocky grinned.

Thankfully, it was too dark behind the hoarding for the other two to see me blushing. I would have to get a new suit – and soon.

'Hey, heard about that Hell's Angel who got stabbed?' Rocky said.

I shook my head.

'When they had that fight this morning, one of 'em was killed. Don't know if he was from the Blackpool or Watford lot though.'

I didn't know either. I hadn't even been sure where they were from, except for what the café owner had said, and I'd not stopped around long enough to see what was on the Angels' colours. Now that Rocky had told me about the murder, I realised that it could have been one of us lying in the mortuary.

'Got any gear?' Rocky said, polishing his glasses on the shirt he'd just put on. 'If not – I've got some in here,' he said, tapping his holdall.

'I haven't got much money left,' I said, surprised by how fast my wages had disappeared at the fairground. I probably had enough for the Mecca, then a bit for Sunday. But I would have nothing left to pay my board when I got home! Worry about that tomorrow I told myself.

'You can have some Dominoes – for what I paid for them,' Rocky said, dropping a handful of small black and white capsules into my palm. 'What about you?' he said, turning to Floyd.

'Don't think I'll bother. I saw what the tablets did to Kenny at the party. If I want to feel like that, I'll just put my head in my mum's spin drier. You should stay clear of them too, Kenny,' he told me. 'Clinton reckons they can make you paranoid – amongst other things.'

'That bastard's always had it in for me,' I grinned, then looked back over my shoulder, as if checking if Clinton was there.

'See, there you go,' Floyd laughed.

'Paranoid or not, no one's gonna spoil my night.'

'I'm taking mine here,' Rocky said, tipping some of the capsules into his mouth, then washing them down with some Tizer. He handed the bottle to me. 'Saves 'em being found – if the doormen – or the police – search you.'

I picked up one of the Black and Whites. You needed a lot of them to get blocked up. I hated taking tablets or capsules and always struggled to swallow the things. The first one stuck at the back of my throat so I took a mouthful of the Tizer. Down it went. I turned the next capsule over in my fingers. It had "Riker" written on it in tiny letters I noticed, before I popped it into my mouth. The next ones soon followed. After the last one was down my throat, we finished getting changed then made our way to the Mecca.

I was all wound up for the club, but was a bit disappointed when I saw it.

'Looks like a fucking car park,' I said, as I looked at the prefabricated concrete building; even the setting sun and the illuminated signs couldn't take away its drab appearance.

'That's 'cause it is,' Rocky told me. 'Or at least part of it. There's a bowling alley too. It's inside what counts. My brother says we should head for the Highland Room.'

It was a hot sultry night and the escalator had just packed in, so we had to walk up it.

As we climbed the, what to me seemed endless, steps, I

155

began to sweat. 'Why do have to wear these?' I gasped, tugging at the tie that was strangling my neck. My mouth was becoming dry, and my tongue felt like it would crack.

'Don't know,' Rocky said, 'but they won't let you in without one.' He handed me a stick of gum. 'Chew on that. It'll help.'

The place was packed. As we pushed through the doors, into a corridor at the top, I saw that most of the lads already inside were stripping off their jackets and ties and handing them in at a cloakroom. No one seemed to be bothering them, now that they were in the place, so we followed suit.

We could hear the music well before we squeezed into the dancehall; the fluttering piano intro of *There's That Mountain* made everyone eager to get in.

It was a tacky place, much like Annabellas, I thought as I gazed at the plastic shields adorning the walls, then the tartan carpet that was supposed to give it a Scottish flavour. But there the similarities ended; here they were playing Northern Soul.

I stood beside Floyd and watched nervously as Rocky took to the floor.

Rocky never seemed to bother what folk thought of him. 'If I can't see them, why should I worry about them?' he would say.

We had practised a few steps at home, even ventured to try a few on the floor of Annabellas, but this was different; everyone here seemed to be such good a dancer. Finally, we plucked up the courage, meandered through the tables and chairs, and joined Rocky.

I forgot all my discomfort, as record followed record. Some were old favourites of mine, like Roscoe Robinson's *That's Enough*. Others I'd never heard before, even though Rocky and his brother had built up a good collection. I danced and danced. I had learned my lesson from the party though; when I took a breather, I only gulped down soft drinks.

Floyd was a brilliant dancer, even without the benefit of speed. Despite being tall, he could do the splits, then spring up effortlessly again. Another brilliant move that Floyd had practised, was to do a back-drop, then jerk his body clear of the floor, clap his hands behind his back, another back drop, then effortlessly push himself onto his feet once more. I had tried it many a time, but only ended up sprawled on the floor; I wasn't going to do that with everybody watching.

I noticed that the clubgoers had different accents. Some were from the Midlands, some from London. There were Geordies as well as Yorkshire lads; others sounded like they were locals. In any other club, they would probably be kicking the shit out of each other by now. Here, they didn't seem to bother and, despite the dance floor being so packed, if you accidentally elbowed somebody in the ribs, they just gave you a bit more room, instead of poking you in the eye.

Duncan and the rest of the gang never appeared in the Mecca; where they finally ended up would have to remain a mystery until we caught up with them again.

As *Any Day Now* slowed the pace, I took the opportunity to take a breather. I was enjoying myself, more than I'd ever done before.

'Sorry folks, that's the last one for tonight,' one of the DJ's said, as the lights were turned brighter.

I screwed up my eyes. 'What does he mean – last one? Thought this place was open until two?'

'It is two – or nearly,' Floyd said, as the dancers began to disperse.

Where had the hours gone? It had all been wonderful, although my shirt was soaking, and felt clammy against my back. But I didn't want it to stop – yet!

'Isn't there any where else we can go – open all night like the Wheel used to be?' I asked Rocky.

' 'Fraid not, mate,' Rocky told me. 'That's all we get.'

15

Time Is Tight

'Wonder what happened to the others,' I said, as I rubbed the sleep from my eyes.

'No idea,' Floyd mumbled from under his sleeping bag.

The rest of the scooters, belonging to the Hole in the Wall Gang, had gone, when we made our way to the blackness of the waste ground, after leaving the Mecca; only Floyd's, Rocky's, and my machine had still been parked there. Untouched as well, we had all been relieved to see. Duncan hadn't left a note to say where they had disappeared to, so we had sought out the caravan that Rocky had scouted for earlier, and spent the night there.

'We'll have to ride along the seafront later. See if we can find them,' Rocky said, as he lit his first cigarette of the day. He sent a ring of smoke spiralling towards the caravan's white-painted ceiling. 'There's a shower block over there,' he said, tugging back one of the curtains. 'Think I'll dodge across before we go.'

I thought I would do the same. Sweating in the nightclub had left me feeling pretty crappy, even though I'd changed into a fresh shirt, and discarded the suit for my jeans again. I had still been feeling high when we sneaked into the caravan, and I had tossed and turned, fully clothed in my sleeping bag, waiting impatiently for the dawn.

'I'm frozen – and starving,' Floyd said as he poked his nose out of his sleeping bag.

'You'd have been a damned sight colder in the tent,' I grinned. 'Unless you'd cuddled up to Duncan for warmth.'

'What a thought,' Rocky grimaced. 'Yeah, you'd have been warm all right. 'Specially if he was drunk and thought you were a tart – and he started screwing you.'

Floyd shuddered; whether it was because of the cold, or revulsion at the idea of being shafted by Duncan, I wasn't sure. 'What're we doing about breakfast?' he said, as he unzipped the sleeping bag and sat up.

'We'll pack up here,' I told him. 'I ain't hungry yet but could do with a drink. There's nothing to be had in here except water. I've already looked.' My mouth had been parched and, in the early hours, I had searched the caravan. The mean bastards who owned it hadn't left us anything. The gas bottles were empty as well I'd discovered this morning, when I'd fetched a kettle of water from the toilets and tried to boil it. Mind you, I hadn't found any tea or coffee to put in it either, so it hadn't really mattered.

At least the water sprinkling from the showerhead was warm when, some fifteen minutes later, it was trickling down my face. There was not much of it, but it felt wonderful as it eased the prickly sensation from my skin.

I dried myself as best as I could, using the shirt I'd worn at the Mecca as a makeshift towel, then got dressed again. 'I've got an idea. Wait here,' I told Floyd, as he stepped from another cubicle, water dripping from his naked body.

I trotted across the deserted caravan site, then returned a few moments later carrying a screwdriver from my toolbox. 'Keep a look out,' I told Floyd.

'What are you going to do,' he asked, as he pulled his trousers on.

I began to prise at the cover of a Durex machine that was screwed to the wall. 'Should be some money in here,' I murmured, as I forced the blade into a gap.

'Somebody might hear you,' Floyd said, becoming ever more anxious. 'There's a few people got their curtains back now,' he warned as he scanned the caravan site.

'Won't take long,' I breathed. A vein in my temple began to pulse, betraying my anxiety; I wanted the money from the machine, but didn't want to be caught nicking it. It was tough going but eventually the metal case yielded.

'Enough johnnies to last a lifetime,' Rocky laughed, as he too finished his shower and saw me stuffing dozens of contraceptives into my jacket pockets.

'Not much cash though,' I grumbled as I counted my spoils. 'Just over two measly quid!'

'Someone's coming,' Floyd hissed from the doorway.

I pushed the cover hurriedly back into place. It hadn't been damaged too much, and you would have to look closely to see it had been opened. Or someone would find it when they tried to get a rubber out. I smiled to myself. Some poor bastard would be spoiling to get his leg over, pop in here for a johnny, only to be disappointed. The poor sod would be even more disgruntled if his girl wouldn't let him near her without a rubber on.

'What're you going to do with the Durex,' Floyd asked when we were back in the caravan.

'Have as many as you need,' I said, spilling the silvery packets onto the table. 'I'll try and sell the rest.' I wouldn't make much from them I knew, and I was a long way short of the cash I needed for my board.

When we had all picked up what we wanted, there were about thirty packets left. Rocky examined one then grinned. 'Let's help nature a bit,' he said, unfastening a metal "Lambretta" badge from his Levi jacket. He bent back its securing pin, then carefully speared it through the foil.

I saw the metal point protrude from the other side; it must have punctured the latex sheath inside as well.

'Give this one to Duncan,' Rocky laughed. He stabbed the next one. 'And this is for Nutter.'

160

'What a rotten trick,' I said, then handed another Durex to him. 'Don't leave Cadger out.' There would be an unexplained baby boom shortly, as well as a few shotgun weddings. 'Let's be off – before someone finds out we pinched the things.'

We fetched our scooters from behind the caravan, packed our stuff, then kicked the machines into life. Minutes later, we squeezed past the barrier that blocked cars from accessing the site at night, then took the road into the resort.

The bikers must have left town I thought as we cruised along the seafront; there was no sign of them. No sign of Duncan either, although we saw dozens of other scooterists, some of whom stared at us as we rode past, then others who waved to us, and then some more who jeered our passage. We found the Hole in the Wall Gang an hour or so later, on our fourth trip along the promenade. They were parked up, chatting to a bunch of skinheads. The other mob was from Walsall I saw; the town's name was pasted, in white stick-on lettering, on several of the scooters' flyscreens.

'Where have you lot been?' Duncan frowned, as we squealed to a halt next to him. 'What a fuckin' night we had. Pillock head,' he said, punching Nutter on the chest, 'suggested we put the tent on the beach.'

'Thought it was a good idea. Nobody would bother us there,' Nutter scowled.

'Good idea!' Duncan scoffed. 'Ever tried knocking tent pegs into sand? They don't fuckin' hold much. Hold even less when you're half pissed. The tent was no use – so we just rolled out our sleeping bags.'

'It was bastard cold,' Cadger said, as he watched Duncan lighting a cigarette. When Duncan ignored his pleading eyes, he continued. 'Even colder when the tide came in!'

'We lost the tent – and most of our stuff,' Duncan glared at Nutter. 'Just managed to get the scooters up the ramp – before they got swamped as well. It'll take me fuckin' weeks to get the salt off my chrome.'

161

I tried not to laugh as I pictured the frantic scenes on the beach, in the dark. That would have been well worth seeing.

'The Walsall lads had a run in with the greasers too,' Duncan told me.

'Yeah, we had heard about them fighting,' one of them, a tall youth with a stubble of red hair said, 'so we were tooled up ready. There was hundreds of 'em but we sorted them out.'

I suspected that after the two Hell's Angels Chapters had beaten each other into pulp, and then the police had done with them, there would have been little fight left in the bikers. I didn't say that though. Let the Walsall skins have their moment of glory.

'Presents for you,' I said, handing Duncan and Cadger some of the booty from the johnny machine.

'Got a few of them to spare?' the red headed lad from Walsall asked. 'Jill likes it at least five times a night,' he bragged, as he rubbed the cropped head of a skinhead girl standing next to him.

'That's why we all have to help Keith out,' another Walsall skinhead chuckled, then ducked his mate's fist.

'Here you are,' I said. 'That's the last of them. Enjoy yourselves.'

'Are we having something to eat yet?' Floyd muttered in my ear. 'I'm famished.'

Duncan overheard him. We left the Walsall lads and went into a nearby Wimpy Bar. 'And this time we aren't paying,' he warned me.

'Up to you,' I told him. Now that I had the proceeds from the Durex machine in my pocket, I could afford to get a decent breakfast for myself and Floyd.

Duncan's plan fell through; unlike the Italian's café, you had to pay at the Wimpy Bar before you sat down to eat. If they hadn't paid, the gang would have had to leg it down the street carrying trays of food.

'We'll have these instead,' Duncan said, and stuffed a

plastic ketchup dispenser, shaped like a huge red tomato, underneath his coat.

Some of the other lads followed suit, gathering up the ketchup and brown sauce containers as they left.

'What do you want them for?' I was puzzled.

'We can have a bit of fun with these,' Duncan grinned as he climbed astride his scooter. 'We'll have one more run along the promenade – then head for home.'

We cruised along the foreshore. As we passed a group of people waiting to cross the road, to reach the beach, Duncan splattered them with ketchup. Other day-trippers, staring wonderingly at the sights, were squirted by the gang. Howls of rage followed in our wake. I shouted for Floyd to speed up; we were at the rear of the pack and bearing the brunt of people's anger, even though we were doing nothing at them ourselves.

Duncan turned his scooter inland, heading for the dual carriageway that led out of town. Our convoy went past a trench at the side of the road. A dozen or so men, naked to the waist, were digging in the ditch. The first man's head bobbed up when he heard the scooters. He tossed long brown hair back from his eyes then stuck his fingers up at Duncan.

'Greaser bastard,' Duncan yelled, then squirted him in the eye with ketchup.

By the time I drew level with him, the man had wiped his face and was scrambling out of the trench. His mates were only a few steps behind, waving shovels and pick axes in the air.

I sighed with relief as I passed the end of the trench. Except for Floyd, the other scooterists had disappeared around the next bend; I wouldn't like to have been caught by the irate roadworkers. Then, my Lambretta misfired. 'What the . . ?' I looked down at the engine, as if I could see what the problem was through the metal side panels.

As the scooter began to slow, I heard a cheer behind me; I

glanced over my shoulder and saw the road menders racing towards me, bent on revenge.

The Lambretta spluttered. I squeezed in the clutch lever then twisted the throttle wide open. It didn't help; the engine died.

'Jesus,' I hissed, as the scooter slowed to walking speed, my mind racing as I tried to figure out an escape. Floyd was circling back, but the two of us would be no match for a dozen angry men armed with all sorts of tools. Should I abandon the Lammy and hop onto the back of Floyd's Vespa? I would escape but my wheels would be wrecked.

The nearest man, the one that Duncan had targeted, was only yards away now, raising his shovel in the air, ready to crack it down on my head. The man must have spotted Floyd racing towards him, and he swung the spade back, poised to knock my mate from his scooter.

Petrol! The fucking scooter was out of petrol, my brain screamed as, in slow motion, I figured out the cause of the problem. Just as the Lambretta was about to stop, I reached down between my legs and twisted the aluminium fuel lever another ninety degrees. The scooter was now on reserve; it would have enough petrol to get me several miles away, if I could just get it started again!

I released the clutch, and the scooter lost almost all that remained of its forward motion as the lifeless engine dragged at it. The fuel in the float chamber of the carburettor would be used up, I suddenly realised; I would have to wait for that to refill before it would fire again. I snatched another quick look back; Floyd had gone wide to dodge the spade then stopped several yards away, offering himself as a target for the men's wrath. Several paused, but the leading road-digger raced towards me again.

I was just about to drop my feet to the floor, to balance the scooter while I kick-started it, when the engine coughed. I prayed the Lammy still had enough momentum to bump-start itself. It had! Nothing ever sounded sweeter to me, not even my favourite Northern Soul record, than the sound of the two-stroke engine bursting into life. The scooter leapt forward as I opened the throttle. I heard Floyd's Vespa closing up behind me. We were safe!

'That was close,' I shouted to Floyd, as he drew alongside. 'Thanks, mate,' I grinned with relief.

'I know you wouldn't leave me,' Floyd smiled back.

That was true I thought, as I reached over and squeezed his arm; I knew that I would never abandon Floyd either. I was glad too, that I usually left the scooter's fuel tap in the halfway position. Several of the other riders never bothered with that, just turned it to the bottom; I would have been well and truly in the shit now if I had done that.

It had been a good weekend and yes, my luck had changed.

Now I just had to face my old man.

I parked the Lambretta next to the garage door, then rubbed the dust from my eyes.

'Where the hell have you been?' my father bellowed as he straightened up from weeding a flowerbed. 'Your mother's been worried sick. We thought you'd been knocked off that thing.' He strode towards me, rolling up his shirtsleeves, anger blazing in his eyes. For a moment, I thought that he was going to hit me, something that he had never done before even when I had been at my worst as a kid. There was always a first time though; I knew just how far I'd pushed my old man.

'Oh Kenneth, you're safe.'

I heard my mother's voice behind me and turned, relieved that she was there. I would never know now if my father would have planted me one. It would have hurt if he had done; despite his age, my father was still a strong man.

My mother hugged me, then began to sob. 'I'm so glad you're home.' She stepped back and held me at arm's length, as if to reassure herself I was really there, and that she was not imagining it, then embraced me again. 'Come into the house.'

I followed her through the front door; my father two paces behind, scowling menacingly at me.

There was a suitcase in the hallway. 'It's your stuff,' my father said. 'If you won't do as I say – then you can leave.'

'Be quiet, Charlie,' my mother scolded. 'He's home safe and that's an end to it.'

'It might be with you – but he's let me down. I shan't forget that. Why couldn't you ring your mum,' he asked me, while she was making us a cup of tea. 'She's been going out of her mind . . .'

'I rang the police,' my mother shouted from the kitchen. 'That nice man, PC Dennis, said he'd certainly keep an eye out for you, but he couldn't do much more. And your boss, Mr Ramsbottom, came round, wondering why you'd not been in to work on Saturday morning. I didn't know what to say – so I told him you were feeling poorly.'

'See! You've got your mother lying for you. I'm fed up with it all,' my father growled.

'We went round to the Edmonds – to see if Floyd could tell us where you were,' my mother said, as she returned to the living room. There were tears in her eyes. 'He was gone as well – but I guess you know that. Floyd will be in trouble too, when he gets in. At least we managed to patch up our differences with them.'

'Yes, just look at the trouble you cause,' my father joined in again.

'I'll go if you want. Find somewhere to live,' I said. 'Get a flat perhaps . . .'

'You haven't the first idea how to look after yourself,' my father sneered. 'I never thought that a boy of mine,' he paused, to take a deep breath, 'would be such a - such a disappointment.'

'Don't say that,' my mother began to weep again. 'Let's put it all behind us now.'

'I'm fed up with doing that. Just let him misbehave one more time. If he wants a place of his own – let him get one.'

'Oh, Charlie, I'd worry about him even more then . . .'

'Last chance, boy.' He wagged a thick finger under my nose, then picked up his tea and stamped out of the room.

'He was concerned too Kenneth, despite what he says,' my mother told me when she was certain that my father had gone. 'He doesn't show it the same – but he made himself poorly. I told him to go to the doctor – but he wouldn't. Just be a good boy for him, please,' she said, teasing a stray lock of my hair back into place.

Relieved that it seemed I was not to be thrown out, I agreed that I would try to be.

Deep down I didn't want to upset my father, but time was passing. I would be an old man myself soon, I was seventeen at Christmas, and I wanted to make sure that I enjoyed myself while I could.

And my father had not mentioned selling the scooter.

Perhaps if I kept quiet . . .

I met up with Cheryl as I was walking towards her home. She was with a boy I vaguely recognised from somewhere.

'Hi, Kenny,' Cheryl said as I came up to them. 'This is Tony. You know him. He was in my class.'

I stared at the youth, then remembered him; he was a right "mummy's boy" and had been a victim of Duncan's bullying. Unlike Floyd though, he had made no friends to help him.

Tony pushed his glasses back onto the bridge of his nose then beamed myopically at me. 'Hello, Kenny,' he said, then offered his hand.

Dipstick I thought, ignoring the proffered handshake. Then a sudden idea struck me. Was this prat giving Cheryl one? I pictured her naked body, as I had seen her that day in the kitchen, then shook my head. Floyd would have something to say to Tony if he was, of that, I was sure.

167

'Is Floyd at home?' I asked, guessing that was where they had just come from.

'He is but papa won't let him out again,' Cheryl told me. 'And he doesn't want him to mix with you either.'

'Will you just tell him I'm here,' I said. 'I don't want to cause trouble with your folks and if I go there . . .'

'We'll be late for the pictures,' Tony said, tugging at Cheryl's arm, trying to urge her away.

Cheryl stared into my eyes. I saw anger there, and wondered if it was because she'd seen me screwing Puffin. Or maybe she was fed up with me, like her folks were. She seemed about to tell me to get lost, but then asked Tony to wait while she ran back home.

I didn't speak to Tony, having nothing to say to him, while she was gone.

Cheryl returned a few minutes later, jogging down the road towards us.

I saw her breasts bouncing beneath her blouse; she was getting even bigger in that department. Perhaps Tony gave them a regular massage, hand rearing them, I thought jealously, then quickly dismissed that idea; the nerd wouldn't know what a tit was if it hit him in the eye. Mind you, Cheryl's would take your eye out if you got too close I thought, as she wobbled to a halt in front of me.

'Floyd says he can't get out. My father's making him go to church with him,' she gasped. 'He says he'll see you at work tomorrow.'

'Thanks, Cheryl,' I said. 'Enjoy yourselves.'

'We will,' she beamed back, then winked at me.

Tony was screwing her, the lucky bastard. I was still feeling a bit horny, after my aborted session with Hazel at the weekend, and would have liked nothing better than to take Cheryl somewhere, strip her naked and fuck her. I sighed. I knew that was just a dream.

But I could see if Puffin was still going out with that other boy.

16

She's Putting You On

I had just started to tighten a gearbox mounting of the truck I was working on, when someone dragged me by the ankles, pulling both me, and the car creeper I was lying on, from under the vehicle. I shaded my eyes against the glare of the overhead lights and squinted up. It was Frank Johnson.

'I want a word with you,' he snarled, his eyes wild with anger.

I struggled to my feet, causing him to back away slightly. 'Can't it wait? Ramsbottom wants this finished before we knock off for the weekend. I shall be in trouble if it isn't done.'

'You're in trouble now – or at least my lass is.'

It took me a few moments to figure out what Johnson had said. 'You mean she's . . ?'

'That's right. In the family way. And it's yours.'

'What do you mean – it's mine. How do you know that?'

'I worked it out. She's about four months gone. That puts it about the time you were – seeing her.'

I shook my head. How could I explain to Johnson that the sprog could be anybody's? I was sure Floyd and me had not been the only ones to screw Shagbag back then. But no father would like hearing that about their daughter; we would end up coming to blows again.

'Doesn't make it mine,' I said finally.

'Well I think it is. She says it must be yours. And you told me that you didn't use anything. You'll have to marry her.'

'But supposing . . .' I tried to think of a diplomatic way to put it. 'Supposing it's Floyd's.'

'No, I'm sure it won't be,' Johnson shook his head.

'A right prat I'd look though – if I married her – then a few months later out pops . . . It would be pretty obvious if it was Floyd's.'

'There's no way that it's his,' Johnson spat. 'I wouldn't stand for it.'

Might have to I thought. 'Why not wait until after she's had the baby? Then we'll know for sure.'

'I'm not having my daughter walking round town with a swollen belly – and no husband. What would folks say? You'll marry her and that's final.'

I bit my lip. Imagine having Johnson for a father-in-law! And Shagbag for a wife. A picture of me pushing a pram around, with her walking alongside, came to mind. I began to feel giddy and sat on the step of the truck. Everyone in town would be laughing at me, and most of the men that we met would have seen her with her legs spread.

'You'll have to start facing up to your responsibilities,' Johnson said.

'What's this about responsibilities?' Ramsbottom said, as he strode round the front of the truck.

'Kenny and my daughter are going to get married.'

'But I thought . . ?' Ramsbottom seemed to be as bewildered as I was.

'His daughter's in the club,' I murmured. My face felt cold with the shock of it all. 'Says it's mine.'

'It bloody well is. She's certain of it,' Johnson snapped.

'You could always have a blood test done,' Ramsbottom suggested helpfully.

Perhaps that was the answer. A blood test would soon prove I was not the father. But then again – what if it did?

'Are you all right Kenny,' Maureen said, as she too appeared and saw me sitting there, my head in my hands. 'I couldn't help but overhear – about the blood test. I hope it's not something serious.'

'Nothing that a vicar can't fix,' Ramsbottom grinned.

'You mean . . ?'

'Yes, he's going to be a father. Congratulations, Kenny.' Ramsbottom tried, but not too hard, to hide the smirk on his face, as he offered his hand to me.

I glanced up and saw a look of stunned disbelief on Maureen's face. That had ruined any chance I had with her, and that hadn't been much of one anyway. I knew that she had finished with King Mod, or maybe King Mod had ended it with her, I wasn't sure which, but, just lately, she seemed to be chatting to Floyd a lot. Maybe she was showing an interest in my friend. Yeah, perhaps we could make up a foursome, me and Shagbag, Floyd and Maureen. Wouldn't the blonde-haired girl impress my family and friends? The floor began to spin and I closed my eyes. This was like one of the comedies on the telly; all it wanted now was for my mother and father to walk in.

'How does he know it's you and not me that filled her up – or even if it's one of us at all?' Floyd said, when I told him the news as we walked home from work.

'I think it's a bit of wishful thinking on Johnson's part.'

'You mean he doesn't want a black lad for a son-in-law,' Floyd grinned. 'Wouldn't it be funny if it was mine.'

'Don't think he'd see it that way. Besides, the odds are that the father is any of a dozen or more blokes. About the only one it won't be is Eddie Duncan – Shagbag can't stand him.'

'What are you going to do? You can't marry her.'

'That's the last thing I'll do. Might ask if any of your relatives in Jamaica have a spare room,' I grinned. 'The trouble is I was getting on so well with Puffin. Now she'll be

171

mad at me again. She hates Shagbag. And some bastard told her I'd screwed Shagbag at the party, after she'd left.'

The day after I had come back from Blackpool, I had gone round to see Puffin. After much persuading, she had agreed to go out with me again. Her only condition had been that I never had anything more to do with Shagbag. Now I was supposed to marry the scrubber. In this town, it wouldn't take long for the story to get back to Puffin, and that would be the end.

'What does your old man say,' Floyd asked.

'Nothing. I haven't told him yet. He'll go ape-shit if he finds out. Thinks I'm being good – keeping out of trouble.' Since my return from the weekend away, I had done my best to keep my mother and father happy.

My old man had said I could keep the scooter, unless he heard of any more misbehaviour, and then that would be it. I'd even turned my Lambretta and gone home again, when I'd spotted Webster and Martin in the High Street one night, to avoid a confrontation.

Luckily, none of my mates had been about else they would have taken the piss out of me.

'Hi, Kenny, Floyd,' a lad walking the other way said as he passed us. It was Tony, Cheryl's boyfriend.

'Reckon he's giving your sister one?'

'What do you mean?' Floyd stopped in his tracks, as if the thought had never crossed his mind. 'He hadn't better be – she's not sixteen yet.'

'By the smile on her face – I think he is,' I grinned. 'Mind you, I don't know that a runt like that could do much good.'

'Hey, come here,' Floyd yelled, causing Tony to turn and look back. 'Yeah, you,' he said when the boy pointed to his chest, as if unsure who Floyd meant.

Tony retraced his steps, looking at us apprehensively.

'I hope you ain't – um – molesting my little sister,' Floyd growled, causing the other boy's cheeks to turn bright red, 'because if you are – you'll answer to me.'

'And me,' I said, forgetting for a moment that I'd often considered molesting Cheryl myself.

'I – I've not touched her. Honestly,' Tony stammered. 'Ask her if you like. I've only ever kissed her on the cheek – and your father was watching then.'

'It had better stay that way,' Floyd told him.

When we dismissed him, he beetled off. Perhaps I'd been right in the first place – the wimp wouldn't know what to do if Cheryl offered it to him on a plate.

We parted just before the Edmonds house.

'Don't be late or we'll miss the train,' I told Floyd as he turned to go.

'Going in your DM's?'

'No, I promised my old man that if he let me go to the match, I wouldn't get into any bovver.'

The town team had been drawn against Coventry in the Cup, and the Hole in the Wall Gang was going to watch them.

My father had thought that he might go himself, causing me to raise my eyes as I thought of how that would cramp my style. Then he said that he was feeling a bit under the weather, and I should go with my mates instead.

'Just behave yourself,' my old man had told me that morning, then placed a couple of quid in my hand. 'Get me a programme – and yourself a hot dog or something with the rest.'

He had forgiven me at last. Now all that I had to do was stay out of trouble this afternoon.

I managed to be good when we changed trains at New Street. As we stood waiting on one platform, a local train disgorged hundreds of Birmingham City supporters on the opposite one. The two opposing sets of fans fought a pitched battle, throwing bottles, bricks, litterbins, and anything else that wasn't screwed down, across the railway lines at each other. Some of the skinheads dashed up the stairs and met on the

173

walkway at the top, punching and kicking at one another, until the Transport Police came along with their dogs and separated them.

When it started, I dragged Floyd into the shelter of a timetable hoarding. 'I'm not getting pulled in – before we even get there,' I told him. 'I need to tell my old man about the match. I won't see much of it from the police station.'

The train to Coventry ran into the platform and the fighting petered out.

'Where were you two,' Duncan said, polishing a scuffmark from his Doc Martens by rubbing his toe against the leg of his jeans.

'I told you Eddie, I'm not getting involved in anything today,' I said.

'Trying to be respectable – now you're a father,' Duncan laughed.

I glared at Floyd.

'I didn't tell him,' Floyd laughed.

'Nutter met Shagbag – on the way to the station,' Duncan said. 'She was telling him of her wedding plans. Can I be the best man? Promise I'll only just kiss the bride – not screw her.' He ducked the punch I aimed at his nose, as the rest of the gang jeered at me, the father-to-be.

'I ain't fucking marrying her – and that's final,' I snarled.

The other skinheads could see I was getting tetchy over the subject and, wisely, decided to drop it.

I kept out of trouble when we arrived at Coventry, despite a mass of Sky Blues fans shouting abuse at us from across the road that led to the ground. The traffic was heavy, and this helped to keep the rival fans apart, much to my relief.

As we approached the ground, we found the road blocked by dozens of policemen. Some were on foot, their arms linked to form a barrier, others had large hungry-looking Alsatians tugging at their leads, eager to get at us. A dozen or so mounted officers were waiting behind the police line.

'What the fuck's going on here,' Duncan said as we came

174

to a halt; the road was soon blocked with milling Town supporters.

'Don't know. But we'll miss the kick off at this rate,' I said.

We found out a few moments later. As we jostled nearer to the line of police, we saw that fans were being allowed past, but only in small groups.

'We're not having any trouble with you lot,' one of the policemen, a Special Constable, scowled as me and my mates squeezed through.

Another bobby directed us past the mounted officers, towards where more Specials were waiting by the turnstiles.

'Boots and shoes off,' a police sergeant bellowed, then pointed towards a heap of discarded footwear stacked against the wall of the stand. 'You can pick 'em up when you come out.'

I was astonished. I had seen the police make skinheads who turned up at matches in steel toe-capped boots remove their laces before going into a ground, or then later force them to take the boots off altogether, when the bovver boys got wise to it and took some spare laces. Never before though had I seen fans wearing ordinary shoes been made to do this.

I was glad that I had left my DM's at home; some other bastard would have nicked my cherry-reds. 'I've only got shoes on,' I told the sergeant, 'and I'm not here for trouble.'

'Doesn't matter. Take 'em off. You lot fight like fairies, kicking at each other. Well, you won't do it here.'

I suspected that the policeman wouldn't need a lot of provocation to arrest me, so I kept quiet.

'Turn out your pockets,' the sergeant said, then made sure we had nothing in them that could be thrown at the other fans.

I had nothing to worry about, but heard a clatter as Nutter dropped his razor onto the floor.

'Lost this son?' one of the Specials beamed as he held up

the razor. He lunged forward and grabbed the Town fan standing behind me.

As he was led off, arm thrust up behind his back, the lad began to wail. 'It's not mine. Don't know who dropped it!'

I breathed with relief; my father would have given up on me if I'd been done for carrying an offensive weapon. The other boy was innocent I knew, but doubted that the police would bother finger-printing the razor to prove that.

I'd seen the police at work before. When I was about fourteen, my father had taken me to watch the Town play Chelsea in another Cup match. We had been in the open end of the ground, as that was the cheapest spot, standing alongside a load of London skinheads who'd come up for the match. There had been trouble before play started, and then during it. The police had formed a line to prevent the Chelsea skinheads from invading the pitch.

Just before half time, one of the Chelsea fans had thrown a bottle. It had been a perfect shot and struck one of the policemen on the back of the neck, just below his helmet, sending him tumbling to the ground.

His comrades had turned as one, then scanned the mob. The Chelsea lads had jeered, and waved knives, razors, and even an axe in the air.

'Come and get it,' they had taunted the policemen.

The bobbies had raced up the steps, but swung to their right and grabbed hold of me instead.

'You bloody scum. You'll pay for that,' one of them, a Special again, had yelled as he wrenched at my arm

'You there! Let that boy go,' a sudden bellow, audible even above the roar of the crowd, made the part-time policeman pause in his tracks. Dazed by events, I realised it was my father who'd shouted.

The Special turned, sensing another customer for the cells, then saw a tough military-looking man, with well-muscled arms, built like, and looking like, Popeye in the cartoon series, stepping towards him.

'Let my son go. He's done nothing,' my father bawled as he gripped the policeman's wrist. He squeezed hard, his fingers crushing into the bones of the Special's arm.

'Help me,' the part-time policeman wailed, tears springing to his eyes as he looked round for his comrades.

'Release him,' another voice ordered and I looked up, expecting to discover that my father was in trouble, but found that another bobby was telling my captor to let go of me.

'Sorry,' the Special murmured as he was freed, in turn, by my old man. 'Somebody said it was him that threw it.' He stamped off, rubbing his arm.

'Let the matter drop there, sir,' the other policeman said to my father. It was more of an order than a question.

My father had stood silently for a moment, composing himself again, then nodded his head.

Since then I had realised that one of the safest places to be was among the roughest and toughest of the fans, away from the Specials who were mostly bovver boys in uniform. Although hundreds of fans were arrested at the matches each week, the trouble between opposing sets of supporters continued. Either there were thousands of hooligans or, as I suspected, many innocent lads were being pulled in. The magistrates were cracking down on trouble at football matches and handing out long sentences, but probably to the wrong people. It would be bad enough to get sent down if you had been in the thick of it, but if you were innocent . . .

'What a bummer,' Floyd murmured, as if he'd read my thoughts, as we tip-toed over the coarse concrete, and went through the turnstile, stone chippings digging into the soles of our feet.

It turned out to be an even bigger bummer when we stepped out onto the terraces. Both teams had just come out onto the pitch and distracted me for a moment. Then I realised that we were surrounded by the other team's fans; we were in their end!

'Fucking hell, Kenny,' Floyd gasped, then pointed to the Coventry supporters' feet; they were wearing miners' boots, with metal toe-cops painted sky blue. So much for the police stopping any trouble erupting; they were making sure the local fans had the advantage.

The referee had barely blown the whistle, when a hail of empty beer bottles, and hundreds of old pennies, surplus to requirements when they were replaced by decimal coins, and now sharpened at the edges, rained down on us.

'The police are going to move – and let them at us in a minute,' a skinhead next to me said, with a tremor in his voice. 'Pass it on. Be ready.'

He had just uttered the words when, with a howl, the Coventry mob surged forwards.

A giant skinhead, with a tattoo of a skull and crossbones on his forehead, shoved through the crowd. He seemed to be heading for me.

'Shit!' I breathed as he lunged forwards; this was one mean bastard.

The skinhead swung a hob-nailed boot towards my stomach, with enough force to have ruptured my insides. My reactions took over. I bent my body away from the crushing blow, then grabbed the skinhead's ankle.

'What the fuck . . .' the youth said as he teetered on one leg.

I swung my foot back and sank it into his exposed groin. It was a shame I had no shoes on I thought, as my toes hit something soft; the kick would have been far more effective then. It did enough damage though. I was sure that he would have collapsed to the ground, clutching his balls, if I had let him. I didn't, just kicked him again in the same spot. The skinhead's fingers took some of the punishment this time, but he still squealed in agony as my toe found its target once more.

Another Coventry fan swung a fist at my temple, stunning me for a moment, but I kept my hold.

'I'll get the bastard,' Floyd yelled, as he stepped between the other fan and me, and began to punch at him.

I wrenched the lace of the Coventry skinhead's boot undone, then dragged it off his foot. I wrinkled my nose as the stench of his filthy sock rose up, but then saw that he was beginning to recover.

'Let me go,' the skinhead wailed, as I made him hop around the stand.

'All right,' I said, but instead of just releasing him, I flipped his leg higher in the air, forcing him to fall backwards onto the concrete terrace.

'You f . . .' the skinhead managed to gasp, then howled in pain as I stamped down onto his privates.

He wouldn't be screwing his girl for a while I thought, as I removed the other boot then laced them both onto my feet. They were a bit too big for me, and I had to pull the laces tight to keep them on. I almost fell over as the fighting fans surged around me, but managed to regain my balance.

The skinhead was writhing on the ground, screaming like a pig being led to slaughter. I booted him again on the forehead, silencing him. I didn't like doing that to someone lying helpless, but was certain that the skinhead would have done it to me if our roles had been reversed. Besides, there were still a hundred or more Coventry fans wading into us.

Floyd had knocked his opponent to the ground and was struggling with another skinhead, his arm locked around the other youth's neck as he thumped him in the face.

Before I could help, someone hit me on the chest with a fist. I looked up, just in time to see another punch aimed at my nose. I parried it with my left arm, then whacked my attacker under the chin with my right. The Coventry lad tumbled to the floor, alongside his mate.

Then, as quickly as it had started, it was over; the Home fans had retreated across the stand, licking their wounds.

Several of the Town fans were lying on the floor too, and some St John's Ambulance staff hurried forward.

Floyd was all right though, a little shaken by the experience but unhurt. Some of the Hole in the Wall Gang, like me, had managed to capture boots from their opponents and were tying them in place.

The Coventry fans attacked us again and again that afternoon, with the police doing little to stop them. The odds began to improve though, as more of us gained boots and shoes. And broken bottles, gathered off the terraces, were used as vicious weapons against the fans who'd thrown them.

Finally, to my relief, the match was over. I'd seen little of the game and wondered what I could tell my father. Perhaps I could buy a paper on the way back and read about the game.

And I was supposed to get a programme as well. I looked around the terraces.

Floyd spotted one lying next to a rail, among some discarded hot-dog wrappers.

'It'll do,' I told him, as I picked it up then straightened it out. It was a bit tatty, but was the best I could do in the circumstances.

Floyd had not been able to get a pair of boots to fit him during the fight, and neither of us could see our footwear in the pile outside the stand when we left. I handed the giant skinhead's boots to him. 'They were miles too big for me anyway,' I chuckled, as I pulled on someone else's frayed brown brogues.

'They're all right. Bit conspicuous though,' Floyd said, as he rubbed at the blue-painted toe caps.

The Town fans set off for the station. I just wanted to get home without further bother.

'Here we go again,' Duncan said. As we turned the corner of the stand, we found another line of policemen blocking the road.

This time they didn't make us remove our shoes; they just split us into small groups before letting us past.

I turned to Floyd. 'What's the idea?'

He shook his head, as mystified as I was. Then, being taller, he saw the answer. 'The Coventry mob are waiting at the end of the road,' he said, as he peered over the other lads' heads. 'The police are letting them have us – a few at a time.'

'Bastards,' I murmured as I saw several curled up bodies, lying on the ground in front of the Coventry fans; some were still being given the boot, even though they were offering no resistance. They must be the first Town fans to be allowed through.

'We're gonna get done here,' Duncan said, his voice increased a little in pitch, as he saw our predicament.

'The pigs won't help,' Floyd said, shaking his head in disbelief at the policemen's action. 'Probably just arrest us – when we come out of hospital.'

Ahead, the Coventry fans jeered as they saw fresh victims approaching.

They were tooled up as well I saw, despite being in full view of the police. Several blades glowed red in the late afternoon sunshine. I hoped it was light reflected on the knives, and not blood. I'd soon find out. The Town fans milled about, uncertain what to do. We couldn't go back, the bobbies were not letting anyone go that way. Any Town fans that tried were being stuffed into black Transit vans. We'd be driven off to the cells and charged with assault or something. To go forwards meant forcing our way through the mob of Sky Blues supporters, and ending up in hospital.

'What'll we do, Eddie?' Cadger said, biting his fingernail.

Duncan seemed dazed by events. 'We'll . . .'

'Let's go down fighting,' I growled. When Duncan still did nothing, I punched Nutter on the arm. 'Let's get the bastards,' I yelled, then began to run forward.

As I raced towards the knife-wielding mob, I realised I'd made a mistake. I was on my own. None of the other lads had come with me. If I stopped now, I would be the laughing

181

stock of my mates. If I didn't, I may soon be badly injured. Or dead!

Then I heard heavy boots striking the tarmac; Floyd was following. I should have known he'd not let me down. We closed on the Coventry fans.

Suddenly, a salvo of empty pint pots, hurled by them, rained down around me, shattering into glistening shards as they struck the tarmac. They all missed me, much to my relief. I guessed that one of the heavy glasses could be painful if it hit you full in the face.

Then, from behind me, came a terrifying roar. The hairs on the back of my neck stood up, as I wondered, briefly, if the Coventry fans had got behind us as well. There was a clatter of racing feet, and I saw uncertainty cross the face of the nearest Sky Blues supporter. The other Town lads must be coming. They would be too late to help me though.

Some of the Coventry fans, at the back of the mob, began to turn and run. Just like in other gangs, they were the chicken-hearted bastards who would stand clear of any fighting, but would be the first to rush in and put the boot into someone helpless on the ground. At least those shitheads will be out of the picture I decided, as I selected my first target. I would get at least one of them, before they had me on the floor.

The other Coventry fans were looking nervously over their shoulders. Their mates' fear was infectious; I could see panic in their eyes.

Then they ran. One moment I had been lunging towards the tightly packed mob, my heart racing with terror, the next they had broken.

'Come on,' Duncan shrieked, overtaking me despite his bulk, as he raced after the Coventry supporters.

It was marvellous how he had appeared, now that they were on the run.

The Hole in the Wall Gang couldn't catch the other fans; the Coventry skinheads ran across a busy road, almost getting knocked over by passing cars, then into some of the nearby shops and department stores, in their panic.

I found that the other Town fans, seeing what lay in store for them beyond the police line, had broken through to join us; that was why the mob had fled. I never wanted to be in that situation again though, I decided.

'Bloody hell, Kenny. Next time you're gonna do something like that – let me know,' Floyd gasped, as he drew up alongside me.

'Didn't know I was going to do it myself,' I shook my head. 'Thought I'd take one of them with me though. Getting too old for this,' I grinned, as I fought to regain my breath and tried to slow my thudding heart. There were better things to be doing on a Saturday than getting your head kicked in at a football match.

This was the last time I'd be going to one.

17

Hey Girl Don't Bother Me

'Can I have your scooter – when you get rid of it,' Cadger asked. 'I know it's old – but it'll do for me. The engine's blown again on mine.'

'What do you mean? My old man is letting me keep it,' I told him. 'Besides – if it ever has to go – I want to make at least a hundred quid for it.'

'You said he was getting shut of it,' Cadger scowled at Eddie Duncan, who was sitting on the wall next to me, munching on a hot dog.

'Thought you'd have to,' Duncan said, raising the bread roll in the air, and tipping the fried onions off the top of it into his mouth. 'What with the baby an' all . . .' He paused to suck mustard off his fingers.

'Bollocks Eddie. I've told you it's not mine,' I said.

Since that dreadful day, when Johnson had broken the news to me, I'd found it hard to sleep. Pictures of me walking arm in arm with Shagbag, behind a pram, crept into my thoughts. I imagined people nudging each other, laughing at me.

I tried to avoid Shagbag, but one day she came to my house, hammering on the door when I didn't answer it. My parents were out shopping, and I prayed they wouldn't come back until she was gone.

'Open up, Kenny,' Shagbag had wailed through the letterbox. 'Your scooter's here – so I know you are too.'

Then, to my horror, I heard my father's car turning into the drive. What had I done to deserve this? I raised my eyes heavenwards, hoping for salvation from that quarter.

I wasn't going to get it I realised, as I saw Shagbag approach my mother as she stepped from the car.

'Hello. It's – Sheila – isn't it?' I heard my mother say. 'I remember you from the – um – party.'

'That's right, Mrs Roberts. I'm here to see Kenny. I don't know if he's in though. There's no answer when I knock.'

'Should be here somewhere,' my father growled.

'Come in, love,' my mother said, and I heard her key turn in the door. 'You look as if you're . . .'

'That's right, Mrs Roberts. And it's your son's. But he won't marry me.' Shagbag began to sob as I scrambled out of my bedroom window.

'What are you up to?' my father said, as he spotted me when he came out of the garage.

'Sorry, pop. I'm trying to avoid Sha – Sheila Johnson. She's telling everyone I've got her pregnant. It's not true. Says we're gonna get married – and that we'll live here with you for a bit,' I said, hoping these last words would get him on my side.

'Well, if it's yours . . .'

'I'm sure it's not. I've told her that I'll take a blood test – to prove it – but she won't listen. Just keeps on that it's mine.'

My old man had stood quietly for a moment. 'I'm a bit old for wet nappies hanging round the place,' he said finally. 'If you're certain it's not yours, then we should fight it. But I don't want you ducking out if it is. You owe that to the girl. It's hard enough bringing up a child. Even more so without a father on the scene.'

'If she'll agree to a test I'm certain it'll prove I'm innocent,' I said, with more conviction than I felt. It would

185

be just my luck, that out of all the sperm that had been shot into Shagbag, it was mine that had done the business.

Shagbag had refused the test. 'It's Kenny's,' she had screamed at my father when he had suggested that having it done would solve all the arguments.

Since then, she seemed to have told everyone in town. Puffin had found out, and had slammed the door in my face when I had called to see her one night. The end of another beautiful relationship.

Her friend Anne told Floyd, who then told me, that Puffin was heartbroken. People knew that she was my girl, and were mocking her about the baby I was supposed to have fathered. Until then, Puffin had hoped we would get engaged, Anne said, but then along came this humiliation.

I hadn't thought of marrying Puffin either; she was fun to be with, and a good shag, but I couldn't imagine spending the rest of my life with her. I've had it with girls I thought. Cheryl was still mad at me for threatening Tony. Mind you, she had been more angry with Floyd, was barely speaking to him now. I saw Cadger climb onto my Lambretta. 'Get off it,' I yelled at him as he reached for the ignition key.

'Like your side-panels,' Cadger said, staying in the seat but dropping his hand from the handlebars, to rub his fingertips on the chromed metal.

The panels had cost me almost thirty quid to get done. With the other accessories, and then having the horn casting and front mudguard chromed as well, I must have spent double what the scooter was worth on fitting it up. The trouble with such a shiny finish though, was that you had to keep cleaning it. 'Keep your hands off them,' I snarled at Cadger, 'else I'll give you a rag to polish them.'

'Only looking,' he muttered then suggested we go for a pint.

Wants us to buy him one I thought.

Duncan whistled as a girl sauntered past me.

She was wearing dark coloured, maybe black – it was hard

to tell in the streetlight – hot pants stretched tightly around her buttocks, and a matching sleeveless top over her white blouse. She must be freezing I thought; although it was still early November we'd already had a few good frosts. She had long hair, that looked like it could be brown, and it hung straight down her back to her waist, drawing my eyes to the rounded cheeks of her bottom.

'Hiya darlin'.' Duncan stepped into her path. 'Where've you bin all my life?'

'Keeping out of your way,' the girl said, as she stepped to one side.

'Don't be like that,' Duncan grinned, as he moved in front of her again. 'Give us a kiss.'

The girl turned her head and looked at us, her eyes wide with apprehension. 'Please let me get past,' she murmured. 'My boyfriend will be here soon and . . .'

'Oh, don't worry about him,' Duncan laughed. 'I won't want to kiss him as well.' He grabbed her by the waist and pulled her to him, one hand grasping at her bottom.

'Don't!' the girl sobbed, twisting her head to one side as Duncan tried to clamp his lips onto hers.

'Let her go Eddie,' I said, never one to resist helping a girl in distress, especially a pretty one. I stood up.

Duncan turned to look at me but kept his grip on the girl. 'Only having a bit of fun,' he scowled, then dropped his arm from around her. 'I'm the leader of this fucking gang,' he spat onto the pavement. 'Keep pushing me and I'll have you,' he told me, then stamped off towards his scooter.

'Thank you,' the girl said. She shivered. I wasn't sure if it was from cold or fear.

'I'm Kenny,' I told her. 'Where are you going? Do you want a lift home?' I nodded towards my Lambretta.

'My name's Lorraine,' the girl smiled. 'I'm supposed to be meeting a friend – at Annabellas. A girlfriend,' she added quickly, when I looked disappointed.

I arranged to meet her in the club later. All my previous

187

thoughts of avoiding the opposite sex for a while were forgotten as I watched her stride away.

'Bastard. Just wanted to pull her for yourself,' Duncan scowled. 'Ain't screwing one girl enough. You won't be friggin' doing that when you're married to Sheila.'

'Fuck off, Eddie,' I said, then waved to Floyd as my friend drew up on his Vespa, with Anne riding pillion.

'We're going to the pictures,' Anne smiled.

'Kelly's Heroes is on again,' Floyd said.

We had threatened to go and see the movie the last time it was on but, somehow, other things had intervened. 'Enjoy yourself,' I smiled at them, a little envious of Floyd. My mate had really hit it off with Anne, and I wondered if they would stay an item. Mind you, that left me free to go after Maureen. I might still win that bet yet. Then I dismissed that idea, as Shagbag's bulging belly came into my thoughts again.

'*Zulu*'s on at the Odeon, Floyd,' Duncan laughed. 'You could see if you can spot any of your relations in it. Or there's *The Nympho* on at the Gaumont.' He leered at Anne. 'You lot can get away with anything in the dark. Folks'll think she's playing with herself. She'll be begging for it by the time the film's over.'

'Leave it,' Anne hissed into Floyd's ear, as he began to pull the scooter back onto its stand.

'Go and see the film, Floyd.' I put my hand on his arm, forcing him back onto his seat. 'He can't help being an ignorant bastard.'

'Fuck off, Roberts,' Duncan scowled as he moved to stand with the other skinheads.

'Get out of here,' I told Floyd again.

'What about you,' Floyd said, staring at Duncan.

'He won't start anything,' I murmured. 'He's just a chicken at heart.'

I hoped that what I said was right. As Floyd's Vespa roared off down the street, I turned to find Duncan muttering to some of the other skinheads. Was he going to have a go at me? I doubted Duncan would take me on, on his own. But would the others help? I wasn't afraid of any of them, one against one, but I didn't fancy getting a kicking off the lot of them.

Rocky would stay out of it, and wouldn't take anybody's side, of that I was certain. What about Nutter? I noticed that he had walked off with Cadger, and they were looking in a shop window, as if to distance themselves from what was about to happen.

That just left some of the younger lads, all out to prove they were hard cases.

This is it, I told myself as Duncan swaggered towards me, the other boys a pace behind.

'If you're in my gang, Roberts – you do what I say,' Duncan sneered, pressing his face up against mine.

I fought back the urge to bop Duncan on the nose. I'd have the bastard before the others could help, but they would lay into me afterwards. And Duncan was the sort to get his own back, when he recovered.

'Got that?' Duncan said.

I nodded. Better to avoid a confrontation now I decided. I was becoming a bit fed up with all the fighting and trouble that we kept getting into. Maybe I should settle down a bit, find a girl to go steady with, like Floyd was doing. But not Shagbag! I shivered at the thought.

I saw a look of triumph on Duncan's face. He thinks he has me scared I realised, but decided not to tell him otherwise

'We're going queer bashing,' Duncan said, putting his arm over my shoulder; all of his previous antagonism towards me now seemed to be forgotten. 'The bastards are shaftin' each other in the toilets behind the market square. Seen it in the papers.'

I wasn't really interested in what he was saying; Lorraine was waiting in Annabellas for me, and I had nothing against the shirt-lifters. Didn't like the idea of what they got up to, but so long as they left me alone . . .

'Coming?' Duncan scowled. 'We'll hide the scoots – then walk up there.'

I knew I'd better go with them, else Duncan would soon be spreading it around that I was one of "them." I nodded, but decided I'd hang back and let the others get on with it.

As we approached the market square, Duncan cautioned us to be silent.

PC Dennis was standing in a shop doorway, watching us. He stared at me as I walked past, but said nothing.

'We'll go and have a piss,' Duncan said, loud enough for the policeman to hear, 'then see if we can catch a bus to the city.' When we had gone a few more steps, he sneaked a quick look back to see if Dennis was following us. 'Think we fooled him,' he whispered.

Dennis stepped from the doorway, and watched where we were going, but, otherwise, seemed not to be interested.

We turned into the alleyway that led to the toilets; it was the one I had raced into when Webster was chasing me, on the first day I'd ridden my scooter. It would be nice if the greaser was here tonight. That was one bit of aggro I wouldn't mind getting involved in.

'I'll go in on my own,' Duncan said, pointing to the stairs that led down to the urinals. 'I'll see if there's any of the puftas in there – then – when I shout – you lot come running in.' He tiptoed across the cobbles and went into the doorway.

A few seconds later, a startled cry came from the bowels of the gents' toilets, followed by a squeal of pain, then Duncan began to yell for us to join him.

The other skinheads dashed down the tiled stairway, and soon I could hear the muffled thuds of their bovver boots as they set about their victim.

'Help me,' I heard a man wail as I went down the steps. Please. Some . . .'

The pufta's cry was cut short; I guessed that someone's toe cap had found his mouth. I turned the corner at the bottom of the steps, to see someone lying face down in the piss trough, the other lads sinking their boots into his ribs.

'Leave him now,' I hissed, as I saw blood streaming into the stinking yellow liquid that lay in puddles in the urinal.

'Queer bastard tried to touch me up,' Duncan grinned, then sank his boot into the man's groin. 'Won't be sticking his dangler anywhere for a while,' he laughed, as the man curled up clutching his balls.

It was Ramsbottom, my boss at the garage, I saw with horror. 'Let him be,' I yelled at Duncan. I tugged at his arm. 'He's not an arse bandit – he's married – got kids.'

'Why did he grope me then?' Duncan scowled.

I couldn't answer that. Duncan had been spoiling for a fight since the run in with me; maybe Ramsbottom was just in the wrong place at the wrong time. 'Get out of here. That copper's coming,' I lied.

The other skinheads looked up in alarm, then raced up the steps again.

'Bent bastard,' Duncan said, then gave Ramsbottom a final kick, before running after the gang.

I saw Ramsbottom squint at me, through one half-closed swollen eyelid, then he sagged against the wet tiles, his battered nose in the trough again.

I couldn't leave him like that, so, despite the fear of being caught by Dennis, I dragged Ramsbottom out of the urinal. I left him propped against one of the toilet doors, then returned to the square. There was no sign of the other lads, but I saw the dark outline of the policeman coming into the alleyway. I quickly made my escape, out the way I had gone when Webster was after me.

I went to Annabellas to see if Lorraine was still there. And still interested. She was. My night was spoiled though, by the thought that, at any minute, Dennis would come into the nightclub and drag me away.

I had a half-hearted dance or two with Lorraine, bought her a few drinks, but my eyes kept straying to the doorway. Soon, the last record had been played and the lights came on. To my relief the copper hadn't appeared.

'Do you fancy taking me home?' Lorraine said, as she gathered up her handbag.

I nodded, but wondered what would happen tomorrow. Ramsbottom would pick me out, even if he didn't know who the other lads were. Maybe the police would be waiting at my house.

'Don't bother – if it's too much trouble,' Lorraine said crossly.

'Sorry,' I said. 'Got a lot on my mind.'

'I noticed.'

'Yeah, I'll see you home.' I forced a smile. At any other time I would have loved to have taken the girl home, or into a darkened alleyway, But tonight . . .

And then again, this could be the last time I got my end away.

Before I went into prison.

18

No Sad Songs

'Heard about Ramsbottom?' Floyd said as he walked into
the garage with me. 'Got beaten up last night. Serves him
right.'

'Duncan did it,' I whispered. 'After you left, he said we'd go
queer bashing. Ramsbottom was in the toilets and Duncan
attacked him. The trouble is – Ramsbottom saw me.'

'He recognise you? Shit!' Floyd said, when I nodded.

'I didn't take part in any of it,' I explained, 'but I'm
probably the only one there that he knew. I expected the
police to be waiting when I got home. I called round at your
place – after I had dropped Lorraine off. That's another
story,' I said, when Floyd looked curiously at me. 'Your
scooter was there, but you must have all gone to bed.' I
hadn't fancied disturbing Mr Edmonds, who had been a bit
offhand with me since the party. 'What will my mother and
father say now? I promised I'd stay out of bother. Anyway,
why haven't the police picked me up?'

'Don't know, but at least this time we know he's not dead,
so you don't have to worry like the time Nutter did the
copper. Maybe Ramsbottom's too badly hurt to talk?'

' 'Kin hell, Floyd. Don't say that,' I sighed. 'I'll be sent
down for months.'

'Are you doing any work today,' Frank Johnson shouted to

us. 'I'm doing the Service Manager's job,' he grinned, when we stared at him.

The creeping bastard was wearing one of Ramsbottom's white coats, I saw.

'Now, let's have you doing something. But I want a word with you first, Roberts,' Johnson said, then beckoned me towards him.

Johnson waited until Floyd had gone in to the locker room. 'About my lass . . .'

'I told you – I'm not marrying her.'

'Well, you can do – if you still want to,' Johnson said quietly, 'but she's lost the baby. A miscarriage. Probably for the best. I haven't forgiven you though. It was all your doing in the first place. Anyway, thought I should let you know.'

Johnson didn't seem very upset about the loss of his grandchild. Not too angry with me either. Maybe he'd realised that it wasn't mine after all. Then I wondered if there was something he wasn't telling me. Whatever, it was one less problem I had to deal with.

'Get a fucking move on,' Johnson snapped, as he spotted Floyd ambling towards the steam cleaner. 'Just because Ramsbottom's not here doesn't mean you're gonna have it easy.'

I saw Floyd stick two fingers up, behind the acting Service Manager's back. 'Have you heard how he is?'

'Who? Oh, Ramsbottom. His wife is at his bedside, or so Mr Beresford said when he rang me this morning, to ask me to come in early. He told me that he'd been found unconscious in the town centre toilets. Someone had rung for an ambulance – the police don't know who – but they are waiting to question him when he's well enough. He was in a bit of a state. The police think he was beaten up by a gang of lads.' Johnson stared at my face, as if he could see the guilt written there.

I hoped the magistrates would take into account the fact that I'd rung 999. When I'd got clear of the market square,

I'd searched for a working phone-box and, after a few moments hesitation, while I debated whether to flee or stay, called the ambulance. I hadn't given my name, but felt sure the call would have been taped. It may help when it came to the crunch.

'I want you to work on that Mini,' Johnson said, pointing towards a cream Austin that stood outside the workshop door. 'It needs a new sub-frame at the back.'

I changed into my overalls, collected a seat cover, and then went to fetch the Mini inside.

Maureen had just arrived for work, and was walking across the car park. She turned in my direction when she spotted me. At least I wouldn't have to worry about Ramsbottom catching me talking to her

'Isn't it awful, about Mr Ramsbottom.' Maureen said, her eyes wide with concern. She placed her hand over mine, where it rested on the car's door.

Despite the cold November morning, her fingers felt hot against the back of my hand. A shiver ran up my spine.

'Who could do such a thing?' she murmured.

I stared at her. Did she know, and was taking the piss out of me? I decided that she didn't, and what's more by asking me that, she mustn't think me capable of being that rotten. 'I don't know,' I mumbled eventually, then noticed her hand still touching mine.

Maureen saw my look and quickly let go of me, then began to search in her handbag for something.

Her face had coloured; she was as excited by the contact as I had been. Well, any feelings she had for me would soon change, once the coppers dragged me off. 'I don't like Ramsbottom much,' I told her, 'but I wouldn't want anything like this to happen to him.'

'I know you wouldn't,' Maureen said. 'And I hear you've had some news too. Word gets around fast in here. I'm sorry about your baby.'

'It's a shame for the poor thing,' I said, quietly. 'But it

195

wasn't mine – despite what Johnson was saying. At least I don't have to marry Sheila now.'

'So you're young, free, and single again,' Maureen said as she turned, then strode into the garage.

It took several minutes before her words sank into my brain. Was she hinting that I should ask her out? The more I replayed the words in my mind, the more I became convinced that she was. Mind you, that was now.

I doubted she'd have anything to do with me, when Ramsbottom pointed me out.

19

Somebody Somewhere - Needs You

A week went by, then two, and still nothing had happened. I stayed in at night, just as I had done after Nutter downed PC Dennis, flinching every time the telephone rang, or looking up in alarm when someone knocked at the door.

My mother had asked me if I felt all right. 'You look so pale these days. It will do you good to stay in for a bit. All these late nights will tell on you when you're older.'

But it was now that I was anxious about, not some distant time in the future.

Everyone was talking about Christmas, what they were going to do, the presents they were going to buy, or hoped to receive, and the parties they were planning. It all seemed unreal to me; here I was facing imminent arrest while everybody else was getting ready to enjoy themselves.

Why hadn't the police come for me? My worries about Ramsbottom being so badly injured that he couldn't talk had been proved unfounded. Both Mr Beresford and Frank Johnson had been to see the Service Manager, and reported that he was doing well. In fact, the hospital had released him after a few days. Ramsbottom had not been ready to resume work they said, but hoped to do so after a week or two's convalescence.

I wondered if he was suffering from memory loss, I'd

heard that this sometimes happened after a head injury, but Johnson told me that the Ramsbottom could remember everything. Then why no arrests? I had kept away from Duncan, and the Hole in the Wall Gang, since the attack, but knew they'd not been rounded up either.

Maybe Ramsbottom was going to sort them himself. He was a big bloke and had once been in the army. Perhaps he was going to get us one at a time. That could be it.

Anything would be better than this I thought, as I parked my scooter at the rear of the garage and walked into the workshop once more. I glanced nervously around, expecting to see blue uniforms waiting for me. I was early again and the building was silent, except for the background wheeze of the diesel heating.

I hadn't been able to sleep and, as I'd done every workday since the assault on Ramsbottom, had come to work expecting, almost hoping, that this was the day that things would be sorted. I had even contemplated turning my Lambretta towards the police station, on my way into work this morning, just so that I could get it over and done with. I had lost my nerve though and ended up at the garage.

I was so early this morning that the only other person in the building was Floyd. He took it in turns, with the other garage labourer, to unlock the doors, fire up the ancient heating system, then mop out the toilets. The door that led to the cubicles was propped open with a fire extinguisher, and I could hear him whistling from somewhere inside, but I avoided him; I didn't feel much like talking this morning. I picked up my spanners and set to work. I wasn't paid until eight, and it was only just turned seven thirty, but it took my mind off things.

It only seemed to be minutes later, when Johnson tapped me on the shoulder. 'After my job,' the acting Service Manager grinned, as the hooter signalled the start of the working day.

'Couldn't sleep,' I mumbled.

'Guilty conscience?' Johnson laughed, then when he saw the look of anxiety on my face, he frowned. 'Not put another girl up the stick, I hope.'

'Nothing like that. Just money trouble,' I lied.

'I can give you some overtime tonight. There are a lot of jobs to catch up on. We'll never shift this lot today otherwise,' Johnson said, pointing to the cars that were squeezed in the workshop.

That was true. With Johnson acting as Manager, we were a fitter short, especially as he didn't think he should get his white coat dirty. I might as well do a few hours tonight; I wasn't planning to go anywhere, and the extra money might pay for my court costs. 'OK, I'll stop over,' I said.

Johnson smiled and strode off. I'd just earned a few brownie points. I was fed up of being at odds with him; it made it even more difficult to turn in every morning. Then again, what good would brownie points do when the police had me?

'Kenny!' Floyd hissed, then beckoned me towards the washroom door. 'Duncan and Nutter have been arrested,' Floyd whispered as I stepped inside. 'Rocky waved me down this morning – and told me. Doesn't know much more – but thought I should warn you.'

I felt my head begin to swim. Thankfully, Floyd grabbed my arm else I would have tumbled to the floor. 'Christ, Floyd. What am I going to do?'

'I don't know. Maybe you should go in – tell them the truth.'

'They wouldn't believe me – and even if they did – what would Duncan and the others do if I grassed them up?'

'Better than going inside,' Floyd said, shaking his head.

'I can't stand much more of this. I'll tell you something Floyd. If I ever get out of this OK, I'm finished with Duncan and the gang. Why go through all this shit – when it's not your fault?' I saw Frank Johnson peer in the washroom window. 'Watch out! Johnson's just seen us.'

'Let him come,' Floyd said. 'I want a word with him anyway.'

I saw a look of determination on my friend's face. 'What's up?' I said, but Floyd didn't have time to answer.

Johnson pushed through the door. 'Get some fucking work done, Edmonds,' he yelled.

'Not until I tell you this,' Floyd said, poking Johnson in the chest with his finger, startling both the acting Service Manager, and me, by his reaction. 'My brother Clinton works at the hospital. Last night he told me about your Sheila. The baby was black!'

That was why Johnson hadn't pressed the matter, I suddenly realised; he must have known that the baby was Floyd's.

'Yeah well. I was too upset to tell you,' Johnson stammered. 'And perhaps it was for the best – what with you courting that other lass an' all. How would she like it if you'd got a kid with another girl.'

I thought that Floyd was going to hit him; I saw my friend's fists clench and I stepped forward. Johnson must have thought the same and spun on his heels.

'Bastard,' Floyd said, loud enough for Johnson to hear as he scuttled away.

'I'm sorry Floyd. I didn't know,' I said, resting my hand on his shoulder.

'I wouldn't have liked the idea of having Shagbag for a wife,' Floyd said, to which I nodded fervently. 'But I was a father. It was a boy. My son.' Tears sprang to his eyes.

'Like Johnson says – perhaps it was for the best,' I said quietly. 'What chance would he have had with a mother like that. No, maybe if you and Anne settle down, you can see about having children of your own.'

'It's strange,' Floyd shook his head, 'but the last thing I ever thought I'd want was a kid of my own. But he was mine!'

'I know. I even wondered what he – or she – would have

been like when I thought it was my baby. What did they do with him? Perhaps we could visit his grave?'

'He was cremated,' Floyd said. 'No name – no trace he ever existed. Just how Johnson would like it.'

'It weren't his fault she lost it though. Just how some things work out.'

'Oh, but it might have been,' Floyd said. 'Clinton told me that Shagbag was covered in bruises. He thinks she'd been punched in the stomach – and that's why she'd lost him. She told the doctors she'd fallen down some stairs. They knew she was lying but couldn't prove it.'

'He has hit her before,' I said, remembering back to the time when I'd dropped Shagbag in it with her father, 'but surely he wouldn't touch her – when she was in that condition? Not even he could be that vicious.'

Floyd shook his head, probably thinking like me, that someone who beat his daughter as Johnson did, wouldn't bother about her being pregnant.

'Anyway,' Floyd took a deep breath. 'What do we do about the fix you're in?'

'You just keep out of it, mate. You weren't involved so don't let's get you jammed up as well. I think that tonight, after I finish here, I am going to the police station. Get it done with. It should count for something if I turn myself in.'

'Doubt it,' Floyd said. 'The others will just deny it and drop you right in it.'

I never got the chance to find out. As I rode my scooter down the High Street, a uniformed figure stepped into the road, waving a torch to flag me down. It was Dennis, I saw with dismay. Should I run the bastard over, then flee? That would really help I decided. Add that to the other charges, and I would be lucky to see daylight again for a long time.

I could ride past; pretend I'd not seen him. It wouldn't take long for Dennis to call for help though; if I did that, it would seal my guilt.

I squeezed the front brake lever and rolled to a halt.

'Been waiting for you,' the policeman said, causing me to tremble with anticipation. 'These mirrors,' he tugged at the metal brackets I'd made in my father's shed, then bolted to the front carrier of my scooter; there were at least three mirrors fastened to each of them. 'I think they're dangerous accessories,' he continued. 'Someone could get hurt by them. And I'm thinking of your safety too. They'd cut you to ribbons if you crashed.'

'I thought you . . . I don't understand,' I stammered. What was Dennis doing? Perhaps he'd already called for back up, expecting me to put up a fight, and was stalling for time until reinforcements arrived. 'I shan't cause any trouble,' I said as I stopped the Lambretta's engine.

'You're in enough trouble anyway,' Dennis grinned. 'At least a ten quid fine – maybe even twenty. Bring it to the station tomorrow.' He wrote something on a slip of paper. 'I'm going to have your scooter photographed – and get one of our traffic boys to have a look at it. See if I can't get you for something else. Why don't you ride off again? Go on, just for me. I'd love to get you in a cell on your own – you cocky young bastard – then we'd see how tough you are.'

Dennis couldn't know about Ramsbottom; that would be just the opportunity he wanted. But what about Duncan? Him and Nutter must have kept quiet – so far.

'Got some of your mates banged up,' Dennis chuckled, seeming to have read my thoughts. 'They're two dozy cretins. Break into the bowling club – smash the bar door open – then stack up all the booze and ciggies. What do our heroes do then? Have a drink that's what. The caretaker found them pissed out of their minds – asleep in the middle of the green. What a stupid pair. Couldn't even wait until they got the stuff home. It wasn't me that arrested them, so I didn't find out that one of them was my old mate Nutter, or whatever he calls himself, until this morning. Boy, am I gonna have fun with him.' Dennis smashed his fist into the palm of his left hand, as if Nutter's nose was there. 'He won't catch me unawares this time. Prison will be a doddle by the time I've done with him. And I'll get you one day,' Dennis said. 'Are you listening to me. You're next!'

I couldn't take it all in. One minute I was expecting to join Duncan, now I found they hadn't pulled him for the assault. I shook my head.

'Well, you'd better take heed. 'Cause I'm gonna have you. Ten o'clock Wednesday morning,' Dennis smiled, then stuffed the paper slip into the top pocket of my coat.

As he strode away chuckling to himself, I debated whether I should still hand myself in. Nutter would really get it now, I guessed. I'd get no mercy from the coppers either and, if they were doing Duncan and Nutter for the break in, not the attack on Ramsbottom, I would face the music on my own – unless I grassed on the others. No, I would leave it for the time being. Now I had the added problem of the mirrors.

What could I do about them?

20

Landslide

'Mr Ramsbottom wants to see you,' Frank Johnson said, as I came back from lunch the next day.

'What? At his house?' I was dumbfounded.

'No. He's here. Upstairs. In Mr Beresford's office.'

I wanted to ask Johnson if the police were there too, but didn't dare. I'd find that out in a minute anyway.

My knees trembling, I ascended the metal stairway. At any other time, I'd have welcomed the chance to come up here, to have a quick chat with Maureen, but today I was dreading it. I hadn't seen PC Dennis or any of his colleagues arrive, but then I hadn't noticed Ramsbottom come in either. Perhaps they'd turned up while I was at the chippy with Floyd.

I went into the outer office.

Maureen had returned from lunch too. She smiled as I entered. 'Hello Kenny. He won't be long. Just making a few telephone calls. Sit there if you like,' she said, pointing to an easy chair that faced her desk.

'Is there anyone in with him?' I said as I sank down into the upholstery; I hadn't changed back into my overalls, and so wasn't covered by the usual layer of grease and oil. My hair stank of the stuff though.

'Oh no, my father's still out. He's taken some friends to

lunch and won't be back for a while. Mr Ramsbottom has called in to see him – wants to tell my father that he'll be back at work next week. He said he'd like a word with you while he was waiting. Not in any trouble are you?'

'Don't think so.' I forced a grin. 'Never know though with me and him,' I said, nodding towards the office where Ramsbottom waited.

'What do you have planned for Christmas? Any parties or anything?'

Was she pulling my leg about the fiasco at my home I wondered? I decided she wasn't. 'I don't know,' I told her. 'I've not given it much thought.'

That bit was true; what was the point of planning anything when I could be joining Duncan inside? 'And you?' I said, then peered into her eyes. As she smiled again, I dropped my gaze; I felt as if she could see what I was thinking.

'Oh, I suppose I shall spend it at home, with the family. Daddy invites everybody over. Pretty boring really.'

I found that I was staring at her legs beneath the desk. She must be wearing one of her short skirts, although I couldn't see it from where I sat. I ran my eyes up her slender calves, following the sheen of nylon encased flesh until I could see her thighs.

Maureen, unlike most of the other girls I knew who wore minis, somehow managed to keep her knees together when she sat.

Often, Floyd and me had timed it so that we saw her getting into or out of her car. Though her slim legs would be exposed to us, that was all we got; never once did we catch sight of her knickers.

Unless she didn't wear any I thought optimistically, then prayed that Ramsbottom wouldn't ask me to come in at that particular moment.

Maureen swivelled her chair, giving me a view of the other side of her thighs, but again nothing else. 'Penny for them,' she said, looking curiously at me.

205

'Sorry, miles away.' I felt my face turn crimson. That I would love to be as well. Miles and miles away, somewhere in the hills, with her on the back of my scooter, her legs wrapped around me.

'Have you ever been to the Torch?' Maureen said. 'It's a bit far but it's supposed to be good.'

'Not yet. One of my mates – Rocky – goes. He travels there on the train. Reckons the club is brilliant – but says it takes the edge of it a bit when you have to wait around in Stoke for five or six hours – until there's a train back again.'

'I think I'd go in the car,' Maureen said.

'Rocky says he might go on his scooter next time. It's just finding somewhere safe to leave it. Otherwise I'd go myself.'

'You could always come with me. I'd like to see if it's as good as they say, but wouldn't like to drive there on my own.'

She was asking me out I realised. This was my chance. What fucking chance? I suddenly remembered why I was here talking to her now; in another ten minutes Ramsbottom would be on the phone to the cops. If he wasn't already. 'I – um . . .' I didn't know what to say.

'Oh, I understand,' Maureen stammered, a blush of red on her pale cheeks. 'It's probably a dive anyway. The Twisted Wheel was a dump when Gary took me there. The air was thick with cigarette smoke. It stank and it was raining in. The floor was covered in puddles. Funny little rooms too. Different from Annabellas. And everyone seemed to be taking something. It wanted closing down.'

Trust her to remind me of King Mod. The bastard earned three times the money that I did and could afford to take her out, give her a good time.

Mind you, she was saying that she hadn't enjoyed herself. Then again, I didn't think she would want to know me either, when Ramsbottom had finished with me.

Maureen told me how much she had enjoyed the records they played at the Wheel though.

I told her of my visit to Blackpool, the bit about the Mecca anyway. I kept quiet about Hazel.

'Is Roberts here yet?' The speaker on Maureen's desk crackled out Ramsbottom's voice, startling me.

Maureen pressed a switch down with a neatly manicured finger. 'Yes, I'll send him in.' She released the button and her eyes sparkled at me. 'I forgot to tell him you were here.'

'Nice talking to you, Maureen.' I forced another grin as I went to the door. And it had been. I suddenly realised that nearly forty minutes had flown by while I chatted to her. She was in another class to the other girls that I knew. And a different class from a soon-to-be jailbird.

'Sit down, Kenny,' the Service Manager smiled.

You never knew where you were with Ramsbottom. He had the kind of smile that never went to his eyes. You didn't know if he was happy, or bollocking you. Mind you, he had called me Kenny, and the police weren't here yet; perhaps there was hope?

'How are you feeling?' I asked, as I saw the bandage on Ramsbottom's wrist, and a piece of pink tape spanning the bridge of his nose. There was another strip stuck to a shaven patch at the side of his head.

'A little better,' Ramsbottom said, nasally. 'I suppose you've heard – I'm back next Monday?'

I nodded.

'Now, about the other night. I know you were there. It's all a bit vague – but that's one thing I'm certain of. Who were those boys? The police have told me to let them know if I find out – or if I see them around town.'

'I don't know,' I lied, deciding that, whatever the outcome, I wouldn't be classed as a grass as well. Better stick close to the truth though, less chance of being caught out that way. 'I'd just followed them into the toilets when I saw them attacking you.'

'I'll never forget the face of that boy who started it,' Ramsbottom said.

207

'Who? Ed . . .' I almost gave the game away by divulging Duncan's name. I cleared my throat. 'The one who head butted you?' I said instead.

'A chubby lad – light brown hair. I am sure I've seen him before. But, as I said, I'll shall know him when I see him again.'

You won't see him for a while I thought. Duncan would probably be inside for Christmas; he usually arranged it so that he was. Probably much better off in gaol; at least there they gave him a proper dinner. At home the only thing Duncan's mother, the wonderful Paulina, would be dishing out, wouldn't be on a table. But then again, it might be, I thought wryly; she seemed game for anything.

The year before, Duncan's plan had backfired. The magistrates had decided to be lenient; it was Christmas after all, a time for goodwill towards all men. Duncan was up before them for burglary; the police had caught him as he returned home with his booty, a stolen TV. Duncan had got on a bus with it, but sat next to an off-duty copper, one who knew him well.

The chief magistrate had given Duncan a ticking off, and then told him that he wouldn't give him a custodial sentence this time.

Duncan had wanted his Christmas dinner, and he had head butted the constable who got up to lead him away. He had got his wish. It seemed likely he would be there this year too, even more so if I spilled the beans on him.

'I haven't told the police you were there,' Ramsbottom continued. 'I know you don't like me – but I know you are not involved with that sort of thing. But I thought if you know them – they were a similar age to you after all – then I could pass their names on to the police.'

'Could have been from out of town,' I fibbed. 'Some seemed familiar – but I don't know.' I shrugged.

'Dear, oh dear,' Ramsbottom sighed. 'I was hoping to get it sorted – without you having to talk to the police.'

He was blackmailing me, I realised. Ramsbottom was as good as saying, "Tell all you know – or you're in the shit yourself."

I sat back and rubbed my chin, wondering what to do. I could give up Duncan and clear myself, or get pulled in. What a choice! Then again, I had no choice; Duncan would name me, if he thought he'd been informed on by me. And I was sure that PC Dennis would tell Duncan who'd grassed on him. 'No, sorry. Wish I could help,' I finally said, deciding that whatever the consequences, I had to sort it myself.

'I'd tell the police how you came to help me,' Ramsbottom cajoled. 'I can recall you pulling me out of that – that horrible thing.' He wrinkled his nose in disgust, as if the urine was still soaking his moustache.

I shook my head again.

'And I'm not a homosexual whatever that boy said. I don't know what the world is coming to, when you can't even use a public toilet without being attacked. Anyway, if you do think of anything, let me know. Otherwise, I'll see you next week.' Ramsbottom got up and shook my hand. 'I'll leave you out of it – for now,' he said.

Was Ramsbottom queer? He certainly had a clammy sort of handshake, if that was anything to go by. Perhaps that was the answer; the Service Manager was bent, despite being married, and didn't want the truth to get out. Well, no one will hear it from me I decided, wanting to put it all behind me. I grinned to myself. No, I would put everything behind me – except Ramsbottom.

Now, relieved that it seemed I would get away with it, I decided to see if Maureen still wanted to go out with me. I opened the office door, but saw that Beresford had returned. He was waiting, with a couple of men in suits, for his office to be free.

'Hello, Roberts,' Beresford said, looking curiously at me as I went past. He turned to his companions. 'Would you

209

give me moment please gentlemen. I want a quick word with my manager.' He went into his office.

The other men being there prevented me from talking to Maureen. 'See you later,' I murmured to her, as I squeezed past Beresford's guests.

Maureen left with her father that night and, despite waiting in the ice-covered car park, I didn't get the chance to speak to her. I wished them both good night, then kicked my scooter into life. The paper that Dennis had given me was still in my pocket; I was supposed to take the Lambretta to the police station in the morning. Then the answer came to me.

I smiled and twisted the scooter into gear.

21

I Need A Helping Hand

'I was told to bring my scooter in.' I handed the slip that PC Dennis had given me, to the constable behind the desk.

The policeman stared owlishly over the glasses perched on the tip of his nose and examined the paper. 'That's right. They're waiting for you.'

'I've got a problem. Someone's stolen it.'

'What do you mean – stolen it?' the constable said, a look of disbelief on his face.

'I left it outside my house last night. When I got up this morning, it had gone. Some thieving sod must have taken it for parts.'

'Wait there,' he told me, then snapped shut the ledger he'd been looking at. He went through a door.

A few moments later, PC Dennis opened another door that led from the lobby into the bowels of the station. 'Through here,' he scowled, motioning for me to enter.

A shiver went down my spine as I stepped through the doorway. There was no going back now.

'Sit there,' Dennis said, pushing me into a sparsely furnished office. At least it wasn't a cell, I saw with relief. Not yet anyway. I sat at the wooden table, and waited for the bobby to settle himself on the opposite side.

Dennis placed a sheet of paper and a hard-backed book on

the table, then took a pen from his pocket. 'Let's get this right,' he said, peering at my face. 'You reckon your bike's been pinched?'

I nodded.

'Bloody convenient that, wouldn't you say?'

'Not for me.' I shook my head. 'I had to catch a bus here today. And I'll have to walk to work now.'

Dennis opened the book. 'Wasting police time,' he said, running his finger down the page. 'Could be three months inside for that.'

'What do you mean wasting your time?' I retorted. 'Just because you don't like me – doesn't mean you shouldn't find my scooter!'

'Oh, we'll find it,' Dennis promised, 'and when we do – we'll soon get at the truth. Yes, if we add deception to the other offences, that should get you another three months.' He turned another page and scanned down it.

'But it has been stolen! I thought you wouldn't believe me. I nearly didn't come in here this morning.'

'What does your father say?'

'He's as upset as I am. Thinks it's shocking that things can't be left outside without somebody having them away. Says the police should be doing something about it.'

That last bit was true. My father had noticed my scooter was missing when he had pulled back the curtains that morning. 'Thought you'd left your bike on the drive,' he had said to me, when he came in to my room to get me up for work.

'I did, pop. Parked it behind your car.'

'Well it's gone now,' my father told me.

I had dragged on my dressing gown then gone outside, shivering in the frosty dawn. There was a dark patch where my scooter had kept the rime off the concrete, but that was all.

'The thieving bastards. What's the world coming to,' my father had ranted. 'I'll ring the police.'

I'd told him that I would go in and report it. Now I was doing just that.

'Does he know that you were supposed to have it examined?' Dennis said. 'Bet he doesn't.'

My father did know though. Since Dennis had given me the docket, I had told my old man of how every time I went out on my scooter the police pulled me. 'Don't even have to be doing anything wrong. No wonder folks turn a blind eye when the police want help.'

My mother had said that if it kept on, she would go into the police station herself to complain. 'It's all very well when teenagers are up to mischief,' she said, 'but, when they're doing nothing, they should be left alone. You should be able to have fun – without getting into trouble.'

'Yes, you can ask him yourself,' I told Dennis. 'In fact he says if you don't look for my scooter – he's going to come in and see you anyway.'

'Clever bastard. You might fool your folks – but you don't fool me,' Dennis scowled. He scribbled something on the paper. 'Now fuck off out of my sight!'

I left, not feeling as calm inside as my appearance suggested. That was another problem out of the way. Now I just had to get my scooter back. Sort this, and I was staying out of trouble from now on.

A night at the Torch with Maureen, or, better still, tucked up in bed against her naked body, were the only things I wanted to be involved in from now on.

213

22

Time's A Wasting

'I thought we'd have a party next Sunday, Kenneth,' my mother said. 'It's your birthday after all. I've asked your Auntie Vi and Uncle Ted over. And Fred and Doris said they might pop in as well. Ask the Edmonds if they would like to come too. It would be nice to see them. Perhaps Mrs Edmonds would help with the food?'

I groaned. I would be seventeen the day after Christmas. At least it didn't fall on Boxing Day this year, with Christmas Day being a Saturday.

Just my luck to be born so close to Christmas. I had always lost out somehow. My aunts and uncles, and everybody, would just buy me one present. I guessed they didn't spend as much on me as they would have done if my birthday had been in the middle of the year.

'You could ask some of your friends from work too,' my mother said.

That would make a wonderful party. Ramsbottom would make it go with a swing. And I could invite Johnson – then he could bring Shagbag as well.

It would be nice to ask Maureen, but, if she agreed to go out with me, I could think of better things to be doing. Here, I'd be listening to my stuffy relatives gabbling on about how tall I'd grown, which I hadn't but hoped that one day I would, or what nice hair I'd got, which I thought I had now that it was longer again.

'Floyd could bring Anne,' my mother continued. 'She seems quite pleasant. I met her in the High Street with him.

She seemed to have forgotten seeing Anne naked with Floyd, in my bed, the day after my party.

'I wish you could find someone like her, Kenneth. That's what you need – a nice girl to settle down with.'

My father coughed then drew on his pipe, probably grateful that he hadn't got Shagbag for a daughter-in-law.

'We could get those spare chairs – the folding ones – down from the loft – couldn't we, Charlie?'

My father grunted and continued to read the morning paper, a blue spiral of pipe smoke rising between the pages.

'The doctor told you to pack that in,' my mother said crossly. 'Your blood pressure will be up again!'

My old man had had a couple of dizzy spells and, eventually, my mother had persuaded him to go and see what the problem was. He had returned from the doctor's and told us that he was fine. 'Says it's hypertension – whatever that is. He's given me some tablets for it. He asked if I'd been under any stress lately. I told him I'd got a teenage son and that was enough to cause it,' he'd laughed. 'What with thinking I might end up a granddad . . .'

My mother had leapt to my defence. 'I know Kenneth's had his problems – but look how good he's been lately. He's not been in any trouble at all since then.'

None that you know about, I had smiled to myself. It was hard to imagine my old man being unwell though. He still kept himself fit and, despite his limp, could walk much further than me, and I was some forty years younger. Then again, there was a tinge of grey to my father's hair now. He looked older than he was anyway, with working outdoors for most of his life. He had never been off work sick though, for as long as I could remember, and he refused to take time off now.

'Plenty of time for resting – when you're in your box,' he'd laughed.

My mother began to rummage in a sideboard drawer. 'We've got some party hats in here somewhere. We could use them. What about inviting some of your scooter friends?' she said, peeved that she couldn't find the hats.

I grinned at my old man. One thing we did agree on was that there would be no wearing of those stupid things this year; he'd thrown them away after the last party.

'That one with the glasses seems nice,' my mother said, as she went into the kitchen to look there. 'Is there anyone else who you'd like to come?'

'The others are inside,' my father mumbled, but not loud enough for her to hear. His mates at the bowling club, some of them magistrates, had been pretty upset about the burglary. He'd found out, from the report of the court case in the local paper, who had done it, and told me I should keep away from Duncan and Nutter in the future.

'I planned to go out next Sunday,' I said. 'Perhaps next year – when it's my eighteenth . . .' That would give me time to think up some way of avoiding it again.

'It would be so nice to get everyone together. Some of them are not getting any younger. They may not be here next year,' my mother said.

That would be a few less then I thought callously, then regretted it. I quite liked my aunts and uncles. But they were old!

'There's a special do on at Annabellas. Everyone's going,' I told my mother.

'You can go there anytime. It's your birthday and I want to make it special. Please, Kenny.'

'Do it for your mum,' my father said, as he rested the paper on his knees. 'It's not much to ask. Stay at home. Just for one day.'

But it was one day that I would rather be doing something else. I was too grown up for jelly and stuff, and that was

216

what my mother would rustle up. Life was too short for boring family get-togethers.

The desk sergeant looked up and glared at me, when I pressed the brass bell at the end of the counter.

'I've come to report another theft,' I said. 'My scooter was stolen last week. PC Dennis knows all about it. Well now I've got it back. But someone's stolen some bits off it.'

'Sit there,' the sergeant growled, then pointed to a wooden bench set against the opposite wall. 'PC Dennis is due back shortly. You can tell him the story.'

Shortly turned out to be the best part of an hour, during which I fidgeted on the seat. By the time Dennis led me into the police station again, my buttocks were numb.

'This way,' Dennis said, but took me down a different corridor this time, then down a flight of stairs.

The walls were brick, painted a dark blue to waist height, cream above that. Although the glossy finish reflected the white light of the overhead bulbs, it still seemed a dingy place to work in. I was glad I had never wanted to be a copper. Fancy working in here; it was almost as bad as being stuck in the garage.

Dennis pulled back an iron gate, then nodded for me to go through. Beyond was a corridor, with blue-painted steel doors to either side of it. Some of the doors were open; others were bolted shut. When I saw the hatchways part way up the doors, I suddenly realised they were cells. 'You can't put me in here. I haven't done anything,' I said, as I turned to face Dennis.

'In you go,' the policeman said, propelling me into the nearest open cell. As I turned to protest once more, the door clanged shut.

'Let me out, you bastard,' I shouted, my voice echoing back from the brick walls. He didn't answer. The only sounds I could hear were his footsteps retreating along the corridor.

I surveyed the cell. There was a bench along one side, with a wooden block, for a pillow, at the end of it. A coarse dark-grey blanket was rolled up at the foot of the bare boards. Facing me was a toilet, not a proper one, just a bowl. There was a handle sticking from the wall that I guessed was for the flush. No seat either, just the cold china rim, with a couple of bits of wood bolted to it, to sit on if you wanted a crap. It stank too. The cell was freezing and seemed to be below ground. At the end though, high up above the toilet, was a small barred window that let in a bit of the weak December sunshine. I tried to picture the outside of the building. There were windows like this at the front of the police station, at pavement level. That was where I must be. The glass didn't open, and the bars were too close together for me to wriggle through.

What was I thinking of that for? I didn't need to escape. I hadn't done anything wrong. I sat on the bench and pulled the blanket over my shoulders, trying to stop myself from shivering. Just the cold I decided, as my teeth began to chatter. The single bulb, mounted in a metal cage above my head, threw out a lurid white light, making the cell seem even colder.

I had always thought they had to charge you before throwing you in gaol. I shook my head, still dazed by what had happened.

Duncan had told the gang that if ever we were arrested we should say nothing, just ask for a solicitor. 'They want you to drop yourself in it,' he had explained. 'They only get the dimwits who cough up. Keep your head and your brief will get you out.'

It hadn't worked for him though; he was still inside.

I had wondered who paid for the solicitor but Duncan had laughed. 'They have to give you one free. It's the law.'

Well, I hadn't even been given the chance to speak to one. How long would I be in here? They couldn't keep me in overnight, could they? My stomach rumbled, to remind me that I'd not eaten since breakfast. Would they feed me, or just leave me here to starve? I could die in here; my mother and father would never know what had happened to me.

To pass the time, I began to read the graffiti that previous occupants had scratched into the paint on the door. I looked for Duncan and Nutter's names, but couldn't see them; maybe they'd been put in another cell before they were remanded to Werrington. The Detention Centre they'd been sent to was somewhere near to Stoke; it would be handy for the Torch if they would just let them out.

She was only the pox doctor's daughter – but she knew the men that mattered, someone had scrawled next to the hatch. I chuckled, but stopped when I felt an itch in my groin. I still wasn't sure if I'd caught a dose off Shagbag at the party. Someone, Clinton I think it was, had told me that it could take months to show up. That was all I needed. Just be my luck for that bastard to be right.

'Come on, Dennis,' I yelled. 'I want to go home.' No one answered. I almost cried when, a half-hour or so later, I heard footsteps returning.

'Good of you to wait,' Dennis laughed as I rose to my feet. 'Follow me.' He took me to the office where he had interviewed me before about the theft of my scooter. 'Thought you'd enjoy a visit to our cells.' He thumped the table, startling me. 'And that's where you'll be spending the night – if you don't tell me the truth.'

The cells were the last place I wanted to be, but I knew that if I did tell the policeman about my scooter, I would definitely be in there. Floyd too.

When Dennis had given me the ticket, I had pondered over how I could avoid the inevitable fines. Then I had asked Floyd to "steal" the Lambretta and hide it somewhere. 'I don't want to get you mixed up in it,' I told him, 'but I don't know what else to do.'

'I know just the place,' Floyd had grinned. 'Next door to us is empty. I'll put it in their coal-house.'

'After a few days – I can find it again – but without some of its mirrors,' I told him.

And that's what we had done. Floyd had sneaked out in the night, wheeled my scooter around the corner, and then started it with a screwdriver. The Lambretta's ignition was a poor design, and so worn that a flat blade would turn it; no key was needed. Floyd had coasted the last few yards to his home, pushed it up the entry between the two houses, then parked it next door, hidden under some sacking.

Now, I had to convince Dennis that someone else had taken it.

'I've told you what happened.' I stared into the policeman's eyes, with more conviction than I felt. 'Somebody stole it – then last night one of my mates said he'd seen it dumped behind the bandstand in the park. I went up there – and he was right. There wasn't any petrol in the tank – that's probably why the thief left it – but some of my mirrors have been stripped off. That's why I've come here. To report the theft of them.'

'Where's the bike now?'

'It's at home. I had to push it to the nearest garage to fill it up.'

'You should've left it where it was. Maybe we could have fingerprinted it. Mind you, there's nothing to stop us doing that now – is there?'

'Well,' I hesitated. 'It was covered in mud – and my chrome was going rusty – so I cleaned it.'

'Why doesn't that surprise me,' Dennis smiled. 'Bet we would only have found your dabs anyway.'

'Suppose so,' I agreed. 'Especially if the thief was wearing gloves.'

'These mirrors,' Dennis said, pulling the top off his pen. 'You've got receipts for them?'

'I don't know. I've not got any with me. Never thought to bring them.'

'I just wondered – because we've had loads of them stolen

from parked cars. But you wouldn't know anything about that, would you?'

'Must be the same thieves,' I smiled. 'Catch them and I may get my stuff back too.'

'Oh, we'll catch them – whoever it is,' Dennis said. 'And when we do – I shall make sure the magistrates make an example of them. That's a promise!'

23

Compared To What

Christmas Day was going to be a nightmare. To my dismay, on Christmas Eve, my father had gone to Boston to fetch my grandmother. It had meant a long drive for him, as she lived some ninety miles away, but my parents had thought it might be the last time she would be well enough to spend Christmas with us. Well enough – the old bastard would outlive us all!

As a kid, I'd always been made to wait until my mother and father were up and about before opening my Christmas presents. Knowing how excited I would be, they usually got up early. I know I'm a bit older now, but I was still anxious to see what I'd got. I had to wait though; my grandmother slept on, her snores rattling the bedroom door.

My father told me to hang on for a bit. 'She'll want to see what you've had. And to watch the look on your face when you open her present.'

He was taking the piss; last year she'd given me a pair of pyjamas that she'd bought for my granddad – and he'd been dead for nearly twenty years.

'Shall I wake her?' I said. 'See if she's all right?'

'No, let her rest,' my mother told me, as she searched below the kitchen sink for the turkey dish. 'She'll be tired from all that travelling. Where is the damned thing?' she muttered, shutting another cupboard. 'Help me look for it Charlie, else the dinner will be late.'

My gran finally got up about ten thirty, but it wasn't until she'd had a bite to eat, and a cup of tea, that my mother and father let me tear at the wrapping paper. They had bought me a Fidelity record player – and it was a stereo one; now I wouldn't have to listen to my records on something borrowed from Floyd's brother. A present from Cheryl was *Festival Time* by the San Remo Strings, which had just come into the charts. Floyd had found me Father's Angels *Bok to Bach* in a shop in Nottingham. I couldn't wait to give them a spin. The trouble was, I didn't have a spare socket in my bedroom; I would have to play them in the living room.

'Listen to them when you've had your dinner,' my gran chided, as I plugged the player in.

'Yes, leave it for a bit,' my mother joined in. 'See what else you've got.'

My aunts had bought me several pairs of socks, all too short in the leg, and which would soon disappear into the toes of my DM's when I wore them. There was a box of Milk Tray from my parents. Cheryl had also got me a bottle of Brut, and a set of air horns, complete with gas bottle, for my Lambretta. The trumpets were red plastic, and chrome ones would have looked better on my scooter, but they were better than the bulb horn I'd fitted since Dennis had started his checks. And they must have cost her a bit. They would have taken the best part of my wages; the last time that I'd priced them up, they were just under six quid. Cheryl, who had started work at a local hairdressers, after she left school, wouldn't earn as much as me.

I felt a bit guilty; I'd only bought her a box of toiletries – soap, talc, and eau de cologne – from Timothy Whites; they'd cost me one pound fifty. I had managed to get all my presents, similar sets, for my mother and gran, my aunts, and Mrs Edmonds from the same chemists; they'd even wrapped them for me.

I saved opening my pièce de résistance, a large parcel wrapped in creased brown paper and tied with much-knotted sisal string, until last, hoping to irritate my gran still further. It was a multicoloured rag rug. It smelt like something her cat had pissed on – regularly.

'I thought it would look nice in your bedroom,' the old woman smiled at me.

'It's – It's breathtaking,' I finally managed to stutter. My mother glared at me, daring me to say more. I didn't. I rolled it up and shoved it next to her. I didn't think she'd stop me binning the thing when her mother had gone home.

'Put it in your bedroom. I can have a look at it later – when I go to the toilet,' my gran smiled.

She knew that my bedroom was private, and she was just saying it to wind me up.

My father saved me from replying. 'Let's have our dinners. You'll miss the Queen's Speech else,' he told her.

We sat at the table. I gnawed at the leathery potatoes that my mother had roasted, then prodded at a part-cooked turkey leg which began to ooze red streaks of blood from under the skin, adding to the puddle of grease on my plate. 'I'm not hungry,' I said pushing it away.

'After your mother's gone to all that trouble,' my gran scolded. 'It's delicious,' she said, shovelling some sage and onion into her mouth.

She wanted stuffing herself I thought, as her skinny jowls wobbled like a turkey; she was the one who had taught my mother how to cook.

'Never threw good food away in my day,' my gran muttered. 'You ought to be made to finish it.'

And you should be done for a couple of hours – at Gas Mark 6 – down at the crem I thought, but didn't say.

The afternoon didn't get any better.

After the Queen, she wanted to watch Billy Smart's Circus. I'd already missed Top of the Pops because she wanted to watch another stupid circus on ATV.

What a load of drivel they'd put on for Christmas – and my gran wanted to watch it all.

'I like seeing the animals,' she said, when I groaned aloud.

She'd have been better off fed to them. Then again, they would probably have spit her out.

All that I was itching to do was spin the discs that Floyd and Cheryl had bought me. The records lay on the sideboard, tantalising me. Finally, the TV was switched off. I plugged the record player in, with the volume down low, but my gran just had to open her mouth.

'What a dreadful noise,' she sneered. 'Turn that row off, Kenneth. Your father's tired,' she said, nodding to the chair where my father was snoring, 'he doesn't want to hear this.'

He doesn't want to hear you either I thought; that was most likely why he had closed his eyes.

And for Christmas night – I had Ronnie Corbett and Ronnie Barker – with their guests Engelbert Humperdink, Vera Lynn, Harry Secombe, The New Seekers and Lulu. They'd really pushed the boat out for Christmas.

Then I just knew she'd want to watch Morecambe and Wise. After that there was the Good Old Days to look forward to.

Annabellas had a special party on – drinks at half price. Why the fuck had I promised to stay in?

I wouldn't tomorrow, that was for sure.

24

Crying Over You

I managed to listen to my records eventually – the next afternoon. I tried to play them in the living room, but my grandmother moaned that the noise gave her a headache. I took the player into the garage, and plugged it into a socket above my father's workbench. It was bloody cold, but at least I could have it as loud as I wanted in there.

After dinner my old man came into the garage, and told me that some of my aunts and uncles had arrived, and that I ought to come in and say hello. I did, but was soon fed up of being pecked on the cheek by the whiskery-faced old buggers; and that was just my aunts.

When my father went out in his car, to collect my Aunt Vi, I sneaked my scooter from the garage.

No one seemed to notice my escape; they were all too busy gossiping, and sipping at the sweet sherry my mother had laid on.

'You can have a drink, if you like,' she had whispered to me. 'I know you're not eighteen yet, but I think you're old enough to have a sip of this.'

A sip of that crap! I would have six or seven rum and cokes tonight, more if I could afford it. I'd miss my Christmas kiss from Cheryl, but I had arranged to meet Lorraine in Annabellas; she would more than compensate.

226

After I'd parked my scooter, I met Floyd and Anne in the High Street.

Floyd had briefly shown his face at the party that afternoon, then as they say in the News of the World, "Made his excuses and left."

'Your parents are gonna be disappointed,' he told me, as I strolled towards him. 'Your mother was so looking forward to it.'

I kicked an empty cigarette packet into the gutter. 'I stayed in Christmas Day. What more do they want?'

Anne leaned around Floyd and looked at me. 'They've gone to a lot of trouble. And Floyd's mum and sister have too.'

That was true I thought, and it was a shame that I'd not get the chance to tuck into the cakes that Mrs Edmonds had made for the party, especially after the crap my mother had laid on over the weekend.

'Pity our new suits aren't ready,' Floyd said, as he admired his reflection in a shop window. 'Could've shown them off tonight.'

'Pair of posers,' Anne laughed.

'Too good for this place,' I told him. 'They're for when we go to a proper club like the Torch.'

'I thought they let you wear T-shirts and things there?' Anne said.

'They do, but everyone meets up in a local pub to buy . . .'

Floyd coughed loudly, causing me to pause.

'Yeah, they have a drink first then get changed later.'

'But you've got a perfectly good suit, Floyd,' Anne said. 'Why spend nearly thirty pounds on another one – when we're supposed to be saving for a ring.'

I stopped in surprise.

'Didn't you know,' Anne said, then punched Floyd in the ribs. 'He said he'd told you.'

'He said something – but I've been busy,' I smiled, as I tried to cover up for my mate. 'So it's no wonder I forgot.

227

But congratulations to both of you.' I gave Anne a kiss on the cheek, then Floyd a hug.

'How touching,' said PC Dennis as he came out of the darkness of a greengrocer's doorway. 'Compliments of the season to you all. Look forward to seeing a bit more of you in the New Year, Roberts.'

'Isn't he the one who you thought was dead?' Anne said, once we were out of earshot. 'I don't like him much.'

'Yeah, and he's still trying to make my life a misery,' I grinned. 'And I don't like him either. The bastard has got to work tonight though. Serves him right. Now, what were you saying?'

'Let's get inside – out of the cold,' Floyd said, 'then I'll tell you.'

I suddenly spotted a greaser coming towards us. I recognised the spindly denim-clad legs of Roger Webster. He was swaggering along, and waving the tassels, dangling from the sleeves of his leather jacket, in a circular motion, as if he was about to whip someone with them. I knew that Dennis was still close by, and Webster must know this also, else he wouldn't be acting so tough now.

Webster came on.

I decided there was no way I was moving aside for the greaser. It would be an accidental collision; I'd make sure of that.

Anne must have sensed what was about to happen. 'Let's cross over,' she said, nudging Floyd towards the kerb.

Walking on the outside, I was forced to step sideways, or else bump into my friend.

'Chickens,' Webster hissed, as he ambled past.

I turned, ready to flatten the greaser, but saw that Dennis was watching. Then I spotted the word "Linda," written in chrome studs pressed into the back of Webster's leather jacket. 'Come on, Linda. Give us a kiss,' I murmured. 'Do a good turn do you love?'

Webster spun on his Cuban heels, his long hair swirling

about his face. 'What did you say?' he growled, stepping closer, pressing his nose against mine.

'Sorry,' I smiled, 'Didn't realise you were so ugly until I got close up.' I saw the policeman hurrying forward, sensing that a fracas may be about to start.

'If he wasn't there,' Webster said, pointing over his shoulder with his thumb, 'you'd be dead by now.'

'Come on Kenny,' Floyd whispered. 'You'll be in trouble.'

'You're both in trouble anyway,' Webster hissed. 'I'm fetching my mates, and we'll be waiting for you when you come out.'

'I'll have picked up something better by then,' I said.

'Dead,' Webster said, then aimed his finger like a mock gun barrel at my head. He turned again, just as Dennis arrived on the scene.

'What's going on?' the policeman growled.

'Nothing,' I smiled, then said in a voice loud enough for Webster to hear, 'I thought it was a girl at first – with that long hair.'

'I suggest you get in there,' Dennis said, pointing to the stairway up to Annabellas, ' and I don't want to see anything more of you tonight!'

'You won't – if I can help it,' I muttered as we climbed the concrete steps.

Lorraine was waiting for us inside, and had managed to save us a booth near the stage. It hadn't been too difficult she told us, as the place was still only half full.

Annabellas was a bit dead I noticed. I'd never been in over Christmas before, and had expected it to be a bit livelier. Perhaps it was because the disco was only open until one o'clock tonight. Rocky and Cadger were there though; they met me at the bar when I went to fetch the drinks.

'Hi, Kenny,' Cadger smiled. 'Getting them in? It's Christmas after all.'

'If it's Christmas – then it must be your turn,' I grinned.

229

'I'll get the next ones. Honest,' Cadger said.

'Yeah, and I believe in Santa Claus.' I bought him a drink anyway.

'We met Roger Webster outside,' I told the two skinheads. 'He says a load of greasers will be waiting for us when we leave. Give us a shout when you're ready to go – and we'll go out together.'

'The other lads aren't here,' Rocky said. 'Don't know where they are. Sort of drifted apart while Duncan's away. I'd help – but I've got my best suit on. Don't want to wreck it.'

'And I promised my old man I wouldn't be late back,' Cadger said. 'I'll stay – if you can't get anyone else . . .'

'Don't bother – mates,' I said, then returned to the table with the drinks. 'Rocky and Cadger are bottling out,' I told Floyd.

'What's this about?' Lorraine said.

'There was a biker outside – trying to cause trouble,' Anne told her. 'Horrible thing he was too.'

'Knowing Webster, he'll chicken out anyway,' Floyd said.

'Well, let's forget about him for now. Enjoy ourselves. Merry Christmas everyone,' I said. We clinked our glasses together, then knocked back our first drinks. 'Now, when is the big day?' I smiled.

'What? Tell me about it,' Lorraine said.

'Don't know yet. We've only just decided. Lots to talk about,' Anne smiled.

'I'm jealous of you, mate,' I murmured to Floyd, while the two girls were talking. 'Good luck to you. Wish I could find someone nice like her. Does that mean you'll pay me that quid?'

'A pound. What's that for,' Anne smiled, as she overheard the last bit.

'Oh, just some money Floyd owes me. I thought I'd better get it off him – before you get hold of his wages.'

'Let's dance,' Floyd said, wanting to change the subject.

'Don't like this one,' I grinned, as Rod Stewart croaked out *Maggie May.*

'Come on, you still haven't told me what the money is for,' Anne nudged Floyd.

'She's just getting you used to married life,' I smiled. 'OK, let's dance,' I said, as Anne waved her fist under my nose. The DJ was spinning the latest release from Al Green, *Let's Stay Together.* It was a slow record, and it would be nice to hold Lorraine close against me. She was wearing hot pants again, and long black leather boots. She looked real sexy as she joined me on the dance floor.

'Happy Christmas,' Lorraine murmured, then placed her lips on mine.

This was better than being at home, listening to my grandmother and aunts gossiping, I thought, as I felt her pelvis press against me.

'I don't believe it,' Floyd shouted into my ear. 'It's my old man.' He pointed across the nightclub.

I tried to focus. I'd sunk a rum and pep at the last round and, with the six, or was it seven, drinks that I'd knocked back already, my head was beginning to spin.

'The embarrassment of it,' Floyd said. 'I'll be a laughing stock when the others hear about it. Keep your heads down,' he waved to us, then ducked below the seat back.

'He's coming this way,' Anne giggled. 'An' he's got . . .' She hiccuped. 'He's got that man – the policeman that was outside – with him.'

'Shit,' Floyd breathed. 'What does he want?'

'Here you are,' I heard Mr Edmonds voice, above the background sound of The Fascinations' *Girls Are Out To Get You.*

'What's up, pop,' Floyd asked.

'It's Ken I wanted,' Mr Edmonds said.

Fuck me I thought. Just because I didn't go to the stupid party! I could do without all this. I began to stagger to my

231

feet, but PC Dennis placed a hand on my shoulder. What was up? I'd done nothing that warranted being shown up in the disco like this.

'Sorry son. It's your father,' Dennis said. 'He's been taken ill.'

'They've got him at the hospital,' Mr Edmonds told me. 'I've got my car outside . . .'

'I'll come with you,' Floyd said, as I reeled and almost fell over. 'Get our coats will you Ann?' He ferreted in his pocket, then gave a cloakroom ticket to her.

I couldn't take in much of what was happening after that. I realised we were leaving Annabellas, was vaguely aware of the drive to the city hospital, then the long walk to the emergency entrance, but it all seemed such a blur.

When the hospital's sliding doors parted, I saw my mother and Auntie Vi huddled together, sobbing, in the foyer. Behind where they stood was a closed curtain.

My Uncle Ted came towards us. 'He's gone, lad,' he said. 'About ten minutes ago. He was asking for you.'

'What do you mean gone?' I swayed, as I tried to fathom out what my uncle was saying.

'He means your pop's dead, Kenny,' Mr Edmonds said, placing his arm on my shoulder.

'He can't be. What's happened?'

'They think he had a stroke,' my uncle said. 'He collapsed in the bathroom. We managed to get him into bed then called for the doctor. He couldn't talk properly.'

'There's got to be a mistake . . .'

'I'm sorry, Kenneth. The ambulance took ages. Suppose it's because it's Christmas.' My uncle shrugged.

'We couldn't find your father's keys and my car was at home – I thought I might have a drink you see,' Floyd's dad said. 'I had to fetch it from there. I could have got him here in it. Perhaps then . . .'

And perhaps if I'd been at home, I could have rushed my father here I suddenly realised. I didn't have a licence, but that had never stopped me before. I could drive. I often moved cars around as part of my job, but I had held back from taking my test as I was hoping to get the garage to pay for me to do it. They had for some of the other staff. I couldn't have afforded a car anyway, so why waste my money I'd thought. Now, vital minutes had been lost before my father had been brought here; if I had been there, he may still be alive. Having no keys wouldn't have stopped me either; I would soon have hot-wired the little Fiat.

'I want to see him,' I said, pushing past my uncle.

'Not yet,' he grabbed at my arm, 'they've just . . .'

I shook myself free and dodged around the curtain. Brown eyes, as lifeless as those I had seen in a stuffed bear down at the pub, stared at me. My father's face was like something from a horror film; his jaw was sagging limply open, his teeth were in a pot at the bedside. He grimaced gummily at me. I shook my head. The whole family was playing a trick on me I suddenly thought, drunkenly, as I saw the white skin of his cheeks. My old man's were brown – and leathery. This was just a mannequin made up to look like him. What a mean way to get revenge – just because I'd bunked off from their fucking party. Clinton worked here; he would be in on it as well. I touched the dummy's forehead; it felt waxy – but was still warm.

That was strange. I bent down to investigate just as a nurse dashed in. There was no mistaking those misshapen ears and battered nose; no one could make something as – as lifelike – as that.

It was my father. And he was dead.

25

And Suddenly

'A good turnout. Shame about the weather though,' Floyd said, as he brushed snow off the bench then sat next to me.

It was a foul day; freezing fog had prevented the snow that had fallen over the last few days from thawing, but I hadn't really noticed it until now. I stared at the pile of soil, brown and stark against the white carpet. It was slowly shrinking in size as the gravedigger and his assistant shovelled it back into the hole.

'I'm glad it's over,' I told Floyd. 'Thought the weather would delay it again. I never expected so many people.'

A load of my father's workmates from the Gas Board, some from the town, others he had known when he worked in Rugby, had turned up. They had held a collection for him and, before they dispersed, a man I remembered visiting our house, when I was a kid, had pushed an envelope into my hand.

'Give it to your mother will you, son.'

I think I said thank you to him.

The Edmonds had done us proud; the whole family, including Clinton, had turned up. 'Sorry, Kenny,' he muttered, when he stood at the graveside.

I do remember thanking him; I know that, despite our differences, he had liked and respected my old man.

'Where's Cheryl?' I asked Floyd.

'Winston's taken her home. She still can't take it all in. Crying all the time. I think some of it's because she knows what you – and your mum – are going through.'

'I'm off now Kenny,' Frank Johnson said, as both he and Ramsbottom came to where I was sitting. 'Take care of yourself.'

I stood up and shook Johnson's hand. 'Thanks for coming.'

'Don't come in tomorrow,' Ramsbottom said, as he too turned to go. 'I've cleared it with Mr Beresford,' he said, nodding towards where the garage owner was talking to some of my father's bowling friends.

Ramsbottom still had the bandage on his wrist, I noticed guiltily. He saw me looking at it. 'Not been a good time for either of us. Your father was a good man Kenny. Don't ever forget that.'

'I won't,' I said, then shook his hand. I guessed he was trying to say that he wasn't going to drop me in it, with the police, for my old man's sake. I was grateful; the last thing I wanted now was to bring shame on my father's name.

'Let's go back to the car Kenny,' Floyd said when they had gone; his face was pinched with the cold. 'You can't sit here all day.'

'You go. Tell them I'll walk to the house,' I said, looking at the crowd of people waiting by the funeral cars. It was bad enough facing them one at a time, but I knew I wouldn't be able to walk up there now, with them watching me, accusing me.

My mother had invited everyone back for a drink and a sandwich. Floyd's mum had asked some of her friends from the school canteen to help lay on the buffet. A good thing too, I smiled wryly to myself, else some of them would end up in here, if they sampled my mother's food.

'Your mum needs you,' Floyd murmured, as if reading my thoughts.

'I'll be along in a minute,' I told him. 'Besides, my aunts are with her.'

'Don't be long,' Floyd said, then gave me a hug. I watched as he walked back to Anne, who was waiting by the cars.

I sat again. The gravediggers were tamping the sticky soil into place using the backs of their shovels. My father's coffin had gone from view forever. Such a small coffin too; I would never have imagined that a bloke the size of my father could fit inside it, and I still didn't believe he was really in it.

I saw Maureen leave her father's side and cross the slush-covered grass towards me, her heels sinking into the mud. 'Put the wrong shoes on,' she smiled. 'Glad I wore this though,' she said, as she huddled deeper into the folds of her black ankle length coat. 'Do you mind?' She nodded to the space on the bench next to me.

I shook my head then shuffled along the seat, so that she could sit on the bit that Floyd had cleared.

'You have to think of the future now, Kenny. What you are going to do with your life.' She took my hand in hers, her woollen glove, black like the bob hat on her head, warming my chilled fingers. 'That's what your father would want.'

I couldn't look at her. I didn't want her to see my tears. Kenny Roberts – so called hard case – blubbering like some kid. 'It was my fault,' I said, staring at the grave through blurred eyes. 'Should've been there.' Instead, I had been out discoing with Lorraine, who I'd not seen since that night. Didn't really want to again, either. 'Yeah, perhaps then he'd still be here now.'

'You don't know that. They might still not have saved him.'

'It would have given him a better chance though. There he was – dying – while I'm out enjoying myself.'

'You can't change things Kenny. I remember when my grandmother died. She was a lovely woman – had a heart of gold. Then she found out that she had cancer. She went from being a robust happy woman to a skeleton. I was only eight at the time. I prayed for her every night, hoping that God would spare her. Towards the end – she was in so much pain – I begged for Him to take her. When she was gone, I thought that it was all my fault.'

I squeezed Maureen's hand in mine. 'It wasn't,' I told her. 'How could it be?'

'And that's what I'm trying to say to you,' she said. 'It's part of life. These things happen.'

'Coming Maureen?' her father shouted from the gate.

'I'll walk up with Kenny,' she called back. 'If that's all right with you,' she said, turning to look into my eyes.

I nodded, then saw that her face was white with cold. 'You don't have to stay. You're frozen.'

'I want to,' she said, linking her arm under mine. 'Say what you have to,' she said, nodding towards the grave, 'then we can go. Walk past the Park perhaps? The holly trees are covered in berries. They look fantastic against the snow and the green leaves.'

That was the difference between us. Never in my life had I looked at the beauty of what was around me, except for girls that is. And Maureen was truly beautiful I thought, as I gazed into her eyes. How nice it would be to get warm together, lying in the glow of a log fire, our bodies naked against one another, I thought, then, guiltily, I looked at the grave. The men had finished and were dragging a piece of imitation grass, like the stuff that greengrocers use to show off their boxes of fruit and things, over the top of the mound.

'I won't be a moment,' I told Maureen, when they had picked up their spades and left.

'I'll wait,' she whispered, pulling her collar up around her neck, then tugging her woolly hat down over her red curls.

I went to the grave, bright green against the slush and mud. I still couldn't take in the fact that he was under there, not my dad. 'Sorry, pop,' I breathed then turned away. I'd said all that I wanted to already, when I'd visited him at the funeral home. He'd looked so different then, from when I'd

237

seen him in the emergency ward, with his shirt torn open and livid bruises among the grey curls of hair on his chest, caused when the ambulance men tried to save him. It was not my father though. The undertakers had dressed him in his wedding suit, tidied his hair, shaved him, padded his cheeks out even, but he never looked that smart in life, except perhaps in a very old picture taken when he'd joined the Marines. Somehow, he was never meant to be that way. I'd ruffled his hair.

'I can't undo what I've done,' I told him, while he lay resting there, 'but I promise I'll keep out of trouble from now on. I'm going to keep on with my college work – perhaps I can get to be foreman, make you proud of me. I'll take care of mum,' I said, then kissed him on his cold forehead, before leaving the little chapel. I didn't cry then, I had to be strong for my mother, but I sobbed my heart out in the sanctuary of my bedroom.

And now I had to face the family.

I wiped my eyes, then rejoined Maureen at the seat. 'Shall we go?'

She stood up and stamped her feet, to get some circulation back in them. The tip of her nose was blue with the cold I saw. She followed me to the metal gate that led out on to the lane past the church. Once through it, Maureen gripped my hand in hers, and we walked up the hill, towards the park, like a couple in love.

And I was in love with her. I had never met anyone who made me feel the way she did, even on such a miserable day as this. I sensed that she felt the same way about me. Perhaps if I could make it work, start a family of my own maybe, my old man would be happy.

Soon, all too soon for me, we were outside my house. 'Let's go around the block again,' I said, when I saw there were still dozens of cars parked in the street outside.

The bungalow's curtains were drawn back, and I could see a lot of people in the living room, reminding me of the party

238

I'd held the summer before, and which had caused my old man such embarrassment.

'I'm cold Kenny,' Maureen stammered. 'And it's going dark.'

It was, I noticed for the first time; we must have been walking for a good hour or more.

'I'll come in with you,' she said, touching my arm. 'You're not on your own.'

As we reached the door at the side of the bungalow, she kissed me on the cheek, her nose cold and wet against my ear. She was chilled through I realised, and though I would love to have dallied there with her, I pushed the door open. A wave of hot air and the sound of a myriad of chattering voices rushed out.

I took a deep breath, then led Maureen inside.

26

You Just Don't Know

Maureen said she would go out with me when I asked her, a few days later, at work. I almost skipped home that night, excited at the thought of it. It was another week though before we had our first date, as I didn't want to leave my mother alone at night, for a while anyway.

'She's going to stay with my Aunt Vi for the weekend,' I told Maureen when I asked if she was free that night. 'Perhaps we could go to the city, to the pictures, then a disco or something.'

'I wouldn't mind a meal,' she told me. 'Chinese perhaps.'

I smiled to myself at that, imagining what my father would have said. He could never understand why folks flocked to their restaurants.

'Never saw them eating that sort of stuff when I came across them,' he told me once, when we were out for a walk. We had been looking at the menu outside the Chinese takeaway in the market square. 'And they certainly didn't feed it to us. Mind you, they gave us enough rats – probably what they put in the curries now.'

'What's up,' Maureen looked curiously at me. 'Don't you fancy that?'

I did, and I fancied her too. I decided that I wouldn't stuff my face tonight though; hot curries and making love didn't

240

particularly go together. 'That would be great,' I said. 'Pick you up at eight?'

'How about I pick you up?' she smiled. 'It's a bit cold to be on your scooter.'

I agreed; it would be nice to be chauffeured for a change, and it meant that I could have a drink too. Not too much though, I cautioned myself. I didn't want the dreaded brewer's droop to spoil things.

I heard the toot of her car horn, bang on the hour. As I pulled the front door closed, the house seemed so empty. I had left here before while my parents were out and never felt this way, but now I knew that I would never see my father again. Cheer up, I told myself, then, as I saw Maureen smiling at me, my spirits lifted once more.

I loved my scooter, but riding in Maureen's Escort, with the heater going full blast, certainly beat having my knackers frozen off on the Lambretta. Maureen's car had a cassette player fitted too, and The Five Stairsteps were singing out, 'I'm so happy to be here by your side,' as she pulled away from the kerb.

'Like it?' she said, nodding towards the player, 'I taped some records to listen to while I'm driving.'

'Please stay close to me,' the singer cooed. That was what I hoped to do with Maureen – later. 'What's that?' I said, as I heard a telephone ring among the music. 'Don't remember that bit.'

'I haven't got a plug-in microphone,' Maureen laughed. 'Seems like I picked up every sound for miles around.'

The miaow of a cat punctuated the next track, *Backfield In Motion*, and we both burst into hysterics. The tape was better than nothing though, and it was wonderful to be able to smile again. And to have such a gorgeous girl alongside me.

Maureen changed into top gear as we left the town behind and took the "A" Road towards the city. In the feeble glow of the dashboard lights, I could see that she was wearing a dark coloured – blue maybe – mini-dress covered in large

241

flower shapes. It was short, very short, I saw as I glanced down. It had ridden up her legs as she moved her feet on the pedals, revealing inches of nylon-clad flesh above the dark knee-length boots she was wearing.

My heart pounding, I rested my hand on her leg, just above the knee. A vein in my temple began to throb, and I began to harden in anticipation when she didn't push it away. As Diana Ross sang *Reach out and Touch*, I took my cue from the lyrics and slid my hand higher, my breath coming in short bursts as my fingers found the hem of her dress.

'Not while I'm driving,' Maureen said. She reached down, then dropped my hand gently, but firmly, back into my lap.

Did that mean she would let me when we were parked? I hoped so, for I wanted so much to have her, make love to her all night.

I couldn't eat much of my meal; I was so excited at the prospect of taking her home. I would invite her into the bungalow, then strip her boots off while she lay back on the bed, my eyes savouring every inch of her legs until . . .

'Do you fancy going on to a club?' Maureen said, as the waiter pushed a plate, with the bill on top, under my nose.

I didn't really. I would much rather have gone straight home, but I wanted to show Maureen a good time. 'OK,' I smiled. 'What do you fancy? The Top Rank – or there's that little place just off Piccadilly.'

'The Spinning Top? Yes, let's go there,' Maureen said. 'I've never been – but I've heard they play lots of soul.'

I'd not visited the club before either; the music they played was a bit too plodding for my taste.

But not tonight. I couldn't get enough of those slow sexy numbers, the Delfonics, with their falsetto sound, or the Chilites asking, 'Have you seen her?' I had the perfect excuse to hold Maureen tight.

We danced, then danced some more, my nose nuzzled into her neck, smelling the sweet soapy scent of her skin, soft strands of her hair tickling my cheek. It would have been obvious to Maureen that I wanted her; she must have felt the hardness of me pressed against her, as we side-stepped slowly across the dancefloor. I had been like this since I'd first held her, and wondered if I could take much more without creaming myself with excitement. I had my left arm around her waist, my right hand at the small of her back, pushing her against me, my knee between the folds of her dress, rubbing against her groin.

She was hot, very hot, against my leg, and I sensed that she wanted me too. I lowered my hand, to hug her buttock, so beautiful, so firm, so rounded. What would it be like when I held her there, naked, while I slid inside her I wondered, then, as my knob twitched, I decided I must think of something else – quickly.

And she had not protested at my fondling, I realised.

Maureen leaned back and looked up into my eyes, then kissed me, her lips soft against mine. A tingle, like an electric shock, jangled my brain.

'Shall we go,' I said, hoarsely; much more of this and I would be embarrassing myself.

Maureen nodded and we collected our coats. 'I have to drive us back,' she said, when I leaned over her in the car. 'Let's get home first.'

It wasn't until we were halfway that I realised that we had hardly touched our drinks in the club. I'd winced when I'd bought the first round. My rum and coke, and a Pernod and lemonade for Maureen, had set me back nearly three quid; you could buy a bottle of whisky for less than that. And then we had barely drunk any, just danced in each other's arms.

As Maureen drove, I put my hand on her knee again.

This time she didn't move it, she just grabbed it when I edged towards her crotch again, as her legs rocked up and down when she changed gear.

'I like it there though,' she told me, moving my palm back to her knee.

243

'I've really enjoyed myself tonight,' Maureen said, as we drew up outside my home.

I looked round in surprise. Were we back already? It hardly seemed five minutes ago that we had defrosted the screen of her car. I stared at the black emptiness of the bungalow's windows. 'Fancy a coffee – or something,' I said as I opened the Escort's door.

'I must go home. Daddy will be waiting up,' she said, to my disappointment. She kept the car's engine running. 'It was wonderful dancing close to you,' she smiled. 'Perhaps we can do it again?'

'I thought that . . . Yes, lets,' I said, then sagged back into the car again. I held her to me, clamped my lips over hers, and cupped a hand over her breast, hoping to persuade her to stay.

She gripped my hand to prevent my exploration of her tits, but left it there while her tongue explored mine. Her nipple was hard against my palm.

'Better go,' she rasped, then leaned back from my embrace. 'See you . . ?'

'Tomorrow,' I gasped. 'Same time?'

Maureen nodded then put the car into gear. I scrambled out and shut the door. She blew a kiss at me then accelerated away. I watched her disappear around the corner, then went inside the bungalow.

'Jesus Christ,' I murmured to the empty building as my prick throbbed with frustration. I found one of my old man's *Titbits* in the rack at the side of the fireplace. It was not the busty bikini-clad blonde in the centre pages that I was thinking of, as I went to sleep.

I dreamt of Maureen, naked, her legs entwined with mine, as the magazine fell to the floor.

27

Touch Me, Kiss Me, Hold Me

'I'm off to the Torch again next week,' Rocky told me. 'You should come with us. They're running All-Nighters now. It's brilliant. Don't have to hang around half the night – in that doss-hole of a town – waiting to get home anymore.'

'I don't know.' I said. I wanted to go, but wasn't sure about it. 'How are you getting there? Don't fancy leaving my scooter where I don't know if it'll be safe.'

'We could thumb a lift,' Nutter said. He was back out again; Duncan was too.

I could imagine that a lot of motorists would stop to pick up a bunch of skinheads, especially if one of them was as mean looking as Nutter. 'Who else is going? Hitching's all right if there's one or two but . . .'

'I'm going,' Duncan said. 'Got the right gear for it.' He waved a black driving glove in the air. 'Keep the faith!'

Duncan hadn't changed much since coming out of prison, but his dislike of me seemed to have grown. I tried not to laugh. He never quite got it right; a single leather glove was cool, a pair of black plastic ones was naff. It was the same when we bought our Italian brogues from Dolcis; Duncan pinched a pair of shiny patent leather ones, the div.

'What's funny, Roberts?' Duncan scowled, as he saw me grinning.

'Just picturing you cutting a groove on the floor of the Torch, Eddie.'

'I've been practising dancing,' Duncan laughed, not realising I'd been taking the sap out of him. 'Should impress the girls.'

Rocky raised his eyebrows at me. We both knew that the Nighters were for dancing, hearing some brilliant sounds, but most of the scoring that went on was with gear, not girls. Girls did go to the club, but to have a good time themselves. Rocky told me that some of them were up for it before the dancing started, he'd even taken a girl into one of the nearby alleyways at the first All-Nighter a couple of weeks before, but mostly they just wanted to dance. In the morning, everyone was too shattered to do anything else.

It was a different scene to what we were used to. And I couldn't wait to try it.

'If you're going Kenny, then I will too,' Floyd told me.

He'd come out with us, on one of his rare nights away from Anne. I hadn't seen much of him since the funeral, what with me staying in sometimes to keep my mother company, or going to the city with Maureen.

'Anne keeps walking me past the jewellers. Don't know if I'm ready to settle down yet,' Floyd said. 'I thought it might do her good if I had a bit of time away from her.'

'You know best,' I told him, 'but I don't know if I'm going anyway. I haven't got much money . . .'

'Have your girlfriends got you under the thumb?' Duncan laughed.

'No. It's just that I can't afford the train fare and things. By the time I've paid to go in – I'll have nothing left for anything else.'

'I'll buy you a pint,' Duncan said, 'I'm going to get pissed anyway. Make a night of it.'

He looked puzzled when Rocky told him they didn't sell alcohol at the Nighters. 'They keep the bar closed. Just sell soft drinks.'

'What kind of a nightclub doesn't sell ale,' Duncan scowled, suspecting he was being made fun of.

I looked at Rocky as if to say, "You explain."

He shook his head; like me, he probably thought it was a waste of time trying.

'We could wear our suits,' Floyd grinned. 'They said they'd be ready this week.'

I pictured the two of us, strutting to the Torch in our threads. I'd ordered mine in light-brown mohair and, if the tailors had got it right, it should have a long centre vent, almost to my shoulder blades, a dozen buttons on each sleeve, pockets everywhere, and a pair of parallel trousers to match. Floyd had gone for more or less the same design, but in black.

The puffy looking shop assistant had shaken his head, dumbfounded, as we told him our requirements. 'Will the young sirs be requiring credit?' he'd lisped, then told us that unless we were eighteen, our fathers would have to sign the HP agreement for us.

'We are both old enough anyway,' I had told him, as I handed over the ten pounds deposit that he asked for. I don't think he believed us, but a sale was a sale after all. Floyd had scribbled down Winston's name, and I had said mine was Charles Roberts. We had ordered them before my dad had died, but I would have just told my old man that the shop had made a mistake if he found out. Now, that didn't matter anymore.

'Don't wear them in the club,' Rocky said. 'Everyone gets changed into T-shirts. Take a pair of cords or parallels with you. You'll be sweating like a pig. 'Sides, you won't be doing much fancy footwork if you're dressed up. And go with at least one spare shirt, then you can swap it again. You'll need a towel as well. It gets hot in there. Anyway, if any of you want to go, you have to be a member – and over eighteen.'

That was no problem for Floyd or me; we had already

applied for and received back our membership cards, although we'd lied about our dates of birth.

As several of the other lads said they were thinking of going, it seemed that there would be a dozen of the gang heading there.

Cadger took me, Floyd, and Rocky, to one side.

Here it comes, I thought. "Can I . . ?"

'I've passed my test,' Cadger murmured, low enough so that Nutter and the others couldn't hear. 'I should be able to borrow my mother's car – if you three can pay for the petrol.'

I had the feeling that we would be subsidising him, but it was better than the alternatives.

'Still not sure if I'm going,' I told him, 'but if I do – you're on.'

I was also not sure if Maureen would be happy if I went. We had both been to the Torch in her car one Friday night. The trouble was, she said that she had to be home by twelve thirty, or her father would be mad at her. That meant we had to leave the club at eleven, just as it was getting going, so that we could make it to her house in time. I couldn't understand her; she would soon be nineteen after all. 'Why not tell him you're staying out late. You're old enough to do what you want.'

'It's not that,' she had told me. 'Daddy insists that while I live with them, I do what he says. But I can come and go as I please if I have my own place.'

'Why not move out then? Get a flat. Then you won't have to bother. Maybe I could move in with you. Just think how nice that would be.'

And it would be fantastic if she had somewhere of her own I thought. None of this rushing back from a nightclub, mostly just having a quick neck in her car, then watching her drive away. We could go home whatever time we wanted, then in the morning . . . It would be a damned sight better than things were now. I could see why Maureen was

248

reluctant to leave her parents though; I would probably have felt the same if I had everything that she did.

One night, after we had been to the pictures, Maureen had invited me back to her home.

'I can drop you off at your house later,' she told me.

Later – after what? I'd wondered. Perhaps she was going to let me screw her at last. In the cinema, she had let me put my arm around her, my other hand resting in her lap. She hadn't objected when, hidden by our coats, I had manoeu-vred my fingers below the hemline of her dress, then slid them along her thigh. She had gasped, then opened her legs slightly, as I caressed her. She had been wearing tights, so my fingers couldn't explore further, deeper, but I could feel the heat and the dampness of her through the fabric. Several hairs had escaped through the weave of the cloth and brushed against my fingertips, as she slid forward in the seat, to press herself against my touch. I wondered what it would be like to feel them rubbing against my groin, when I was ramming away inside her.

Maureen slid her left hand onto my leg, then higher still, resting against my bulging penis. My heart began to hammer, as, hidden by the blackness, her slender fingers unfastened the buttons of my jeans. Tonight was going to be the night, finally, I thought, as her hand slid between the fly of my Levi's, touching me through the soft cotton of my boxer shorts. I twitched in response as she gripped me through the, by now damp material, praying that she would put her hand inside my pants, touch me. She didn't, just held me as I slowly writhed against her palm, seeking fulfilment that way.

'Not yet,' she breathed into my ear, just as I was about to explode. Maureen withdrew her hand, then pushed my own away from her groin. The lights came on, a minute or so later. The film was over and I had hardly seen it.

We left the cinema. My prick was still hard, and I had to cover the damp patch at the front of my jeans with a film guide. Maureen was smiling misty eyed at me. It was then as

I was bursting with frustration, that she asked me back to her home.

As the car crunched along the short gravel drive to where she lived, I could see why she was reluctant to leave. A large double-fronted Georgian-style house was illuminated by the Escort's headlamps, as Maureen braked to a halt in front of the white columns that framed the porch.

The building was in darkness. 'Is your old man out,' I asked, as she unlocked the front door.

Maureen whispered for me to keep quiet. 'They're in, but once they've gone to bed, so long as they know I'm home, they don't bother me.' She led me into a small sitting room. From the magazines, records, and stuffed toys scattered around the room, it didn't look as if Beresford used it much. 'This is my place,' she told me. 'Daddy's got his own study, and Mummy uses the lounge, so I flake out in here.'

I had been hoping that she was going to sneak me to her bedroom, but this would do I thought, as she moved a smiling teddy bear from the end of a large sofa, so that I could sit there.

'Drink?' she said, as she put an LP onto a record player at the side of the fireplace.

I nodded. 'Rum and coke – if you've got it.' I don't know why I said that; someone who lived in a massive house like this would be sure to have everything.

As Otis Redding began to croon out *Dock of the Bay*, Maureen adjusted the sound down a bit. 'My parents' bedroom is at the other end,' she said, 'but I don't want to wake them. Shall I put the fire on?'

I was still in a daze, thinking of what was to come, and I'd nodded before I'd realised what she'd said. I was feeling hot, remembering back to when she'd touched me, and anticipation was making me warmer still.

Maureen took a match from a box on the mantelpiece, struck it, then bent to apply it to the gas fire.

My prick sprang up again as her mini-dress tightened over

250

her buttocks, as she reached for the gas tap with her free hand. It took all my willpower not to jump to my feet, roll her dress up over her back, tear down her knickers, and stuff myself between her cheeks. You must wait, my brain cautioned; it would be ecstasy for me, but not the ideal way for Maureen to experience her first lover. And that's what I would be, if everything that she had told me was true.

I smiled at her as she left the room to fetch our drinks. Every time I had tried to take her further she had resisted. The rumours were right; she was a virgin. King Mod must have been surprised; bet the great lover hadn't let on that he had failed.

'My mother always told me to respect myself,' Maureen told me, when we had left the pub one night and were sitting, necking, in her car. 'And that's what I'm doing. I treasure my body – and I want the first man who makes make love to me to do the same.'

This was all strange to me. Other girls I had courted had let me shag them within the first few dates, some on the first night even. Those that resisted longer, perhaps for a day or two, had let me finger them, or fondled me in return. Maureen was different; until this night, I'd not been allowed to touch her or caress her. But this was it, at last.

Maureen came back into the room with two sparkling crystal glasses on a silver tray.

Very posh I thought, as she set them on the table in front of me, then closed the door that led from the hallway.

We sipped our drinks, then kissed. As Otis moved on to *My Girl*, I ran my hand over her breast then down and along her thigh, feeling the warmth of her flesh as I found the waistband of her tights. She didn't resist, just eased herself off the cushions, as I pulled both her tights and her white panties down together. I knelt on the floor in front of her, then tugged them down further still, over her knees, until they were tangled around her ankles. Her mini-dress still covered paradise, and I pushed it upward over her flat white belly, revealing a tangle of gold-red curls. She was a genuine redhead I thought as I nuzzled at her body, my nose investigating the softness of her; her hair was not as bright a red as that on her head but still looked wonderful to me.

'Oh Kenny, I like that,' Maureen sighed, as my tongue probed deeper.

She was wet, in fact she was soaking, and I couldn't wait any longer. I leaned back then unbuttoned my jeans. What about a condom I wondered, as I shrugged both my jeans and boxers down; I had a pack of three in the pocket of my Levi's but Maureen had not mentioned using anything, or said she was on the Pill. Play it by ear I decided, as I manoeuvred my throbbing prick between her thighs.

'No, Kenny,' Maureen gasped as the wet tip of me touched her leg. 'Not yet.'

What did she mean, not yet? I was bursting for her. Another minute or so and I'd be splashing over her belly.

'Let's lie on the floor,' she murmured, shrugging her tights free of her feet.

This was more like it. Maureen was right; it would be nicer to have her naked alongside me. As she slid off the cushions, I reached behind her and unzipped her dress. By the time she had pulled it over her head, my jeans and shirt were on the floor too, piled on top of my socks and shoes. I hugged her to me as we knelt there, my prick pressed against her belly, burning to be inside her. My fingers found the clip at the back of her bra and it sprang undone. As Maureen shuffled her shoulders, it fell clear of her boobs. I snatched it out of the way then cupped one breast in my hand.

I had her naked – and she was the most beautiful girl I had ever seen, far prettier in every way than the girls I had ogled over in magazines. Her tits were not as big as some of the other girls I had undressed, but they were firm, and her nipples were surrounded by dark red, almost brown, areolae, almost two inches across.

I gasped with delight then eased her down onto the

252

sheepskin hearthrug, in front of the fire. I positioned myself astride her.

'Lie down beside me, Kenny,' Maureen whispered.

I looked at her curiously, wondering what she had got in mind. As I stretched out next to her, she reached over and grasped me. 'Jesuuus,' I breathed as she moved her hand slowly up and down. 'Do too much of that girl and I won't be . . .'

'I don't want to – I don't want you to sleep with me – but I like this.' She rubbed her thumb over the glistening tip of me.

What did she mean, sleep with her? I didn't intend to do that. I just wanted to screw her, again and again, until morning came. I began to roll on top of her.

'Please, Kenny. Not until we're married.'

Married? I didn't remember saying anything about that. She tightened her grip, then relaxed it again, then tightened it again . . . 'Oh, Maureen,' I cried, as I soaked her hip, her breasts, the carpet . . .

Since then, although she would let me finger her, strip her, kiss her, she would not let me go the whole way. She would caress me until I came, but that was as far as it went. I had some beautiful sensations and thrilled at her touch, but was beginning to get a bit frustrated with it all.

'If you really love me,' Maureen had told me on our last date, 'then you'll wait for me.'

Would I? That was the question. Well, I wasn't going to be waiting for her next Saturday. Perhaps if I began to lose interest she would crack.

Yes, sod it. I would go to the Torch All-Nighter.

28

Music

'Are you sure we're at the right place? ' Floyd said, as we walked across a cobbled market square.

All around us were dingy shops and pubs, none that I recognised from my previous visit to the Torch. Then I saw the stone clock tower in the middle of the square. I could remember that. I turned. Yes, there was the Sneyd Arms at the bottom of the square; there was no mistaking the pub where everyone met, before going to the club. 'Said we should have driven on a bit more,' I thumped Cadger on the shoulder. He had told us he knew where to go, and had ignored both mine, and Rocky's, directions.

'It's a shortcut,' he murmured, when we said he should have gone left, and not right, at a roundabout.

It was some shortcut; we had nearly ended up in Crewe. Still we were here at long last, and, unlike other clubs, we had until after eight in the morning to enjoy ourselves.

We had left the girls at Annabellas. I'd told Maureen, earlier in the week, that the gang was planning to go to the next All-Nighter, and suggested that she come with me. We could go in her car.

'I'd still have to be home for twelve thirty,' Maureen said, 'and I thought it was a bit of a dump.'

Perhaps she was right, the imitation marble décor and the

"stone" pillars had looked a little jaded at our visit, but the music more than made up for that. The locals hadn't been very friendly either, they'd scowled at us as we went in and I'd thought we were going to get done over. Rocky said it was different at the Nighters though; everyone was there to have a good time. The bar was shut too; that meant the divs who wanted to get pissed, then have a fight, didn't bother going.

'And I never got the stains out of my cream jacket. I had to throw it away,' Maureen added.

On our way up the steps, to the balcony overlooking the dancefloor, Maureen had stepped away from the wrought-iron stair-rail, with its spear shaped bars, to let a girl coming down get past her. Unfortunately, Maureen's jacket had rubbed against the wall underneath one of the twin torch lamps. Her sleeve had gained a damp brown mark, from cuff to shoulder, where the nicotine from hundreds, maybe thousands, of cigarettes had found a home.

'Perhaps we could go to the pictures again. *Love Story* is on this week. Or maybe ten-pin bowling,' Maureen said.

Carnal Knowledge was on too. I'd seen it advertised in the evening paper. If I went to the cinema with Maureen, I would have preferred to watch that, maybe get her juiced up a bit. No way did I want to see a soppy film instead. 'I shall be going to the Torch anyway – I've promised the lads,' I told her. 'Perhaps we could meet up before I go.'

Maureen said at first that she was going to stop at home that Saturday and wash her hair. Then she had changed her mind. 'Why should Anne and I stay in – while you're out having fun? No, we'll go to Annabellas. See us there if you want.'

And that's what the girls had done. When, at just after nine, Cadger had beckoned to us from the top of Annabellas stairs, I had kissed Maureen then got up to go.

'Enjoy yourselves,' both Maureen and Anne chimed in unison. 'We shall – while you are away.'

As Floyd and me circled around the dancefloor, King Mod had grinned at me as if to say, "I'm in there, while you're away."

I glared at him, deciding that if I found out he'd been anywhere near Maureen, he'd be spitting teeth for a week or more. He'd need some more work doing on his mouth; wouldn't be much of a ladies man with a set of dentures clacking away.

'Think the girls will get off with someone else?' Floyd said, worriedly.

'No,' I told him, although I wasn't all that sure myself. 'They're just trying to stop us going. Besides, if that's how they feel – what's the point of us getting serious with them?'

Floyd seemed doubtful, but he began to look a bit happier the closer we got to Stoke.

'Call in at the next services,' Rocky had told Cadger, as we rumbled along the motorway in Cadger's mother's Triumph Herald. 'I've heard we should be able to get some gear there.'

'And I need a piss,' Eddie Duncan said.

He'd found out about ·Cadger giving us a lift and had browbeaten a place in the car for himself. His bulk had made it a bit crowded in the Herald, and Duncan hadn't forked out his share of the petrol money yet.

We had stopped off at Keele, and had a quick coffee. Rocky told us that some of the dealers hung around the Services and asked if we wanted anything. I told him yes, as I was determined to make a night of it. Floyd declined. 'I enjoy myself without them,' he said. 'And my old man would kill me if he found out that I took anything.'

Duncan pulled some cash from his pocket.

I took a quid of it then tossed it to Cadger. 'That's towards the petrol,' I said.

Cadger picked up the note then put it with some money he took from his jacket. Our petrol money presumably. He handed it to Rocky.

'I've already paid my share – to fill the car up before I fetched you,' Cadger explained.

More likely, his mother had done, and he was getting a free ride off us.

Duncan scowled at me, then pushed some more money towards Rocky. 'Bombers if you can get them.'

'I'll try,' Rocky said, pushing his spectacles back onto his nose.

He came back, some ten minutes later, then tucked a small paper wrap in my pocket, then palmed another to Duncan. 'Could only get Green and Clears,' he whispered. 'Keep 'em hidden. There's some black guys waiting to roll folks for their gear at the bottom of the stairs. I've heard they're tooled up as well.'

'So am I,' Duncan chuckled, flicking his cutthroat razor open onto the table. 'Put that away,' I hissed as I saw the cafeteria staff staring at us. 'Don't want to get searched now – and lose our stuff.'

We finished our coffees then got up to go, believing we still had plenty of time to get to the club.

That was before Cadger's shortcut. As we made our way to the car park, we met up with the black lads that Rocky had been on about. They were from Manchester I realised, as I heard them speak, and they were mean looking bastards too.

Floyd gave them five as we passed and, perhaps because he was with us, or because we looked ready to take them on, they let us pass without incident. I wouldn't have liked to come across them on my own though.

We had finally made it to Tunstall.

The pubs were closed, so it was lucky that we had picked up some gear on the way. I had my bearings now. So had Rocky. He led us across the top of the square, and then along Forster Street. As we turned right into Phoenix Street, I could hear the music even from that distance. I loved the sounds, but wouldn't have liked to live in one of the little terraced houses near the club, especially when there was an

257

All-Nighter on. At the bottom of the road, I saw the Roman chariot sign above the entrance to the Golden Torch. In another few minutes we would be inside. I couldn't wait.

A rush of hot air, the smell of sweating bodies, cigarette smoke, and various scents, some of them fragrant, hit me as I pushed through the glass doors. Then a tingle of excitement raced up my spine – and it wasn't just from the capsules I'd swallowed. Decibels of raw energy were vibrating the air. We paid our money over. Fifty pence for members – sixty for guests – for twelve hours of fantastic, foot-stomping, Northern Soul. Then another pound for the deal. I'd spent almost as much for a crappy few hours in Annabellas.

'*Exus Trek*,' Rocky grinned, as an instrumental pounded at our eardrums. He held up his BOAC bag, then winked. 'Don't want to put this in the cloakroom. I know some of the locals,' he said. 'Let's find their corner – then we can leave them there.'

We had stripped from our suits in the car, but had brought our bags with us, so that we had a change of clothes for later.

As my eyes adjusted to the darkness, I saw that the club was packed. There must be at least double, maybe treble, the number of punters that had been in on my Friday visit. It was only a small place, and the dancefloor was perhaps only twenty-five paces end-to-end.

How would we find room to do a few moves among that lot I wondered, as I looked over the railing that circled the oval wooden floor.

Rocky led us up the narrow stairway, which twisted its way to the balcony, at the opposite end from where Maureen had spoiled her coat.

He introduced us to several lads he knew from previous soul nights, or had met at the first couple of Nighters. 'This is Mickey,' he shouted into my ear.

I shook hands with a massive youth, who had short black hair, a boxer's nose, and hands like shovels.

'He's from Stoke,' Rocky said, 'that's Dave,' he waved to

a fair-haired lad, a similar height to me, 'and this gorgeous girl is Wendy.'

Wendy was gorgeous too, I decided, as she kissed me on the cheek. She had long dark hair, parted in the middle, held back, by a loose ponytail, from her oval face. Her curved eyebrows, high cheekbones, and soft brown eyes gave her a "come to bed" look. I wouldn't have minded taking her there either. She was wearing a black low-cut halter-neck dress that flared out wide at the bottom, white ankle socks, and dancing pumps. And little else I guessed as my eyes drifted to her cleavage; she certainly wasn't wearing a bra.

'Mickey's girl,' Rocky said, as if he knew what I'd been thinking.

I didn't fancy upsetting the giant Stoke lad, so decided that I would act like a monk where Wendy was concerned.

Rocky finished his introductions. I forgot most of their names that first night, but there was a lad called Martin, another Dave, Max, someone called Tomcat, a girl called Karen, and – I forget the rest. I had never met such a friendly bunch though.

'Should've been here last night,' Mickey shouted to us.

I could barely tell what he was saying as a fanfare of brass introduced a great sound that I'd never heard before; the sweet voice of a woman singing, 'I'm gonna love you a long long time,' echoed off the walls, almost drowning out Mickey's words.

'Edwin Starr was on. Brilliant,' he said as I leaned forward.

I nodded. 'Rocky told us he was on. Would have liked to see him.' I had debated whether to go or not. Rocky's brother had watched Edwin's performance at the Top Rank, a few weeks before, and told us how good he was. But, with tonight, that would have been two nights away from Maureen . . .

'Leave your bags there,' the fair-haired Dave said as the record faded. He pointed to where their stuff was stacked

259

under the table. 'No one will touch it,' he told me, when I looked uncertain about leaving it there.

Suddenly, everyone seemed to make for the stairs, as the insistent beat of a piano, then the sawing strings of the Tymes *What Would I Do*, began to echo around the club. We followed them, my body swaying along with the beat, as the already crowded dancefloor filled even more. I hurdled the last two steps in my eagerness. I wouldn't be able to move much I thought, but began to side step in a tiny gap at the edge. The atmosphere was amazing. The Torch had been good on that Friday night, but this was – different.

Great sound followed great sound. Some I recognised, like Sandi Sheldon's *You're Gonna Make Me Love You*, then came others that were new to me.

I would have to see if I could borrow Maureen's tape recorder; we could listen to them in the week then. Someone was belting out the words of *Angel Baby*, but it wasn't the Darrell Banks version I was familiar with. Rocky would know who it was, I felt sure, and he'd be trying to get near the DJ's about now if he didn't. As I swayed nearer the stage, I peered into the gloom but couldn't see him there, just the DJ's and some of their friends.

I didn't know the lad spinning the sounds either; maybe I'd find out when the DJ's swapped over.

'Fancy a drink,' Floyd yelled into my ear, as *Devil with the Blue Dress On* began to reverberate across the floor.

It was one of my favourites, by Mitch Ryder, but I was spitting sawdust despite the gum I was chewing, so I nodded and trailed him to the bar. They didn't seem to have any Coke so I settled for a bottle of Hubbly Bubbly cola. It helped quench my thirst anyway.

'What do you reckon?' I shouted to Floyd, as he wiped the sweat off his forehead with the back of his hand.

'Unreal,' he grinned. 'Trying any fancy moves?'

I didn't want to make a prat of myself out on the floor, so I shook my head. 'Think I'll practise a bit more – at home.'

Some of the crowd seemed to be novices like we were, but other, mostly older lads, must have been regular Wheel and Mecca goers; they made backdrops and spins look so easy. They could only do the moves when the rest of us left them a bit of room though; the floor was so tightly packed that I'd had a job to lift my arms up to clap. Try a high kick in here and you'd probably knock someone's teeth out, or they would yours.

'Did you see that lad near to the stage?' Floyd said. 'Thought I could dance until I watched him.'

I hadn't really noticed who Floyd meant, I was still taking it all in. I'd have a look though when we went back. He must be good if Floyd admired him; my mate was no mean mover himself.

The music faded briefly and the dancers suddenly started clapping. 'Another DJ's coming on,' I explained to Floyd as I realised what it meant. On my Friday night visit the dancers had applauded the exiting DJ, something I had never noticed before at other clubs. I missed the name of the lad who'd just finished, as well as the one who came on next; his words were drowned out by hundreds of hands cracking together.

'Let's have another spin,' I said to Floyd; I was eager to get moving again. My arms and legs just would not stay still as the blaring horns, then staccato drumbeat, and piano chords, of the intro of *Cracked Up Over You* sounded out. As we stepped onto the floor again, the female vocals chorused the singer's words. A great record for spins and drops, but it was so popular that the floor was crowded. It didn't matter though. I was enjoying myself.

More fabulous sounds followed. The DJ's introduced a few records they'd imported from the States, that none of us had heard before. We clapped the best and cleared the dancefloor if we didn't fancy the others. To my surprise though, they never took the record off, even if it was obvious that we didn't like it; just played it to an empty floor, to the bitter end. The DJ's would then try to salvage the situation by playing a favourite sound. The twanging guitar of *Sliced Tomatoes*, or the jerking rhythm of Sam and Kitty's *I've Got Something Good*, would soon get us on our feet again.

Later, when I went down the steps to the bogs, some of the lads queuing there stared menacingly at me. Were they debating whether to roll me for gear? Or did they think I was from the Drug Squad and were waiting for me to leave so that they could get back to their deals? I didn't care which; I just wanted to take a leak and then get out of there.

Rocky had told me that the police came in to the club undercover, but found it hard to pass themselves off as soulies. When we were taking a breather, halfway through the night, he had nudged me then pointed to a couple of lads who must be in their late teens, maybe even early twenties, and who were standing, stiffly, to one side of the dancefloor. 'Evenin' all,' he shouted, as we walked past them. They had turned and glared at us. The lads had close-cropped hair, but done as short back and sides, not skinhead or smoothie cuts. They were wearing Fred Perrys and cords but looked uncomfortable in them. I almost expected them to stand with their hands clasped behind their back. I decided that no one could mistake me for one of the squad, as the queue shuffled forward.

I was glad when my turn finally came and I was at the urinals; some of the other lads had given up waiting and had pissed on the floor. The place stank and the tiles beneath my feet were soaked. My nose wrinkled as I turned and squeezed out of the place again. Suddenly, a hand grabbed my arm. I spun round, fists clenched, expecting to be attacked.

'I know you, don't I?' the lad behind me said. He had a Midland accent, a bit like a Benny. He was tall, with long spiky ginger hair.

I stared at him. I knew him from somewhere. But where?

'Blackpool,' the other lad grinned.

Now I knew who he was. It was Keith, the big Walsall

skinhead we'd met there. We shook hands. 'Still with that girl,' I asked. 'Jill, wasn't it?'

'Yeah mate, he is,' another lad, a friend of Keith's said. 'They're getting married soon.'

'Like fuck we are,' Keith spat onto the floor.

'She's got a bun in the oven,' his friend grinned.

'And it's not fucking mine,' Keith scowled. 'Always used something.'

I tried not to smile as I thought back to Rocky and the Durex; Keith would kill him if he knew. Mind you, it was no laughing matter to be in that situation either, as I knew from experience. 'Nearly ended up the same myself,' I said, then told him about Shagbag. 'I could have been pushing a pram round by now.'

Keith told me that it was the first time he and his mates had been to the Torch. 'There's some good clubs round our way – but nothing like this. We'll be coming here again. See you later,' he said, as they headed off to get a drink.

I found Floyd and we hit the floor again. We danced and danced. As the night wore on the club became a little less crowded, as some of the people who hadn't dropped any gear, or those that had bought crap stuff, fell by the wayside and slumped over tables or against the wall.

Floyd kept going, despite not having indulged. 'Can't keep my feet still to these sounds,' he said, his shirt plastered to his ribs.

I think I'd overdone it a bit with the dexamphetamine though. As the lights came on and the DJ's played some slower numbers, to try to bring us down to reality, I was still raring to go. Then, after Jimmy Radcliffe's *Long After Tonight is All Over* finished, there was an eerie silence. But it wasn't silent I realised as, like many of the other soulies, I stared dazedly around. There was the noise the DJ's made, as they began to pack their records and the clatter of bottles being rounded up. Footsteps echoed around the building as people began to descend the stairway and cross to the exit.

263

Most of the clubgoers seemed to be talking in muted voices, unless it was just that it sounded that way to me. After a night of pounding Northern Soul, my ears seemed to be filled with cotton wool. I looked at my watch. It was eight-thirty. It had been just before midnight when we'd walked past the tower in the town square. Nearly nine hours had gone – just like that.

Soon, much too soon for me, we were blinking in the cold dawn of an April Sunday morning, shaking hands with the friends we'd made, promising we'd meet up again soon. I shivered as we made our way to the car, my clothes soaked with sweat. I wanted to go on somewhere but just like after the Mecca, this was it, nowhere else to go.

What a great night it had been though. It was another week until the next All-Nighter. A week of fixing some miserable bastards' cars, my face, and hands, covered with rust and oil. All for a measly few quid. Yes, a whole week. Nearly seven days – six of which I'd be stuck in that fucking garage, barely seeing daylight.

Roll on next Saturday.

29

Out On The Floor

'What time does the coach go,' I asked Rocky, as I secured the fan cowling of Floyd's Vespa back into place.

'Half seven. Gets us there for about nine o'clock. That gives us time to go to the Sneyd Arms first.'

'If I can get this finished in time, I'll come with you,' I said, as I searched for a missing bolt. 'Otherwise I'll go on my Lambretta and meet you there.' I knelt down, placing my eye level with the garage floor, hoping to spot the fastening silhouetted against the daylight. I couldn't see it, so I ran my fingers over the oil-covered concrete, to try and find it that way. It was a shame my father hadn't got round to putting more lights in the garage; it would have made it so much easier to work. I found the bolt, it was hidden by the rubber foot of the scooter's stand, and I screwed it into place. Not much more to do now, then I'd just need to get cleaned up.

'You ought to let Floyd fix his own scooter,' Eddie Duncan said. He was leaning on the wing of my father's little Fiat, smoking a cigarette. 'Met him in town earlier. He's taking the piss out of you. He says why should he get dirty – fixing his scooter – when he's got you to do it for him.'

'Lying bastard,' I said, as I tried the Vespa's kick-start.

'It's true,' Duncan scowled, then tossed the cigarette butt into the fishpond that my father had made behind the house.

The scooter coughed into life, filling the garage with blue-grey smoke. As it warmed up, and I eased the choke in, the engine settled into a steady tickover. I must admit I was getting a bit browned off with sorting the machine, but I didn't believe that Floyd was saying that. We had drifted apart a bit over the summer. Now, it seemed the only time I met up with him was at work, or, like this dinnertime, when his scooter had let him down again, and he'd pushed it round to me.

I didn't see him at the Torch much either; after his first All-Nighter, he had only been to a couple more with me.

'I enjoyed it, Kenny,' he said, 'but Anne won't come with me. If I keep going, I might lose her. I don't want that.'

And, probably at Anne's insistence, Floyd had signed up for college. I still hadn't got around to enrolling for the new term myself. I know I'd promised my old man, when he lay in the funeral home, that I'd keep it up, but there was always next year.

Floyd was doing a course in electronics, much to his family's delight, hoping that, one day, he could get a job repairing televisions and things. 'Might even try to open my own little business,' he told me.

That would have been Anne's idea again; she was always pushing him to better himself. I had no objection to that; it would be nice if Floyd could escape the drudgery of his labouring job. But it meant that, now, he spent two nights a week at the local Tech.

It was the same with the scooter. I didn't mind fixing it for him; I'd done that ever since we'd had them. I just wished he'd service it sometimes. Most of the problems came about because he hadn't changed the plug for ages, a simple job that anyone could do, or because the points were worn, things like that. If he'd spent an hour or so each week looking after the Vespa, it would save me all this hassle.

'Yeah, Floyd's not so dumb,' Duncan tried to stir again. 'There he is in town, clean as you like, with a pretty girl beside him. Why should he get his fingers black,' he chuckled at his own joke, 'when you're dumb enough to do it for him.'

I glared at him.

'Two pretty girls,' he went on. 'Your Maureen was with him. Is he giving her one as well?'

He fled as I dashed around the scooter. My spanner hit him between the shoulder blades before he got to the front gate, but it was only a small one, didn't hurt him. He was out of range before I could find anything bigger.

'See you tonight,' he yelled back, as he jogged off down the road.

'Take no notice of him,' Rocky said. 'He's only jealous 'cause you and Floyd have found someone.

'You're right. Who the hell would have him?'

'Why don't you go in this tonight?' Rocky said, opening the door of my father's Fiat.

'I haven't taken my test yet. I'm hoping to, soon. Be nice to use that when it gets colder.'

'Since when have things like tests and all that stopped you?'

'It's different on my scooter. But this was my father's . . .'

Rocky nodded, then pushed his spectacles back onto his nose. He probably understood me better than anyone; his father had been killed in an accident at work, a couple of years before.

No, it would be nice to use the little car, and roll the roof back on a beautiful summer's evening as I drove to Tunstall, but I just couldn't risk being pulled up in it. It was still registered to my father, although my mother had agreed that I could keep it. I didn't want any summonses in his name dropping through the letterbox.

Just have to be patient I told myself. A few more weeks and I could probably drive it legally.

I'd suggested to Ramsbottom that it might be useful if I could get a full licence. 'I'd be able to go out on breakdowns then. Or road test customers' cars,' I told him. 'Trouble is, I can't afford the lessons.'

'I'll see if Mr Beresford will agree to us paying for you,' the Service Manager said. 'You seem to be settling down now – putting all that skinhead nonsense behind you.'

I was doing it for my old man more than anything. And partly because I was fed up with getting into trouble. It gave you kudos with your mates, but things like that didn't impress Maureen, or her father. 'I shouldn't need many lessons,' I told Ramsbottom. 'I can drive a bit – and I've got my road sense from the scooter.'

He told me he'd do his best to get it sorted.

'You could get rid of the Lambretta. See if Gary can fix you up with a nice car,' Maureen said, when I told her later what Ramsbottom had proposed. 'And then you could chauffeur me around for a bit.'

I told her that there was no way I could buy a car from the garage, not on the money her old man paid me. If I could, I certainly wouldn't have wanted any favours from King Mod.

Beresford did agree to finance my driving lessons. I think Maureen had a bit to do with it. Plus the fact that the garage owner, while not liking the idea of me courting his daughter, probably thought that anything that would improve my status, and not lower his family's too much, might help.

'No, the coach sounds fine to me,' I told Rocky, as he sat in the Fiat and rocked the steering wheel. I refitted the engine cover, then rolled the Vespa outside. I stopped the engine and pulled the scooter onto its stand. 'You steer the car – while I push,' I told Rocky, motioning him towards the garage. The Fiat's battery was duff. It would start easily enough by bumping it, but here there was no need; it was a light car and the drive was level.

'That'll do,' I shouted as the front bumper nudged the wall at the far end of the garage. 'I'll get washed up,' I told him, as he squeezed out of the driver's seat. 'Then get ready. That'll give us time to go round to your place.' We were going to take some of his record collection to the All-Nighter, to see if the DJ's would spin a couple of obscure tracks that he'd found. They were on the B-side of some discs that had charted in the states; put there just to fill up the vinyl, but great dance tracks all the same.

Rocky was earning himself a bit of brass each week, buying and selling records. He didn't have any of the real rarities that were fetching up to twenty or thirty pounds in his boxes, but had a good range of discs that most of the clubgoers could afford. He was doing pretty well out of it. When we arrived at the Torch, he usually managed to sell several records. Then, as the night wore on, and some of the dancers wanted more gear, but had no money left, or they had spent their train fare home, they would come and ask Rocky if he would buy their records back again. He usually did, but not at the price they'd paid him earlier.

'It's business,' he would tell them. 'I can't sell it again for that much – halfway through the night.'

Some would tell him to get lost; others would do the deal. The following week, they'd often ask him if he still had the one they'd sold back to him. If he did, would he sell it to them again, for what they paid before! Some, desperate for cash, would bring a disc they'd paid perhaps ten quid for, to Rocky, or the other record dealers, then sell it again for a fiver, or whatever they needed for gear. And on it went.

I loved the music, but on my wages could only just about afford to get there each week, have a pint in the pub first, buy a bit of good stuff for myself, then a few colas. All I'd have left after I'd paid for petrol and things for the Lambretta would be swallowed up on my nights out with Maureen. My mother had never bothered to ask me for any board, since my father had passed away; he'd left her with a good pension and she was happy with that. I was too. It gave me a bit more cash for clothes and things.

I had once bought a record, *Queen of Fools*, with some money one of my aunts had given me. Rocky had been going on about how much it was worth, and I'd met up with a lad selling it in the Sneyd Arms for three quid. I was sure Rocky had said it was fetching ten quid or more. Pleased with my bargain, I had taken it to him.

'It's a boot,' he told me, shaking his head in disbelief. 'So long as you didn't pay much more than fifty pence . . .'

'Oops,' I said, my face turning crimson.

'If you paid more than a pound you were robbed.'

I daren't tell him how much; the rest of the lads would be taking the piss for months. I searched for the youth who had sold it to me but, wisely perhaps, he had disappeared. That was the one and only time I had a dabble in record buying. I was the "King of Fools" where they were concerned.

All the talk of what label a sound should be on, red, or white, or whatever damned colour, just baffled me. A big red "A" on the label meant it was worth something; a black one seemed to mean the opposite. Sort through that minefield, and there was the problem of knowing which record company had produced it. Buy something that labels like Chess, or Cameo Parkway, or Ric Tic, or Stax, or Mercury, had put out, and it was worth a bit, but buy the same sound on Decca, or MCA, or Pye, or Warner, and it could be worth fuck all. Something from Tamla, or Motown, the American labels, might be collectable, but buy it on Tamla Motown, the British label and it wasn't. Or was it all the other way round? It was all a bit above me. All that I wanted to do, every Saturday, was get blocked up then dance all night to fantastic sounds.

I didn't really give a toss what label they were on.

'Got any stuff Kenny?' Duncan whispered in my ear, as I stood at the balcony rail, watching the dancers below.

'Piss off Eddie,' I told him. 'You still haven't paid me for the other stuff I fixed you up with.'

'I'll give it to you on Monday,' he wheedled. 'My mother owes me some money – then I can settle up with you.'

I could just picture his mother, Paulina, humping away with some man, just to give Duncan some money. No, she would blow it all on drink.

'Please Kenny. It's no fun when everyone around you is smashed – and you aren't.'

'Ask Rocky – or Cadger.'

'I have done. They said you had bought some Blueys in the pub.'

'They're down my neck,' I told him. 'I have got some . . . But no, you wouldn't want that.'

'Want what? I'll take anything you've got.'

'I brought a twist of whizz with me – just in case I couldn't get anything better,' I said. 'Don't know if it's any good though. That's the trouble when you don't know the dealer.'

And that was a problem we were facing. The police were trying to crack down, and were searching anyone they suspected of pushing gear. What a joke calling the dealers "pushers," they could sell everything they got their hands on without much difficulty, especially when the police raids caused a shortage.

A lot of clubgoers' cars, and many of the coaches that brought us here, were being pulled up as they left the motorway and headed for Tunstall. The vehicles were thoroughly searched, the soulies would have their bags, clothes, and pockets checked. The locals managed to get through, as they knew how to detour around the police roadblocks, and they had told us the way too. The trouble was the police had discovered that the motorway services were another popular dealing scene, and they kept a close watch on them. Slowly, we were being forced to buy our stuff further and further away from the club.

The local Chief Constable had said, in the papers, that he was going to stamp drug taking out, even if it meant closing the Torch. So far, thankfully, he had been unsuccessful. My Aunt Vi had seen the report, as well as reading in her local

271

paper, the Sentinel, about some lads being fined for possessing drugs. The divs had told the police they were going to the Torch, causing the club to attract even more interest from them. Helpful as always, my Aunt had sent the newspapers to my mother.

'They're on about that place you go to in here, Kenny,' she said, one Saturday night, as I got ready to go. 'Does all this drug taking go on there?'

'I've never seen it mom,' I lied.

'Oh Kenny, be careful you don't get mixed up in all that,' she told me. 'I've read about people dying from heroin.'

'They don't take hard drugs – or so it says in there,' I added quickly, pointing towards the Sentinels piled on her chair arm. 'None of this injecting or anything goes on.' That wasn't strictly true; I had seen one youth, in the Torch bogs, squirting amphet powder, and water, into his arm to get a buzz. I would never do that; I hated needles too much.

'Just be careful,' she said. 'They say you can't stop taking them once you're on them.'

What a load of crap I thought; I could stop whenever I liked.

'I'll give you a quid for the whizz,' Duncan said, bringing my thoughts back to the present.

'Two quid,' I told him. 'And I want it Monday.'

'Deal,' he said, holding out his hand.

I knew he had no intention of paying, whatever the price. I peered around the gloom of the balcony. No one was watching so I dropped the twist into his palm. 'Don't forget you owe me,' I reminded him, as he scuttled away.

Rocky came over to me. 'Has he swallowed it?'

'No, but he soon will,' I told him.

Like me, Rocky was pissed off with Duncan tapping him for gear. The previous week I had fixed Duncan up with some tablets.

'What are these,' he'd asked, looking at the small white tablets that I tipped into his hand.

272

'Same stuff as Chalkies – but they're tablets,' I said. 'Or so I'm told. The dealer says they're homemade – but good.'

We saw him half an hour later that night, at the edge of the Torch's dancefloor, chewing frantically on some gum, his eyes staring. 'It's fuckin' good gear,' he told me, loud enough for the nearby dancers to turn and look at him. He did a spin. 'I'll be up all night on this,' he laughed.

Rocky had winked at me. We both knew he wouldn't be. Puffin now worked in a chemists, and, although I was no longer seeing her, she had agreed to help us with our trick. She had hesitated at first until I told her who the victim was; last Saturday, Duncan had swallowed – and got high on – some worm tablets.

He had still come back for more this week though. I had persuaded Puffin to get us some laxative powder. Mixed with a bit of whizz, to get the required smell and taste, and Duncan would definitely be up all night. And for most of the following day. I was still courting Maureen, but wondered if it might be worth chatting up Puffin again. Perhaps she could fix me up with some proper gear.

Would she supply me? It was worth thinking about. 'Let's hit the floor,' I said to Rocky, as a heavy guitar beat, then the shrill of horns, was replaced by the bass voices of the Dramatics, as they growled out *Inky Dinky Wang Dang Doo*. The lyrics were crap, but it was a record that always got my feet moving.

We passed Duncan at the bottom of the stairs. He was sitting on a bench talking to two older lads. There was something strange about them. What was it? Then I knew. They were the Squad. There's something about policeman and soldiers that, even if you see them out of uniform, you know who they are.

'Kenny,' Duncan beckoned me towards him. 'Got any more of that powder?'

Was he just being dumber than normal – or trying to drop me in it?

'What do you mean – powder?' I acted ignorant.

'I've taken some of it,' he said chewing away. 'It's good stuff. But these lads are looking for some as well.'

'Don't know what you're on about,' I said. I shrugged and began to walk away. I saw the two policemen look at each other. They must have decided that – a bird in the hand – and all that. They dragged Duncan away.

Guy Darrell was echoing out *I've Been Hurt*, by the time I mingled among the other dancers. Out of the corner of my eye, I saw Duncan being propelled past the pay desk. He'd be mad at me when they finally let him go, but I'd worry about that later.

The jerky beat of the Cooperettes' *Shing A Ling* filled the air, then a couple of sounds I didn't recognise; great to dance to though. The Blueys had been good gear; I was up and running. *Girl Across the Street* was another favourite of mine. The trouble was I loved them all, wanted to dance to every one of them.

Another gem was JJ Barnes with *Please Let Me In*. As he sang 'Same old two feet – walking down your street,' everyone in the Torch seemed to be side-stepping to the record, clapping in time with the beat. A shiver went up my spine as the noise bounced back from the bare walls. He was supposed to be coming to perform live at the club, any time now; that was one night I'd make sure I was here!

Mitch Ryder's *Breakout* was another smash with me. The rolling drums and screaming horns, of the intro, were followed by the plaintive guitar sound that came to my mind sometimes, when I was cruising along on my scooter.

As Mitch burst into song, it seemed to be the signal for some of the dancers to begin doing their stuff, in a sort of unofficial competition.

I had practised for hours, but didn't feel confident enough to stay out there. I could do the moves, but the art of it was to make one action follow the next – smoothly. Do a spin then stop at the wrong place, or stagger because you were

274

giddy, and everyone thought you were a right div. I wasn't going to risk it. All around me, other soulies were spinning and backdropping, but two lads, one of them the dancer that Floyd had been on about before, made it seem effortless. They would spin, drop back to the floor, flip up and forwards, touch the floor again, or spin then do the splits. It was fantastic to watch, and the rest of us just gave them room to perform.

It was a pity that Floyd hadn't come; he might not outdo them, but he could have given them a run for their money.

We clapped them, as the horns shrieked out for the last time. Mind you, no one could keep that pace up all night and they just side-stepped, along with us, for most of the other sounds.

I was getting quite good at some of the slower stuff though. At the tango-like sound of *One in a Million*, I started to glide across the floor. It looked effortless if you could perfect it, and your shoes didn't stick to the floor. Though I say it myself, I could make it look easy. Do too much of it though, and your calf muscles would be hurting for days afterwards.

You're the One, then another couple of floaters, and the pace changed again. I went to get a cola as the guitar, then female backing vocals, of *Love You Baby* began to sound out. I had tried many a time, but had never been able to find a pace to match Eddie Parker's rendition of the record. It was time to cool down.

I took the cola back to where I had left my bag, and sprawled into an empty seat. I took the, by now tasteless, piece of gum from my mouth and stuck it beneath the table. As I took the first swig of my cola, Rocky joined me again.

'What a great night,' he said, taking off his steamed up glasses and wiping them on his shirt.

It didn't seem to help; his clothes, like mine, were soaked.

'Hi, boys,' Mickey's girl, Wendy, said, as she came across the balcony to us. 'It's all right. Don't get up.' She plonked

275

herself on my knee. 'Just need to get my breath,' she told me, as she leaned back against my chest.

As usual, she was wearing a halter-necked dress, but white this time. She looked fantastic in it as she spun on the dancefloor. It flared out to reveal her long slim legs, and gave us all a flash of her skimpy white briefs.

The lads in the club would move back to give her room, so that they could watch her as they jogged nearby. The size of her boyfriend deterred any of them from moving in on her though, and now, as she sat on my knee, I was careful where I placed my hands. I had become friends with Mickey, and knew he wouldn't be bothered to see her there; he might think differently though, if he came back to find my hand on her butt.

'It's hot,' Wendy sighed, tugging the front of her dress away from her breasts and flapping it, backwards and forwards, to cool herself.

I couldn't help but look as her pointed tits jiggled under my nose. Despite the fact that she was soaked with sweat and stank of cigarette smoke, I felt my prick beginning to respond. Although I'd tipped a load of pills down my neck, I became hard.

'Naughty boy,' Wendy murmured, as my body began to press at her thighs. It was obvious what my reaction to her closeness was. 'If only . . .' she said, then leaned forward. She threw her arms around my neck and planted her lips on mine. It was only a quick kiss, but her tongue darted between my teeth, making me rise even more.

Rocky dropped me in it, the twat. As Wendy drew away again, the straps of her dress fell from her shoulders. Instinctively, I grabbed for them, but only succeeded in catching her breasts instead. I gasped as her nipples pressed against my palms.

Barely had the shock of what had happened sunk in, when I saw the grin drop from Rocky's face. He stared sheepishly over my shoulder. I didn't turn round. I just knew that

Mickey was there. Rocky must have been wondering if he had spotted him untying her dress.

'Shove over,' Mickey said as he perched on the end of the bench.

My mouth was dry again as his bulk pressed against me.

'Biggest pair of tits in the place,' he growled, as Wendy reached behind her neck and tied the straps together.

'Who? Me and Rocky?' I tried to force a grin.

Mickey roared with laughter then punched me on the shoulder, almost breaking my arm in the process. 'She's got a younger sister – looks just like her – if you're interested.'

I told him that I was going steady with Maureen.

'Why don't you bring her with you next time?' he said. 'Could make up a foursome.' He winked at Wendy, who was by now properly dressed again. She slid forward over me to sit on his knee.

'Maureen's not really into the scene,' I stammered.

'You'll be a happy couple. One of you going to Nighters – the other staying at home. Does she indulge?'

I wondered what he meant for a moment, then realised that he was on about speed. 'Not really,' I told him.

Maureen had admitted to me that she'd tried a reefer, when one of her previous boyfriends had given it to her, but that was as far as she wanted to go where drugs were concerned; she had been terrified then that her old man would find out.

'Yeah, you're a well matched pair,' Mickey grinned.

Perhaps he was right. We didn't share the same tastes in music either. OK, Maureen liked soul, but it was the slower moodier stuff. She liked pretty clothes, wanted a nice house, kids even. I just wanted to have a good time while I was still young enough to enjoy it. Was it because of the difference in our ages? Or perhaps it was money; her family had never been short of that, since her father managed to make a success of the business after he came back from the War

Maybe we were just too different and our relationship

would never work. I still wanted to screw her though, and one day I would.

'Coming next week,' Mickey asked, as both he and Wendy rose to their feet and began to towel themselves down.

I suddenly realised that the DJ was playing *I Love The Life I Live*. A few more slow tracks and another night would be over.

'We're going to the All-Dayer – in Bolton – after here next week,' Wendy said. 'Why don't you come with us? You could have a quick wash at my flat – and something to eat.'

'Yeah, have a lift in my van, ' Mickey said. 'You too, Rocky.'

'I don't know,' I told them. Although I was still up, and desperately wanted the night never to end, Sunday was the day I recovered. By the time I got home, I would usually be coming down. A shower and a quick change, and I'd meet up with Maureen in the afternoon. I was not much company then, or Sunday night, I knew, and I was knackered the next morning at work. What would I be like if I followed a night like tonight with an All-Dayer?

'Perhaps another week,' I told my friends as we jostled our way down the stairs. It could be the end for Maureen and me if I did it too often. She grumbled about me going off every Saturday as it was. One thing I was certain of though.

There was no way Maureen would stop me from going to the Torch.

30

Hold To My Baby

In the reflection of the jeweller's plate-glass window, I saw Eddie Duncan crossing the road towards us.

'Shopping for a ring?' He spat onto the pavement next to the shop door.

'Yes, we are,' Maureen told him, coldly. She didn't like Duncan at all.

'He gives me the creeps,' she said, after we had left a pub where he was drinking one night. 'He's always staring at me.' She thought that I should have as little to do with him as possible. That was one thing I'd already decided on anyway.

'When is the big day?' Duncan spat again, causing Maureen to raise her eyebrows at me. 'Don't forget to invite us. Be yer best man again if you want,' he grinned. 'Like I said I would be – when you was gonna marry Shagbag.'

Maureen knew about that; a good job she did too, else Duncan would have dropped me in it with her.

'Floyd will be my best man,' I snarled at him. If ever it came about I thought, but didn't say. 'Besides, it's a long way off yet.' And I hoped it would be. A few nights earlier, I had been lying naked, next to Maureen, in her den. Once again, even though she had let me strip her, and toy with her body, she wouldn't let me go the whole way. I'd produced a pack of Durex from my pocket, hoping that she would go further if she knew that she was safe.

'I would love to, Kenny,' she had whispered into my ear, as she slicked her fingers along me, 'but . . .'

'I know,' I growled with frustration. 'You're saving yourself.' I stared down at her slim body, slid my fingers through the curls of gold-red hair, felt the moistness of her. I should just stick it in her, fuck her anyway. That would be the end of us, but it would be better than this. One day I wouldn't be able to stop myself. 'I don't know why you're holding back,' I said, wishing that it was my prick, not my fingers, probing at her body. 'We've been going out for months now. You must know how much I care for you.'

'But do you love me, Kenny? I need to know before . . .'

'Course I do,' I smiled down at her. 'But do you love me?'

'I wouldn't be here with you – doing this – if I didn't.'

'Then I don't understand why you won't . . .'

'It's not easy for me either,' she whispered. 'But it will be wonderful when we are married.'

Perhaps that was the answer. 'Supposing we were to get engaged?'

Maureen smiled at me as she gripped me tightly in her hand. 'Is that what you really want?'

Was it? What I really wanted to do was to push her back onto the rug and slide inside her. I nodded.

'You're sure?'

I nodded again.

'Oh, Kenny, it would be wonderful to be yours,' she murmured, then leaned forward to kiss the tip of me. I almost exploded onto her face as her tongue fluttered out. I waited for her to take me in her mouth, like other girls had done, but she didn't, just held her lips there while she caressed me.

Maureen moved her head away and smiled up at me. 'I've never done this before,' she said huskily. 'But it's nice . . .' She kissed me again.

'Maureen . . .' I wailed.

Whether she had done it before or not, she must have sensed what was about to happen and covered me with her hand.

Later, as we lay dozing together, I wondered if she would give herself to me when she had a ring on her finger. What a prize I thought as I drifted into sleep, my hand resting on her nipple.

Now, in our lunch hour, we were looking for an engagement ring, and Duncan would blab about it to everybody.

'Going to the Torch again on Saturday,' Duncan asked.

I shook my head. Although I hated missing an All-Nighter, I had another chore to do; I had to ask Beresford for his daughter's hand. I didn't really want to, but Maureen said that, if I was sincere about her, it was what I should do. She'd told me she wouldn't feel engaged until we got the ring, and her mother and father would ask her what it was when they saw it. I had suggested that she could just wear it when we were out together, then take it off when she got home. 'Just until we are sure,' I explained when she looked disappointed. She told me that she would be proud to wear my ring. So, if that was the price I had to pay to sleep with her . . .

'You can give me your gear, if you're not goin' then,' Duncan said. 'You owe me that. The bastard sold me some laxatives,' he told Maureen. 'The Squad told me they were,' he said, when I shook my head.

I wasn't denying that, but I didn't want Maureen to know that I dabbled in drugs. When the police had pulled Duncan, I'd guessed that she might find out that I gave him the stuff, so I had told her, part truthfully, that it was to stop him from pestering me.

Since then, I'd thought the matter had died down. It seemed that Duncan hadn't forgotten about it though, although he'd never paid me anything.

'Yeah, they said it was laxatives and just a bit of whizz,'

Duncan told Maureen. 'Not enough to do me. Twats kept me in all night though.'

'I'm surprised you didn't go on the run,' Maureen smiled thinly at him.

'They would have caught me again,' Duncan said, not getting her joke.

I was relieved that she could smile about it. Perhaps she wouldn't delve further, I thought, as Duncan spat again, then went on his way.

'You're not getting into drugs and things, are you Kenny?' Maureen said, pulling me round to face her.

'No, like I told you, it was just a joke we played,' I said. 'Anyway, let's find that ring.'

'Two rings. You said you would wear one as well. You will be careful, Kenny,' she said, as she watched Duncan disappear out of sight.

Was she talking about Duncan – or drugs, I wondered?

'What wonderful news, Kenny,' Mrs Edmonds said, as she heard me tell Floyd about the engagement.

I'd not said anything before, hoping that it wouldn't be necessary, but now that Duncan knew . . .

'Congratulations mate,' Floyd said, gripping me in his arms, then picking up my hand to examine the ring that Maureen had bought me.

'Perhaps we'll be having a double wedding,' Floyd's old man said, winking at his son.

I doubted that; although things had been getting serious between Floyd and Anne, Floyd had told me that he didn't want to settle down just yet. I knew the feeling.

'How do you fancy being a bridesmaid for them both,' Mr Edmonds said, putting his arm around Cheryl's waist.

'I – I couldn't,' she stammered. 'Everybody looking at me.'

I was sad about that. If I ever did get married, I would have loved Cheryl to be the bridesmaid.

Cheryl shook herself free of her father. 'I'm happy for you, Kenny,' she said, then kissed me on the cheek, before running out of the room.

I was dumbfounded. I had felt the wetness of her tears on my face. 'I'm sorry. I didn't mean to upset her,' I told the Edmonds.

Her father looked at me. 'She's – um – she . . .'

'She's fallen out with her boyfriend,' Mrs Edmonds said, interrupting her husband. She gave him a funny look, as if to say, "It's Cheryl's business and don't tell Kenny."

'Oh, I'm sorry. I didn't know. Maybe I should go talk to her,' I said, turning towards the door.

'Let her be, Kenny,' Mrs Edmonds said quietly. 'She'll get over it. Do you fancy one of these Porcupines,' she asked, holding out a bowl of mango pieces.

I nodded my head. I had tasted them before and they were delicious, especially when the weather was as hot as today. The only thing nicer would have been one of the coconut and rum drinks that she sometimes made. The Edmonds called them "milkshakes" but they were nothing like those that Payne's café sold; the Jamaican ones would blow your head off. Not much use if you wanted to drive after.

This time, with the Porcupines, I remembered to take the "spines" out of the fruit and not swallow them. Cloves, I think the spiky bits were called. Cheryl had whispered to me that I didn't have to eat them, when she saw me grimacing at the taste.

It was a shame that she couldn't find a boy to love her I thought, as the fruit melted into my mouth. She was a pretty girl, and blossoming into a beautiful young woman. Cheryl would make someone a wonderful wife one day. And a fantastic lover I thought, as I imagined her athletic young body astride of me. I envied whoever did take her.

I was just wondering whether she would hold back until she was married, as Maureen was doing, when I realised that Mr Edmonds had spoken to me.

'What does your mother think of you getting wed,' he repeated, when I apologised and said I'd not heard him.

'She doesn't know yet. We only sort of decided today,' I told him. 'That's my next job.'

I'd not seen much of my mother just lately. Since my father died, she seemed to hate being in the house. Instead, she preferred to stay with one of her sisters. And she'd joined all sorts of clubs, even gone to night school just to get out a bit more; she'd done almost every course going – except learning how to cook.

'Your father would have been proud of you,' Mr Edmonds smiled.

And he would I thought. His son finally settling down at last.

But was that really what I wanted to do?

31

I Love The Life I Live

The Lambretta still went well I decided as I hurtled along. It had been several weeks since I'd given it a good run. I travelled to work on it every day, but that was different. It was great to feel the wind whistling through my hair.

What would it be like when everyone had to wear a crash helmet I wondered? They had changed the law to make it happen. It just wouldn't give the same thrill, this wonderful buzz.

I should turn for home soon. I needed to get ready for tonight. Maureen had suggested that I dress up smartly, even wear a tie, so that I could impress her father.

I wasn't looking forward to it one bit. Mr Beresford had never said anything about Maureen and me going out, but he made it pretty obvious that he didn't approve. I don't suppose that I would have either, in his position. Why invite a penniless young troublemaker into his family, when Maureen could have her pick of the local businessmen's sons. Maureen had told me how her parents tried to matchmake, when they took her to Conservative Club dinners. Not a scene I fancied much, I must admit. Would I be expected to go to them when we were married? I hoped not; I couldn't see them playing Northern Soul at their dances. Perhaps I could suggest that they hire Rocky as a DJ for one of their do's. It would be good to see their faces, when I did my first backdrop.

I blinked my eyes and turned my head, to deflect a wasp that had bounced off my screen. I had learned long ago to keep my mouth shut when riding the scooter; it was bad enough swallowing a fly . . .

My last day of freedom, a voice said inside my head. Was it? Or was it the start of something better? I loved the Lambretta, but was becoming spoilt by being driven around in Maureen's car. As well as the lessons that the garage paid for, Maureen had put L-plates on her Escort, and then sat in the passenger seat to give me more time behind the wheel. I preferred her to drive though; it meant my hands were free to wander over her body. We had sometimes gone out in my father's little Fiat too. Maureen had said that, when we had a mortgage and things, we would need to sell it, as well as my scooter. I was unsure about that; the car was virtually all I had left that was my father's, except for a few medals, in a drawer, that my mother said would be mine one day. And the Fiat cost sweet FA to run.

Would I sell the Lammy? Might have to, the voice inside my brain said. I'd certainly had some good times on it. I smiled as I remembered screwing Puffin, or some other chick, after they had ridden on the back. There was something about a scooter that made a girl who'd sat with the engine throbbing below her, want something else to be throbbing inside her. They already had their legs wrapped around you, so you were halfway there anyway.

I wouldn't be doing any of more of that, once I was married. But then again, would I want to? I could easily imagine how fantastic it would be, to sleep next to Maureen every night, reach out in the bed to find her lying there. No, she would be more than enough for me. I had never met anyone who made me feel like she did. And not just in a sexy way either; she was always behind me, believing that I could do better. It was working; I had kept out of bother and didn't have a lot to do with the Hole in the Wall Gang nowadays. The things they did seemed childish now.

Then I thought back to last week's All-Nighter, when Junior Walker had appeared live. He was more mainstream soul than Northern, but what soul! I'd shivered as his saxophone almost spoke to me, as he blew into it. And him and the All Stars had remained on stage for ages, coming back to give us more when we all shouted for him again. Junior played *How Sweet It Is* and *What Does It Take*, bending over backwards at the knees, until his head almost touched the stage behind him, all the while playing his sax. Then he raised himself up again without losing a note. What a performer.

Mickey, the Stoke lad, told me that the band had also been on at another club earlier that night. 'Two pounds to go in and he was only on for an hour or so, is what I've heard,' Mickey said.

Well, at the Torch he was on for at least twice that long, and for about half the admission money. We loved him, and just wanted him to keep playing that sweet soul music of his. Junior must have been enjoying it just as much; although sweat poured off him, he gave everything that night. And we had hours of non-stop dancing, to some great sounds, after that.

That's something else you'll have to cut out, my mind nagged again. No more All-Nighters when you're married! Then again, it wasn't as if I was going there to pick up another girl; it was just to get blocked up, have a good time, then home again. Maureen wouldn't go with me. I'd tried to persuade her, but she just wasn't into Northern Soul like me. And it must be a bit of a bummer if you didn't take gear, and everyone around you was having a good time while you were ready to drop. It was a shame, but it wasn't her scene at all.

It won't be yours either soon, the voice said.

Maureen had told me that she wouldn't stop me going, but wished that I didn't. She was frightened that I'd get mixed up in all that went on there. She said that it would be the end of us, if she thought that I did gear; her father would not allow her to see me then.

What she doesn't know won't hurt her I thought, as I pulled out to overtake a slow moving lorry.

Out of the corner of my eye, I saw someone waving to me from the grass verge on the opposite side of the road. There was nothing coming the other way, so I risked a quick glance. It was Webster; he wasn't waving but shaking his fist at me. What was he doing there I wondered, as I returned to the right side of the road. Then I recalled there had been a can in his other hand; he must have run out of petrol – somewhere close by. I scanned the road ahead, then saw his Anglia. It was in a lay-by that had been formed when the road had been straightened at some time; I could just see its black bonnet poking out from behind some bushes that separated the lay-by from the road.

I looked in one of my mirrors, then, when I saw there was nothing close behind, swung into the far end of the lay-by. I rolled towards the Anglia, wondering if Martin or any of Webster's other mates were in the car. It was hard to tell because of the tinted windows. I guessed that if any other greasers had been inside, they would have soon bundled out when they heard my Lambretta approaching. Easy Rider could be in it though, keeping her head down until Webster returned.

I pulled the Lambretta onto its stand. I couldn't see anyone. The front windows were half open, to let out the heat, so I peered into one. Nobody! I looked around the lay-by. There was another car at the end of it, but that was empty too. This was a popular spot for fishermen to leave their vehicles while they dangled their rods, or whatever, into the nearby canal. The other driver would probably be gone all day.

I lifted up the seat on my scooter, and took out the large monkey wrench from between the springs. I normally used it to secure the large nut on my rear wheel if it came loose, but it would do for this job too. I would sort the car, then go after Webster. I owed him that before I finally settled down.

Passing traffic couldn't see me; they would have to come into the lay-by to do that. I whacked the Anglia's nearside headlamp with the wrench, and glass shattered over my shoes. The offside one quickly followed. Then I smashed the taillights, sprinkling red and amber fragments onto the tarmac. It took a couple of hits to break the windscreen; the first impact cracked it, the next broke it into tiny shards. The side windows were a different proposition; they were made from tinted Perspex and my spanner just bounced off them. I opened the passenger door and leaned inside, gasping as hot dry air seared at my throat, even though the screen had gone. The Anglia must have been sitting in the sun for a while; Webster obviously didn't like walking, and must have tried for a lift first.

The car's dashboard had been customised. Webster had fitted some fancy gauges, to show fuel level and oil pressure, as well as a tacho. He'd put them in a black plastic centre-console that went downwards, from the bottom of the screen, to cover the transmission tunnel. The Anglia switches had been replaced, and added to, by those long black ones that were fitted to some Minis. Here they were for effect; on the Mini, they had been needed so that people could reach them with a seat belt on. There was also a radio tucked in another plastic housing that hid the metal parcel shelf. And the normally Spartan upholstery had been covered with black fake fur; it looked really naff. The switches flirted in the air as I swiped them off with my hand; it needed the weight of the wrench though to wreck the gauges.

I decided that I ought to set fire to the Anglia, for I was certain that Webster would smash my scooter and burn it if he found it. I slid out of the car to get away from the dry heat, then began to kick dents in the door panels. I didn't have any matches, but figured that, if I split the fuel line, I

289

could easily find some way to spark a fire. I whacked the sloping rear screen of the Anglia, sending a shower of glass across the back seat.

'You fucking bastard,' someone howled.

I turned, just in time to see Webster swinging the petrol can at my head. Thankfully, it was empty. But it still dazed me for a moment. The greaser must have suspected that I would find his Anglia, and raced back.

'I'll teach you to wreck my car,' Webster howled, then hit me with the can again.

This time it caught me on the shoulder. I grabbed it and wrenched it from his fingers. He kicked at me as I flung it into the car, making me wince as his steel toe cap scraped across my shin. His boot would have broken my leg, if it had connected properly, he'd put so much effort into it. But now he was off balance, so I thumped him at the side of his face, spinning him away from me.

'You're dead,' Webster spat, then wiped his mouth.

There was a knife in his hand. I hadn't seen it at first but I realised that, if I hadn't hit him, it could have been in my ribs by now. Still might be I thought, as I searched around for something to defend myself with. I'd dropped the wrench at Webster's first attack. It lay on the ground, next to the Anglia's rear tyre. Webster saw me glance at it; I knew that he would have me long before I could get my fingers on it. There was nothing else. The can may have helped, and acted as a shield, but it was too far inside the car now.

Webster grinned. 'I shall enjoy this,' he said, crouching, then moving forward, just like I'd seen Indians do in some corny cowboy films.

I looked at the blade. It was a bit like a Bowie knife too; it had a long wide blade, sharpened for a short distance on the top, as well as the lower edge. The blade gleamed where it curved back from the tip. Designed for hunting, or for ripping into my guts! Involuntarily, I sucked my stomach in, as if my taut muscles would stop such a vicious weapon!

Webster lunged forward, swiping the knife sideways across my ribs. I jumped back. He'd missed me. What could I do? I tried to remember what my father had said when, much to my mother's disgust, he had shown me some of his unarmed combat skills. My mind was blank though.

Webster stabbed forward this time, the steel blade jabbing at my belly.

I spun to the right, my right arm deflecting the knife away from my abdomen, my left grabbing his elbow. As he struggled not to fall over, I grasped his wrist with my free hand then smashed his arm down across my knee.

That's it lad, you've got it, my father's voice seemed to say to me, as the knife clattered from Webster's fingers onto the ground. I hadn't broken his arm though, as my old man would probably have done to someone who attacked him in this way, but I knew I'd hurt the greaser. Webster wailed in agony, as I used his momentum to throw him to the floor. I kicked the knife out of his reach, before he could grab it again.

'Come on then,' I yelled, as Webster began to scramble to his feet. I let him stand then flattened his nose, sending a spray of blood down the front of his shirt. Another punch closed his left eye. 'You won't ever try to knock me off again, you bastard,' I said, as my left fist found his other eye.

'I've had enough,' Webster sobbed, peering dazedly through swollen eyelids.

I hadn't though! I hated the bastard for what he'd tried to do on the first day I rode out on my scooter, and now it was payback time. I kicked him in the balls.

'I – ooff,' he exhaled noisily and bent forwards, clutching his groin.

My knee connected with his chin, jerking his head back. Even above the sound of passing traffic, I heard his teeth snap together.

He collapsed to the ground.

'Come on – I haven't finished with you yet,' I yelled,

291

kicking him in the buttocks. Webster didn't reply, just moaned as he curled into the foetal position. I kicked him again.

Somewhere within my brain, I knew I was releasing all my pent up anger and frustration on Webster. I booted at his ribs; he curled up tighter. I hated myself, for not being there for my father, and for all the pain that I'd caused him. I booted the mop of black hair on the top of Webster's head, making him sob with terror. I hated my job; my hands always covered in cuts and bruises, the pores of my skin always filled with oil. I kicked his legs, but he gripped his shins tightly, preventing my foot from penetrating deeper. I hated Maureen, for being the prick tease that she was. I kicked at his hands, trying to make him let go. I saw gold rings on his stubby fingers, reminding me of my own forthcoming engagement. I drew back my foot again.

'Oy. Leave him alone,' someone bellowed.

I turned angrily.

A tipper lorry had come into the lay-by. I hadn't heard or seen it arrive; I had been too busy sorting Webster. Its driver had climbed out the cab and was wobbling towards me. He was a big fat bastard, maybe twenty stones or more in weight, with a round piggy face. His belly strained at the holed once-white vest he was wearing, and it sagged down over his waistband, only prevented from bursting his fly buttons by a two-inch wide leather belt. Curls of black hair escaped over the top of the vest's neckline, and there were tattoos on his flabby arms. He had brought a jack-handle with him, and he was waving it in my direction.

'Let him be,' he said. His voice had the high pitch of most fat men.

'Stay out of it,' I snarled. 'He tried to knock me off my scooter – was going to kill me. Now he gets it.'

Webster moaned, as if to argue the point.

'OK kid, but he's had enough,' the lorry driver said, as he came to a halt several yards away from me.

As he faced me and saw the anger in my eyes, he seemed to have changed his mind about getting involved. He'd done his Good Samaritan bit, and could tell his mates later, in the pub, how he'd broken up the fight, but that was about as far as he wanted to go.

My arms and legs were beginning to tremble now that I'd stopped. I knew that if the truck driver hadn't intervened, I would probably have killed Webster. I looked down. The greaser had had enough; snot and blood trickled from his battered nose, mixing with the tears that streamed down his face.

I bent down, dug my fingers into the strands of Webster's greasy black hair, and tugged his head back. 'It's finished now. Got that!'

He nodded; his eyes puffed shut.

I rose to my feet again, saw that the lorry driver had not moved, then climbed on to my scooter. I glared at the driver as I kicked the Lambretta into life, as if to say, "You're next if you interfere," then I rode off. He may call the police, but I wasn't too worried about that; Webster had a reputation as a troublemaker, and I didn't think they'd be too keen to investigate.

Now, all I had to do was get home, get changed, then into the lion's den with Maureen's folks.

32

Our Love Is In The Pocket

'What's happened to your face?' Maureen said, running her fingers across my cheek.

'Bumped my head in the garage,' I told her, as I tugged at the tie that was trying to suffocate me. 'These are for your mum.' I stuffed a bunch of red roses into her hands.

I'd felt a right prat walking through town with the things. I didn't even get my mother stuff like that normally, but thought it may keep Mrs Beresford sweet. And if Mrs Beresford was kept sweet, then perhaps Maureen would be sweet to me – later tonight.

'Oh, she'll like these,' Maureen said, sniffing at the petals.

I doubted it; I'd seen a garden full of the things as I walked up the gravel drive.

'Do come in.' Maureen waved me into the hallway. 'Mummy and Daddy are in the lounge.'

I almost wiped my feet on the coir mat, set in a metal frame in the porchway, but knew it was because I felt I should, not because my shoes were dirty. I swallowed hard then followed her. She had a gorgeous arse I thought, as she swayed along in front of me; I could easily picture those soft round cheeks, feel the smoothness of her skin.

Well, that was why I was here. I fancied her rotten, loved her even, and if the only way to win her over was this . . .

'Come in Kenneth,' Mr Beresford said, rising from an armchair, then shaking my hand. 'You've met Grace?'

I nodded. I had met his wife briefly when I'd called to collect Maureen for a date. And I'd sometimes seen her at the garage. She was like an older version of Maureen, smaller, and a bit plumper, and with flecks of grey in her red hair, but still good looking. She reminded me of a film star who had lost her youth, but kept her beauty. It was obvious that Maureen took after her mother in everything but her height, that must have come from her father.

Mrs Beresford – "do call me Grace" – took my hand in hers and squeezed.

I saw her eyes swivel away from mine, to look at the livid bruises on my cheek and forehead, where Webster had struck me with the can.

'Bumped into the axle of a truck I was working on,' I lied.

'Big compensation claim next, eh?' Mr Beresford smiled wryly.

Maureen gripped my arm, as if to defend me from her father's taunt.

'It was my fault,' I said. 'Should have looked where I was going.'

'Drink, Kenneth?'

I nodded. 'Whisky will be fine.' It would be as well, no cheap rotgut stuff in here.

'What time did cook say dinner would be served?' Mrs Beresford looked at her daughter.

Cook? I almost expected to see Floyd's mum appear; that was the only time I'd seen cooks, in school kitchens or hotels. No wonder Maureen didn't want to leave home.

It seemed that I had another hour to wait before I embarrassed myself at the dining table; more than one knife and fork and I'd be bollocksed.

'Sit down, sit down,' Mr Beresford said, handing me a glass tumbler, half-filled with brown liquid, then waving me towards a large overstuffed leather sofa.

It was a chesterfield, and it faced a marble fireplace in which several logs were spitting and crackling. Two other sofas were at right angles to the one I sat on, flanking a large polished coffee table. My hands were shaking, and I wanted to set the drink down, before I spilled it on the expensive-looking rug spread out at my feet, but the glossy finish of the table didn't seem the place to put it.

'Glad you've come round,' Mr Beresford said. 'You've been going out with Maureen for some time now. It will be nice to get to know you better.'

I could only nod again. I took a sip of the whisky. My throat was dry but the spirits only made it worse. There was a small table next to the arm of the sofa. A lamp, its base made from an intricately detailed porcelain eagle, shone an amber glow onto a man in RAF uniform. He had the same bristling moustache as the garage owner. It was Beresford, but taken many years before. Maureen had told me that he'd been one of the "Brylcreem Boys" in the War.

That table wasn't the place to put my glass either I decided, as lamplight reflected off the French polish.

Soon, to my relief, we moved into the dining room. They had certainly pushed the boat out for my visit; silver dishes gleamed and cut glass goblets sparkled above a white linen cloth. Unless the family ate like this all the time! The table could have seated a dozen or more people in comfort and, now that Maureen was sitting opposite me, no longer there to support me, my confidence waned altogether. I could face up to Webster, or some mean-faced skinhead, but this was different.

I prayed for the meal to be served, then prayed that it would soon be over.

A grey-haired lady, who must be the cook, ladled some soup into a bowl in front of me. I don't know what sort it was, but I managed to splash it on the cloth. I dabbed at it with a stiff linen napkin, but only succeeded in spreading the stain further.

'It's all right, Kenneth,' Mrs Beresford said. 'Accidents do happen.'

She was only trying to put me at my ease, but it made me feel worse; I had hoped that none of them had spotted it.

As each course was served, I watched which piece of cutlery Maureen picked up first, where she placed her napkin, how she used her fork to gather the peas into her mouth. I didn't want to make a bigger prat of myself, but it was just one of those days; the sort where a potato has to roll off your plate, or a piece of carrot flirt onto the tablecloth when you try to slice your meat. Would Beresford want a clown like me for a son-in-law? I doubted it. I knew I wouldn't!

As I worked my tongue at a gap in my teeth, hoping to dislodge a chunk of beef that had jammed there, I felt something touch my ankle. It was Maureen's foot I realised, as she smiled at me, hoping to reassure me.

I gave her a feeble grin in response.

Her toes slid up my shin, beneath the edge of my trouser leg, touching my bare skin.

It had better be worth it I thought, and, as I looked into her eyes, I knew it would be.

Soon, pudding, or dessert, or whatever it was called, was out of the way too, and I'd only managed to get a bit of the cream onto my jacket.

'Shall we leave the menfolk to it,' Mrs Beresford said, rising to her feet.

I stood as well. This was one bit I knew from the films on TV; here was where the women went off to chatter, while the men drank port.

Maureen and her mother smiled at me, and Maureen touched my hand, as they left the room. This was it. The moment I'd been dreading.

'Cigar?' Mr Beresford said, then indicated I should sit in one of the leather chairs at the side of the dining room grate.

I had nodded again before my brain realised what he'd

said, and I stared at the box he held in front of me. Not wanting to look a twat once more, I took one of the cigars out. Thankfully, they were not those damned big things that Churchill used to smoke; at least I could stuff this one in my pocket.

He passed me some sort of nail clippers. 'You need to take the end off,' he said, then showed me how.

Now, the tobacco would all come out in my jacket.

He stooped to the fire, lit a spill, and then held it in front of me.

Shit! I was expected to smoke the thing! 'I don't – um . . .' I stuck it between my lips, and watched, almost hypnotised, as the flame danced in front of my nose. I sucked, just enough to get the tobacco glowing. And my stomach churning. Better not drag on it too much I thought, else I'd be throwing up over the hearthrug.

Maureen's father handed me another whisky. My head was really swimming now, what with the wine we'd had at dinner, then the cigar smoke filling my lungs. Much more and I would be lucky to remember why I was here. Better get it over with, as soon as possible. I steeled myself.

'Mr Beresford – I don't know if Maureen's said anything to you – but we would like to get married. She says that I should ask you first.' I breathed a sigh of relief. There it was, out in the open now.

He didn't answer for a moment, just stared at me, cigar poised in mid air. 'We always wanted a son, Kenneth,' he finally said. 'After Grace had Maureen, she lost . . . Well, let's just say we couldn't have any more children. I hoped that one day I'd have a son who would follow me, take over the business. It wasn't to be. It's how things work out sometimes,' he shrugged, then puffed on the cigar. 'What I'd want now, is for Maureen's husband to do that instead. Help her run the business when I retire. I'll be honest with you, Kenneth. I'm not sure if you could do that.'

'You mean I don't talk properly and didn't go to the right

school?' I muttered, then watched in horror as a lump of ash fell from my cigar onto the carpet. Beresford seemed not to have noticed and, surreptitiously, I scuffed it into the pile with my foot.

'It's nothing like that at all. It's just that you're not – a businessman.'

He was right there; running the garage had never entered my head. 'But I love Maureen – and I want the best for her,' I told him.

'And so do I – but I'm not convinced that it's you. Let me put my cards on the table. It's fairly obvious that we are let's say – well off – and that whoever marries my daughter could do all right for himself. I don't want her to be unhappy though – find that someone has married her to get all this,' he said, waving his arm around the room.

I told him that his money was the last thing I was after. I loved Maureen for what she was.

I wanted her body too, but didn't think he'd want to hear that.

'What I'm proposing . . .' He paused, drew on the cigar again, then blew a ring of smoke into the air. 'What I suggest is that we both save Maureen a lot of heartache. Have you seen those new Firenzas in the showroom?'

I nodded, then looked around for an ashtray, wondering what he was getting at.

'Well, how would one of those suit you?'

'I've got my scooter – and there's my father's car when I've passed my test,' I stammered. 'Maybe in a few years – but I couldn't afford . . .'

'What if I gave you one?'

I looked at him, curiously. Why would he give one of those away? Perhaps he didn't want his future son-in-law chugging into work in a little Fiat 500. 'I'm not with you,' I said.

'You get a new car – free. I'll even tax it and everything – but you stay away from Maureen.'

'But I don't want a car – and I love her,' I almost shouted, as my face began to burn with rage.

'If that's not enough – I can give you some money as well. How much?'

'How much what?' I glared at him. 'Oh, I see. This is some sort of test,' I grinned. 'You're just seeing if I really do love her.'

'Two hundred? Three?' Beresford pulled a chequebook from his pocket. 'No more than that, surely,' he said, when I didn't answer.

I suddenly realised that he was serious. He was trying to buy me off. I might be a bit of a bastard, but even I wouldn't sink that low. I fought back the urge to stamp the cigar into the carpet, then throw the whisky in his face. I put them on the table instead. 'I'd better go,' I said, then turned towards the hallway door.

'Five hundred,' he shouted, as I stormed out of the room.

Maureen came out of the sitting room as she heard our voices. 'Well?' she smiled, and then her face froze when she saw my eyes. 'What's . . ?'

'Ask him,' I said, pointing my thumb towards her father. I saw Mrs Beresford standing behind her. 'Thanks for the meal,' I said, then tugged open the front door.

'Kenny, what's up?' Maureen said as she ran after me. 'Has he said no?'

I turned, saw the tears in her eyes, and would have loved to hug her to me. Beresford would have just thought I was trying to put up the price though. Perhaps he was right; we weren't meant for each other.

'Come in the house, Maureen,' her father shouted from the doorway.

'You go in,' I told her. 'Let him explain.'

'Meet me at Annabellas later,' she sobbed. 'Please, Kenny.'

I looked at my watch. It was just before nine o'clock. If I hurried, I could still make it to the Torch. Nip home, grab my kit, get the Lambretta from the garage then away. How much petrol was there in the scooter? Enough to get me to the motorway I guessed, then I could fill it up at one of the service stations. It would cost a bit more, but I needed a good night out.

'Please, Kenny,' Maureen repeated, wrapping her arms around me, as if to hold me there.

'Gotta go,' I said, 'I'm off to the All-Nighter.'

'I'll come with you. Wait while I get my things.'

I watched her run to the house. The door slammed behind her. I didn't think Beresford would let her out again, so I headed for home. Once out of the drive, I began to run. I needed to think, but not tonight.

Tonight I was going to get smashed.

33

Good Time Tonight

'Thought you weren't coming tonight,' Rocky said, as I bumped into him at the top of the flight of stairs that led to the Torch's dance floor. His pupils were wide, made even more so by his thick glasses. He had obviously scored.

'Changed my mind,' I told him. 'Got any gear left?'

'No, but I think Mickey's got some Bombers. He's asking a bit for 'em. See what he says. I'll sniff around too – see what I can find for you.'

Mickey was not at the usual table, although I could see his things were there. I dropped my bag alongside the others, then went in search of the Stoke lads.

I stood by the rail that circled the dance floor and peered into the gloom, as the thrumming guitar, and whip-crack sound, of the Shakers *One Wonderful Moment* bounced around the club.

When my eyes adjusted, I saw Mickey's head and shoulders bobbing above the other dancers. No backdrops or spins for him, he was just too big. Mind you, he never had any problem finding room on the dancefloor.

Wendy was dancing near to him. She saw me at the rail and waved. Mickey turned then, when the record finished, they came over to me.

'Are we invited to the wedding?' Mickey grinned, as he

leaned against the wrought-iron rail. Even though the dancefloor was a couple of steps down from where I stood, his head still towered above mine.

'How did you know about that?'

'Rocky,' Wendy shouted up to me.

She was only about five feet tall, and I often wondered how the two of them managed to make love; there was no way Mickey could lie on top of her, he would crush her.

'Think it's all off,' I told them. 'Her old man's not keen on me. So I thought, bollocks to the lot of 'em.'

The jingling cymbals, then snorting saxophone of *Hit and Run* were blasting over the speakers, and I wanted to be out there. 'Can you sort me,' I shouted into Mickey's ear.

He looked thoughtful for a moment, then handed me a pack of cigarettes and a box of matches. 'In the fag packet.'

'I am a bit stuck . . .'

'Settle with me next week,' he said, as Rose Batiste faded away, to be replaced by *Free for All*. There was no pause; the DJ spinning the records rarely told anyone what he was playing.

I made my way to the toilets but when I saw the queue for the cubicles, decided to drop the gear somewhere in the darkness. I got myself a drink, then moved into the corner near to the bar. Surreptitiously, I flicked open the fag packet and tipped the contents partway into my palm. My fingers touched a couple of cigarettes then found several capsules. Without making it obvious, I couldn't look at them, so would have to trust Mickey.

Rocky had said he'd got Bombers, so I hoped that's what they were. They felt about the right size. It was unlikely that whoever had sold them to Mickey would have doctored them either, not if they wanted to live a bit longer. They would be expensive, but I would have a brill time on them. I popped the first one in my mouth, then washed it down with a swig of the soft drink. The others soon followed. A few more would have been nice, but, as the saying goes, "beggars can't be choosers." My tongue tasted a few shreds of tobacco, which must have stuck to the capsules, so I took another mouthful of cola.

As I put Mickey's fags on the table where our bags were, I saw a lad watching me. I didn't know him, and wondered if he was going to rifle through our things. So, although I wanted to hit the floor, I decided to hang around for a bit. Things had been going missing since the Squad had cracked down, and a few lads, desperate for gear, had taken to pilfering from other clubgoers. A dangerous occupation though; if caught, they would have the shit kicked out of them.

Another lad joined the first and, out of the corner of my eye, I saw his mate point to me. I moved to the balcony and looked around, to see if Mickey was still there. Being a regular, and local, he may know who they were.

Mickey was still dancing, but a few moments later, a mate of his, Dave, came back to the table. 'Surprised to see you here,' he said, as he slumped onto a chair.

How many more folk had Rocky blabbed to I wondered, as Dave towelled his face dry.

'Listen, Dave. See those divs next to the rail. Don't know who they are, but they've been looking at our bags – and watching me. I wondered if they were gonna roll me. They'd be out of luck – 'cause I've swallowed it.'

Dave rubbed the towel across the back of his neck, then turned his head, casually, towards the balcony rail. 'One's wearing a red shirt – the other a check Ben Sherman.'

I nodded, then tipped more cola into my mouth.

'Squad,' Dave muttered. 'Some they've brought in from London, hoping we don't recognise them. One of the Cockney lads remembered being pulled by them though, and pointed them out to us. Shit! I've got some whizz in my pocket. Hope the batards don't search me. '

Almost as he said the words, the two policemen came over. The tallest, a rough looking type, with a broken nose, leaned over me. I wasn't too bothered, all the gear was in me now; they would have a hard time pinning anything on me. But Dave could be in a fix.

'Got any gear you can sell us?' the policeman said.

I shook my head.

'What's in here?' He tipped Mickey's fags on the table.

'Nothing. Just my cigarettes,' I told him, and began to put them back in the pack. 'Come on, mate,' I said to Dave, and stood up. 'Let's go for a dance.'

Dave got to his feet to follow me.

Suddenly, the tall one grabbed my wrist; his mate wrenched Dave's arm behind his back. 'Come outside with us,' he said, as he twisted my arm behind me. 'We want to search you.'

'Who are you? I haven't done anything,' I yelled, as I was forced towards the stairs. Only the tight grip he had on me prevented me falling headfirst onto the hard steps. We were propelled towards the exit. I thought of the moves my father had shown me, and wondered whether I could kick back at his shins. I didn't have anything to worry about, but thought it might give Dave the chance to slip away. The policeman must have read my mind; he twisted my arm higher, making me squeal with pain.

Suddenly, the policeman shoved me forwards, violently, and I tumbled to the floor, my face pressed into the musty carpet. He landed on top of me, winding me.

'What the fuck. . ?' he rasped in my ear, his breath stinking of garlic and fags. He lost his grip on my hand.

As he struggled to his feet, I tried to squirm free.

'We're police . . .' the one who had been holding me shouted, trying to make his voice heard above the music.

'Like fuck you are,' said another voice, then, out of the corner of my eye, I saw a giant fist swing at the policeman's head.

'Help,' my captor wailed as more fists, then feet, began to pummel into him.

305

As he rolled to the floor, blood spattering from his nose, I struggled to my feet. I saw Mickey yank the other policeman away from Dave, then smash his elbow into the undercover officer's face. He went down as if pole-axed.

Whistles shrilled in the doorway as dozens of uniformed police began to pour into the building. The other clubgoers were deliberately slow in moving out of the way though, and by the time they reached the spot where their colleagues lay motionless we were well away.

No one moved to help the injured men.

'Get back,' a fat Inspector bawled, then shouted for one of the other constables to get the music stopped. As the sound died away, he turned and examined the soulies encircled around him. 'Why didn't you help them?' he said, as one of his men bent to check on the unconscious officers.

'Didn't realise who they were,' one lad said. 'Thought it was just a fight.'

'Well, you know who we are – so let's start having a look in your pockets.'

There was a low, angry murmur, throughout the club. Some of the flatfeet began to look around nervously.

'Get the dogs in,' the Inspector bawled, then waited until two more officers, holding back savage-looking black Alsatians, came into the club.

The dance floor began to clear of soulies. Small wraps of silver or white paper, or the odd tablet, or capsule, lay strewn in their wake on the polished floor. The dogs began to sniff at them suspiciously.

The search was soon called off; the Inspector must have known he would be lucky to catch anyone with gear on them now.

As the battered drug squad officers were stretchered out, he got some of the policeman to sweep the litter into a black rubbish bag.

'Make a good job of it,' someone shouted. 'Don't want to spoil our dancing.'

'Cheeky bastards,' a police sergeant growled. He went among the crowd, asking for witnesses to the fight, but, to no one's surprise, was unsuccessful.

Eventually the police left, scowling at us as they went.

'They're fucking spoiling it for us,' Mickey said. 'Why don't they just leave us be.'

I wondered that too. No one in the Torch was being forced to take speed and stuff; you only did it if you wanted to. Many of the dancers, like my mate Floyd, had a good time without it. It was your choice. And I couldn't see the harm in it. I didn't know of anyone being hurt by the sort of drugs we took; only if some bastard laced your whizz with Vim, or rat poison, or talcum powder, or stuff like that, were you likely to suffer. And that was happening more often as the raids caused a shortage in supply. The dealer would suffer as well though, if you caught him later.

All that the police were doing was making the price go up. That meant some of the lads had to thieve to get the money; other harder sorts would roll Torch-goers for cash, their gear, or their records. Turn up at the club for the first time, with only a few mates, and you'd be dragged into one of the nearby alleyways. Resist and you'd be given a good kicking. Hand your stuff over, and your night would start on a real bum note. The soulful atmosphere was being spoiled.

It was all pointless anyway. You only had to look at me, and my mates, to see how harmless speed was. We had been getting blocked up most weekends, and we weren't affected. If the police kept on, they would eventually get the Torch closed, but that would only move the scene elsewhere, just like had happened after the Wheel was shut down.

What really irritated me, was that you could get pissed anywhere, without any bother. I knew of loads of people being injured in drunken brawls, glassed in the face even, but nobody thought of banning alcohol. A lad I'd known from school had been killed by a drunk driver. He had broken down late at night, and was pushing his scooter to a nearby lay-by, when a drunken twat ran into the back of it, crushing him. My schoolmate was killed outright, but they never thought of shutting the pub down where the driver got pissed. No, it was so unfair. They just wanted to stop us youngsters having a good time.

Rufus Lumley's *I'm Standing* began to play, breaking the silence, and I followed the others to the floor.

No one, Maureen's dad, the police, or anybody was going to stop me enjoying myself tonight.

34

I Don't Want To Cry

I peered blearily at the alarm clock. It said eight o'clock. Bollocks! I was going to be late for work again. It would give Beresford an excuse to get rid of me.

The catch was across the top of the clock, stopping the bell from sounding; I either hadn't set it, or had switched it off, without knowing, in my sleep.

I struggled into my work jeans, then staggered into the kitchen.

My mother came through a few moments later, tying the belt of her dressing gown. 'What time is it?' she yawned, as she lit the gas under the grill.

'Just after eight,' I said, as I peeled back the foil top from a bottle of milk, then began to pour it down my throat.

'Are you feeling all right, Kenneth? You don't look very well.'

'Must be something I ate yesterday,' I said, then told her I wouldn't have time for breakfast. 'Gotta go, else Ramsbottom will be after me.'

'Surely you could have a drink of tea at least – while I get your sandwiches ready? It's no wonder you're so thin.'

I wasn't hungry, just incredibly thirsty.

Not surprising really. When we'd spilled out of the Torch on Sunday morning, blinking in the cold dawn, I had agreed to go on, with Mickey and the others, to the All-Dayer. We'd bought some chips, from a shop around the corner from the club that opened early for the likes of us, then called at Wendy's place, to eat them.

I'd collected my Lambretta from the narrow cobbled alleyway that ran behind the Torch, then parked it outside Wendy's flat. A quick freshen up, a change of shirt, and we'd all crammed into the Escort van that Mickey drove.

His boss had a painting and decorating business and allowed him to use the van; or at least that's what Mickey said. The vehicle stank of turpentine, and oil paint, and made my stomach a bit queasy, but it was better than going on the scooter. I don't know how Mickey managed to drive after all those hours in the club, but he did.

The other lads, Rocky included, had squeezed in the back, among the paint tins and dustsheets, but Mickey had told me to sit in the front. 'I don't trust them,' he said, as Wendy climbed in and sat on my knee.

I wasn't sure what made him think he could trust me either; if I hadn't still been a bit smashed, and he hadn't been sitting in the driver's seat next to me, I wouldn't have minded shagging Wendy. We bounced our way to Bolton, but the close proximity of her had little effect on me; I was out of it.

Coming back, several hours later, was different though. I'd used the last of my wages to pick up some more gear.

Mickey had been happy to wait for his money for the other stuff. 'Just don't forget,' he'd told me.

Once again, I'd been lucky enough to get Black Bombers. By the time we were in the van going home, I was starting to come down again.

Because I had managed to stick to Bombers, I wasn't suffering as I'd done other weeks, even though I'd been up for most of the weekend. No cramps, or blurred vision – except from being tired – and no tremors.

The only prickly sensation I got was from Wendy being on

my knee. As the van droned along, she settled back against me, her cheek resting against mine, her hair soft against my face. I glanced down, to see the delectable valley between her breasts. Her dress hung loosely and I could see her nipples, just as I had pictured when I'd once dreamt of screwing her.

To my surprise, despite the gear I'd dropped, I felt myself harden.

As my prick rose against her, Wendy shuffled position so that the bulge in my jeans was tucked between the cheeks of her bum. My prick leapt up again and, as each bump in the road bounced us together, I thought that I would burst.

I gulped then looked at Mickey.

He diffed the cigarette he was smoking out of the part-opened van window, then looked at me.

My face flushed as his eyes met mine.

He grinned, as if he knew the effect that his girl was having on me. I had told Wendy of how Maureen was holding herself back from me, and she must have guessed how horny I would be by now. I wondered if she had told Mickey.

I never found the answer; I fell asleep myself, dreaming of slipping myself between Wendy's thighs for real.

'Do you want me to make a flask up?' my mother said, bringing me back to Monday morning with a jolt.

'No, mum,' I said, then kissed her on the cheek. As I grabbed my coat, and made for the door, she called to me.

'Stay in tonight, love. You've hardly been in all weekend.'

I told her that I might, then dashed to my scooter. Although I had left it outside overnight, it fired up on the second kick, much to my relief.

I raced to the garage, leaning the Lambretta right over, scraping the stand on the tarmac as I sped around the bends in the road.

I was still twenty minutes late, despite my haste.

Ramsbottom was waiting near the door.

I cursed under my breath.

'Kenny,' he waved to me. 'Start on that Beetle over there. The back brakes need looking at.'

I was stunned; I'd been expecting a bollocking, maybe even getting fired, after Saturday night. Was he keeping quiet because of what had happened in the town toilets?

He must have seen the puzzled look on my face. 'I know a bit about what went on, on Saturday night. If Mr Beresford wants to . . . Well, if he thinks I'm doing his dirty work for him,' he muttered, then began to walk away.

What did he mean? Had the garage owner asked him to get shut of me? I glanced around the car park. No sign of Maureen's Ford Escort, or Beresford's Daimler. Perhaps I would see her later.

But should I tell her what her father had said? It would drive a wedge between them I thought, maliciously. No that wouldn't be fair on Maureen. She hadn't done anything wrong. It was all over between us now though. I couldn't see how we could go on after what had happened.

I went in search of Floyd, to tell him the story.

'Where've you been,' he grinned when he saw me. 'Off for a dirty weekend?'

'I wish,' I said, then told him what had happened.

'I'm lucky,' he told me. 'Anne's parents have taken to me, and I like them. That's not my problem. I just ain't sure if I'm ready for settling' down. Anyway, I've got some more news for you. Duncan's been done again – but you'll never guess what for?'

'Burglary?'

Floyd shook his head.

'Assault?'

Floyd shook his head again.

'No idea then. I wondered why he'd not been at the Torch.'

'Gross Indecency,' Floyd grinned.

'But that's . . .'

'Yeah. He was caught in the toilets, behind the market place.' Floyd looked about the workshop to see if anyone was watching. 'The one where he duffed up Ramsbottom. He was sucking another bloke's pecker through a hole in the wall.'

When desperation had forced me to use the stinking bogs, it was either that or crap myself, I had wondered why someone had knocked the jagged holes through the chipboard walls from cubicle to cubicle. I'd been in there one day when a man had stuck his eye against the hole; I'd spotted him and told him to piss off. Now I knew what their purpose was.

'Bet they use them to shaft each other as well,' Floyd said. 'Wouldn't look as suspicious as two of them going in the same shithouse. Anyway, the police were watching and burst in. Caught Duncan – and his friend – with their pants down.'

'The dirty bastard,' I said. 'But he was always so keen to go queer bashing.'

'Takes the suspicion away. Who'd believe it, if someone said he was bent?'

'Explains why he likes it so much in prison. Go down well there. Fucking shirt lifter,' I scowled.

I thought back to my party; I'd woken up in the same bed as Shagbag – and Duncan. I had thought, back then, that he'd crept in and given her one while we were out of it. Had the bastard been messing with me? I'd fucking kill him if he had. Would I know?

I tried to think back. Had my arse been sore? It hadn't, not as far as I could remember. Surely, I would have been aware. Shagbag had gobbled me off while I lay in my stupor, that I could recall. Unless that had been Duncan? Fuck me – or then I hoped he hadn't. That was the last time I would get smashed like that.

I remembered Rocky at Blackpool, joking that Duncan might shaft Floyd in the tent at night. Did Rocky know something that we didn't?

'What're you thinking?' Floyd said, as he realised I'd fallen silent.

I hoped my mate had forgotten about the aftermath of the party; he had been pretty hungover too. 'Just wondering. You never know who the bastards are. First Ramsbottom – married – with kids – and now Duncan.'

'Nutter told me. Heard about it from his brother. I don't think Duncan will dare show his face again. He'll get a good kicking from the other lads if he does.'

'He'll get one from me as well, the bloody pervert,' I said, still wondering just how out of it I had been.

35

Money Won't Do It, Love Will

'Don't know why we're going to Annabellas – it's crap compared to the Torch,' I grumbled at Floyd as we walked along the High Street. 'Why not come with me tomorrow night?'

'Anne would give me grief then. Bad enough that I'm having one night out with the boys. Still, she's got to learn,' Floyd grinned.

When he had knocked at the door earlier that night, at first, I had thought he wanted his scooter fixing – again. I had gone to the gate, then looked along the road. 'Where is it?' I'd snapped at him.

'Where's what?' Floyd had said, a hurt look in his eyes.

'Your fucking Vespa. Broke down again?'

'No! It's going fine. I walked here. Just thought – we'd not seen much of each other lately and we could go somewhere.' He turned to go.

'Sorry mate,' I said, grabbing his arm. 'Still a bit down over what happened with Maureen.'

Floyd had paused for a moment, then smiled. 'That's OK, Kenny. Let's have a good night out together. Go to Annabellas, or somewhere, and get pissed. Perhaps it'll help.'

'I ain't got any gear. Is Rocky going?'

'Don't know,' Floyd told me. 'Why not have a night off the stuff – have a good natter instead. You can make up for it Saturday.'

I had eventually agreed, although I couldn't wait for the next Nighter; it was great for us to hit the town together once more though.

'Look who it is,' Floyd nudged me, bringing my thoughts back to the present.

I scanned the street.

Duncan was coming towards us on the other side of the road, spitting into the gutter. He was on his own now that the Hole in the Wall Gang had cut him out.

'Hi, Kenny, Floyd,' Duncan said as he crossed over to us. 'Going to the disco?'

'Piss off, you bent bastard,' I growled.

'You've got it all wrong,' Duncan said angrily. 'I went in there to beat one of the bastards up.'

'Beat his willy up, is what I heard,' I told him.

'You know me. I ain't one of them. Remember when I did that one who worked at your place?'

'What was up with him? Wouldn't he pay you? Now, piss off,' I repeated.

'I came to tell you about Webster,' Duncan whined. 'He's going round town saying he's going to kill you. Did you damage his car or summat?'

'Something like that,' I said, not wanting Duncan to blab it all around town.

'I'll help you get him.'

'What? Hit him with your handbag? Now fuck off before I give you a good kicking.'

I moved towards him, but Floyd grabbed my elbow. 'Leave the pufta be,' he said. 'Why spoil our night out?'

'It would be a good start to the night,' I said as Duncan scampered away.

When he was fifty or so yards away he turned. 'I'll get you back, the pair of you. I promise.'

316

'I'll fucking have him,' I shouted, then dashed towards Duncan.

He legged it. I didn't go after him; I just wanted the bloody pervert out of my sight.

'My round first,' Floyd said as we handed our coats to the girl at the cloakroom. 'Grab a seat if you like.'

Annabellas was quiet; it was only just past eight and the disco wouldn't be busy for another hour or two yet. I had suggested that we go on a pub-crawl first, but Floyd had shaken his head. 'Cheaper to get in early,' he told me. 'Gives us more to spend on drinks.'

Mary Wells was singing *My Guy,* as I crossed the polished dance floor to the corner booth that we normally took over when we were at the club. There were probably only a dozen or so people in the place. Bit of a dead loss. The disc jockey was playing the records at half volume, one after another, as if saving himself for when it livened up.

'Hello, Kenny,' Maureen smiled at me, as I went into the booth. She was sitting in the corner, watching for the reaction on my face. Her eyes had dark circles under them, exaggerated by the lights positioned overhead. 'Please don't go,' she said, as I turned to look for Floyd.

Floyd must have set it all up. All week he had been on about how upset Maureen was.

'She wants to see you, mate,' he kept telling me. 'Her old man has told her to stay at home. Says he'll sack you if he catches the two of you together. She'll meet you after work – but is frightened her father will see her.'

'Tell her to get lost. The fucking prick tease. I don't want anything more to do with her.'

'It's not her fault,' Floyd said. 'She must think a lot of you,' he said, 'to even consider going against her old man.'

'Gives you a chance to win the pound,' I told him, but felt a bit of a bastard when I saw the wounded look on his face.

'I'd give everything I've got – if it helped you two get sorted,' Floyd said.

317

Now, this was another attempt of his, to get Maureen and me back together.

'I just want to talk, Kenny,' Maureen said, patting the seat next to her.

She looked so lost sitting there, on her own, that I just wanted to hold her. But where would we go from there?

'Please,' Maureen said again. 'I got you a drink.' She pointed to a glass next to hers on the table.

That confirmed it had been no accident. 'OK, just for a few minutes,' I said. 'I'm here with Floyd. We may be moving on soon.' I knew in my heart though that Floyd would keep out of the way, now that he'd got us face to face.

I sat down opposite her.

Maureen shuffled along the seat towards me, her scent wafting into my nose, reminding me of . . .

'What do you want to talk about?' I said, as I sat there stiffly. 'It's all over between us.'

She put her hand on mine. Her touch sent a quiver up my spine. There were tears in her eyes.

She looked at our clasped hands. 'I just don't understand. You and Daddy seemed to be getting on so well at dinner – then suddenly – you're leaving and going off to the Torch. I came after you – but you'd gone by the time I came outside. What did I do to you – for you to hurt me so? I asked Daddy what had happened but he wouldn't tell me. Just said he never wanted you in the house again. What did you say to him? He was so angry.'

Tell her that her old man tried to buy you off, a voice said inside my head. Yeah, that she's worth a few hundred pounds. That would make her feel as shitty as you do.

But what had Maureen done to deserve that?

'I asked Floyd what I'd done wrong. He wouldn't say. Just said that I should ask you. But you wouldn't talk to me . . .'

Deep down I knew that I loved her, but where was the future in that. 'Me and your father just didn't see eye-to-eye,' I told her instead. 'He doesn't want me for a

318

son-in-law. And I don't particularly want to be part of your family either.'

'It's not what he wants that's important to me,' Maureen said quietly. 'I love Daddy but I want to be with you.'

I wanted to crush her against me, but knew that I would be lost if I did. 'I don't want to come between you and him. Perhaps it's better that we're through.'

'Is it just – my father?' Maureen began to cry, her shoulders shaking. She blew her nose on a tissue. 'Or is it because I won't – I won't let you make love to me?'

'Nothing to do with it,' I said.

That was only partly true; I was also pissed off with ending up frustrated every night. I'd read in one of Cheryl's magazines, when I'd been waiting for Floyd, of how a boy should be patient with a girl.

"If he loves you," the writer said, "then he should be prepared to wait for you."

Well, I had – did love Maureen, but couldn't wait any more. If she wouldn't come across there were plenty of other girls who would.

'I want to – just as much as you,' Maureen said. 'But I want the man I marry to be the first. I love you – and I don't want to lose you. If you still want me – we could try again. Then perhaps . . .' She smiled at me. 'Just give me time.'

I wanted nothing more than to take her to bed, sink myself deep inside her, and hold her close all night. And to wake up next to such a beautiful girl was more than I'd ever dreamed of.

But where would her old man fit into the picture? Perhaps I could screw her, and then, after that, it wouldn't matter. I knew that I could never do that though. She did matter to me. I was in love with her.

Rocky came into the booth, along with a girl he sometimes went out with. They must have sensed, or known, what was going on, because they studiously ignored us.

The disco was filling up now I suddenly realised, then

319

saw, by Maureen's watch, that a good hour had passed. It was strange how time flew by when I was with her.

I saw Floyd dancing with Anne. They must have set this up together. 'Shall we dance?' I said to Maureen, as the DJ played another slow record.

She nodded, then rose to her feet, and followed me onto the dance floor, squeezing my hand in hers.

She was truly gorgeous I thought, as she came into my arms, her face pale in the disco lights, tresses of hair spilling down her back, almost to her waist. She was wearing a black mini skirt, and a white silk blouse underneath a black woollen cardigan that came down to the hem of her skirt. Knee-length black leather boots showed off her slim legs.

I must be the envy of every boy in the place I thought, as she snuggled her cheek against mine. The smell of her hair against my face was wonderful. Soft strands of it brushed against the back of my hand as I held her close. She smiled at me, then kissed me, the taste of aniseed on her lips as her body pressed into mine. I responded immediately, just as I always did when she was next to me. She pressed herself closer still.

Jackie Wilson's *I Get the Sweetest Feeling* came next. Maureen's perfume was making me feel dizzy. I placed my hand in the small of her back, forcing her against me.

Maureen nibbled at my ear, her breath warm on my cheek. 'I do want you, Kenny,' she murmured as the record finished, 'but I can't – just yet. Not this week.'

I understood, but I didn't want to move away from her. The DJ, or God, must have been on my side; the gentle sound of *You Fooled Me* began to drift across the disco.

It was a great song for dancing to, slowly, with a girl in your arms, but the words were sad. As the singer, Virgil Henry I think he was called, crooned 'It's over – there ain't nothing to say,' Maureen began to sob against my shoulder. My eyes began to water too as he sang of how his girl broke his heart.

'Oh, Kenny, I'm sorry. Don't ever leave me again,' she snuffled.

The split hadn't been her fault. It was her father's, but how could I tell her what had happened? I knew that I never wanted to be away from her side.

I just had to find an answer.

What was up with everybody? Just over a week to go until Christmas, yet all my mates were miserable as fuck. In another couple of weeks I'd be eighteen, and no one seemed bothered. They hadn't even mentioned it, just kept on about what they were getting each other for Christmas.

And Maureen seemed to have the hump with me because I planned to go to the Torch again.

'You go – if you want to,' she had told me. 'I don't mind. Honestly.'

Well she said she didn't mind, but I suspected that she was getting fed up with me disappearing every weekend. Since we'd been back together, she'd said that she trusted me, and wanted me to go, but that she didn't like the place herself.

Maureen had surprised me though, by how she had faced up to her old man. She had driven me to her house the night after we made up, then took me into the lounge where Beresford was watching the TV.

Her father had leapt to his feet. 'What the . . . What's he doing here?' he'd snapped.

Maureen had stood between us. I didn't know if she was trying to keep him away from me, or stop me from belting him. 'I love Kenny, Daddy. Either you accept that – or I shall leave with him – and you'll never see me again.'

I was dumbfounded. I looked around at the expensive furnishings and the, what must be very valuable, clocks and ornaments. How could she think of giving this up for me? I had nothing to offer her. I wouldn't even have a job if she left with me now; Beresford would make sure of that. Would I do the same for her? I decided that I would, but then again, it might be different if I had all this to lose.

Beresford's face had turned crimson. 'Out,' he bellowed at me again, his moustache bristling.

'Come on, Kenny,' Maureen said, taking me by the hand. 'Help me pack my things.'

'You won't come back here – if you leave,' her father had ranted.

'No, that's right – I shan't,' Maureen said, then led me towards the stairs.

'Where will you live?' he scoffed. 'Bet you haven't thought of that.'

'We can live with my mother,' I told him. 'There's lots of room.' I hadn't asked her though, just thought of the idea.

'Stop her, Henry,' Maureen's mother shouted. 'I don't want her to go.'

'It's her decision.'

'But if they're in love . . . Remember back to when we met. My father didn't like you. You didn't let that stop you.'

'That was different. I had something to offer you. What does he have?' he said, waving his hand towards me. 'Besides, he's not – not good enough for my daughter.'

'He's the boy I'm going to marry,' Maureen said, biting her lip in defiance.

'Over my dead body.'

'Your parents thought that I was common too, Henry,' Mrs Beresford said, 'just because we didn't have much money – and my father worked for the Council. You said then that it didn't matter to you.'

Her husband scowled at me, probably hating the fact that I was hearing all this personal stuff. Then he stamped off. 'Do what you damned well like,' he shouted back over his shoulder. 'I'm going to the Club.'

'Please stay, Maureen,' Mrs Beresford had begged her daughter. 'I'll talk him round.'

Well, she had – eventually. Since then, Beresford had tolerated me, but didn't exactly make me welcome. He didn't stop Maureen going out with me though, but was probably hoping that our relationship would fizzle out.

Now, some three months later, it seemed like he may get his wish after all. I wouldn't see Maureen tomorrow if I went to the Torch, and she had said she wanted to stay in tonight, when we normally went to Annabellas, or the pictures, or for a meal, or somewhere together. She had seemed angry when I told her that I thought the club might be open just before Christmas. I wasn't sure if it was, but I hoped so, or I would have to go at least two whole weeks without a Nighter.

'But you won't get back until Christmas Eve,' she said. 'Then you won't be fit for much. I hoped we'd spend all of Christmas together.' She had told me that her parents normally held a dinner for their relatives, and some of Beresford's business colleagues. 'You're invited too,' she said.

I could imagine the pressure that she, and her mother, must have put on Beresford for me to be present; I would get a very grudging welcome.

I wondered what would it be like at the Torch at Christmastime. Last week had been one of the best All-Nighters I had ever gone to. Major Lance had appeared there and given his all. It would take a lot to top that night. He'd performed there a couple of months before and the club had been packed out. The Torch was licensed for six hundred people, or so I'd heard, and I guessed there must have been nearly fifteen hundred in to watch him. The club said there were only twelve hundred, but it felt like a lot more than that. It had been such a great night that the manager of the Torch told us they were going to bring the Major back again, make a recording of his performance, and turn it into an LP. I didn't buy many discs, but that was one I was going to get.

It had been just as packed again at the Major's next visit, or I should say performance; he enjoyed the club so much that he came back to other Nighters, as one of the crowd, just to enjoy himself. Last Saturday, when I'd walked down Hose Street, past the recording vans, and fought to squeeze my way in, it seemed there were as many people inside again, if not more.

From the minute the Major set foot on stage, we barely stopped clapping. A guy with him, called Otis Leavill, could make such wonderful sounds from his guitar. I had never heard anyone play like him before. Sometimes I couldn't wait for the live acts to finish, so that I could hit the floor again, but I just didn't want the Major to stop. He bounced around the stage, enjoying it just as much as we were. We stood spellbound on the dance floor in front of him, some soulies waving their arms slowly in the air, two fingers on each hand pointed skywards, swaying to the sound of *Um, Um, Um, Um, Um, Um*, while others clapped and clapped. We sang along to *The Beat* until we were hoarse. I clapped so fast and hard when he sang *Ain't No Soul*, and *Investigate*, that my hands were numb for days afterwards. I was just about deaf too, from the sound of hundreds of palms cracking together close to my ears. Never felt it at the time though; I was just lost in the Major's performance. The atmosphere was electric. I couldn't believe it when he finished. We shouted and clapped for him to come back on again, but, eventually, he could give no more. I had told Maureen what she'd missed, but she still thought it wasn't her scene.

'I don't like the drugs and things there. Promise you won't get involved,' she said again.

I had promised her that. What else could I say? I think she suspected that I was lying, but I planned to stop when we got married. Until then . . .

I was a bit miffed with Floyd too. I had called at his house to see if he fancied a night out, but Mrs Edmonds said he'd gone somewhere earlier. 'Don't know where,' she said. 'He was acting a bit mysterious.'

Floyd seemed to be avoiding me lately, and when I met him at work, he didn't have a lot to say. 'Just got a lot on my mind, Kenny,' he explained when I tackled him about it. 'Don't know whether to finish with Anne. She's so posses-sive.'

'Thought you two would get married before Maureen and me,' I told him.

'I've still got things I want to do – before I settle down. I find myself looking at other girls and wondering . . .'

'So do I,' I grinned. 'Don't see the harm, so long as we don't do anything about it.'

'Yeah, but sometimes I'd like to,' Floyd said.

I had to agree with him. I did too. Maureen always seemed to find an excuse for us not to go the whole way. She was either on the rag, or wanted to wait until we had our own place, or something.

'I'd just like it to be – special,' she said, when I had knelt on the floor of her Escort, between her legs. 'Not cramped in here.'

I would have preferred to be in her bed myself, instead of having a cold dashboard pressed against my arse, but she wouldn't do it at her parents. "I should hate to think they're listening." And she wouldn't come with me to my bed either. "I couldn't relax – what if your mother came home." A hotel was out of the question with her as well. "Too seedy."

'It won't be long, Kenny,' she had told me, 'Let's get Christmas out of the way, and then . . .'

Would we ever do it? I was getting hornier every week that went by; I wouldn't be able to stop myself one of these days. A further temptation was that Mickey, my mate at the Torch, had finished with Wendy and was going out with another girl. Wendy seemed to have a thing for me, and I knew that if I wanted to, I could be in there. I liked her a lot as well. And she loved the Torch. Maybe we had more in common than I had with Maureen. Wendy and me had left the Torch together, after the Major's performance, totally drained by the experience. She had invited me back to her place, for a cup of coffee, and to freshen up. As we sat on her settee, Wendy with her legs curled under her, her knees pressed against my thigh, she had said that I could stay there if I wanted.

I had read the message in her eyes and smiled at her. 'I really like you Wendy,' I told her, 'but you know how it is with Maureen. We're supposed to be engaged.'

'No strings,' she told me. 'Just feel a bit on my own – now that Mickey's gone.'

She was too beautiful to stay on her own for long as well. Reluctantly, I had climbed astride my Lambretta instead, and made my way home. I'd got Sunday dinner with Maureen's folks to look forward to; that was if I didn't fall asleep on the sofa when I got home, as I'd done the week before. That had not helped Maureen's humour either. I pictured Wendy, waving to me from the window of her flat. Perhaps if things were different? Maybe I'd not be able to stop myself if I went to Tunstall again this week. I'd have to see if I could persuade Floyd to go with me. He'd act as my chaperone, nag me if I was tempted.

Doing his boy-scout thing would cheer him up a bit.

37

They Say

Annabellas was pretty lively by the time I got in; it looked like some people had started partying for Christmas a bit early.

I'd called into several pubs on my way, but not one of my mates was about. I felt a bit of a prat on my own, so had gulped down a quick pint at each place, then decided to see if they'd gone to the disco.

I met up with Rocky at Annabellas bar. 'I've got a lift organised for tomorrow,' he told me. 'Save you freezing on your scooter.'

'You're on,' I said. The week before, after I'd left Wendy's, and before I had gone many miles, my fingers had almost been stuck to the twistgrips with cold. It was made even worse by me spending most of the previous twelve hours in the jungle-like atmosphere of the Torch.

'Your mate's here,' Rocky grinned at me, as the disco's glitterball bounced light off his glasses.

'Floyd. Where?'

'No, not him. I ain't seen him tonight. I mean Duncan.'

'Fucking shirt lifter.'

'He's over there. In our corner. Sobbing into his beer about how the police have fitted him up. Reckons he's as straight as the next man. It's all a big mistake.'

'He'd better keep away from me,' I growled; I was still not sure what had happened at my party.

'Hi, Kenny. On your own,' a girl's voice said behind me.

I turned. It was Anne. She was with Puffin.

'Yeah. I've been looking for Floyd. Thought he was with you?'

'No, I've not seen him tonight. He said his father wanted him to do a job for him.'

I just stopped myself from telling her that he wasn't at home. Why hadn't Mrs Edmonds said that Floyd had gone on an errand for his old man? Perhaps it was just a cover up. Maybe Floyd had done what he had threatened and gone out with someone else?

'Fancy a drink?' I said, hoping to change the subject. I turned to Puffin. 'Still on rum and coke?'

'Please,' she smiled.

Reluctantly, Ramsbottom had given me my Christmas bonus, so I had plenty of money to go at for the weekend. I'd earned it, I told the Service Manager; I'd turned out more work than any of the other fitters.

'True,' he said. 'Just a shame you can't get here on time in the morning. Sort that – else I shall have to act.' He was also desperate for me to go in, tomorrow morning, to finish a customer's car.

My problem was, after a night at the Torch, then the drive home, then spending the Sunday afternoon and night with Maureen, I was shattered; he was lucky I turned in at all. Once there though, I tried to prove Beresford wrong about me and worked my balls off.

Tonight though, I would forget all that. I was feeling a bit bloated from all the beer I'd knocked back, so I changed to drinking shorts. I sank the first one when the barmaid put it in front of me. 'Fancy another?' I asked Rocky and the girls. 'Gonna have a good time tonight,' I told them.

A few more drinks and I was dancing with Puffin, Rocky with Anne.

Puffin leaned towards me. 'Is Floyd seeing someone else?' she shouted into my ear, above the jingling sound of Archie Bell and the Drells getting ready to sing *Here I Go Again*. 'Anne thinks he is.'

I swayed towards her, almost falling over her handbag which was on the floor between us. 'Not as far as I know,' I answered truthfully. 'Think he wants to cool things a bit though. Perhaps she's pushing a bit too quick.' I hoped she would pass the message to her friend. Maybe if Anne knew that, they could work things out.

The pace changed as the DJ played a Stylistics number. There was an awkward pause as I looked at Puffin and she looked at me. I hated dancing to slow tracks on my own.

She stepped forward, pushing her handbag out of the way.

I put my arms around her, but noticed she kept her body slightly away from me.

'Are you still with Maureen?' she said.

I nodded.

'Where is she tonight?'

'Staying in.'

She snuggled a bit closer, as if relieved that Maureen was not about to catch her with me, then closer still for the record that followed.

Damn! Puffin still turned me on and she knew it. I felt myself harden, then decided it would be a good idea to sit the next record out. I led her to the bar, to get us another drink, and then we went to sit in one of the booths.

'I still fancy you, Kenny,' she whispered into my ear. 'And I know you still like me too. You know, I wouldn't mind if later . . .'

I wouldn't have minded either; in fact, I could think of nothing better. And Puffin was on the Pill too. No rubber to put on – I could just slip into her . . . But that would be betraying Maureen. Maybe just this once? I slugged back my drink.

No, I was supposed to be getting married soon, and yet

330

here I was thinking of shagging Puffin behind Maureen's back. Except it probably wouldn't be behind her back for long in this town. 'I'll get us another drink,' I said, then staggered to the bar again.

Duncan was there. I went to the opposite end.

'Kenny, I want to tell you something,' he shouted, then forced his way through the queue towards me.

Here we go again I thought, "Webster is going to kill you!" or some crap like that. 'Piss off,' I told him when he reached me.

'No, listen Kenny. It's important. I know you'd want to know.'

'I told you – fuck off.'

'It's about Maureen. OK – if you don't want to hear about it . . .'

Duncan was trying to shit stir again I knew, but I asked him what he was on about anyway.

'Don't like telling you this, mate,' he said, 'but she's two-timing you.'

'Lying bastard,' I said, swaying towards him.

'It's true,' he said, stepping behind a barstool, as if it would offer some protection. 'Floyd's seeing her. I saw him go into her house tonight,' he added quickly as my fist rose. 'His scooter's still there – if you don't believe me.'

I felt like flattening the bastard, but then he would have thought that I doubted my girl. 'Look Eddie, just get out of my sight before I kick your head in.'

He must have seen how close he had pushed me to whacking him one, so he sidled away, muttering.

I took two more rum and cokes back to Puffin.

'What's up?' she said, when she saw my face.

'Just that bastard Duncan winding me up.'

'He's horrible. When I heard that about him – I could well believe it,' Puffin told me. 'Fancy another dance?'

I felt a bit better when I was pressed against her again. Where had that twat Duncan got that idea from? OK, Floyd

331

wasn't here, but that didn't mean . . . Maureen's not here either, my mind nagged. No, it was impossible. Maureen was mine.

Unless Floyd was giving her one.

I leaned my head on Puffin's shoulder; the room was beginning to spin – it was all those stupid thoughts. I'd kill Duncan, I promised myself. As I shuffled with Puffin across the dance floor, I spotted him at the end of the stage, next to the DJ. He was keeping well away from me. Very sensible of him.

Puffin moved closer, the fingers of her left hand buried in my hair. The DJ was spinning *Backstabbers*. 'They smile in your face,' sang the O'Jays. Where was Floyd, if he wasn't with Anne? And he wasn't at home. That bastard Duncan had started me fretting. I was mad at myself for doubting Floyd – or Maureen.

As I swayed about the floor in Puffin's arms, I thought of the bet Floyd had made with me. Was Maureen holding back all this time – because Floyd was already getting it? Had he won the pound?

'Come on over to my place,' sang the Drifters as the DJ swapped the record.

Had Floyd "gone over to her place?" Was he there with her now? I couldn't believe that; Beresford hated me being in the house, never mind Floyd. But Maureen's father was at the Bowling Club tonight, and her mother had gone to a WI Meeting or something; Maureen was there alone. Or was she?

You've Been Cheatin' came on next. That was one of Rocky's records; it was strange that the DJ had that in his collection. As the backing strings reverberated around the club, and the Impressions sang 'another lover – you discover,' I glanced towards the stage to see Duncan handing the disc jockey a record from a box on the floor. The damned pufta was trying to wind me up by getting him to play those records.

332

'Back in a minute,' I said to Puffin as I slid from her arms.
She looked at me. 'What's up?'

I didn't answer, just strode towards the stage. Duncan saw
me coming and ran for the fire escape. I was only a few steps
behind him, as he fled down the metal stairway, but I lost
him in the darkness of the alley below. 'Show your face near
me again – you lying bastard,' I yelled into the night, 'and
I'll kick your fucking teeth in.'

I heard a scooter start up. My Lambretta was down the
alley. Had Duncan done something at it? That would be the
last straw. I went to check on it and, to my relief, found that
it was all right.

I still had this picture of Floyd screwing Maureen in my
mind and, no matter how I tried, I couldn't wipe it out. It
would be easy to check, just jump on the Lammy, and go
past her house. But I was pissed and I didn't want to be
pulled up. I could make it with Puffin too, if I wanted. I
shivered. My coat was still in the cloakroom. I looked at the
scooter. Ten minutes and I would know.

I leapt onto the seat, stuck the keys in the ignition, and
then started it. As I swung onto the High Street, I knew I'd
made a mistake; I hadn't put a jumper on, was just in my
jacket, and it was fucking freezing. It'll help me to sober up I
thought, as I wobbled around the roundabout at the end of
the street. The trouble was, I looked a bit odd riding like
that, if the police spotted me. As I straightened the scooter
again, I accelerated towards the park; Maureen's parents
lived at the back of it. I remembered the night I took Puffin
into there. Could be doing that now instead of going on this
wild goose chase.

I turned another corner. At the end of the next avenue, I
would have the answer. I sped up then switched off my
engine, dropped the scooter in neutral, and coasted towards
Maureen's house; I didn't want her to think I didn't trust her,
and was checking up on her.

As I drew level with the double wrought-iron gates, I saw

that the gravel drive was empty, except for Maureen's Ford
Escort. Beresford's Daimler wasn't there, so he was out, and
her mother's Rover was gone too. The house was in
darkness. Maureen must have gone to bed early. I turned my
watch so that I could read it in the weak glow of the
streetlights. It was just past ten thirty.

I got off the Lambretta. I could wake her up, or go back to
the club. What would I say to her though when she asked
why I was there? And she would wonder why I didn't have
my coat. No, I would just push the scooter a bit further away,
then kick-start it again, out of her hearing.

Something glimmered on the concrete path that led to the
rear of the house. I pulled the scooter onto its stand then
walked a few paces up the drive, chippings crunching under
my feet as I peered into the gloom. It was a bit foggy, and it
was especially dark at the side of the house, being well away
from the street lamps.

Then I knew what had caught my eye; it was one of the
mirrors on Floyd's Vespa. My heart thumped against my
ribs. Duncan was right! There was no doubting it. I had
worked on the fucking thing enough times to recognise it,
even at that distance. I sank to my knees in disbelief. How
could they? My two best friends!

There must be some explanation. But why was Floyd's
Vespa hidden? There was plenty of room on the drive. All
sorts of stupid reasons for it being there came to my mind.
Perhaps Floyd had sold it to Maureen. I knew, as soon as I
thought it, that that idea was ridiculous; Maureen was not
keen on scooters and she had her car anyway.

Supposing Floyd had called there looking for me. That
was it! He was in there now, drinking coffee, and chatting to
Maureen, wondering where I was.

But the house was silent. I staggered to my feet and
walked along the drive. As I went past the Vespa, I reached
down and placed my fingers near the exhaust. It was stone
cold. Mind you, that didn't mean anything I reasoned; it was

a frosty night and would have cooled quickly anyway. Floyd could have been here for just a few minutes. Or a few hours, my brain argued. I approached the window of Maureen's sitting room. It was in darkness. So was the kitchen. The only window that was lit, and that only by a feeble glow, a lamp or something, was the one where I knew Maureen's bedroom to be. He was in there with her!

Should I kick the door in then run upstairs? Supposing I was wrong? And Floyd was my best mate. If that's what the two of them wanted – then so be it. Stuff the marriage. If it meant they were both happy . . .

My teeth began to chatter and I thought of Puffin waiting for me at the disco. I decided to go back there, think things through. Lying bastard, my mind nagged at me; you just want to get your leg over Puffin again. I suppose I did, but I was still flabbergasted by what Floyd and Maureen were doing behind my back. I was angry that neither of them had the decency to tell me; I wouldn't have got mad with them.

Twenty minutes later, I was at Annabellas bar.

The bastard doorman wouldn't let me back in without paying again. I told him that I'd been in before, but he said he hadn't seen me, and, as I hadn't had my hand stamped when I left, it was pay up or fuck off. I paid. I just wanted to get warm again.

'Where've you been?' Rocky said, when he saw me shivering there.

'I – I went after Duncan,' I told him, my teeth clattering together. I ordered a double whisky for myself, then asked him what he was having.

'Do you think you should be having anything else?' Rocky said. 'Thought you said you'd come on your scooter?'

'I can leave it out back until tomorrow. Got any gear on you?'

'Shh,' Rocky cautioned me, then nodded towards the girl behind the bar, who was looking curiously at me.

I handed her a note.

'Well, have you?'

'You don't want to be taking anything in your state,' he murmured into my ear.

'It's for tomorrow,' I lied. 'Just thought I'd get fixed up now.'

Rocky looked at me for a moment. 'I'll see you tomorrow night anyway,' he said. 'I'll give it you then.'

'I've got the brass now,' I said, as the girl dumped some change into my palm.

'OK. Pay me now – and I'll give you the gear when we're on the bus.'

'What if I pay you – then you don't give it to me.'

'Fuck off, Kenny. Look how many times I've trusted you. I thought we were mates. I'll put it down to you being drunk.'

He was right; you should trust your mates. But then Floyd was screwing Maureen. Who could you depend on? 'Here's the money. Just give me the fucking stuff,' I snapped.

Rocky shrugged then walked off. He came back a few minutes later and dropped a small packet into my pocket. 'Only got powder,' he said. 'Don't take it tonight. The club shuts soon anyway. And Kenny – get it from somebody else in the future.'

'Sorry, Rocky,' I muttered. 'You were beginning to sound like my father.' That was the first time I had thought of my old man in ages, I realised guiltily.

Rocky shook his head then left me there.

I decided to go to the bog and get the powder down my neck; I would be set for the night then. I bought myself a pint, shorts were no good for washing whizz down, then made my way to the toilets with it. Some of the couples dancing looked at me curiously as I wove across the middle of the dance floor, but I negotiated my way to the bogs successfully. I rested the pint pot on a shelf underneath a mirror, untwisted the wrap, and then tipped the powder into my mouth. A guy having a piss stared at me but said nothing.

It was a good job for him too; I was in no mood for some wise arse to interfere.

The whizz tasted foul, just like cat piss, and stuck to my tongue. It was all over my lips and nose, I noticed in my reflection. I took a glug of the beer but it frothed up, bursting out of my nostrils. 'Bastard!' I shouted, as a mix of powder and ale splashed down the front of my shirt. I wet my hands in the sink, then dabbed at the wet cloth.

A trickle of snot, amphet, and beer, ran from my nose, and I blew it into a wedge of bog paper. Another swig of beer, and I was feeling much better.

Now – where was Puffin?

38

Crackin' Up Over You

'You're drunk,' the girl I was leaning on said as she pushed me away.

I glared at her, then looked around the dance floor. Still no sign of Puffin. The cow must have gone home. Well bollocks to her then, there were plenty of other girls here! As Smokey Robinson was crooning that he was 'sadder than sad,' I spotted Shagbag staggering from the ladies and went over to her.

'Hi, gorgeous. Fancy a fuck,' I shouted to her.

'You're pissed, Kenny,' she laughed. 'But so am I. Buy me a drink – then we'll have a dance.'

'Stuff the dance – I want to shag you,' I yelled. Unfortunately, *Tears of a Clown* finished just at that moment, and everyone in the club turned to stare at us. Shit! Now some big mouth would tell Maureen what I'd said. But that didn't matter – did it? She was being fucked herself tonight.

'Shhhhh.' Shagbag fell towards me and placed her finger on my lips. 'Let's have a – a drink first.'

We propped each other up, then made our way to the bar. Shagbag managed to perch herself onto one of the high stools. I did the same, on the one next to her, then ordered a couple of doubles. Shagbag had another of those skirts on,

338

the ones that split almost to her waist, and it slid off her legs as she crossed them. I leaned my head against her chest, feeling her heart thumping against my cheek, her tits warm against me, then groped at her thigh.

'Not now,' she giggled. 'Everyone's looking.'

There was one thing about her, everybody might have been through her, but she certainly knew how to use her body to make you feel good. Screwing her would be better than nothing.

Marvin Gaye and Tammi Terrell singing *Two Can Have A Party* crackled from the tinny speakers above the bar. Floyd and Maureen were doing just that. 'Lights down low and I'm holding you near,' sang Marvin. Floyd would be lying naked, next to her, right now. The cheating bastards. I didn't mind it when we shared a girl, when someone like Shagbag or Eddie's mother was willing, but Maureen was special – she was going to be my wife.

I pictured his black rump pumping away between her thighs. Or was I remembering when he had shagged Paulina? My thoughts were getting a bit mixed up. Was Maureen sucking him off, just like Shagbag had done in the scout hut? The fucking cheating, lying, double-crossing bastard! I tossed back my drink then slid off the stool. There was only one way to find out.

'Where you going,' Shagbag slurred. 'Wait – I'll just finish . . .'

I didn't answer her, the fucking slag. She'd sleep with anybody. Just like Maureen. Except that Maureen wouldn't sleep with me!

Somehow, I don't know how, I found myself at Maureen's house again. Floyd's Vespa was still there, and now her parents' cars were parked up too. The house was still dark though. Fucking great! Beresford didn't like me being there, but he lets Floyd stay the night. I hammered on the door.

A light came on in the house across the road, and a woman leaned out of a window. 'What do you want,' she shouted.

'Fuck off, you old cow,' I yelled back. As she ducked back inside, threatening to call the police, I kicked at Beresford's front door again. Had they gone out? Perhaps I'd made a right balls up and they had all gone somewhere? But their cars were here!

The fanlight above the door lit up as someone turned on the hall light. There was the crash of a couple of bolts being opened, and then Beresford was standing there.

'Who is it?' he bellowed, staring out into the darkness of the porch, as he knotted the cord of his dressing gown around his waist.

'Just me,' I said, then pushed past him. Mrs Beresford was standing at the top of the stairs. Maureen was by her side, dressed in a flimsy peach-coloured gown, peering anxiously over the banister.

'What . . ?' Beresford exhaled, as I raced up the stairs.

'Kenny, what's up?' Maureen said, stepping towards me.

'Out of the road,' I said, shoving her to one side, then dashing towards her room. The door was part-closed, and I kicked it back. The bed was rumpled – but empty. Perhaps Floyd was sleeping in a spare bedroom. Yes, that was it. Maureen would pretend to her parents that he was staying the night in another bed, then, later, Floyd would creep in there . . .

'Where is he?' I screamed, as Maureen and her mother followed me in to the room.

'Who? I don't know what you mean . . .'

'Floyd. His fucking scooter's here – so where is he?'

'None of that language young man,' Beresford bawled from the bedroom doorway. 'You're drunk. A disgrace. Get out now. I've called the police.'

I dropped to my knees and peered under the bed.

Maureen reached down and touched me on the shoulder. 'What's the matter?'

I shrugged her hand off. 'Fucking whore,' I yelled. 'Where is he? Don't tell me Floyd's not here. His scooter's outside.'

'He was here – but he's gone now,' Beresford snapped. 'And you'd better be off too.' He began to drag at my collar, pulling me to my feet.

I swung at him. He fell backwards and sprawled across Maureen's bed. I'd missed him, but the shock of my attack had stunned him. He cringed as I reached for the lapels of his dressing gown.

'Oh, Kenny,' Maureen sobbed, tugging at my arm. 'Please stop it.'

'Keep your hands off me you slag,' I hissed, 'save it for the other pillocks you string along.

'Floyd went home ages ago,' Mrs Beresford said coldly, as she hugged Maureen to her. 'And I suggest that you do the same.'

They were siding with him I realised. Maureen's parents had never liked me; they wouldn't tell me the truth. I staggered to the door. Floyd's place next. I'd beat the shit out of him.

'That's right – get out,' Beresford raged as I took the stairs two at a time.

I didn't fall, despite being pissed.

'And you're fired. Don't come into work again. Told you he was no good,' I heard him say, as I flew out of the front door.

As I started the Lambretta, a picture of the look of despair on Maureen's face came into my mind. I felt a tinge of sadness. I hated hurting her that way. But she hadn't worried about my feelings – so stuff her. As I wobbled along the road, I heard sirens in the next street. They were going the opposite way. What if I was wrong and I had dropped the biggest bollock of my life.

I had to find Floyd.

39

Too Much

As I steered my scooter past the local recreation ground, I passed a couple walking arm in arm, going the same way as me. Although the girl had the hood of her coat over her head I recognised the lad. It was Tony, Cheryl's boyfriend. They had made up again Floyd had said, so that must be her with him now. Cheryl would tell me if Floyd was seeing Maureen. I swung the Lambretta into a tight turn. It had been raining and, although it had stopped now, it had frozen on the icy road. I skidded, almost tumbling off.

'Bollocks,' I murmured as I recovered my balance, then rolled to a halt next to them. I switched the engine off. 'Where the fuck is your brother tonight?' I said as the two-stroke shuddered to a halt.

'Don't use language like that in front of my girl,' Tony said, stepping towards the scooter.

'Piss off, squirt,' I told him, then pulled the Lammy on to its stand.

'I – I told you not to say that,' he chirped, clenching his fists in front of him.

I stared into his eyes. He'd got more balls than I thought, but he was going to get a good kicking in a minute; I was not in the mood for being pissed about.

'Leave it Tony,' Cheryl said, gripping his arm.

She could probably see the anger in my eyes, and knew very well what I was capable of in a fight.

'Are you all right, Kenny? What's the matter?'

'It's private. Don't want spunk brain here blabbing it all over town.'

Tony stepped forward again, then changed his mind. 'I'll take you home,' he told Cheryl.

'I want to talk to her,' I said. 'It's all right. I'll give her a lift home,' I grinned when Tony scowled at me.

'I'll be OK. You go home. I'll see you tomorrow,' Cheryl said, then kissed Tony on the cheek.

'If you're sure . . .'

'She's sure,' I growled. 'Now run along.'

He looked doubtful for a moment but then walked away, his shoulders slumped.

'It's not nice how you spoke to him, Kenny,' Cheryl said, anger in her eyes.

It began to rain again. 'Let's step in there.' I nodded towards a bus shelter that stood with its back to the rec. It was a brick building, with a concrete roof. There was a long black-painted wooden seat along its length, sheltered from the wind by the side walls. I sagged onto the bench, then waited while Cheryl waved to her boyfriend before she joined me.

She was wearing a full-length suede coat that I had seen her in before. It had long strands of white fur at the end of the sleeves, around the hood, and down the front. Cheryl pushed the hood back from her hair, then sat next to me. She had a parcel in her hand, wrapped in Christmas paper. It was shaped like a bottle.

'What's that?' I said, as she balanced it on her knees.

'Oh, this. We won a bottle of brandy in the youth club raffle. I'm going to give it to my dad,' Cheryl said.

I reached for it. 'I need a drink. I'll get you another – I promise. I've just found out something that's knocked the stuffing from me.'

343

Reluctantly, she let go of the bottle. I tore the paper off, then twisted the cork out. The brandy burnt at my throat as I gulped it down.

'Just one drink,' Cheryl said when I offered her the bottle, 'then tell me what's upset you.'

'Where's Floyd tonight?'

'I don't know.' She wiped her lips, where some of the brandy had spilled. 'He went out early. He's been acting funny this week. Won't let on what he's up to.'

'I bet he won't. He wouldn't want to tell you he's shafting Maureen behind my back.'

'I don't believe that. Not Floyd. You're his best friend.'

'That's what I thought. Duncan told me about it . . .'

'You didn't listen to him?'

'He said Floyd was with her tonight. I'd have hit him – if I could've caught him. But he was right.'

Cheryl shook her head. 'It can't be true. If Floyd was anywhere – he'd be with Anne.'

'Then how come she was in Annabellas – on her own – looking for him?'

Cheryl had another drink while she thought about it. 'He could have gone out with Clinton. He's gone to the City.'

I took the bottle from her and had another gulp. 'I didn't want to believe it myself. I went to Maureen's house. Floyd's Vespa was there.'

'Perhaps he . . .'

Like me, Cheryl had probably run out of excuses. She reached for the bottle again.

'I knocked on the door,' I told her, underplaying the actual event a bit. 'Her parents told me he'd been there – with Maureen.' I sagged forward, my head in my heads.

'I'm – I'm sorry if it's true,' Cheryl said, passing the bottle to me, then placing her hand on my back. 'But I still don't believe it. Floyd loves you – like a brother.'

I sat in silence for a moment, trying to figure out how, if he felt like that, he could do this to me.

344

'I'd better be getting home in a minute, Kenny,' Cheryl said. 'Else my pop will play hell.'

'Stay a bit longer – please. I don't know who to talk to. I would've . . .' My voice trailed off; I didn't need to tell her that it would be Floyd or Maureen I would normally turn to.

'Just for a bit then,' Cheryl said quietly. 'But I'm cold.'

It was getting frostier I noticed. Perhaps we could go back to my place. I didn't want to face my mother though. 'Come here,' I said. Cheryl snuggled under my arm, her cheek against my chest. 'Better?'

She nodded. I could see her breath steaming in the air.

'I – I don't know why Maureen would do anything that might lose you. I never would if you loved me,' Cheryl murmured.

It took a few seconds for her words to sink into my drink and speed fogged brain. I looked down at her. Her eyes were wide as they met mine, and her lips were there, just waiting to be kissed. 'Do you mean . . ?'

'I've always loved you Kenny, but didn't think you fancied me.'

'Fancied you? You don't know how much . . .' I kissed her, feeling her lips soft against mine, the smell of brandy on her breath, the scent of lemon in her hair. Cheryl opened her mouth wide, and rocked her head from side to side, her lips tickling mine, sending a shiver through my body. She slid her tongue between my teeth and, despite the ale and gear I had stuffed down my neck, I felt myself getting hard. I knew that I should stop, before I got carried away; this was Floyd's little sister after all. I moved my head away.

'Oh Kenny, that was nice. I've waited so long,' Cheryl said, her eyes shining in the gloom.

But then again, Floyd hadn't given a shit about me when he'd been screwing my girl. I kissed Cheryl again. She twisted her body around facing me, then put both her arms around my neck, pulling me closer.

I felt her breasts pressing against my chest, and I moved

my left hand underneath her coat flap, then upwards, to cup one beautiful rounded tit in my hand. Even through her jumper and bra, I could feel the heat of her body. I ran the palm of my hand over and round her breast, feeling her nipple stiffen.

Cheryl moaned, then sank her tongue deeper into my mouth.

I tugged at her jumper, dragging it from the waistband of her skirt. She gasped as I caressed her stomach. I worked my fingers under her bra, pushing it up, until it slid over one soft brown breast. Her nipple stood up between my fingers as I cupped her in my hand. Cheryl flicked her tongue around my teeth, then moved her body closer.

I drew back from her, to get a breath, but when I saw her nipple, proud against the dark circle of her areola, I lowered my head and began to suck on it.

'I like that,' Cheryl whispered, then lifted my head. She began to undo my shirt, her tongue protruding sexily between her lips as she concentrated on the task. She slid her hands behind my back, they were icy cold against my flesh, but were soon warm again.

I reached around her, under her coat, and freed the catch of her bra. A minute later, her jumper and bra were rucked up under her neck. 'Jesus,' I gasped, as she pressed her tits against my bare chest. Even though the night was freezing, I just didn't notice any more.

As I kissed her, I moved my body so that her nipples rubbed against the hair on my chest. Cheryl trailed her fingers down my spine, sending shock waves of pleasure to my brain.

My hand found its way to her thigh. I almost creamed myself as I slid it under her skirt; she was wearing stockings, the hold up kind, and not tights!

I don't know who moaned the loudest, Cheryl or me, as my fingertips traced along her naked skin. She parted her legs slightly, as I found the hem of her knickers. Cheryl was

346

wet, very wet, when my fingers began to probe into her body. In fact she was soaking. How wonderful it would be when I slid into her.

'That's gorgeous, Kenny,' Cheryl breathed, as she moved back slightly, so that I could ease my fingers deeper. I felt her rock against my hand. Jesus Christ, she was begging for it.

Her hand was resting against my ribs and I grasped it, then lowered it to press against the bulge in my jeans. Between us, we freed the buttons and I guided her fingers below my boxers.

'Bloody hell, Cheryl,' I hissed, as her fingers closed around me. She moved her hand slowly up and down, gripping me tightly. It wouldn't take much of that . . .

I pulled her towards the floor.

She stopped for a moment, resisting me. 'Not down there, Kenny. It's filthy.'

I took my hand from her, then shrugged the coat from my shoulders. 'We can lie on that,' I murmured, then tugged her forward again.

'Please, not here Kenny. I want you – but it's so cold – and somebody might come . . .'

Me in a minute I thought, as I pulled her down.

'Please, Kenny,' she said, as I forced her onto the coat. 'We could go to your place . . .'

I couldn't wait that long; all those months of frustration, waiting for Maureen, were bubbling inside of me.

'You've not got anything on,' Cheryl whispered, as I tugged at her knickers.

I would have ripped them off, if I had the strength and the time, but I just wanted to be inside her.

'Please don't Kenny. I love you – and want you – but not like this – here in this dirty place. Please – please,' Cheryl began to sob, as I dragged the gusset of her knickers to one side. 'It will be the first time for me,' she cried, as I thrust myself against her. 'I want it to be special.'

347

Another fucking prick tease claiming to be a virgin I thought, as I positioned myself between her lips.

'Oh no, please don't,' Cheryl wailed, and began to struggle beneath me.

Yeah, says she's supposed to be saving herself, then letting every boy in town fuck her I thought, as I felt her wetness against me. What had Tony been doing all these months – tossing himself off?

Cheryl began to pound at my back, as I slid backwards and forwards. The elastic of her knickers began to dig into me, hurting me, when I let it go so that I could grope her breast.

'Stop! Please Kenny,' Cheryl sobbed, beating her fists against me.

I pictured Floyd ramming himself between Maureen's legs as she pounded his back, urging him deeper. He might be fucking my girl, my ex-girl I corrected myself, but I was screwing his sister.

I laughed, then yelled with pleasure as I exploded into Cheryl.

40

Don't Be Sore At Me

Where the hell was I? I stared, bleary-eyed, into the gloom.
That was it – I was in the bus shelter where I'd screwed
Cheryl. I must have dozed off. It was freezing. My arse was
icy cold where it was bared to the December night.

Cheryl was underneath me, sobbing quietly.

She had been right; it was a bit of a doss hole to be making
love in. A stench of urine, from dogs or humans, or both,
met my nostrils. The floor next to Cheryl's head was covered
with soggy leaves, bits of chewing gum, fag ends, and, under
the seat, several condoms, including one that looked as if it
was full of spunk. Somebody else had brought their girl here
as well.

Cheryl must have sensed that I was awake. 'I want to go
home,' she said, struggling to get up.

I raised myself to my knees, my prick plopping from under
her knickers. Had I been inside her or just trapped under her
knicker leg? I'd been so far gone, and so horny, that I hadn't
noticed.

Cheryl sat up and began to wipe between her legs with a
hanky.

What if I'd put her up the duff? It was too late to think
about that now. I took a tissue from my pocket and held it
out to her. She ignored me. When Cheryl had finished, she

tossed her hanky under the seat, then scrambled to her feet, refusing my outstretched hand.

'I'll run you home,' I mumbled, ashamed at what I had done. Floyd might be a cheating fucker, but Cheryl had never done anything against me.

'I shall be all right on my own,' Cheryl snapped.

'I don't like to think of you going home alone,' I muttered.

'What could happen to me that's worse than – than this,' she said, waving her hand to where my coat still lay among the rubbish. 'Just leave me alone Kenny. I never want to see you again.'

'I'm sorry,' I said, putting my hand on her shoulder. 'I didn't . . .'

'Just get lost,' she said, pushing my hand away then gathering up her bag. She tugged her bra and jumper down, then belted the coat around her waist. A quick look round the shelter, to see if she had forgotten anything perhaps, then she walked off towards home. I could still hear her sobs when she was many yards away. What a bastard I had been to her. I sank back onto the seat, then checked to see if there was any brandy left. There was, so I swigged some back, to warm me, while I tried to sort my head out. Where did I go from here? My best mate was screwing my fiancée, I'd lost my job, of that I was sure, and now I'd fucked a young girl who doted on me, loved me even. And I'd loved her too.

I looked at the Lambretta, sitting by the kerbside, the chrome bodywork frosted with dew.

Perhaps I should just get on that and ride away?

41

If This Is Love – I'd Rather Be Lonely

I woke up just after dawn; my fingers and nose were dead from the cold. I was huddled in the corner of the shelter, my coat tugged around my ears. I ran my tongue across my teeth; they were coated with something foul. My bottom lip cracked in the middle as I grimaced at the taste. Staggering to my feet, I stamped on the concrete floor, trying to get some circulation into my toes. What a dickhead! A mile away I'd got a comfy bed and yet I'd spent the night in this freezing dump.

The brandy bottle was lying on the seat and, although my head told me I didn't want any more, I needed something to freshen my mouth. It was empty.

I tossed it into the corner of the bus shelter, where it shattered against the wall. As the cork, now freed of the glass neck, rolled to a halt under the seat, I saw the screwed up handkerchief that Cheryl had thrown there.

I sighed as I thought back to the night before. It hadn't been all my fault though; Cheryl had been willing. Perhaps she was just upset because it had been a bit of a flop, literally. A couple of minutes of me trying to poke myself into her, before coming all over her, would have been a bit of a disappointment to any girl. And it wasn't exactly the most romantic place in the world I thought, as I peered at the paint peeling from the graffiti-covered walls. Maybe we could put that right some other time. Cheryl had a beautiful body, firm and rounded, a real love machine. I shivered as I thought back to when her breasts had been in my hands. Wonderful. Yeah, perhaps if I took her somewhere nice she would put last night behind her.

What should I do about that cheating pair of twats, Floyd, and Maureen? I looked at my watch. It said seven o'clock. What day was it? I peered at the dial again, as if it would give me the answer. The fingers just ticked away the hours and minutes though, as the cogs in my brain began to unstick. It was Saturday! I'd be late for work by the time I got home and changed, and I'd promised Ramsbottom I would be in to finish the engine job that I'd been working on.

Then I remembered that Beresford had fired me, the bastard. He had never liked me. He was in on it with Maureen. They wanted to get me out of the way altogether, so that Floyd could step in. But then, I'd thought Beresford didn't like Floyd much either. He must realise that he'd got even less to offer Maureen.

No, that was the odd part about it. Unless, after the run-in with Maureen, over me, he'd just given up? Why had Maureen gone against her father, got him to accept me, then done this? Perhaps I was step one in her plan; get him used to the idea – then get Floyd in there. Then why the engagement? Was that all part of the cover-up, to convince her father?

Or was it all just a spur of the moment thing? Maybe they'd just had the urge - and the opportunity. Mind you, Maureen hadn't let me screw her, so that blew that argument. And Floyd had planned it anyway, because he'd dropped Anne for the night. He'd not just gone round to Maureen's and then it had happened. I thought back to how he'd been telling me that he fancied someone else; it had all been there in front of me but I'd not seen it coming.

Even so, I still couldn't believe they would do that to me. But Floyd's scooter had been there; I'd seen it with my own eyes, touched it even. Why hadn't they both said? They owed me that. None of it made sense. What was up with everybody?

I tipped the Lambretta's seat forward, then brushed my hand down it to get rid of the wet from the cover. It was still damp though when I sat astride it, and I felt the cold strike through my trousers. To Floyd's house? No, I'd not be able to tackle him there with his family eavesdropping on everything. And I didn't particularly want to meet up with Cheryl yet, not until she'd forgiven me a little.

Would I ever forgive Floyd? I doubted it. Not after what he'd done behind my back. I could go to the garage later, to have a go at him there. But what would Beresford do if he saw me? Fetch the police in again, that's what. And Maureen might be there too. I wanted Floyd to be on his own, so I could get at the truth. I didn't think that I could have looked at Maureen either. I had never hit a girl, but knew I would have a job to stop myself from smacking the prick-teasing slut if I bumped into her. Better keep away for now.

Then I had the answer. Ride to Payne's café, they opened at seven for passing truck drivers. I could warm up and get some coffee into my stomach; then perhaps, my hands would stop trembling. After that, I could catch Floyd on his way to work.

And give him his fucking pound!

42

The Cheater

'You fucking bastard, Edmonds!' I yelled as I stepped from the shop doorway.

I saw a look of surprise, then alarm, on Floyd's face as I stepped towards him. I'd caught him unawares. I grinned as I swung my fist at his face. My right hand missed but then my left thumped into his ribs.

Floyd gasped but recovered his balance. 'You're fucking dead,' he snarled, then aimed a blow towards my head.

I may have been a bit boggy-eyed, and still a bit hung over from the club, but he was way too slow. I ducked the punch then hit him on the chin. I'd aimed at his nose again but, with him being taller, I'd missed my target when he leaned his body away.

It hurt him. That would teach him. We'd often wrestled together, and sparred together, but I'd always won despite Floyd's build. That had been for fun though.

Now I wanted to hurt him. He may have taken Maureen, but he wouldn't be screwing her for a long while by the time I'd done with him.

I took a hit to my chest, felt Floyd's hand crack against my ribs, but got him again. Blood trickled down his cheek, from a cut to his eyebrow.

'I'll make you pay for what you did,' Floyd growled.

He flinched as my fist skidded across his cheekbone, leaving a livid bruise on his skin, but he managed to hit my ribs again.

That one hurt. I'd lost a bit of weight, with all the dancing I'd been doing every weekend, and there wasn't much to pad my bones now. I bit my lower lip and felt blood trickle from the split that had opened earlier, but then I landed a beautiful right on his chin. Floyd's head snapped back, his teeth clacked together and he swayed away from me.

'Come on, you double-crossing fucker,' I screamed, beckoning him towards me.

'Stop that,' someone yelled.

Out of the corner of my eye, I saw a man walking towards us. He was the newsagent from the nearby shop, where we normally called for papers on our way to work.

'Piss off,' I told him. 'This is personal.'

He wavered for a moment then hurried back to his business. The police would be here soon, I guessed.

Floyd straightened up, just in time to get a punch on the nose. Blood sprayed onto the pavement as he staggered again. I would have to sort him out good, and be quick about it, before the filth came. What was that he'd been saying about making me pay? He had started it all.

'You should have left Maureen alone,' I told him as I smacked him in the mouth again. More blood ran down his chin; I'd cut his lip. The engagement ring that Maureen had bought me had done the damage I realised; it was still on my finger. That was fucking apt I thought, as Floyd snorted blood and snot from his nostrils. 'But while you was fucking her – I was screwing your little sister.'

Floyd snarled then ran at me. I punched his nose, then whacked him in the ribs. He came on, wrapping his arm around my neck. As I fell backwards, under his momentum, I hit him in the chest again. The pavement jarred against my spine and I was almost strangled as Floyd's free arm pressed against my throat.

'Why'd you do it, Kenny?' Floyd sobbed, his blood and tears spotting down onto my face as his weight trapped me there.

I tried to think of a way to get free. What would my old man have done? I wriggled my body, trying to get a leg hooked around his.

'You broke her heart,' Floyd spat more blood into my face.

'Broke her fucking heart. What about mine? You and Maureen didn't give a shit about hurting me.'

'What the fuck are you on about? We thought Cheryl had been attacked when she came in. Then we found out she was with you. What's all this got to do with Maureen?'

'While you were shagging her – I was giving Cheryl a good fucking,' I grinned.

It was then he nutted me, his skull smashing into my cheek and forehead. Stars swam before my eyes and I squirmed to get free. As I looked up his head cracked into mine again. I had to get him off me. I couldn't take much more of that. I reached around his shoulders, my fingers grasping for his eyeballs.

'We were planning your fuckin' party,' Floyd said, as he bent his body back, away from my hands. 'Your eighteenth birthday. Maureen wanted it to be a big surprise.' He spat blood from his mouth, onto the paving stone next to my head. 'Make it special after what happened last year – your dad and all that.'

'Yeah, good excuse. How'd you think that one up.'

'Because it's fucking true that's how. Then my bastard scooter wouldn't start. It had been playing up all week. But you seemed pissed off with fixing it . . .'

I shook my head, trying to clear it. Could he be telling the truth? I tried to move, but Floyd tightened his grip again. Behind him, I could see people staring at us. A car slowed. I thought it was the police, but it accelerated away again, past my head. It was a Daimler. And I knew who the driver was.

'You hadn't been the same this year – and Maureen thought it was because of your father. Now you do this. What did you do to Cheryl?' Floyd's eyes were cold as he stared into mine.

'We just met up – and got carried away a bit that's all. Then she regretted doing it.'

'My mom and pop were going spare, wondering where Cheryl was. Me and my brothers had been out looking everywhere for her. Then she comes home – crying her eyes out – and her clothes all dirty and torn. We thought that somebody had – had raped her – but she said it wasn't that. Wouldn't tell us what had happened though. I only found out this morning from her boyfriend, Tony. I called on him before my brothers did. He said that she'd been with you after he left her.'

What a fuck up I'd made of my life, I thought.

Sirens sounded, coming our way. Floyd pushed himself off me then shook his head. 'It's over between us,' he said, wiping his face on the front of his shirt. 'Just keep out of my way.'

'I'm sorry Floyd. I just thought that – that you and Maureen . . .'

Floyd began to walk away, back towards his home. 'How could you? Clinton was right. The drugs have made you fucking paranoid – addled your brain. You should've listened to him.'

I scrambled to my feet and followed him. 'Can't we still be friends? We've been together a long time.'

'That's what hurts,' Floyd said. 'Now, I don't want anything more to do with you. It's because we were friends that I'm not hurting you more for what you've done to Cheryl. Better keep out of the way of my brothers though. Clinton's after your blood. He's guessed what happened. He won't be so forgiving. I should leave town before he gets his hands on you. And he's waiting outside your house.'

'Please, Floyd,' I said. 'We can't just stop like this.'

357

He turned and faced me. 'I can. So, fuck off Kenny. And I should imagine Maureen will tell you the same thing – if she finds out what you've been thinking.'

'She already knows. I went round there.'

Floyd shrugged and walked off.

I saw a police car stop at the newsagents, so I dodged between two shops to where I'd left the Lambretta. What was I going to do now? Floyd hated me, Cheryl must think I'd crept from under a stone, and Maureen would never forgive me. What would my mother say if she knew? And my old man would have been real chuffed with me. I'd blown it with my job at the garage. And now Clinton was after me.

Well bollocks to him. I'd soon show that uppity fucker if he messed with me.

43

It Keeps Rainin'

It was a shame, but the scooter would have to go. Unless I could get another job – and soon. At least the Lammy never let me down I thought, as I banked it into another corner. The icy wind made tears run from the corner of my eyes, but it was good to be on the open road, forgetting all my troubles as I concentrated on my riding instead.

Rocky had turned out to be a miserable git too. Said he didn't want to go to the Torch with me again. Bastard wouldn't fix me up with any stuff either. Well, he could get fucked. Nutter had sold me a couple of dozen Maroon and Greys, and some Pirellis. More than enough for the Nighter. After my fight with Floyd, my head had been pounding and I'd thought I was going to have a stroke like my old man. You just never knew; I could have inherited that from him.

I should have gone home, got my head down ready for the Torch, but that bastard Clinton had still been waiting in his car when I'd gone past the end of my street.

I dropped a few capsules and washed them down with a bottle of coke. They would help me stay with it until tonight; the rest would set me up for the All-Nighter. I needed to get my suit and things, so I had decided to ride around for a bit while I thought things through. Hopefully, by the time I got back, Clinton would have got fed up and pissed off home.

I was still cold, had never warmed up properly from my night in the bus shelter, but it was just great to leave my problems behind.

The Mini tyres had made a big difference; the Lammy went round corners as if it was on rails now. Perhaps I could sell my old man's Fiat; it was in the garage waiting for the moment when I'd have my full licence. I couldn't afford to pay for the test myself and, without a job, I'd never be able to run the car. Selling it might give me enough cash to keep going for a bit.

Maybe I could shack up with Wendy for a while? That would solve a few problems. I wouldn't have my mother nagging at me. And I wouldn't keep bumping into Floyd – or Cheryl – or Maureen. I nodded my head. Yeah, that was it. I would be away from the Edmonds brothers too. I could try to get a job in Stoke, there might be more of a chance there, and then chip in with Wendy to help with the rent. I made up my mind to call on her on my way to the Torch.

Although it was only two in the afternoon, the streetlights were on in the villages that I raced through. It started to rain again. What miserable fucking weather. The tarmac glistened, and the tyres hissed as they sprayed the water aside. At least it wasn't icy; I would have had to slow then, and I just felt like a good burn up.

A car came close behind, its image reflected a myriad times in my mirrors. The driver must be shifting a bit, to catch up with me; I was really moving on the Lammy. A police car? No, it was green.

It came closer still, the shape of its bonnet filling the mirrors.

Why didn't the prat go past me? A sudden terrible thought sprang to my brain as the car followed me around the next bend. What if it was Clinton? I came to a long straight. I'd find out now. The driver should have plenty of opportunity to get past. If he didn't . . .

Should I ease off and see?

No, that would be a big mistake if it was Floyd's brother. I heard the car's engine roar, as the driver floored the throttle pedal. I moved towards the kerb to let him pass.

Thank fuck for that I thought, as the car accelerated.

Then my body jerked as the vehicle rammed the back end of my scooter. I clung onto the handlebars. It was Clinton, and he was out to get me! In my panic, I twisted back the throttle so hard that the rubber sleeve slid round on the tube beneath, but thankfully, the scooter responded. It was a good job I'd tuned the engine when I'd rebuilt it; fitting a racing piston, and smoothing the ports, among other things, had given me back the speed I'd lost by fitting all the accessories. A gap opened between us.

What sort of a car was it? I took a glance over my shoulder, to see if I could outrun it. It was a Ford Zephyr. Shit – some of them had three litre engines! No way I could leave that thing behind on the straight. Corners were another matter though; the Zephyrs were big lumbering lumps of metal and I should be able to shake Clinton off. There was a series of bends about a mile ahead. Just had to make it there.

I saw the Ford close up again and gritted my teeth. It was a big thing to smash me into the road with too!

Hang on though my mind reasoned, Clinton had a little Datsun, a purple one; I'd often ragged him about it, said it was a pufta's car. It wasn't him, unless he'd borrowed another vehicle. Who the hell did I know who owned a Zephyr?

The first bend was coming up. I was going to hit it a bit fast; I just prayed that my tyres would grip.

They didn't; they slid a little as I leaned into the bend but the kerb stopped me from losing it. I went round the bend, just like I was riding the Wall of Death, my scooter almost horizontal. My heart began to pound again, and my mouth was dry. I licked my lips, tasting the salt spray that had settled there. I came out onto a short straight and recovered my balance.

A squeal of tyres, from behind, told me that the Zephyr driver was in trouble too. I looked back; the rear end of his car skidded towards the verge before he could control it. He overcorrected and the vehicle went broadside the other way.

Blue smoke and steam rose in the air, as the driver fought for control. As I banked into the next corner, he disappeared from view. Had he gone off the road?

My hopes were quickly dashed; he was behind me again. I risked another glance over my shoulder. 'Christ!' I hissed. I now knew who the driver was. It was Webster, the greaser. He must have swapped his Anglia for the Zephyr soon after I'd "modified" it for him. I'd not seen the bastard since the day I'd beat the shit out of him. He would "modify" me too if he caught me with that thing!

Another bend was approaching. It was tight. I should slow for this one, but the car was too close. Fear made me keep the throttle wide open. I held my breath. The tyres squealed, complaining at what they were being asked to do, but they gripped. The Lambretta's stand scraped along the road, with the floorboard beneath my right foot almost touching the ground. I moved sideways from the saddle, sliding my right knee towards the flashing tarmac, my left leg hooked over the seat, as I tried to lower the scooter's centre of gravity.

I would have made it – except for the bus. It had pulled up smack bang in the middle of the curve.

Don't they put the stops in stupid places I thought, in the millisecond of time I had left before I smashed into the back of it. Choices? My brain raced to come up with an answer. I couldn't steer round it – I was on the limit now. I would skid if I braked, and crash into the bus anyway. Frantic now, I scrambled back onto the seat, my change of position forcing the Lammy upright.

Too late. I was going to hit it!

The bus began to pull away in a cloud of sulphurous grey-blue choking smoke. I missed the corner of its rear engine cover by inches. My relief lasted about another millisecond, and then I was jolted from my seat as the Lambretta's front wheel hit the kerb.

As I bounced down on the saddle again, both my legs now at the nearside of the scooter, I grabbed for the front brake lever and squeezed. I couldn't get my foot to the rear brake pedal on the floor. I tried to twist my body round, get back into position. It was all pointless though; the grass was so wet I couldn't have stopped.

The Lammy skidded across the tussocks, bucking me like a rodeo bronc. At least it stayed upright.

Then I saw the bridge parapet in my path. It was like the ones you see where the road crosses a railway, with large stone blocks at the ends. Bloody solid as well I knew, as I wrenched at the handlebars. There was no chance. The front wheel turned but that was all. The scooter slammed into the bridge at what must still have been about fifty miles an hour.

Mirrors flew to left and right like shooting stars as the Lambretta destroyed itself on the stonework. I laughed as I thought back to when PC Dennis had said how dangerous all that glass would be. None of it cut me.

Then I felt a terrible pain in my knees and wrists. I saw the sky flash past, then the ground, then the sky again, grey and dismal, then the ground once more. I slammed down onto wet earth.

Eventually, I stopped rolling and gazed up, dazedly, wondering where I was. I had been right; the bridge was over a railway line, and I had tumbled down the batter to lie next to the tracks.

A tangled mess of metal, that looked like it could have been my Lammy, lay among the gorse bushes that covered the bank. It was my scooter. The engine screamed. The throttle had stuck open, and with no road to hold it back, the little two-stroke was racing. That ended suddenly as, with a terrific bang, then a cloud of smoke, it died.

I lay on the cinders at the side of the line, staring up at the bridge above me. I could hear traffic passing as if nothing had happened. Had anyone seen me crash? Would I lie here for hours?

Someone must have spotted me. A head appeared over the parapet of the bridge. It was Webster! He must have stopped then come back. What would he do to me?

I tried to move but found I couldn't. I noticed something white sticking through the thin cloth of my trousers. It was one of the bones in my leg. Funny, but it didn't hurt as I thought it should. Was I paralysed?

I glanced up again. Webster had gone. I waited, expecting to see him scrambling down the bank to put the boot in me while I lay there helpless, but he didn't come. I don't know if I was relieved about that; no one else came either. Would there be marks on the bridge to alert someone to my crash? Had the passengers on the bus seen it? I turned my head to look at the railway. I was in no danger of being hit by a train where I lay. The rusty rails of a freight line were dull in the rain; not much came along here.

I could be here for hours – days even. I tried to get up again, but, when I pressed my palms against the sharp cinders, a burning pain seared to my brain. I must have broken something in my wrists. I remembered my tight grip on the handlebars. My fingers had been wrapped around them when I smashed into the wall; that wouldn't have done me much good.

My knees were beginning to hurt. I had some sensation in them then. I looked down. My trousers were torn, revealing a bloody mess where my kneecaps should have been. They must have hit the legshield, then the handlebars, as I was thrown forward. Probably smashed as well. My left foot was facing the wrong way, confirming the broken leg. At least I'd not hit my head on anything when I'd landed. Lucky that, because I hadn't had a helmet on.

What a fucking mess. I'd never be able to get my scooter fixed now I didn't have a job. And as I'd only gone for Third Party, the insurers wouldn't want to know.

Perhaps Floyd would . . ? Then I remembered. No help there.

I could forget the scooter anyway; I might never walk again – could be a cripple. No more backdrops and spins for me. Didn't see many wheelchairs in the Torch. And Wendy wouldn't want to know me now.

That assumed I survived at all. Who knew I was down here except for Webster? He wouldn't be calling an ambulance. Most likely, he'd be fetching Skunk Martin so that they could really do me in.

It began to rain a little heavier, just to make my day. I shivered as the cold began to soak into my already damp clothing. Water dripped from the bridge overhead. The wind whistling through its arch, as well as chilling me, blew drops of it into my eyes. It could be worse, snowing even, I supposed.

My teeth began to chatter, from shock perhaps. I'd heard of people dying from that. Tears ran down my cheeks, as I thought of my life ending, all alone, in this God-forsaken place. I began to pray, thinking back to when I'd watched my old man being buried. Then I prayed for my father to help me too. Who would be at my funeral? Not many people, that was for sure.

Then I remembered I still had the gear in my pocket. If I took that, at least I'd go out on a high. I couldn't get at it though; my coat was twisted beneath me and the pain in my hands stopped me from tugging it free. The police would find it on my body. Something else for my mother to remember me by.

I wondered how long I'd been lying there. My watch was gone, it must have come off my wrist in the crash. It was getting darker. The night was drawing in. I could see the lights of car headlamps flashing over the bridge, but none of them stopped. No one would spot anything amiss now; I would be here until tomorrow at least.

What had I done to deserve ending up this way? I'd just

wanted to have fun, not really wanted to hurt anyone. Some of the other skinheads had been real vicious bastards, going out Paki-bashing, or slashing folk with razors; some had even gang-banged a drunken girl they met going home one night. But it was me lying here, not them. It was so unfair.

A terrible pain raced to my brain when I tried to move again. What was that? Voices? Someone was coming. I peered into the darkness.

But it was just the sound of my screams echoing back from the bridge arch.

You're Gonna Make It

'Keep still,' a woman's voice muttered.

I felt cold metal against my stomach. I opened my eyes and was dazzled by a blare of lights from above. Car headlamps? No, they were too bright. My vision cleared. Some people dressed in green gowns were surrounding me. What was going on? Then I clicked. I was in hospital. I shivered, partly from cold and partly from relief. I had been found.

The icy sensation returned to my belly, and I looked down to see that one of the green-coated figures was snipping my clothes free, using a large pair of scissors. Soon, I was bollock naked, and freezing. Someone else tugged at my arm, making me cry out with pain.

'This will help,' a man said, his voice a mumble because of the mask he wore. He jabbed something sharp into my flesh.

Who had found me? I owed them a lot.

The curtain twitched and a face appeared above me. It was PC Dennis, without his helmet. 'You're a lucky boy, Roberts. Another ten minutes or so and you'd have been gone. One of the people on the bus – an old woman – saw you crash,' he said, answering the question in my mind, making me wonder if I had spoken it aloud. 'The old dear wasn't sure at first. She looked back then, seeing no sign of you, thought she had imagined it. Finally decided she'd better report it, just in case.'

'You'll have to leave us now, Constable,' one of the other figures, a nurse said. 'Oh, and we found this in his coat.'

She handed him a paper wrap. My remaining stuff. I tried to recall if Duromine was a controlled drug. Didn't think it was, and I'd swallowed all the Pirellis. I couldn't focus my thoughts. Not many of them left, from what I could remember. I guessed Dennis wouldn't be able to do me for them. He'd be disappointed about that.

'Don't forget – I want a blood sample,' the policeman said. 'Be seeing you later Roberts. Got to break the news to your mother now.'

The nurse jabbed at my arm again, then connected up a drip. I'd be like a fucking pincushion at this rate.

Another gowned figure ducked around the curtain and began to poke at my body. 'Looks like he'll lose that leg,' I heard the figure say.

It was a man's voice. A doctor perhaps? At last!

Then a cold shiver ran down my spine. It was not because I was still naked, and cold, and damp though; I now knew who the speaker was.

Clinton's eyes gleamed over his mask at me. He ran his fingers higher, towards my groin, prodding at my bruised and battered thighs. 'Even if he keeps it – he'll walk with a limp,' he growled.

It sounded more like a promise than an observation. My lips were dry with fear, as well as from the stuff that the nurse had pumped into my arm.

I tried to rise up, to protest. God knows what Clinton would do to me while I was out. 'Please, don't let . . .' I managed to gasp.

I saw Clinton pull his mask down and grin at me.

Then, I sank into oblivion.